leisure

girl GONE Viral

ALISHA RAI

piatkus

PIATKUS

First published in the US in 2020 by Avon,
An imprint of HarperCollins Publishers, New York
First published in Great Britain in 2020 by Piatkus

13 5 7 9 10 8 6 4 2

A CIP catalogue record for this book
is available from the British Library.

ISBN 978-0-349-42405-7

Printed and bound in Great Britain by Clays Ltd, Elcograf S.p.A.

Papers used by Piatkus are from well-managed forests
and other responsible sources.

MIX
Paper from
responsible sources
FSC® C104740

Piatkus
An imprint of
Little, Brown Book Group
Carmelite House
50 Victoria Embankment
London EC4Y 0DZ

An Hachette UK Company
www.hachette.co.uk

www.littlebrown.co.uk

For those who have fought for a place to call home.
And those who are still seeking theirs.
It's out there. I'm sure of it.

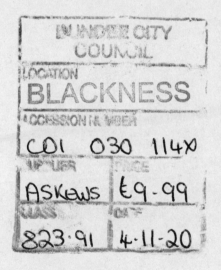

Chapter One

KATRINA KING LOVED love. Even when it didn't love her.

The concept of love, the stories, how it was and how it should be. She loved giving it, receiving it. She cherished the rich platonic love her friends and roommates brought into her life, the generous kindness of the love her late husband had shown her. Though she'd spent much of her adolescence and early adulthood starved for it, she was comfortable with the emotion. Or, at least, forms of it.

Still a mystery to her was the kind of sweeping love she'd started to crave fairly recently, along with everything that went with it: sex and kisses and mutual consideration and respect and the zing of romance. Occasionally getting to big-spoon someone.

Those things seemed far away. Especially when she was aimlessly swiping on her dating app of choice.

"Walk me through this again." Andy squinted at Katrina's phone, her tortoiseshell glasses perched on the tip of her nose. "You swipe left if you like someone, right if you don't?"

Katrina settled into the comfortable leather armchair

across from Andy's. The office they were in was cramped, dominated by a large desk and two bookshelves lining the walls. It was a little musty and windowless, but Katrina only needed privacy for her therapy sessions, not luxury. "Switch those around. Swipe right if you like someone."

"My God, has the world changed in ten years. I met my wife online but on Matchmaker, and I thought filling out that long questionnaire was difficult then." Andy turned the phone around to face Katrina. "What about this one? He's an entrepreneur and CEO."

"This close to Los Angeles, every guy is an entrepreneur and CEO if they're not a music producer." Katrina dutifully looked at the profile and scrolled through the photos. "I do like this photo of him shirtless holding two puppies, though."

"You know he's not allergic, at least. Important, since you aspire to own a menagerie someday."

"Someday." Katrina only had a cat so far, but she was working her roommates up to a dog. Or three. "Let's give him a chance." She swiped right, and another man filled the screen.

Andy swiveled the phone around and perused this one carefully as well, taking much longer than the average 0.6 seconds the average app user spent on a profile. "Oh look, this one answered one of the question prompts, put a little work into it. Two truths and a lie: *I've been to Guatemala, I have a twin, and I think women should be barefoot and pregnant.*" Andy paused, eyes widening. "Um, I really hope the first two are the truths."

"Yeah, some people are really bad at playing two truths and a lie."

Andy tapped her finger on her chin. "Are you a misogynist, or have you never been to Guatemala, sir?"

"The eternal question. Left on him."

Andy paused. "But what if he *has* been to Guatemala?"

"My rule of thumb for two truths is, if we have to play the *did you really visit that country or do you think I'm a second-class citizen* game, it's a left."

"Fair enough." Andy swiped confidently, with the kind of ease only a happily coupled-off person could display, when swiping was a novelty and not a way of life. A minute later, she turned the phone around. "This guy mentions his height four times in his profile."

Katrina glanced at the bare-chested stud. She didn't need to read his bio. "Is he six-foot-four?"

"How did you know?"

"People who are six-foot-four really like to tell the world they're six-foot-four."

Andy chuckled. "Yea or nay?"

Katrina considered the gentleman. She wasn't a height snob, but she wouldn't kick the extra inches out of her bed. "Yea."

Andy swiped right and a little ding sounded. The high-pitched squeal of victory that came from her lips might have surprised a person who made a snap judgment based on Andy's all-black leather ensemble, heavy eyeliner, visible tattoos, and septum, ear, and eyebrow piercings. "It's a match. That's exciting."

Katrina tried to work up the same degree of eagerness. "Yes. So cool."

Andy placed the phone on the arm of Katrina's chair and regarded her with kind eyes. Katrina had run through . . . well, she couldn't count how many therapists she'd run through at this point in her life. But Andy had been around longer than most, a few years now. "Thank you for letting me see what it's like. It feels like a game, but I can see how this must get exhausting after a time."

Katrina spun the phone around. "I don't think it helps that I know how the sausage is made, so to speak."

"Yes, of course, your equity in Crush."

Katrina's investment in Crush was a fact not many people knew. She was a fairly silent partner, even if she took on a more active role than in her other investments.

Andy steepled her fingers under her chin. "I'm sure you know the numbers and all, but you seem pretty savvy on the ins and outs of people's profiles. You've been spending time on here."

"I told you I was going to." When she'd decided she wanted a romantic partner, she'd made a deal with herself, one she hadn't really shared with anyone but her best friend and roommate, Rhiannon.

If she could make it out of her house to ten places, ten places where she felt comfortable and cozy and safe, then she could date.

She'd hit ten last month. Had managed road trips to ever-farther destinations. And then she'd had no excuse, right? She had to start going after the thing she wanted.

The thing you said you wanted.

Crush had seemed like the easiest way to go about that. Beyond the fact that it was as woman-friendly as a dating app could get, with Rhiannon as CEO and herself as a minority shareholder, she'd felt safe in creating a profile there. Her roommates had helped her take some blurry, unidentifiable photos—her looks had changed since she'd been a model, but she was cautious—and she'd drafted a short bio after much agonizing.

Looking for a partner in mostly legal activities. Enjoy cooking, gardening, the outdoors, romance, art, reading, and animals. Please be kind and have more emotional intelligence than a turnip.

Rhiannon had written the last part, and it had made Katrina laugh, so she'd kept it in.

Andy leaned back. "How many people have you messaged since we last spoke?"

"Two."

"How many messages did you exchange with them?"

She winced. "Um . . . two."

"Each?"

"No. I said hi and ghosted when they replied. Which I'm not proud of," she hurried to tack on. Ghosting wasn't a good thing to do to people, even if it was digitally. "But I did message, so I technically did my homework."

Andy cocked her head. "I suggested you try talking to some of your matches. It wasn't homework."

If I do this thing my therapist says, then she will give me an A-plus, was a thought process she was trying to shake. The people-pleaser in her made life rough. "Right, of course."

"What are you looking to get out of this app, Katrina?"

"I want to meet someone." Katrina looked down at her hands. "Feel that . . . zing."

"Zing?"

"Yeah. You know? That little zing, when you talk to someone or touch someone that you're attracted to and like? That's a thing, right?"

The lines around Andy's eyes crinkled. "I think we all call the zing something different, but yes. How long has it been since you've felt that zing?"

Since about an hour ago. Katrina carefully avoided glancing in the direction of the office door. Or more accurately, at the man who was waiting for her outside it. She wasn't ready to talk about that yet with Andy. She kind of hoped she'd never need to. "I don't know. I've always been a romantic, but . . . I didn't think it was for me, and I was at peace with that. These urges are kinda new."

"Not wanting sex and romance is totally natural. So is wanting sex and romance. Going back and forth between those wants, depending on where you are in your life, that's also fine."

"I'm not doing this because I feel pressured or anything, don't worry." She lifted her shoulders. *I want to figure out if these things I've started feeling for this one particular man will translate over to other men, because I can't . . . with him.*

Later. She'd discuss *him* with Andy later. She needed to process *him* first.

"I might be scared to actually meet someone face-to-face."

"You fear you won't be able to mask?"

"That's part of it." *Masking* was a nice word Katrina had learned from Andy. It covered what she did when she went out in the world and pretended she wasn't sweating over what her brain and body might do to her.

Fear of fear. That was what her very first therapist had called her panic disorder, and it was accurate.

"It's always an option to tell someone up front that you may have a panic attack, if you feel comfortable doing so."

She inwardly shuddered. That *was* an option, but only a select few people knew about her panic attacks. They made her vulnerable, and she knew how vulnerability could be used against her. "I don't think I'm there yet."

"You don't have to be. Only do as much or as little as you feel comfortable doing." Andy grinned. "I'm not telling you to be a serial ghoster, but don't beat yourself up."

Katrina picked at her cuticles, then stopped when she noticed the quick glance Andy shot her hands. "Got it." Andy's nonjudgmental face was calming, but Katrina didn't know if she'd ever be at a point in her life where she'd stop judging herself.

"It's one step in front of another. Downloading the app, texting, talking, having a coffee. You're in charge."

Find someone else. Anyone else. "Okay."

They spoke for a few minutes about other, more casual matters, until Andy discreetly checked her watch. "Is there anything else going on that you want to talk about?"

Katrina kept her face placid. When she exerted a small amount of effort, she was a stellar actress. "I'm good, thanks."

"Same time next week?"

"Absolutely. Thanks as always for meeting me here." She politely stood when Andy did and walked her to the door. Andy's leather jacket creaked when she grabbed the helmet from the coatrack. She and Andy had started meeting in person relatively recently. Before this, they'd conducted most of their weekly sessions via video.

"No thanks necessary." Andy embraced her and patted her on the back gently. "I can see myself out. Text or call if you need anything."

"I will." Katrina waited for Andy to make her way down the hallway to the back door of the building before heading in the other direction, toward the café's dining area.

The large place was usually filled with sun, but the blinds were still closed, giving it an intimate, quiet air. This street didn't get much foot traffic in the early morning, so the owner opened late and focused on brunch and lunch.

Katrina went straight to the counter. She avoided looking in the mirror behind the register that reflected the whole café.

And the tall, dark, and handsome man sitting motionless near the door.

Instead, she visually traced the sign hung above the mirror, made up of driftwood and rope, the kind of thing you could get at a stall on the beach.

Happiness is a radical act.

She mouthed the words to herself, as she had since the first time she'd come in here, pushing them into her soul.

A slight silver-haired woman bustled out of the kitchen

and beamed at Katrina. Her face was wrinkled from sun, weathered by wind and the ocean. The eighty-year-old café owner remained an avid surfer. Every morning before she came to this shop, she hit the beach. "How was your visit with your little friend?"

"Lovely, thank you." Mona Rodriguez knew Andy was her therapist. For a year now, every Thursday morning, Mona had graciously provided the use of her back office before the business opened. She treated Katrina like her granddaughter and the sessions like they were playdates.

"Are you staying for a bit? Can I get you more coffee?"

Katrina nodded. Sometimes she left before Mona opened, but today she'd like to be around other people. "Yes, please. Two, actually, and a croissant." She handed over her mug and tapped her smart watch to pull up her credit card.

Mona shook her head firmly as she poured the coffee. "No charge on refills."

Katrina raised an eyebrow, not swayed by this new tactic. "We both know that's not your policy, and one of those isn't a refill. Well, two of those, since a croissant can't be refilled."

Mona smiled. "It's my policy for investors, especially when those investors are friends."

Warmth filled her heart and Katrina couldn't help but smile back, though her sigh was exasperated. "We've been over this. That wasn't an investment, I want no equity."

"When someone saves my business from a big shitty corporation trying to steal it from me, and tells me they don't want to be paid back"—Mona scooped a croissant from the display case onto a plate—"I consider them investors, and they get a free cup of fucking coffee every now and then."

Katrina's cheeks turned hot. The situation hadn't been nearly as dramatic as Mona made it sound. A few months ago, Katrina had learned that French Coast had been served notice of a sky-high rent increase. It was a common ploy to force older mom-and-pop shops out in favor of big-chain money.

Mona had started this business with her husband forty years ago. Her spouse and son were gone. She needed the café and not only for the money it provided.

Katrina didn't lack for money. It hadn't pained her to give Mona a cash infusion to make up the difference in the higher rent and float her through a couple years. She'd earned that money back easily on her actual investments.

Her gift had been partially made out of sentiment. This had been the first place she'd managed to step inside of, after almost five years, where her PTSD and panic disorder had narrowed her range of activity to her own home and the grounds around it. The coffee shop was a simple place, but coming here had given her the confidence to try to go to another place, and then another.

"Instead of the free coffee, of course, I could set you up with my neighbor as thanks." Mona beamed at her. "He's beautiful. Has a nice head of hair, always has a lady wandering in and out of his house. I talked to one of them once, when she stepped on my petunias. He's got a huge—"

"Mona."

The older woman widened her eyes in faux-innocence. "Bird. Also, his prison conviction was just expunged."

Katrina stifled her grin. She might have to start dating somewhere, but she felt like she had to aim a little higher than "has hair follicles" and "prison record clear," big . . . bird or not. "I'll take the coffee."

There was a savvy glint in Mona's eye as she pushed the order forward. "That's what I thought."

Once Mona's back was turned, Katrina slipped a fifty-dollar bill out of her pocket and dropped it in the tip jar, burying it under the dollar bills Mona filled it with in the morning to stage the thing.

When Katrina was in her early teens and starting to model, her father had made her spend an hour every day in the living room, smiling. Constant, unceasing smiling. Different kinds of smiles, big smiles, small smiles, smiling with her eyes, smiling as she sat motionless, smiling while talking.

Yes, her dad *had* been quite the prince.

It had been the worst hour of her day. The only possible upside was that she was now excellent at smiling, even when her stomach was roiling in the throes of an impossible crush.

She balanced the tray and pasted a cheerful smile on her face as she made her way to the occupied table.

Jasvinder Singh was many things: her friend, her bodyguard, her medical contact, her shadow.

He was also beautiful. Today he was dressed casually but fashionably, his tall, lean frame displayed in camel-colored slacks and a red sweater. His beard was sharply trimmed to showcase the line of his jaw and the curve of his cheek, and he carried himself with the ease of someone who was utterly comfortable with their own body.

She'd met him almost a decade ago, when she'd married his wealthy boss, international jeweler and investor Hardeep Arora. Hardeep had kept a whole security team on their toes, and Jas had been in charge of it.

He'd been in her life for so long; she'd always been objectively aware of his beauty. She'd only recently started taking it personally, tracing his bold features repeatedly with her gaze. She'd become especially obsessed with his eyebrows. They were slashing and black and thick and prominent, and she didn't understand why her sexual awakening was tied to a man's eyebrows of all things, but here she was.

When she neared, he glanced up at her from behind the book he held, a thick biography, and as those black eyes pinned her she tripped on . . . well, she wasn't sure what she stumbled on. Air? Could one's feet fumble over the strong breeze from an AC vent?

With some fancy juggling she managed to salvage the coffee, though it sloshed over the sides of the mugs.

The plate, however, flew right off the tray. It could have crashed on the floor or clattered onto the table. But no.

It landed in his lap. Facedown.

Just a plate.

And a croissant.

And jelly.

And butter.

Her smile gone, she groaned and set the tray down on the table. "Yikes, I'm so sorry." She reached for the plate, but caught herself. A few months ago, she would have cracked a joke and helped him clean up, but she couldn't possibly now. What if she, like, touched him? She'd die.

His reflexes were quick, and before she could act, he scooped the food and plate off his lap. "Don't worry about it."

Katrina grimaced. "I was going to ask if you wanted to stay awhile." There were few things in life that were certain: death, taxes, and Jasvinder Singh's sense of responsibility. He was her employee, so she could technically tell him that they would be staying, but their relationship had never worked like that.

The doors might remain locked for another twenty minutes, Mona and her the only ones in here, but Jas wouldn't leave her alone in public. Hell, it had taken all of Katrina's negotiating powers to get him to sit out here during her therapy session. He'd wanted to stand outside the office door, and had only acquiesced when she'd told him that would make her too self-conscious to talk.

He arched a perfect eyebrow at her. "We can stay."

"You'll probably want to go home and clean up."

Mona popped up, holding a small bowl of water and a towel, as well as a new croissant. "Here you go."

"I can clean up here." Jas accepted the items. "Gracias, Mona."

Mona said something to Jas, too fast for Katrina to catch. Her Spanish skills were limited, and Mona and Jas were definitely advanced-level. Jas's family was mostly Punjabi

American, but he had a Mexican grandparent or great-grandparent, if she remembered correctly, and had grown up in a multilingual community where English, Punjabi, and Spanish were spoken fluently.

Jas chuckled at Mona's comment, but flushed. Without being asked, he translated once Mona winked at her and left. "She said it was a good thing it wasn't the coffee that landed in my lap."

Knowing Mona as she did, she assumed the woman had cracked a ribald joke. Katrina puffed out her cheeks. She'd have to download that language app again.

"See?" Jas blotted his thighs. "Good as new."

She'd take his word for it. There was no way she was going to inspect those finely clad appendages for leftover jam and butter. "Okay, sure." She picked up his mug and handed it to him. "Speaking of coffee, here you go."

"Thanks." Their fingers brushed as she passed the warm ceramic to him.

Katrina indicated a table across the café. "I'll be over there." It was common for them to sit separately. She liked the routine of the same spot, and he preferred to be able to see the whole room.

She stuck the hand he'd touched into her sweatshirt pocket as she walked away. Her fingers brushed the stone she always carried with her. She'd found it on a walk a few years ago and decided it was a perfect fidget stone, smooth and a good size for her small hand. She ran her thumb over the dip in it, the cool rock grounding her.

But it couldn't get rid of the tingles racing up her arm.

One might call them zings.

She settled into her seat and pulled a baseball cap and a book out of her bag. She adjusted the cap on her head and knocked the brim down lower over her face. She wasn't a celebrity anymore, but the café would start filling up soon and it calmed her to have the illusion of anonymity.

She opened her book and stared down at the page, thinking of what Andy had asked her just before she'd left.

Is there anything else going on that you want to talk about?

I can't stop thinking about my bodyguard, and I'm not sure if it's because he's the only eligible bachelor in my life, or because I'm genuinely in love with a man who sees me as nothing more than a responsibility he takes very seriously.

She cast a glance at Jas. He'd returned to his own reading, but she knew he was entirely, fully aware of his surroundings. He hadn't been a military man in over a decade, but he always had that air of hyperarousal around him. Something else they had in common. She hated being startled.

As if to taunt her, he slowly scratched one perfect eyebrow, and another zing ran down her back, to the hand he'd touched. She refocused on her own book, and curled her fingers into her palms.

Yes. Something else is definitely going on, damn it.

Chapter Two

As LUNCHTIME APPROACHED, more of the red-cushioned chairs in the café became occupied by locals, students, and tourists. Occasionally Katrina glanced up to people-watch. Since so much of her brain was occupied with her crush, she couldn't help but notice the couples in the room. The two giggling college girls who walked in holding hands, wearing goofy smiles. The older couple at the counter, familiarity in the way the two men stood and chatted with each other. The newlyweds in the corner, rubbing noses and cooing. The young parents who sat nearby, harried and yawning while they passed their chubby baby back and forth so they each could eat.

It was almost too much to bear. She tried to get lost in her book and nearly succeeded until she heard footsteps pause next to her table.

"Excuse me?"

She used her finger to hold her place and casually glanced up.

Her finger slid out of the book. The thriller was no longer the most thrilling thing around.

The man looming above her was so breathtakingly attractive she had to battle a sudden urge to scrub her eyes like a cartoon character of old.

The stranger had the jaw of a Disney prince, with a cleft in his chin to match. His unzipped red sweatshirt revealed a soft blue-gray shirt that matched his eyes, and his auburn hair was artfully tousled.

He held an absurdly tiny espresso cup in his big hands. "Hi. It's so crowded in here today."

Her back was against the wall, so he must be talking to her? "Um. It is," Katrina agreed.

He gestured to the seat across from her. "Is this taken? Do you mind if we share a table?"

"Oh." She glanced around. The young woman sitting at the table next to her, a leggy blonde in yoga pants and a sweatshirt, gave her a curious look before leaning forward to whisper something to the dark-haired man she was with.

Katrina's gaze skipped over them to meet Jas's. He'd placed his book facedown on the table, and he was making no secret of the fact he was watching carefully, his face hard and suspicious.

When Katrina had first started coming here, she hadn't wanted to talk to anyone other than Mona and her employees. It had taken her a while to get to a point where she hadn't felt nervous about a stranger sharing her table, especially when it was crowded.

Having panic disorder meant she could have an attack at any time. Sometimes anxiety or her PTSD triggered it. Sometimes she couldn't tell exactly what pushed her body into it. Between years of therapy and meds, she'd learned how to occasionally catch a warning.

Katrina often felt like she had a perpetual scanner checking her vital signs. Heart rate, breathing, headache, adrenaline surges. It ran in the background like a sleeping computer program.

Jas started to rise, and she gave a barely perceptible shake of her head. He paused, then sat down, though he kept his attention on them. "Sure, no problem," she said to the man.

She continued her internal check as the man sat down, the same way another person might check their pulse.

No alarms going off. Was there anything else, though?

She searched for anything other than appreciation of his beauty, but there was . . . nothing. No interest, no zing. Only the same detached interest she felt when she swiped through hundreds of men's profiles on her app.

This could be your meet-cute, though. Give it a chance.

Her romantic side perked up a little as she envisioned this story playing out on a movie screen, like it was happening to someone else. Sharing a table in a crowded café was the cutest of meet-cutes! Maybe only matched by bumping into a man in a grocery store and having him pick up the peaches knocked out of her basket.

Or the croissant knocked into his lap.

Nope, she was not thinking about the croissant.

The man gave her a smile so perfect, even she, a smile expert, was impressed. "Hey, new seatmate," he said.

"Um, hello."

He scooted his seat closer to the table. "I'm Ross."

She angled her baseball cap down. "Hi," she repeated.

"What's your name?" he prompted, which was an utterly reasonable thing to ask.

"Kat." Only her inner circle of friends and staff knew her full name.

"Pretty name." His grin widened. He produced a paperback from his sweatshirt pocket. A sci-fi novel, if the cover was anything to go by.

"Thanks." She tugged on her T-shirt. If this was a meet-cute, she wished she'd worn something a little more attractive and form-fitting today.

"Thank you for letting me share your table." He shifted, and before their knees could bump under the small table, she pulled her legs back instinctively.

Fool! You were supposed to let them bump.

"No big deal." Since she'd lost the bump opportunity— the bumportunity—she ought to say something clever. Damn it. She shouldn't have gone down the meet-cute alley in her brain. She was feeling too much pressure now.

You're good at talking to people, at evaluating them. She'd never been a shy person, even if life had made her wary.

She slid her hand into her pocket and caressed her fidget stone. "Do you live around here?"

Ross put his book on the table. The spine was cracked.

That's not a deal-breaker for a meet-cute. Still, she protectively cupped her own carefully intact book spine.

"No, it's my first time in Santa Barbara."

"Oh, you're a tourist." Her shoulders lowered, some of the

pressure relieved. Meet-cutes didn't happen when someone was on vacation.

Her inner romantic, that bitch, squinted at her, and quickly filled her brain with the fifty-seven and a half romantic comedies that started exactly that way.

"Kind of. My mom just moved here. Thought I would make sure she and her golden retriever are settling in well."

Most people might be more touched at the man's care for his mom, but she perked up for another reason. "Golden retriever?"

"Yeah." He unlocked his phone, scrolled, and turned it around to face her. "That's her. Well, my mom and Sandy."

She ignored the mom, and zeroed in on the dog. "Oh my God. She's so cute."

"She knows." He swiped right, and a helpless noise of adoration escaped Katrina's mouth. "Yeah, she's even cuter dressed up."

She grinned at the pup in a tutu. "What a beautiful creature."

"Inside and out. Her sister was my dog, actually. She passed away last year."

"I'm sorry."

He shrugged, though sadness tinged his eyes, turning them a darker gray. She swayed toward him, eager to ease the upset. Katrina pulled her phone out of her pocket and turned it on. "Here's my cat. Her name's Zeus."

He visibly cheered as she showed him a few pictures of her tuxedo cat. Jas had found the cat for her at the humane society, so she wasn't actually sure what breed she was, but Zeus had a nice hold on her heart. "Gorgeous."

"She is. Very cuddly. A dog is next on my list."

"I got Sandy and her sister at a shelter a few years back. You can find the sweetest dogs there."

"That's my plan. Sometimes I scroll through the adoption websites."

"I heard someone say that pet adoption websites and real estate sites are like dating apps for married people." His gaze dipped to her left hand.

She resisted the urge to touch her bare ring finger. She'd taken off her wedding ring ages ago. "I'm not married."

"Cool." He cocked his head. "Significant other?"

Her cheeks heated. She might be naïve, but she couldn't tell herself he wasn't interested now. "No."

His eyes warmed. "Me neither. What do you do? For a living?"

She hesitated. The phrasing was odd, because she had the privilege of not needing to really do anything for a living.

It was a circumstance that filled her with a vague sense of guilt. She'd been a regular middle-class kid growing up, with a regular divorced single mom, and would have stayed middle-class had it not been for a freak series of events: her mother's death, her father taking custody, an agent discovering her in a mall, being catapulted into the kind of circle that would lead her to marry a rich, childless jeweler, his death, her own interest in investing and growing the nest egg he'd left her.

That wasn't to say she didn't work. She worked on herself, her businesses, her charitable donations, her cooking, and an ever-changing selection of art, crafts, research, and books. She picked one at random. "I make jewelry." Her latest interest, one she'd picked up a little over a year ago in a nostalgic mood for her late husband.

"Oh. Wow, that's so cool. An artist, huh?"

She lifted a shoulder. A therapist had suggested she try painting a few years ago, and she'd cycled through a million different forms of art since then. She parroted his question back at him. "What about you?"

"I used to coach rugby. Now I'm a nutritional coach."

Rugby. That explained the thighs.

"Hey, do you mind watching my stuff for a minute? I need to use the restroom."

"Sure."

He rose from his chair and she tried to avoid checking out his aforementioned (in her head) massive thighs as he walked away.

She snuck one peek, though. Okay, well. It wasn't news that she could feel lust over a pair of well-formed legs. It didn't rise to the level of a zing, though.

She waited a second or two and got up as well. Katrina caught the eye of the blond ponytailed woman at the table next to her, no easy feat, since she and her companion were sitting silently together, furiously typing something on their phones.

Writers, she bet. "Do you mind watching our table for a

second?" There was no real need, Katrina wouldn't go far, but she didn't want someone to poach it.

The woman nodded. "Of course."

She walked to the counter and grabbed an extra couple of napkins. A large shadow fell over her. Jas leaned on the counter and signaled to the waitress for a refill for his empty cup.

"Everything's fine," she said. "He had no other place to sit. He's not bothering me."

She got a barely audible grunt in return. Grunts were one of Jas's favorite methods of communication, and she'd learned to decipher them the same way someone else might learn to decipher Morse code. This grunt was a satisfied grunt.

The grunts weren't as sexy to her as his eyebrows, but they were still pretty cute, damn it.

She glanced up at that rope sign. *Happiness is a radical act. Focus on the new guy. Find a zing there.*

She made her way back to the table. "Thanks for holding it," she said to the blond woman, and got a wave in return, the lady not even looking away from her small phone screen, her thumbs moving at the speed of light.

Definitely a writer. Bet she's in the middle of something juicy.

Katrina sat down and returned to her thriller. A few minutes later Ross returned. He placed a plate with a giant cookie on it between them. "I went biking this morning and worked up an appetite. Please help me eat this."

She never turned down a good cookie. "Happy to assist."

She was careful not to let their fingers brush as they demolished the cookie. Despite her brain urging her to let it happen, the bumportunities were bump-blocked by her own instincts.

Ross sat back. "The weather's so nice today."

Mona had all of French Coast's windows and doors open, and the salt-tinged air was perfection. "It's nice most days. Have you been to the beach yet?"

"Not yet. That's on the agenda for tomorrow. I didn't bring my flip-flops today."

She named a popular park. "If you want to see the sunset tonight, you can see it from there. The view's incredible."

He smoldered and leaned over the table. She hadn't been on the receiving end of a smolder in a long time, but this was most definitely a smolder of the highest caliber.

And like most smolders in the past, she was left cold. It was a sad day when a grunt could make her heartbeat accelerate, but a perfectly good smolder barely caught her attention.

"The view's good from here too."

She stifled the sudden urge to laugh. Were this a book or a movie, she might have sighed, but in real life, the line was cheesy and heavy-handed. "Uh, you mean the décor? Yeah, we call rope art *beach chic* over here."

"Partially," he said, the smolder turning down to a simmer. "Hey, you know of any good pizza places around here? No chains."

The subject of food was never cheesy. Unless there was literal cheese involved. "There's a place around the corner from here." She gestured. "I order delivery from there a lot, and love it. I'm pretty sure they have a nice place to eat in."

"Perfect." He crossed his arms over the small table and leaned forward. This time, she forced herself to keep her body still. They touched, his forearm against hers.

Nothing. No zings. Not even a spark.

"Would you like to join me for pizza and a sunset tonight, then?"

She blinked. This was a bona fide meet-cute!

Except she didn't care. It was flattering to have such a handsome guy flirting with her, but she could quite easily turn him down. "No, I'm afraid I can't."

He shrugged good-naturedly and, bless him, didn't press. "No problem."

"You should try Crush," she offered. "I'm sure you can line up a date for the evening pretty easily."

He made a face. "Never used one of those dating apps. I prefer meeting people like this. Face-to-face contact, you know."

Katrina could at least tell Rhiannon she'd tried to convert another subscriber. "Totally get it."

He gathered up his stuff. "Thanks so much for letting me share your table. I enjoyed having the company and the local tips."

"Me too. Pet Sandy for me."

He laughed. "She wouldn't settle for anything less."

He held out his hand and she shook it, expecting no feelings and getting none. This time she did watch him leave, satisfied at the contentment she felt.

One step after another. She could repeat this, message some of those guys lingering in her matches. And next time, maybe she'd want to go out with the guy.

She dawdled for a few more minutes, then tucked her paperback in her bag and collected her trash, depositing her stuff and the plate and cup Ross had left behind in the bin.

"Ready?"

She turned to find Jas behind her. She noted the bookmark sticking out of his hardcover with approval. No cracked spines here. "Yup."

They went out the back door, to the alley where Mona allowed them to park.

Jas walked a step in front of her but within reach, leading her to the car. She slid her gaze from his straight black hair, down his strong neck and back, and tore it away just as it got to his butt.

Your employee. Your friend. But also, your employee. You're his responsibility. Nothing more.

She'd message more men on Crush. She had to find someone else.

He opened her door for her, and she slid into the back seat. The windows were darkly tinted, so no one could look in and see her. She could look out, though.

Riding in cars was still a relative novelty for her. Almost two years ago, when she'd decided she wanted to try exposure therapy under Andy's guidance, they'd come to this vehicle, parked in her driveway, and sat inside it. She'd wrestled her way out of the car when her throat had constricted so much she could only gasp. Not quite a panic attack. Fear of fear. The terror of a potential panic attack.

The second time had been easier. The third time, she'd managed to travel within a mile radius of her house.

She'd tested herself up to six hours straight in the car now, round-trips where Jas had driven her up the coast and back, the sight of the ocean something she'd missed dearly. Twice she'd hyperventilated to the point where Jas had had to pull over. She'd survived, though, and that was what she told her fear every time she got inside the SUV.

She watched the city pass her by as they made the short ten-minute drive back to her home, in between sneaking glances at Jas.

"Did you have a good time?" Jas asked.

"Yes. Did you try the cookies? Oh, never mind." Jas didn't like sweets like she did. "They were delicious. I'll have to get the recipe from Mona. Jia would like them." Her new housemate liked to eat, which delighted Katrina, because she liked to feed people.

Jas grunted. "What about the guy? What was his deal?"

She lifted her head from the window. "He was a tourist." She'd never know what prompted the next confession. "He asked me out."

Katrina immediately wanted to recall the words. In the nine years he'd worked for her, she'd never spoken to Jas about something like this, had no idea what was going on in his personal life. She considered them friends, but they had clearly defined boundaries. Her relatively recent desire for physical companionship was something only her girl-friends and Andy were privy to.

There was a short pause. "What?"

She met her bodyguard's dark eyes in the rearview mirror. *Gloss over it. Don't talk to the man you want about a man you don't. It's not like he'll be jealous or anything.* Anyway, jealousy was something high school girls sought.

She opened her mouth and heard herself say, "That man I was sitting with? The cute guy? He asked me to go to dinner with him tonight."

Jas's gaze flicked back to the road, his thick black eyebrows furrowing so deeply she wanted to smooth them out. "Cute? Is that what's considered cute now?" He snorted. "Fake teeth and a fake tan?"

She paused. The fake tan was possible. As for the rest . . . "Fake, huh?"

"Definitely. No one's teeth are naturally that white."

She couldn't help but grin, a real grin. Not many people saw this side of Jas. "Cosmetic procedures are not something I shame a person for," she said primly.

He gestured. The sunlight glinted off the iron bracelet he wore. "I'm not saying Sir Teeth-a-Lot should be ashamed, I'm saying he needs a better dentist." Jas took a sharp right. "I'm sure he has many other excellent qualities."

If she didn't know better, she might think there was a caustic bite to Jas's words.

Jealousy?

She strangled the surge of hope in her soul, shoved it down deep. "He seemed okay."

"Where are we going on this date?"

Katrina squinted at the back of his head. His hair was short, always in the same tidy style. "We?"

"I would prefer to accompany you until we have a chance to vet him."

She opened her mouth and then closed it again, flummoxed. She hadn't thought about the logistics of dating. Jas lived on her property, in the guest cottage. When they were at home, he had an uncanny ability to fade in and out of the woodwork as she needed. When she left her home, Jas was always at her side.

She'd have to take Jas on a date? With another man? And he sounded . . . fine about that prospect. Utterly, totally fine.

So much for him thinking of her as anything other than a job. "I'm not going out with him. I turned him down. Wasn't feeling it."

"As you wish." His attention returned to the twisting road. "Your wrap is next to you."

She hadn't realized she was shivering until then. It was cool out, the chill multiplied by the air-conditioning. She picked up the shawl and drew it around her shoulders. "Thank you, Jas. What would I do without you?" Truth.

A grunt. That was the grunt that told her he didn't know what to say in response. He wasn't great at handling compliments.

She leaned her forehead against the window. After a second, she pulled her phone out of her purse and opened Crush.

She studied the man Andy had matched her with. He

said he was six-foot-four five times in his profile, not four, and she had no doubt he'd say it ten more times when they got together. Tall people were very proud of hitting the genetic lottery.

Jas was tall, though, and he rarely mentioned it.

Stop it.

With a surreptitious glance at Jas, she clicked on the guy's profile and sent a waving-hand emoji. Not the most creative opener, but if he was interested, he'd get back to her.

What would I do without you? They hadn't been empty words. Jas was such an integral part of her life. If he left, she'd survive, but she'd mourn his loss.

Longing shot through her. She wanted him to feel the same way about her. She wanted him to share his needs with her, so she could do things for him, too.

Katrina wrapped her shawl tighter around her. That wouldn't happen, though. So she could never jeopardize their working relationship or their friendship with her stupid, too-big feelings.

Chapter Three

THERE WAS A time in his life when Jasvinder Singh had always been prepared for a fight, for an enemy around the next corner.

But if the military had taught him anything, it was that the lines between friend and foe were blurry, and there were some attacks you could never prepare for.

He asked me out.

Jas ramped up the speed of the treadmill, his feet pounding on the track. His breath was coming fast and hard. It had been far too long since he'd properly pushed himself.

He asked me out.

He tapped the incline button, forcing himself up to a steep elevation. He welcomed every second of the pain in his calves.

He asked me out.

The doorbell interrupted his savage thoughts, and he hit the pause button on the treadmill, jumping off before it came to a complete stop. He winced as his knee protested. When Hardeep had been alive, Jas had woken up every morning at four and worked out for at least a couple of hours.

Then again, his job had been much more physical then. Hardeep had been a massively wealthy jet-setter who was also highly visible, with an equally visible wife. Every day had brought another event and security challenge.

When Hardeep had died six years ago, Katrina had disbanded the rest of the security team with hefty pensions. Jas had assumed she'd give him notice as well.

Instead she'd summoned him to her office and quietly told him she wanted him to find her a nice house with an ocean view in California, and would he like to remain her bodyguard?

His yes had come very fast.

Jas picked up the phone from the weight bench and checked the display for the fifteenth time since he'd woken up an hour ago. He accompanied Katrina on all outings and was otherwise available to meet her needs, but he'd shifted into handling cyber security for her, her investment fund, and a number of the businesses she had shares in. His phone was always on him, and he was attuned to every noise it made.

For the past few days, though, he'd been on hyper alert for a 202 area code. No good news came out of Washington, not for him.

Nothing right now, though. The doorbell chimed again and he tucked the phone into the pocket of his shorts. He walked to the door, peered out, and silently groaned at the sight of the man standing on his doorstep.

Jas contemplated slinking away, but it was impossible to pretend he wasn't home when his car was in the same large garage this man parked in. He unlocked the door and opened it, leaning against the doorjamb. Wait, did that look like he was trying to bar the guy from his home? He straightened.

Jas had never been a man who made friends easily, even before his life had turned upside down and he'd left the military. He was too slow to open up to people, or at least, that's what more than one exasperated family member had told him.

Katrina's part-time roommate, Rhiannon, had started dating Samson Lima about six months ago. Jas didn't know exactly how Samson had slipped in under his guard. Possibly because Jas had been slightly starstruck: Samson had played pro, but he also came from a pro-football dynasty. Jas had grown up watching Samson's uncle and father play ball. He'd owned a Lima jersey. A few of them, in fact.

The guy didn't spend that much time at Katrina's house—he and Rhiannon were usually together at Samson's apartment in L.A. But when he was in Santa Barbara, he and Jas had settled into a habit of getting together for a workout or coffee.

Samson surveyed his sweat-soaked shirt and raised an eyebrow. "Whoa, there. You training for something?"

Jas swiped his hand down his chest. "Nah. Pushing myself a little, is all. Need to get my stamina up. I've been slacking."

"You could have texted. I would have come and spotted you."

Jas scratched the back of his neck. "Thanks, but I'm done now."

"I actually came over to see if you wanted to go for a run or play some basketball. It's been a while." Samson was dressed in an old T-shirt and gym shorts. "Since you've already got your workout in, why don't we have some coffee?"

Jas would rather they work out. Working out meant they didn't have to talk. "Oh no, I wouldn't want you to miss getting your—"

"I insist." Samson took a step forward. A former linebacker, he was big enough to crowd Jas, and Jas took an automatic step back, enough to let the younger man slip through. "I'll make the coffee."

Jas's smile probably looked more like a grimace. Short of tossing Samson bodily out of his house, he didn't know what he could do to get the man out. And he couldn't bounce him. Samson was much heftier, and also there was the whole thing about him dating Katrina's best friend.

People and all their connections. So complicated.

He trailed after Samson as the other man went to the kitchen, a short walk in the cozy two-bedroom cottage. Katrina had partially bought this property because of the in-law quarters in the back. Jas had been happy to take her up on her offer to live in the small home. Situated a few hundred feet away from Katrina's bigger house, its location struck a good balance between the protection he wanted to offer her and the distance he struggled to maintain between them.

Samson made a beeline to the coffee maker, familiar with the place in a way that made Jas nervous. It hadn't made him nervous a month ago, or even a week ago, but then Jas had gone and opened his usually tight-lipped mouth. "Isn't the French press making better coffee than that terrible machine you had?" Samson remarked. He pulled a coffee can from the cupboard.

"Yes, it is." Coffee was always coffee, in his opinion: hot bean soup he occasionally drank when other people around him were drinking it. He preferred not to depend on any chemical on a day-to-day basis.

Samson set the electric kettle to boil and measured out the grounds while Jas fetched the mugs and cream for Samson. "How have you been?" Jas asked, because that was what you asked friends, even friends you were mildly embarrassed to talk to.

"Busy as hell with boring corporate stuff." Samson leaned against the counter.

"Meetings for the new merger?" Rhiannon and Katrina's dating app was merging with Samson's aunt's dating website, and it had kept Rhiannon and Samson busy in L.A.

"Yeah. Rhiannon and my aunt love each other, but they're both two strong-headed CEOs. They need a pretty face to buffer." Samson poured the hot water over the grounds. He brought the press over to the counter.

Samson took a seat on one of the stools. "I see you've added some new rosebushes."

Jas remained standing and folded his hands in front of him on the counter. "Trying to get them in before the first frost."

"How are your orchids doing?"

"Good."

Samson rolled his empty mug between his palms. "Does this feel as awkward to you as it does to me?"

Jas tensed. The good thing about not having many friends was that he didn't really have anyone to confide in, which meant no one later brought up the unpleasant things he told them.

But last week, when Samson had caught him moodily digging up some weeds in the garden at the big house, Jas had cracked. *I got a call from an old friend*, had been the first words out of his mouth, and then it all came out. They'd sat in the sunshine, Samson quiet while Jas had spoken.

So now he did feel awkward, damn it. "I don't feel awkward," Jas lied.

Samson poured the coffee. "I know awkward when I see it, man. What I don't know is why."

Because Jas had felt good after he'd told Samson everything, for a few hours. Then he hadn't.

When Jas didn't speak now, Samson nodded. "Look, I don't have many friends."

Jas squinted at that, because it made no sense. Samson was too . . . what was the word? Charming.

Samson nodded. "At least, not ones I've made in the last ten years. Except for Rhiannon, and Katrina, and, well, you. So I know it can feel weird, telling someone something personal. I haven't told anyone what you told me, not even Rhiannon." Samson shrugged. "I know it feels weird, letting someone in, but it can be helpful too."

Jas wrapped his hands around the warm mug. "I didn't mean to, uh, burden you."

"Hardly a burden. If you feel embarrassed, you don't have to be." Samson braced himself on his elbows on the counter and nodded. "You know they used to call me the Lima Charm?" His smile didn't quite reach his eyes.

Jas nodded.

"I thought that meant I couldn't show anyone anything but a smile. I hid everything else. It worked, until it didn't."

He had a feeling Samson didn't tell many people how he felt about his nickname and the pressure to be a smiling face. Jas opened his mouth, then closed it again, the words slow in coming, but they emerged. "You're right. I'm not used to telling anyone my problems." The friends he'd had via forced proximity, in the Army or as part of a security team, were all scattered across the world now. They occasionally connected, but he was isolated here. Which had been what he'd wanted.

Samson took a sip of his coffee. "You're going through something. We all go through things. I didn't run and google you or anything, by the way. I only know what you've told me."

"Thank you." Googling wouldn't bring up much. The military had kept McGuire's trial under wraps as tightly as possible, and fourteen years ago, the news cycle hadn't been quite like it was now.

Jas thought the man had gotten off pretty lightly for flagrantly disobeying orders and wounding two people, including Jas: a twenty-year sentence, and he'd been out in five years with parole. The pardon McGuire was now rumored to be up for would lift his parole restrictions. It would be like nothing ever happened, except for the scars Jas carried.

McGuire was an apple-cheeked Midwestern boy, the son of a prominent prosecutor and a judge. His pardon would make news in a way his trial hadn't. Surely some enterprising journalist would try to track Jas down for a statement.

Jas controlled his full-body shudder. *Exposure.* Plus, the potential emergence of all those memories he'd spent fourteen years shoving down deep, so deep he'd never have to think about them. He'd run away after the trial, and a big part of him wished he could run away now.

"Hey," Samson placed his hand on Jas's shoulder. "It's okay, Jas. There are things I have trouble thinking about, too."

That, Jas believed. Samson's parents' and uncle's tragic deaths were public knowledge.

"You can talk about the stuff you feel comfortable talking about, and not about the things you don't. That's how I operate with my friends, okay?"

Friends. Another shot of that good feeling, like a drug coursing through his veins.

Tell him about Katrina, too.

Haha, nope. Jas wasn't going to magically be able to spill everything. Some things, though, might be okay. "I am . . . concerned about the thought of this pardon." *Concerned* was an understatement. "My friend who called me about this is pretty well-connected, and she's put in calls to a couple of people higher up to let her know which way the wind is blowing."

Samson's face turned grave. "You just have to wait, huh?"

Wait for the other shoe to drop. Jas nodded.

"In that case, you should try to get your mind off it. You know, Rhi's leaving for her trip to India today, so I was thinking of going out with some of my football buddies tonight. You'd like them. You know Dean and Harris Miller? I played with them on the Brewers. Dean's retired, Harris is retiring soon. Come with us."

Did he *know* the Miller cousins? Uh, yeah.

You are not a child, to be impressed by professional football players. Only he kind of was, damn it. He didn't really work conventional hours, but he was technically off today. There was no reason not to go. "I know them."

"Harris can be a bit of a smart-ass, and Dean will probably tell you all about his baby's poops, but they're good guys."

Jas blinked. "Did you say—"

"Poops, yeah." Samson waved his hand. "I don't get it, either, but I guess different colors and consistencies of poops all mean different things. I think it's a parent thing?"

"To be obsessed with poop?" That didn't sound right.

Samson shrugged. "I try to give Dean the benefit of the doubt, he's a great dad."

"You're going out in L.A.?"

Samson's smile widened. "I know people here hate to drive, but yeah. It's not so far, I promise."

It wasn't far. Rhiannon regularly commuted to Los Angeles from here when she stayed in Santa Barbara on long weekends.

"I'm not really one for bars or clubs." Jas shied away from places that had too much alcohol and too much testosterone and too much music. Loud noises and raised voices made his head throb and made sleep difficult for days after.

"Clubs? Oh no." Samson laughed and took a big gulp of his coffee. "I'm too tired for a wild Friday night like that, and Dean's parenting a toddler. No, Dean wants to go out to a new Mexican vegan place, and then maybe our regular pub for a nightcap. It's usually filled with older players. Nothing too rough. It'll get your mind off things. You can crash at my place, or drive back here after, whatever works for you."

Jas drummed his fingers on his thigh. What would he do tonight, if he didn't get away from the house? Sit here and fret over McGuire?

Or over Katrina checking out that strutting asshole yesterday?

He agreed before he could change his mind. "Okay. I'll drive separately." He'd go down early to avoid rush-hour traffic and poke around the city. He made a mental note to beef up security here. Out of an abundance of caution, there was always a guard posted at the gate of the property, but he posted two when he left the premises, even for a few hours. One of his old Army buddies had started a security company as a second career. Lorne had also testified against McGuire, and had been the one to call Jas about the possible pardon. Jas trusted her to hire good people.

"No problem." Samson rose and stretched. "I'm going to

go shower and then head down. Rhiannon's probably just waking up, and I want to say goodbye before she leaves for her trip."

"See you tonight." Jas showed Samson out, then loitered on the porch for a moment and checked his watch. Katrina was a creature of habit, so he knew at this exact second she was finishing reading her newspaper, catching up on the events of the world. She might be an angel investor by trade, but she was a collector of knowledge by nature. He'd never seen anyone inhale and synthesize information the way she did, on every topic imaginable, not just the ones related to the companies she invested in.

She'd carefully fold each piece of the paper when she was done and then make her way to the kitchen to cook breakfast. She cooked for him and Gerald, the housekeeper, as well as herself and her roommates. She'd always cooked for staff, even when she'd been married to Hardeep, and commanded a much larger number of employees. He'd never been a breakfast-eater, but he'd become one, which was no surprise. He clung to the crumbs of her affection, hoarding them carefully. He would eat brussels sprouts if she put them in front of him, and that was really saying something, given that they were tiny alien brains.

He'd been just shy of thirty when he'd first laid eyes on her. She'd been rushing to the courthouse for a surprise wedding with his ultra-rich boss, both of them wearing what was clearly the previous night's evening wear.

Jas had been suspicious, as he was of all new people, and

he'd only had an hour to run a background check on Katrina. Twenty-four, half–Thai American and half-white, no criminal record, no bankruptcies, financially sound, lived with her father who also happened to be her manager. No red flags.

The bride had worn green for the wedding, a rumpled dress made of emerald silk. Her hair had been loose, thick brown waves cascading over her gleaming shoulders. Her gaze had been downcast for much of the ceremony, her responses to the justice quiet but sure. When Hardeep had kissed her, it had been a quick, dry peck on her upturned cheek.

Jas had met her eyes only for a brief moment during the ceremony, when he'd signed as witness, and something about her stark vulnerability had cracked through his suspicion.

He hadn't fallen in love with her right then and there. His love had come later, as he trailed along behind her, protected her, discovered her quirks and quick wit. It was her small acts of kindness that had sucked him in, her clever intelligence and sweetness that had kept him hooked. She flowered open daily to receive and give affection and care to everyone in her orbit. She fascinated him. He had always dated sporadically, but his interest in other women had dwindled to zero over the past few years.

He asked me to go on a date with him.

Jas closed his eyes and counted to ten. *You're upset about this because you want to focus on something other than McGuire.*

Bullshit.

You could tell her you love her.

No, he absolutely could not. His pining for her was his own concern. As was his intense jealousy of Mr. ToothyGrin.

He'd learned how to control his emotions at an early age, before he'd even entered the regimented world of the United States military. His grandfather wouldn't have allowed anything else. Calm control was essential on a farm, where humans were often at the whim of animals, the weather, the land.

He knew how to strangle his feelings down deep, so deep he barely thought about the blood-and-horror-soaked event that had ended his career, or the backlash that came after from people he'd respected and sworn vows to, or how difficult it had been to readjust to civilian life. So difficult Jas had taken a position as a bodyguard for a man his grandfather had disdained, crossed continents to be away from all the reminders of what his life was not.

So he wasn't about to go spilling his feelings all over Katrina. He shuddered. Imagine if she pitied him, or worse, was horrified. At the very least, their working relationship would never be the same. Then he'd be deprived of even the crumbs.

His watch beeped, reminding him that breakfast would arrive soon. The world was often unreliable, but Katrina was not. Another thing he craved about her, that tight, perfectly predictable schedule. It was like a soothing balm to the part of him that missed his regimented life.

He went inside to get ready for the day. As he stood in the shower, letting the heat permeate his bad knee, he came to terms with the harsh truth.

Katrina hadn't shown interest in any romantic connection since Hardeep had died. He hadn't believed that would last forever. He didn't want it to last forever, if it would make her happier to seek someone out. He'd have to follow her and her prospective date around, watch them fall in love.

What was the other option? Quitting?

He scrubbed his face. Nope.

Chapter Four

Katrina was in an upbeat mood when she entered her kitchen, purring black-and-white cat in her arms. The sun streamed in through the huge east-facing windows, bouncing off the sparkling stainless steel appliances.

Morning people had once annoyed her, until she'd become one. She woke around five A.M. now and got so much done before the rest of the household started to stir. There might be some variation in her schedule during the day, but she preferred her start and end to stay the same. Routine comforted her.

She placed Zeus on the kitchen tile and gave her a good rub. The feline twined around her ankles as she filled her water bowl with clean, distilled water and served the food she made specially for her. "Spoiled," she cooed at her love, and stroked the black spot on Zeus's forehead.

Once her baby was taken care of, Katrina grabbed her wireless headphones and placed them over her ears. "Sienna, play Prince's *Love Symbol*," she said aloud, and the black cylinder on the counter lit up red. Her hips swayed as the music poured through the headphones. She danced her way to the counter where her other baby sat. She opened the lid of the glass jar and inhaled the yeasty aroma that greeted her.

Her mom had loved to cook. Katrina retained a couple of memories of key comfort dishes, like tom yum goong and mac and cheese . . . and sourdough bread. Using this exact starter.

It had been the one thing she'd been able to take with her when she'd gone to live with her father, just a few ounces of it. It was a miracle in Katrina's mind: all you needed was a small amount of the white stuff, and it would grow like magic once it was fed. It had been surprisingly easy to travel with over the years. Katrina added flour and water to the jar in the appropriate quantities, as she did every morning, and placed the starter back in its spot.

It took no time at all to whip up enough waffles for Gerald and Jas. She arranged the heaping plates on a tray with butter and syrup and glanced at her watch. She pulled her headphones off one ear as Gerald silently appeared in the doorway. Her small crew knew how much she hated to be startled or sneaked up on, so they adhered to her strict schedule or stomped loudly when around her. Even Zeus had a bell around her neck.

Her housekeeper was dressed casually, in jeans and a long-sleeved T-shirt, with his silver hair combed neatly over his bald spot. He wore a suit every day when Hardeep was alive, but he'd relaxed significantly since her late husband's death, even going so far as to tell her what foods he preferred for breakfast.

Her queries to Jas about the foods he loved had been met with shrugs and assurances that he liked everything she made. The fact that he always cleaned his plate was her only sign that he was telling the truth.

"Good morning, madam," Gerald intoned. His British accent was softened from years of living in the U.S. He kept his gaze pointedly on hers, which was standard for him. She wore a robe today in deference to the cooling temperature, but usually she was in short shorts and a tank. One of the small pleasures of pleasing only herself was that she could wear whatever she wanted in her own house. Almost ten years since she'd left life under her father's thumb, and she was still savoring the taste of freedom.

She liked clothes that revealed some skin, because she loved every inch of the body she'd finally been allowed to care for and nourish how she saw fit. She'd even come to love the faint scar on her face, though she'd received it traumatically. It was *hers*.

"Good morning, Gerald." She handed him the tray and he inclined his head.

"Thank you." A man of few words, he left with his and Jas's breakfast.

She went on to the next round of meals, cracking eggs, folding them into the batter, and warming the maple syrup. Her mood swung ever upward as the music lifted her and she created a meal for her friends. She found joy in cooking for people who were loudly appreciative of her efforts. Providing sustenance for others was her love language.

Katrina pulled her headphones off when she heard the

loud sound of footsteps. Rhiannon. She'd known her best friend and part-time roommate for going on a dozen years. The other woman got her in a way few people did.

Except Jas. He got her real well.

Okay. No more thinking about Jas for the rest of the morning, that's the rule. It was his day off, so it was her brain's day off from him, too. "Morning," she called out to Rhiannon, when her friend entered the kitchen.

Rhiannon yawned loudly. "Good morning."

"Is Samson joining us for breakfast?" She critically surveyed the amount of food she'd prepared and considered increasing it. Samson may not be a football player anymore, but he ate like one.

"Nah, he left to go back to L.A. He'll be scarce while I'm gone, he has some work to do with his foundation." Rhiannon pulled her sweatshirt together and zipped it up.

After so many years, Katrina was well versed in what Rhiannon's clothes meant, though her ever-changing wardrobe of hoodies and jeans might look the same to anyone else. The blue hoodie was her power sweatshirt, but it was also one of her more loose ones. Her travel power sweatshirt. "Ready for your trip?"

"As ready as I'll ever be."

"I loved India when I was there." She'd traveled quite a bit in her youth. It hadn't always been enjoyable or anxiety-free, and she was in no hurry to hop on to a transatlantic flight anytime soon—or ever—but there had been a few trips she was glad she'd taken.

Rhiannon went to the cupboard where the plates were

stored. Katrina was aware she was biased, but she thought Rhiannon Hunter was surely one of the most beautiful women in the world, with her high cheekbones, glowing dark-brown skin, and big black eyes. She'd cut her hair recently, and the curls brushed her shoulders and framed her heart-shaped face perfectly. "I'm kinda nervous."

That was a big admission for Rhiannon, who prided herself on being tough. "There's no need to be nervous. We are prepared for this."

Usually, Katrina didn't concern herself with the day-to-day operations of the start-ups her fund invested in. Because of Rhiannon, she was more actively engaged with Crush, and had happily taken the lead on a lot of their tentative expansion into foreign markets. India had its own dating apps, but Crush's arrival into the huge smartphone-armed population was an opportunity to expand their footprint significantly.

Rhiannon made a face. "I've been working on this Matchmaker merger so much, I feel like you know more about the expansion than I do."

Katrina shook her head. "That's because you're used to being a hundred and forty percent prepared, so when you're actually a hundred percent prepared, you feel underprepared."

"How dare you utter the truth first thing in the morning."

Katrina smiled and slid the last waffle out of the waffle iron. "There's nothing about this company you don't know. And honestly, I'm a phone call away."

Rhiannon set three places at the table. "And thank God for that."

Katrina smiled. She was grateful, too, that she'd reached out to Rhiannon with an investment offer four years ago, when she heard her friend had left her previous employment.

Do you have any idea how much a start-up costs? Rhiannon had asked her.

Do you have any idea how much my husband left me? she'd countered.

Rhiannon had never asked for that number, but it had been a lot. Hardeep had been a jeweler for the stars, yes, and that had brought in a tidy sum, but he'd also invested in a certain then-obscure search engine in the nineties.

Katrina had taken the multiple zeros she'd inherited and turned them into even more zeros.

"You'll be gone for less than two weeks. Meet with the team we assembled, lay the groundwork, and we'll be rolling in the rupees shortly." Katrina slid her friend a sideways glance. "I'm surprised Samson's not coming with you." Rhiannon had only ever been a part-time roommate at best, but she'd been gone a lot over the last few months. Rhiannon had her own apartment in L.A., but Katrina suspected that her friend had been spending most of her nights with Samson.

"I asked him, but he's got a fund-raiser he's committed to, so it was a no-go."

"Gotcha." Inside, her inner romantic pumped her fist at Rhiannon's admission. Awwwww. As far as she knew, this was the first trip Rhiannon had invited her boyfriend along on.

A loud yawn preceded Jia's entrance into the room. The internet would be stunned to see Jia Ahmed in baggy cotton pajama pants and a sweater, her hair uncovered and in a simple braid, but the toned-down fashion and beauty influencer was still glamorous, the pep in her walk not diminished by the early hour.

She had put on makeup, though it was only a brush of eyeliner and a slight tint of lip gloss. In fact, Katrina didn't think she'd ever seen Jia without some makeup in the five months since she'd come to live with them.

Katrina wasn't quite sure how this living arrangement had come to be. Rhiannon had gone home back east for about twenty-four hours, and returned with the news that she'd invited a childhood friend's baby sister to live with them.

Katrina had been mildly anxious about whether the semi-famous Pakistani American influencer would like her. That fear was put to rest about five minutes after meeting Jia. The younger woman was goofy and lacked a filter, but she made up for her chattiness in the pure earnest warmth and sweetness she exuded.

"I'm dying of hunger," Jia announced.

Katrina's lips quivered. Jia very much liked to announce things. "How do you feel about waffles?"

"Ooh yes, love them."

"Can you grab the juice, Jia?" Rhiannon asked.

"Yes, ma'am." The younger woman stuck her head in the fridge. "Orange, apple?"

"Both."

Katrina took her seat at the small breakfast table in the

sunny nook and neatly placed a napkin on her lap while the other women joined her. The much larger dining room was rarely used, except for holidays. The last few Christmases had been fun, with Rhiannon, select Crush employees, and her own staff.

What's going to happen when Rhiannon leaves you?

She swatted away the anxious thought. Nothing. She would be fine. People came into her life, and they left, and Katrina had learned to enjoy the parts in the middle. That was really all a person could do. "How was your party last night, Jia?"

Jia was at the point in her career where she was getting invites to various product launches. As far as Katrina could tell, being an influencer meant a whole lot of visibility. Like modeling, but with more access.

Inwardly, Katrina shuddered. Jia could have that.

"I couldn't enjoy it." Jia tapped on her ever-present phone and showed Katrina the screen. "Would you look at this jerk?"

Katrina peered at the photo of Jia contemplatively staring out at the ocean. "Ah. It's you, Jia."

"I know it's me! Look at the comment from the motivational model."

"What's a motivational model?" Rhiannon asked.

"You know. A model who captions all his pics with inspirational quotes? Like, from Gandhi or Mother Teresa or the Dalai Lama."

Rhiannon pursed her lips. "Lovely. I'm sure Gandhi would be delighted he went on a hunger strike so his words could caption thirst traps."

Katrina took the phone from Jia and read the comment out loud. *"Wow, the west coast really agrees with you. Your skin has never looked better."* She handed the phone back to its owner. "I'm sorry. I don't see what the problem is."

"You're reading it wrong." Jia raised the pitch of her voice. "The *west coast agrees* with you. Your skin has *never looked better."* She scowled.

"That bitch," Rhiannon commented, and took a sip of her juice.

"You're saying that sarcastically, but let me assure you, this guy is the worst." Jia sneered. "He's implying my skin hasn't always been flawless. How dare he?" She stroked her smooth cheek. "Look at this. Like a baby's bottom."

"Your face is like a baby's bottom?"

Jia growled at Rhiannon. Their relationship had quickly settled into a sisterly squabbling. "You know what I mean. Trust me, I'm reading this exactly right. I have good instincts about this. I couldn't sleep a wink, I'm exhausted."

"You can't tell. Ah, to be dewy and twenty-five again."

"I'm twenty-seven," Jia answered pertly.

"You'd probably sleep more if you didn't stay up all night texting a guy."

Jia's flush confirmed Rhiannon's guess.

Rhiannon poured a generous serving of syrup on her waffles. "Where in the world is your mysterious boyfriend now, anyway?"

Katrina gently kicked her best friend under the table. Jia had moved cross-country to expand her empire and get the kind of opportunities that were only accessible in close proximity to L.A. When Rhiannon had proposed adding her as a roommate, she'd told Katrina that Jia's family had been worried about her moving here and living alone.

About ten minutes after meeting her, Katrina had understood Jia's family's hesitance. The girl was social-media-savvy and clearly brilliant, but she had the kind of sheltered, wide-eyed eagerness and innocence that came from not having been exposed to the worst of mankind yet.

Katrina wasn't that much older, and not nearly as cynical as Rhiannon, but she felt about eighty years removed from Jia when it came to street smarts.

Which was why she wasn't eager to crush Jia's spirit. Especially when it came to this mystery guy Jia had been texting for the past month. A guy Jia hadn't met or seen yet.

"He's in Hong Kong this week," Jia said blithely, unaware of or uncaring about Rhiannon's sardonic tone. "He's finishing up his business in Asia and then he should be in the U.S. in a few weeks."

Rhiannon nodded. "Uh-huh, uh-huh, uh-huh. And what is his business, again? Or his name, for that matter? Asking for science."

This time, Jia's flattened lips told Katrina she'd picked up on Rhiannon's disbelief. "Stop playing big sister, Rhi. I've got enough of those."

Rhiannon pointed her fork at Jia. "None of your biological big sisters know about this guy. I do. I'm looking out for you. It's weird you guys haven't even video-chatted yet."

"It's not weird. He'd rather we meet in person first."

Rhiannon scoffed. "Have you ever heard of this thing called catfishing?"

Jia's face turned red and Katrina cleared her throat, eager to ease tensions. She hated arguments. "How about I tell you guys about the guy *I* met yesterday?"

A pair of light brown and dark brown eyes turned immediately to her. "Where did you meet a guy?" Jia asked.

"At French Coast. We sat at a table together. I talked to him and we flirted a little and then he asked me out."

"What?" Rhiannon's scowl deepened. "What's his name? When are you going out? What does he look like?"

Katrina shook her head, having expected nothing less than this third degree. Rhiannon might be protective of Jia, but she was overprotective of Katrina. She would happily internet-stalk any guy in Katrina's vicinity. Possibly even real-life-stalk them. The amount of data Rhiannon had at her fingertips was a little frightening. "His name was Ross, and he was very cute. He likes to bicycle, and his mother has an adorable puppy. But we're not going out. I didn't feel a spark."

Rhiannon harrumphed. "Okay. I won't run a background check on him then."

"Now *I'm* going to tell you to stop playing big sister." Only she wouldn't, because deep down, Katrina adored Rhiannon for caring so much about her. Having a sister had always been her dream.

"You can't go out with some stranger you meet in a café. Or on the internet," Rhiannon tacked on, giving Jia a meaningful look.

Katrina cut into her waffle. "You made a fortune for both of us by building an app where people literally go out with strangers. Strangers on the internet. You met Samson on that app."

Rhiannon swallowed the bite in her mouth before answering. "That's different."

"How is it different?"

"It . . . just is."

Katrina rolled her eyes. "Okay then."

"Wait a minute." Jia's silverware clattered onto her plate. "Is French Coast the place with that blue-and-white wall? And the red chairs?" The youngest roommate's perfectly arched eyebrows drew together in a frown.

"Yeah, it is. Why?"

Jia bit her lip and glanced at Rhiannon. "Uh. No reason."

"Pretty sure there's a reason."

"Um . . ."

Her hesitation worried Katrina. "What? You can say it."

Jia reached for her phone. "There was something I saw yesterday on Twitter, but I didn't have much time to look at it, because I was—well, that's not important." Her fingers tapped on the screen.

Rhiannon cocked her head. "Spit it out, Jia."

Dread balled up in Katrina's stomach when Jia's face turned pale. She placed the phone faceup on the table so they could all see.

It was her.

Katrina's face wasn't visible, hidden by both her baseball cap and the way the camera was angled, thank God. But

Katrina could still make out the curve of her round cheek and the light brown strands of her hair.

"What is this?" she whispered. "Paparazzi? Was he someone famous?" Ross's face was more distinguishable than hers in the shot.

"Actually . . . you're both famous now." Jia exited out of the picture she'd clicked on, and the tweet it had come from was revealed.

The thread of tweets, rather.

Katrina was barely aware of Rhiannon scooting closer to her. She read through the thread with growing disbelief, each tweet more ridiculous than the next.

This guy just sat down at this girl's table and they make such a cute couple.
♡ 496   ↻ 10k   ♡ 36k   ⬆

OMG! Wouldn't it be adorable if he's her soul mate???
♡ 68   ↻ 386   ♡ 1k   ⬆

I don't see any wedding rings. 👀
♡ 42   ↻ 1.3k   ♡ 10k   ⬆

They touched legs!
♡ 565   ↻ 368   ♡ 889   ⬆

Aw, they're talking about each other's families.
♡ 2.7k   ↻ 1k   ♡ 4k   ⬆

The fuck.

She looked at the avatar of the tweeter. It was the smiling blond woman from the table next to theirs, the one she'd thought was in the middle of writing something juicy.

You. You were the something juicy.

"You talked to him about your parents?"

Katrina shook her head at Rhiannon's skeptical question. The surprise was valid. She didn't talk about her parents with anyone, save Rhiannon and her therapist. Jas knew about some pieces of her family history. That was it. "We were talking about his mom's *dog*, and Zeus," she muttered. She waded through the meticulously detailed play-by-play of her and Ross's interaction, each innocent action and part of their conversation taking on a rom-com spin.

"Jesus, there's like over fifty tweets—" she gasped.

Breaking: #CafeBae and #CuteCafeGirl went to the bathroom AT THE SAME TIME 😊
♡190　⟲6.4k　♡14k　↑

"What the hell, we didn't go to the bathroom together. We definitely didn't do what this is implying. He went to the bathroom. I went to get some napkins. I was barely gone for a few minutes."

"This is so creepy." Rhi took the phone from her and kept scrolling. "Jeez. *He's got a peach to die for.*"

Katrina raked her hands through her hair. "Not entirely inaccurate, but irrelevant, since I wasn't personally moved by the peach."

Rhiannon shook her head. "They overheard him asking you out, and said you agreed."

"I didn't." Katrina's words were too loud, but she couldn't

dial back the volume, she was so agitated. "I mean, he did ask me out, but like I told you, I turned him down."

Rhiannon *kept* scrolling. Oh God, was it never-ending? "After a bajillion tweets of buildup, she probably had to make up a happy ending to satisfy her followers."

Katrina scrubbed her face. "This lady doesn't have a lot of followers, at least, does she?"

Rhiannon was silent for a moment, then she cleared her throat. "As of this morning, she has about two hundred thousand."

Two hundred *thousand*.

"Some of those have to be bots, though," Jia tagged on in a hurry. Like it mattered if even two-thirds of them were bots.

Two hundred thousand people had seen her face on the internet.

"The thread went pretty viral. She probably got a lot of those followers overnight," Rhiannon said.

"Why? I mean, it was an unusual encounter for me, but it was, like, utterly typical to most people."

"People love to ship other humans, real or fictional." Rhiannon slid the phone back to Jia. "This woman spun a story, and the world went with it. They got invested in your happily-ever-after."

Happily-ever-after? No, this was a disaster. "She took my photo," Katrina whispered, and picked at her cuticles. Save for the vague pics on her dating profile, no one had taken her photo since she'd disappeared into relative obscurity.

She didn't have any social media. Every photo of her on the internet was from years and years ago, and that was how she preferred it.

Anonymity had been the main thing that had comforted her when she'd gone for that first drive. The assurance that no one would know who she truly was if she had a panic attack in public. The certainty that anyone who wanted to hurt Katrina King would stay far away.

"At least you had that hat on. You're pretty unidentifiable in it," Jia reassured her.

It did reassure her, but only for a moment. "You identified me."

"Only after you told us about the encounter. And honestly, I live with you. I know your face."

Katrina waited for her heart to start racing, but an odd, icy cold had settled over her. It might not be a huge pool, but other people knew her face too. And the woman—Becca, according to her username—may have given a halfhearted thought to hiding her identity, but she hadn't pixelated her face out entirely.

She pushed her plate away. "Okay, so odds are no one will recognize me, right?"

"Right." Jia nodded. "And these things blow over. A cat will learn how to play the tuba in like an hour and you'll no longer be a viral phenomenon."

A phenomenon. She tried to smile, but feared it was a baring of teeth. "Cool. Cool, cool, cool, cool." This wasn't a big deal. It would be fine.

"I'll put my trip off. I'll get Lakshmi on it. We'll figure this out."

Rhiannon's assistant was amazing and possibly a warlock, but Katrina feared even Lakshmi wouldn't be able to do anything about this. "No. You go. Don't say anything to Lakshmi, or even Samson yet, please? I'll monitor it and it'll be fine." The numbness was nice, a new way to manage her emotions.

"Should we tell Jas?" Rhiannon asked.

"No." The single word was sharp, but she couldn't help it. Maybe she should tell Jas, but that would mean bugging him during his time off.

You're being foolish. He is your core security, and should know about this.

But that was the problem with getting romantically interested in one's bodyguard, eh? The embarrassment of her crush finding out about this debacle outweighed her need to tell her employee that she'd gone viral, albeit anonymously. For now. "I'll tell him if it escalates."

As if she sensed her distress, Zeus came to rub herself against Katrina's legs. She scooped the cat up, scratching under her chin. Zeus immediately collapsed in a boneless heap against Katrina's chest. She wished she could relax as easily. "Do you guys mind cleaning up?"

"Of course," Jia murmured.

"Excellent. Will you excuse me, please?" She didn't wait for either of them to respond, just got up from the table and made her way to the door.

It'll blow over. It'll pass. No one will be able to identify you. The words played in her head as she walked down the hallway to her sunny little office. They had to be true, those words, or the tendrils of panic would grab hold of her and never let go.

No, no, that wasn't true. The panic always let go. It did. She'd survive.

It'll pass.

You're safe.

Chapter Five

"Here's Miley in her Halloween costume. She's going to be a Tootsie Roll."

Jas dutifully perused the photo on the phone shoved under his nose. The baby was about a year and a half old and sported a solemn expression on the chubby face that poked out of the cutout in the candy costume. "Very cute."

Dean Miller took the phone back, swiped a few times, and then showed it to Jas again, beaming. "Here she is dressed like a peppermint patty."

Jas expected the photo to be from a previous year, but the girl looked the same, if more resigned, as a foil-wrapped square. "I thought her Halloween costume was the Tootsie Roll."

"Oh, that's for trick-or-treating. We're having a party, too, to celebrate her second Halloween. I can't pick one look, so I got her a bunch of different outfits and took photos." Dean flipped through the photos. "Here she is as peas, and a piggy, and a roll of pennies, and a dinosaur, and a—"

"Can I see the dinosaur?" Harris, Dean's cousin, interrupted from across the table.

"Sure thing." Dean passed him the phone.

Harris didn't glance at the device. Instead, he tucked it into the inside of his jacket. "Thanks."

Jas coughed to hide his sudden laugh.

"Hey!" Dean glared at his cousin.

"No one wants to see your kid dressed up like food and animals, cousin."

"Jas was interested."

"No, he wasn't. He's new, so you were taking advantage of his politeness to make him suffer through a slideshow of your kid's every move."

Jas was grateful neither man seemed to want his input at all. Dean growled at Harris and placed his hands on the table, rising slightly out of his chair. "Give me my phone back."

Harris smirked, unconcerned. The two Black men had the undeniable stamp of family about them, similarities in their face and build, both clearly athletes—or former athletes, since Dean had retired a couple years ago and Harris was on his last season. Their comfortable squabbling held the ring of near-brothers. "Come and get it, green bean."

Dean slammed his big fist on the table. "Veganism is good for the environment and your body!"

Samson walked back to the table at that exact instant, holding another round of drinks. "Guys, simmer down, drinks are here."

Dean bared his teeth. "He took my phone."

"He was over-dadding." Harris rolled his eyes.

"You try having your heart walking around outside your body, Harris."

Samson placed the tray in front of them. Jas grabbed his Coke. Since he was driving, he hadn't wanted to drink.

"Harris, give him back his phone. Dean, your mother-in-law came all the way from the Valley to stay the night with Miley so you can have a break, remember? Enjoy the time off," Samson said.

Harris and Dean both grumbled, but Harris handed back the phone and Dean subsided in his chair. "I didn't even get to show you her as a bag of potatoes," he grumbled.

Harris opened his mouth, but Samson cut off whatever teasing remark he had locked and loaded. "Harris, that woman at the bar was checking you out."

Harris's attention was immediately diverted. He straightened and puffed out his chest, then casually glanced over his shoulder. "Holy shit, she's hot. Be right back, guys."

Dean shook his head as his cousin left. "Was she really checking him out?"

Samson grinned. "She glanced this way a few times while I was getting the drinks. I suppose she could have been checking any of you out." He shrugged. "If she's not interested, Harris will come back or find someone who is."

"Samson's been running interference between Harris and me since we were in college," Dean informed Jas.

A pang of . . . something hit Jas, and he had no idea what

it was, but it was sharp. Wistfulness, maybe? Over their obviously deep, long-running bonds?

"Sorry we've talked your ear off, Jas. Haven't let you get
a word in edgewise." Dean's smile was friendly. "Tell us
about yourself. What's your story?"

What *was* his story? "I'm in security. I work for Rhiannon's roommate."

"Security work sounds so cool. Like Jack Ryan."

"Jack Ryan was CIA," Samson said.

"Well, who was a famous bodyguard, then?"

"The guy from *The Bodyguard*?" Samson suggested.

Dean shook his head. "Don't know that one. Still sounds
glamorous."

"It's not really. You spend a lot of your time hoping
nothing happens." Only once had something happened to
Katrina, and that memory still gave Jas nightmares. "I do
mostly cyber-security now. It's basically a desk job." His
degree was in computers. It had taken a little self-study to
get back to them, but he genuinely enjoyed designing digital
lockboxes for information.

"Let me have my illusions. My life is pretty boring, all
playdates and poop." Dean took a sip of his beer, and Jas
eyed him warily, hoping he wouldn't go more into detail on
that poop thing.

Luckily, or unluckily, depending on how one viewed his
next question, Dean didn't go the poop route. "How'd you
get into that line of work?"

Jas gave the bare bones explanation. "I was in the military

until I was about twenty-five, and medically discharged. I called up an old family friend to ask if he had any jobs available. He needed someone to head his security." *Family friend* was simplifying Hardeep's complicated relationship with the Singhs. Hardeep's grandfather had started a farm in NorCal with Jas's great-grandfather, and then bounced to go back to India. Jas's grandfather was still salty over that old slight.

Dean raised his eyebrows. "Military, huh? Army?"

"Yes. Rangers."

Dean gave a low whistle. "That's, like, elite, right?"

Jas shrugged. He'd thought it was. He'd been really excited to be accepted.

"Were you deployed?"

"Yes," Jas said, and he couldn't help how short his tone was. "Iraq."

"Hey, Dean, have you seen that new movie—"

Dean cut off Samson's change of topic. "You know, we should put you in touch with the nonprofit Samson and I work for, right, Samson? We help people with Chronic Traumatic Encephalopathy, head injuries. Trevor's looking to expand the organization to include veterans. A lot of service people are diagnosed with CTE, too."

Jas leaned back in his chair. "I don't know how I could help."

"Trevor's looking to consult with some veterans, get an idea as to needs and resources, especially when it comes to mental health. The symptoms no one can see and often slip through the cracks."

"I'm afraid I'm not a typical vet." He hadn't had to rely on the government's dubious assistance.

He'd had advantages his brothers and sisters hadn't, even with his discharge, his injury, and the trial that had pitted him against his own man and left him a snitch in the eyes of many of his colleagues. He'd had a job and money and health care and a place to lick his wounds. "I don't think I can assist anyone."

Samson cleared his throat. "Dean—"

"Even so—"

"The girl was checking *Dean* out, you asshole." Harris dropped down in his seat, cutting Dean off and entirely distracting him.

"Is that so?" Dean preened, and stroked his beard.

"It's cool. I told her Dean was married and had an *adorable* baby. Informed her all about how my precious niece was going to be a sushi roll for Halloween." Harris wiggled his phone. "Got her number."

"She's a tootsie roll, not a sushi—oh shit." Dean stopped. "A sushi roll would be really fucking adorable."

Jas sipped his soda and relaxed at the banter resuming. The last thing he wanted to do was talk about vets and mental health, a subject he was ill-equipped to handle when he was actively trying to avoid thinking about the time he'd spent in Iraq.

"Anyway," Dean said, and raised his glass to toast his cousin. "I'm sure you'll have a great date. Try not to think too much about the fact that she thought I was hotter than you."

Samson snorted, and Jas couldn't help but chuckle as

Harris's smug smile vanished. The football player growled. "Fuck."

JAS GRABBED HIS coat from the passenger seat of his car and clambered out. His personal vehicle was a hybrid. It barely fit his body, but he mostly drove long distances when he left the house, so he preferred to save some gas.

The evening fall air nipped through his lightweight cotton Henley as he walked up the driveway. A dark figure separated from the wide porch of the big house. Jas stilled until the man fell under one of the lights, and then he relaxed. "Richard. Anything going on?"

The blond-haired man shook his head. He'd maintained his high-and-tight haircut, though he hadn't been in the military for a while. "No, sir. Quiet night." He hesitated. "Except there is one thing. I was doing a round and Ms. Smith opened the door to her office and yelled at me."

Ms. Smith was the name the guards used for Katrina. It was a simple way to make sure no one who overheard knew who their client was. "Yelled at you?" That was very unlike Katrina. In all the time Jas had known her, he'd never heard Katrina raise her voice to anyone. She was unfailingly polite to contractors and people on her payroll.

"Yes. She said I scared her, that she couldn't see who I was." The boy's eyes widened. "I swear I didn't mean to scare her, and the exterior lights were on. But I thought you should know. She seemed calm when I left her."

"Thanks." He didn't reassure Richard. He'd talk to Katrina first, in the morning. "Will you be relieved soon?"

"Yes, sir. John's arriving in about an hour for the night shift."

"Excellent. Good night."

Richard all but saluted him. Jas stopped when he was almost at his cottage and looked over his shoulder. From this angle, he could see the dim light from Katrina's office spilling out onto the patio. It was late. If he wasn't her bodyguard, if he was someone . . . else . . . to her, he'd go check on her now.

He wasn't, though.

He went inside and shut his door firmly. If only he could shut the door on his wayward feelings as easily.

His phone buzzed and he smiled faintly when he saw who it was. He put the phone on speaker and toed off his loafers, depositing them on the shoe organizer next to his front door. "Hello, Mom."

"Hello, dear. How are you?"

"Fine. Just got home." He went to his bedroom and tossed his cell on his bed. He pulled his shirt off over his head, placing it neatly in the hamper.

"Where were you?"

"I went out with some friends in L.A."

His mother paused. He could imagine Tara Kaur sitting in the living room of his parents' small two-bedroom condo. They lived in a more affordable suburb of the City, but nothing in the Bay Area was affordable for the middle class anymore. The fact that they had a second bedroom was a miracle and a product of tight rent control and a generous landlord.

"You went out with who?"

"Uh." He took off his socks. "Friends?"

"You have friends?" his mother asked, and he tried not to be offended by her skepticism, since he had basically been marveling at the same thing earlier in the night.

"What did he say?"

Jas winced at the booming voice of his stepfather. Oh no, this was about to become a family affair. He crossed his fingers that his stepbrother, Bikram, wasn't also lurking on the call.

"He said he went out with his friends in L.A., Gurjit."

"What friends?"

His mom spoke to him. "You're on speaker. Jas, your father wants to ask you who these friends are as well."

"I can hear him. That's what speaker does." Jas sat on the side of his bed.

"What friends are these, in Los Angeles?" his dad demanded. "We don't know them." Gurjit was a high school history teacher and he spoke with the gentle firmness of a man used to handling shenanigans.

"You don't know all my friends," he said, and was immediately annoyed by how defensive he sounded. He was thirty-nine years old, for crying out loud.

"Dear, of course we do," his mom said. She had a sweet lightness to her voice, as if the peach farm she'd grown up on had infused her with the fruit's essence. "Who is in Los Angeles?"

"Rhiannon's boyfriend and his friends." Though his parents had never met Rhiannon or Katrina, they knew everyone's names. They peppered him with a million questions about his life when he was with them.

"Samson Lima?" There was excitement in his dad's voice now. "Say, when are you going to get me a football signed by him?"

"I don't know him well enough for that sort of thing." Samson would probably happily sign a football for his dad, but Jas wasn't accustomed to asking anyone for anything.

"Don't make him hit up his little buddies for autographs," Tara admonished.

Jas bit the inside of his cheek, amused at the idea of his mom calling anyone who had once been a linebacker a little anything.

"Did you have fun?"

A stab of guilt ran through him at the eagerness in his mother's voice. They worried over him so much. It would have been easier if he had gone home after he was injured and lived on the farm or in their small condo for the last fourteen years. Easier for them, not for him.

That worry was the reason he hadn't told them about the potential pardon for McGuire. His mother had wept when Jas had come back home. For his injury, for what he'd seen. He couldn't tell her now that she might have to relive that. "I did, yes. Thank you."

"Good. I'm glad you're getting out. Widening your circle," Tara said.

"I'm going to get ready for bed," Gurjit announced. "Good night, son."

"Good night."

There was the unmistakable sound of a brief kiss, and though it was his parents, Jas smiled. He didn't know his biological father. He'd been fourteen when his mom had met and married Gurjit. He was glad his mother had found happiness with a man who loved her dearly.

Tara came back on the line, and Jas could tell she'd taken him off speaker. "I called to ask if you were going to come to the parade," she said quietly, in a rush, and Jas knew immediately that his stepdad had probably told her not to ask him this exact thing.

He rubbed the bridge of his nose. "That's a while off."

"Not that far now. A few weeks."

"I haven't gone to the parade in years." Not since he'd come back from Iraq, for sure.

"I know." Her voice dropped lower. "They're honoring your grandfather this year."

"I'm aware." He shifted. There it was, that tug of longing followed by fear. How to tell his mom that while he deeply missed their hometown's annual Sikh parade, and would give anything to attend it again, the event was too big and loud and crowded for him. He avoided such places to the point that he used to have to delegate security detail to other guards back when Katrina and Hardeep had gone to areas where there might be fireworks or intense crowds. "Mom—"

"It would mean so much to him. And to me. But really to him."

"I see Grandpa all the time." He kept the emotion out of his tone, which pleased him. He definitely saw his parents more, but he did see his grandfather quite a bit, even went to the farm for monthly dinners with the whole family. He never stayed more than a night, but he went.

"He's all alone and he's getting older. This is all he wants."

"Did he say that?"

The beat of silence told him that his grandfather hadn't said anything of the sort to his only daughter.

Stubborn old man.

"He would have told me, but our calls have been so rushed lately. He's out of the country for the next couple of weeks. He had to go to Mexico to work on that school he's established."

Is he well enough to make a trip like that? Mexico wasn't far, but his grandfather wasn't young. "Does he have someone with him?"

"Yes, he took a few employees." His mother tried a different tack. "We're all going to be there that night. It will be so apparent if my eldest isn't here. What will people say? Come for me?"

His lips twisted. His mother played dirty. Yuba City was a relatively small and gossipy town. His absence would be felt.

"You can stay at the little house. It's all yours. No one will bother you there. You can have your privacy and come to this one little award ceremony and then you can either go back to Santa Barbara or stay in your own home on the farm."

When Jas was nineteen, his grandfather had deeded over the empty house his great-grandparents had built, as well as a small tract of the surrounding land. No one was living in it, his grandpa had said, so Jas might as well have it.

Deep nostalgia shot through Jas. He loved that house. Jas had known it was a lure and a bribe when his grandpa had given him the deed. A way to tie him to a business and life he didn't want.

He had few emotional ties to the huge home his grandpa had built later in life and now lived in, so it was easier to pop in there for their monthly dinners and leave. The farm sat on hundreds of acres. He didn't even have to see the little house.

Jas tugged at a loose thread on his comforter. Oh, but he missed every inch of that place.

It might be different now. You could go and see. Not the parade, but at least the house.

He shook that thought away. It would surely be too painful, and to what end? He and his grandfather narrowly avoided getting locked in their usual battle of wills during a once-a-month dinner. An extended visit would be rough.

"You don't have to commit this minute. Think on it?" Tara asked.

He gritted his teeth. *Tell her why you don't want to go. Tell her about the loud noises, and the fireworks, and the heat, and the crush of people.* His mother was kind and empathetic, a kindergarten teacher. She would understand. "Fine," he said reluctantly. "I'll think on it. No promises."

"Good enough for now. I love you. Have a good night."

"Good night. Love you too." He hung up and sat there for a moment, taking a beat to collect himself. The doorbell roused him.

Who on earth would be looking for him at this hour?

Jas strode to the door and yanked it open to find Jia. He'd never seen the girl without a full face of makeup, a coordinated outfit, and a matching hijab, but tonight she wore lounge pants, a cotton shirt, and a scarf tied over her hair.

"What's wrong?" he demanded when she didn't speak, but merely stared at him.

"Um." She dipped her gaze down his body and then back up, and he flushed as the cool air hit his bare chest.

"Hang on." He shut the door, grabbed the shirt and shoes he'd taken off, and pulled them on. He was back in under a minute.

She snapped to attention and cleared her throat. "I'm sorry to bother you, but something's come up, and, well . . . I hate tattling or anything, but Rhiannon's on a flight across the ocean, and it seems like you've known Katrina the longest of all of us, so I thought I would come and see if we can—"

Jas cut off her rambling. "What's wrong?" he repeated.

Jia bit her lower lip and looked torn. "Katrina said not to tell you."

"Jia."

"But she didn't say you couldn't guess, I suppose."

"I am not playing charades with my Katri . . . my employer's well-being."

Jia didn't seem to notice his almost-slip. She typed something on her phone. "Whoops, dropped my phone." She tossed it at him and he caught it automatically against his chest. She gave him a meaningful look.

He stared at the tweet blankly. *He has a 🐻 to die for!* "What is this?"

"Scroll up to the first tweet in the thread. Katrina's viral."

Jas started to read. "What?"

"It means she's internet-famous."

"I know what going viral means. But I don't understand how Katrina—" He stopped as he got to the first photo of her. She was instantly recognizable to him, despite the baseball cap she wore and the halfhearted blurring of her face. He scrolled through the tweets and embedded photos, his disbelief and fury growing as he read them. "What the hell?" He pinned Jia with his glare, though it wasn't meant for her. "I was there. I couldn't hear what they were saying, but it wasn't . . . this." He'd been silently seething in dismay the entire time, trying to read their lips, but even he knew this was a fabrication.

The second-most-liked tweet was the one implying they'd hooked up in the bathroom. That for sure wasn't true. Katrina had never been out of his sight.

"That's what Katrina said. I have no doubt it's all lies this woman spun to fit her own narrative."

He stepped outside and closed the door behind him. "How is Katrina handling this?" He thought of Richard saying Katrina had snapped at him, and immediately realized that was a foolish question.

Katrina craved anonymity. She invested and gave charitably, yes, but it was all done through layers of paperwork and systems he'd helped her design. Even the local small business owners who knew her, like Mona, didn't know her full name.

"She was definitely . . . upset. I tried to tell her that no one will recognize her, which seemed to be Katrina's main concern, but I don't think she bought it. Her face is pretty hidden, though, right? You're the security expert. What do you think?"

He went back to the first photo of Katrina and used his fingers to zoom in. It might be hard for a stranger to recognize Katrina from these photos, but for someone who was familiar with her? He examined the photo further for other identifiable details, grimacing when he caught a tiny clue. He turned the phone around to show Jia. "Look at her handbag on the back of the chair. It has her initials embossed on the strap." He couldn't believe he'd missed that until now, or he would have stopped her from ever carrying that purse.

Jia squinted. "I can barely make it out. Besides, lots of people have the initials KKA."

Katrina King Arora. Her married name. Hardeep must have given Katrina the purse. The man had been unfailingly generous to everyone in his orbit, which had put Jas in a pickle. It was hard to be jealous of a good man.

"No one will identify her off it, but it's confirmation for anyone who has their suspicions," he said grimly. "The idiot who took these photos should be sued." And Jas should be fired. What kind of a bodyguard was he? How had he not caught the woman at the next table taking creeper shots of her?

"Oh, hey. I can take secret photos so well a CIA agent couldn't spot me. Don't beat yourself up over that."

He hadn't realized he'd spoken that thought out loud. Jia's condolences were nice, but he didn't want to be consoled. He handed Jia back her phone. Not now. He'd feel like a failure later. "Where is Katrina now?"

"In her office." Jia worried her fingers together. "I stuck close to home today and checked in on her, and she's been glued to her computer. I've been monitoring too. The story's gaining steam, it's starting to get picked up by mainstream news outlets."

Which meant the threat to Katrina's anonymity was growing. He gave Jia a short nod and stepped around her to head to the front doors of the main house. "I'll take care of this."

"It'll be okay, right?"

"Yes." He'd make sure it was okay.

Jia trailed him all the way to Katrina's office. Jas paused. "Give us a moment alone, please."

She bit her lip and nodded. He knocked once on the heavy wooden door of Katrina's office, and waited impatiently for her faint "Yes?"

The light from the overhead halogens lit up Katrina's shoulder-length light brown hair. She didn't glance up from her computer screen when he walked in, which worried him even more. Katrina was given to dreaminess, but she was hypervigilant if she was completely alone. His heart ached every time she jumped at a noise.

He stopped in front of the desk. He tried to put himself in

the shoes of someone who may not have seen her for years. He remembered when her hair had been darker and longer. A carefully screened stylist came to the house every few months and touched up her highlights—balayage, Katrina had once told him, was the correct term—and trimmed her hair. Her round face was fuller now, her body different. Still beautiful, though. She'd been beautiful then, she was beautiful now, and she'd be beautiful sixty years from now.

Now is not the time for waxing poetic.

"Jia told you," she said, forestalling his greeting. Her voice was flat, which ratcheted his worry up more. He hadn't heard her sound like this in a long time. Generally speaking, her voice was as warm and golden as her skin, bubbling underneath, like she was barely suppressing laughter.

He linked his hands together in front of him, because he wanted to grab her. "It's a security breach. *You* should have told me."

The rare rebuke did catch her attention. She blinked up at him. Her robe gaped at the neck, revealing her collarbones.

He came around the desk and glanced at the computer screen, which was open to the tweets he'd skimmed on Jia's phone. The numbers on the faves and retweets were flipping every second. God, had she been watching this counter all day? He infused calm into his voice. "It will be fine. These things blow over. What's viral today will be a forgotten meme by tomorrow."

"Oh God," she whispered. "I'm a meme too?"

"No," he said instantly, though she could very well be a

meme. He understood computers, but memes still baffled him. "Of course not. It's a figure of speech."

She rubbed her temples. "Who would do something like this? This is such a . . . gross invasion of privacy."

What was privacy now, anyway, in a world where everyone carried a recording device? "She probably assumed it was harmless."

Katrina swallowed. "Maybe for her." She straightened and clicked on another window to bring up the spy's Twitter page. BeccaTheNose was her handle. "Look. Reporting gigs, endorsement offers, a book deal. She got hundreds of thousands of followers today alone. Off of me as content."

Katrina's bitterness actually eased Jas. Anger was better than fear or panic.

"It's bullshit," he agreed.

"She's going to benefit from this and I'm . . ."

"Nothing will happen to you, because no one will know it's you."

Her breathing deepened. He knew the sound of all of Katrina's breaths now, and these were long and deliberate, the kind of breaths she took when anxiety was creeping in.

A few weeks after he'd met Katrina, he'd witnessed one of her panic attacks. He'd spent enough time around soldiers with PTSD to have an idea of what was happening. Her attacks didn't always have a clear trigger, but getting twisted up with anxiety didn't help.

"What if someone figures it out? How long will it take to track me to this house?" She picked at her cuticles.

"A long time," he said firmly. He couldn't touch her, but

he eased closer. "Katrina King didn't buy this house. They'd have to unravel shell company after shell company. Or bribe someone who knows, and that's a handful of extremely trustworthy people who can't be bribed." Katrina's investment fund consisted of three employees, all vetted and there for the long haul. A couple of select people at Crush knew who she was. Him. Her roommates and their families. Samson. That was it.

After the incident that had scarred her, Katrina had made it plain she wanted nothing more than to disappear. Jas had done his best to give her what she needed. If she wanted to disappear, she'd disappear. If she wanted to stay in her house forever, he'd facilitate that. If she wanted to venture out, he'd have her back there too. She was a grown, smart woman. She knew what was best for her.

She fiddled with her collar. "It used to be I was scared of having a panic attack in public. The fear, the embarrassment. What if I couldn't get away, or if people saw me, or someone hurt me when I was incapacitated?"

She didn't seem to need him to respond, so he didn't. He didn't know the full history of Katrina's panic disorder. She didn't talk much about her life with her father, but he imagined it hadn't been pleasant.

"Then that man kidnapped me. And I had something else to fear."

His heart clenched, hard. He often forgot about the scar that ran down Katrina's cheek. It was simply a part of her now, the same as her hair or legs. But right now it seemed like it was pronounced and white, more obvious than ever.

Her voice dropped so low, he had to lean forward to hear. "If I'm . . . nobody, then no one will want to hurt me, no one can capitalize off me, no one can use me, do you understand? I *have* to stay nobody."

Oh, he understood. He understood perfectly what it was like to want to go someplace where no one knew who you were, to want to run from attention and the spotlight.

He didn't fully realize what he was doing until her soft, smooth hand was in his. A part of him was aghast at the liberty he'd taken.

Another part of him was dying at the warmth that simple touch filled him with.

He tightened his grip when she looked up at him, her eyes pools of worry and fear. She wasn't a small woman, but she felt fragile and delicate, and if he hadn't already felt protective of her . . . well, it was all over now. "When you were kidnapped, I wasn't with you." She'd been shopping on crowded Oxford Street in London. He'd been with Hardeep when he'd gotten the panicked call from her security detail. "I'm with you now. I promise you. Anyone who wants to hurt you will have to get through me first."

Chapter Six

Katrina looked down at Jas's hand. He'd never touched her before. Not like this, not bare palm to bare palm, for no other purpose but to touch her.

The kicker? She couldn't even properly enjoy it!

Thanks a fucking lot, Becca.

Katrina had watched with an ever-growing knot in her belly as the metrics for that god-awful Twitter thread climbed ever higher. She'd watched as the woman who had photographed her and narrated a made-up encounter batted her lashes at her new followers and watched hashtags be born and trend in real time: #CafeBae and #CuteCafeGirl.

They weren't even good hashtags.

"Katrina?" Jas squeezed her fingers, grounding her better than any fidget stone.

She gathered herself and put on the hat that allowed her to eyeball start-ups and pick apart any BS to find their core. "To summarize, no one will be able to identify me from these photos. Even if they do, it would be almost impossible to track me to this house. Even if *that* somehow happens, there's an even smaller chance there's a bogeyman lurking out there to hurt me." Her kidnapper had been arrested during the ransom handoff when she'd been recovered. He'd been wanted for a laundry list of crimes, and would be in prison for a long, long time. Her father was the only other person who might hold a grudge against her, and he'd been quiet since Hardeep had paid him off. Katrina kept tabs on him, and had checked in today to make sure he was still tucked away in Vancouver.

Jas's beautiful eyebrows came together. "Right."

She lifted her shoulder. So logical. So rational. "Right. Thank you."

A knock came at the door, and Jas slipped his hand away from hers. Katrina had to swallow twice at the loss before she could speak. "Come in."

Jia poked her head around the door, her forehead creased with worry. A rush of affection coursed through Katrina. While she'd been consumed by this viral phenomenon, Katrina had neglected everything else, including work and food. At some point, a messy sandwich had appeared at her elbow, and her water bottle had kept getting refilled. She had some vague recollection of Jia trying to distract her with chatty conversation. "Come in, Jia."

"How's everything going?" Jia asked.

"It's . . . fine." She shoved back from the desk. She had to . . . do something. What could she do?

Pain ran through her legs when she got up, and she wondered how long she'd been sitting in the same position. At the very least, she could move. Make something. "Gosh, look at the time. Nearly ten. Are either of you hungry? Did you eat dinner?"

"Oh, I'm fine."

Jas shook his head. "Katrina . . ."

"Let me put something together."

"That's not necessary."

It was necessary. Katrina placed her hand in her pocket, but there was no rock, because she hadn't gotten dressed today either. No shower, no perusal of her wardrobe to decide what she felt like. No rock. Nothing to hold on to.

"I'm hungry." Katrina scooted past Jas. Her head was a jumble of thoughts and feelings, her stomach in turmoil.

Katrina rubbed her arms as she power walked through the hallway to the kitchen, Jia and Jasvinder trailing behind her, murmuring to each other.

She opened the fridge and stared inside. Oh shoot. She'd forgotten to place a grocery order. What on earth would she make?

She swiped the back of her hand over her cheeks, though there was no wetness there. She was anxious, but that numbness from the morning continued to protect her. "How do you feel about sandwiches?"

Without waiting for an answer, she gathered up sandwich fixings and brought the goods to the counter.

Out of the corner of her eye she caught sight of a movement outside the window and jumped and whirled.

"What's wrong?" Jas crossed to the window and peered outside.

She relaxed once she realized it was a tree branch knocking against the glass. "Nothing. Sorry."

It was awfully dark outside. And light inside. She placed her knife on the counter, then walked briskly over to the window and snapped the blinds shut. She glanced behind her with a frown. There was the sliding glass door, and she'd never put blinds over it, since it faced the backyard. Why had she bought a place with so much glass?

She'd hang a blanket there tonight. Tomorrow she'd rig up proper curtains.

By tomorrow her name might be all over the internet.

She spun around. "Jas, I yelled at Richard," she blurted out.

"It's okay."

"It's not." She stalked back to the counter. "He startled me while he was doing his rounds, but that's no excuse for my short temper. Is he here? I'd like to apologize. Does he have any dietary restrictions? I'll make him a sandwich too."

"He's already left. You can talk to him when he's back on shift."

"Do you have his number? I can call him. It's not kind to be so short-tempered. I wouldn't want him to worry about it."

"He won't. Trust me, he's fine."

She applied mayo to a slice of bread like her life depended on it. "Okay. Thank you."

"Why don't you let me make the sandwiches?" Jia asked. "It's basically the one meal I can handle."

She gave Jia a halfhearted smile. "No, it's fine. Jas, is grilled cheese okay?"

"I— Fine."

"I make it with mayo, you know. That's the secret." She pulled out a pan and placed it on the stove. "The mayo has a high fat content and crisps the bread. It works better than butter."

A small meow distracted her and she glanced at her feet, startled. "Zeus." She pressed her fingers against her lips. "I'm so sorry. I completely forgot about you today." She bent over and petted the cat. "How could I do that?"

"She's a cat," Jia said. "She's probably thrilled you forgot her for a day."

She smoothed her hand along her kitten's back. "What a terrible cat stereotype. Zeus loves me." Ah, there it was. A thawing of the numbness, the prickle of tears behind her eyes.

I love you, Katrina. This is all for your own good.

Katrina straightened. Her breath was coming faster, the floor wavering in her vision, her head aching.

This is your kitchen. You are safe.

"I need some air," she managed, and the next thing she knew, she was outside, damp grass under her butt, sucking in great gulps of precious oxygen.

Jas crouched in front of her, his no-nonsense voice cutting through her panic. "Name five things."

She closed her eyes, and opened them again. This was one of her handiest coping mechanisms. Five things she could see or hear or touch. "The grass." It was cold.

"What else?"

"The moon. The flowers." Jas took care of her garden, he had since they'd moved in. It was a work of art, filled with dark greenery and bright flowers, a colorful paradise. She'd told him he didn't need to do that, it wasn't in his job description, but he hadn't listened. So she'd quietly increased his retirement plan contribution.

"Two more."

She swallowed, tasting the ash of fear, but her heartbeat was returning to normal. She came to her knees. "Smoke. Trees."

"Good." He inhaled and exhaled slowly, and she matched his breathing without thinking.

Jia knelt next to her. "Here, drink this."

Katrina accepted the water. "The stove—"

"You never turned it on." Jia sat cross-legged. A flash of embarrassment ran through Katrina at Jia witnessing this, but she swallowed it. Though she wasn't prepared to share her issues with everyone, when Jia had come to live with her Katrina had told her what to expect. This had, frankly, been nothing.

She shuddered, though the cool air was nice. She took a sip of the water, letting it wet her parched throat.

Jia leaned against her side, giving her comfort. "Do you want to go back inside?"

Katrina looked at the house. It had been her haven for so long, the place where she'd felt safe and sound.

This wasn't about the house. This was about her identity. She'd had no idea how much safety she'd derived in staying anonymous. "I'll stay out here for a moment, thanks."

Jas also joined them on the ground. He was dressed in crisp dark jeans and a gray Henley, the lines of his beard extra sharp. Had he gone somewhere today? She vaguely recalled Gerald delivering a message in the afternoon that Jas would be absent until later in the evening, but she'd been too preoccupied to pay attention, even to news about Jas.

He linked his arms around his knees like he had all the time in the world. "What do you want, Katrina?"

Wow, what a question. Where to start?

I want to not have been under my father's thumb until I was twenty-four.

I want him to have not used my condition against me.

I want to not have been kidnapped all those years ago.

She bit back the bitter answers and answered him honestly. "I want to run away."

Jas nodded. "Where can you go where you will feel safe?"

The words didn't have a single ounce of mockery in them. It was a simple, soft query.

Still, she inhaled. Where could she go? This was the only property she owned, the only one she'd bothered to buy. Hardeep had left her with substantial cash, but he'd deeded all his other properties to his extended family and charity and she hadn't quibbled with that. He'd been more than generous to a girl he'd married out of kindness.

Ten places.

Her goal for a while now. She thought of the ten places she felt comfortable going to, all eating or working establishments in the city. She couldn't very well go sleep at the pho place. A hotel would mean strangers all around her, and that wouldn't help.

She accessed her mental fear ladder, her hierarchy of

things that scared her. Getting on a plane? Ugh. No, that was outside of her abilities.

She looked to the east, where her house hid her driveway. She could get in her car, though.

"What are you thinking?"

"I'm wondering what remote cabin I can go hide in until this all blows over." Her smile was wobbly.

He stared at her for a minute. "Is that really what you want?"

"Yes . . . I—"

Before she could finish, Jas rose to his feet and walked away to a corner of the garden, pulling his phone out of his pocket. She watched him for a moment, but turned her attention to Jia when the younger woman gently took her water out of her hand and set it on the ground. "Do you want me to call Rhiannon?"

"No. She's still in the air." Rhiannon would rush back, and Katrina didn't want that. She'd put on a convincing show when Rhiannon had left that morning, even if most of her brain had been on the likes racking up on that post.

What Rhiannon was working on was an important next step for Crush. What kind of partner would Katrina be if she distracted the CEO from their business plan? How was that looking out for the good of the company?

Jia nodded. "What about your therapist?"

"It's a little late for her." Besides, Andy wouldn't tell Katrina what to do, but she'd make her think, and Katrina was so tired of thinking.

Jas ended his call, walked back, and crouched in front of

her again. "How do you feel about going up north? It would be about a seven-hour car ride, with no stops."

Perhaps she may have to think a little more tonight. "Wait, are you serious? Where would we go?"

"To my family's place."

"The Bay Area?" Katrina had never met his parents or his younger brother, but she knew his parents were teachers who lived in a suburb.

"No, my grandpa's farm, north of Sacramento. I have a small house on the land."

"You grew up on a farm?" Jia's tone was incredulous, and it matched what Katrina's reaction had been the first time Jas had told her about his family farm in Yuba City years ago. With his pressed clothes and buffed nails and groomed beard, Jas didn't look like a farmer at all, yet he still went there at least once a month.

As tight-lipped as he was, some information inevitably leaked through.

Jas didn't take his gaze off Katrina's face but answered Jia. "Yes. It's remote. Quiet. The house is nice, isolated, even from the rest of the farm. My grandpa's out of the country right now, so no one would question us being there." He held up his fingers, counting each point off. "*If* the internet figures out who you are, and *if* they somehow trace you to your house, you wouldn't be here. You'd be in a place no one would connect to you. No need to worry about bogeymen."

Huh.

She'd grown up in a suburb, and then had lived purely in large cities. She thought now of what a farm meant. Trees, maybe a barn. A small kitchen with a gas stove, hopefully. Cute woodland creatures.

Solitude. Solitude and total anonymity.

The words buried in her soul, the exact thing she needed right now.

Plus you'd get to see where Jas grew up.

Personal information about the man would always be tantalizing, even if she was preoccupied with a crisis. "We'd be alone?"

"Yes. We can stay as long as you'd like."

We. That *we* was extraordinarily comforting to hear.

She wrapped her arms around herself. Was she actually considering this?

She checked in on herself. Yeah, she was. The thought of leaving the house felt right, the same way not leaving the house often felt right. If it didn't work out, she could always come back. It could be a good exercise.

For you. Not for Jas. "It's a long ride."

"We've driven at least that long round-trip. I'll be there with you. We can turn around if you find it unbearable."

"I'm not talking about me, I'm concerned about you." She could always knock herself out. What she couldn't do was drive. The thought of having an attack behind the wheel had terrified her so much, she'd never learned how. "If we were to, perhaps, leave in the morning—"

He cut her off. "No, I'd rather leave now. No traffic."

Damn it. She was relatively new to driving in California, but even she knew all plans revolved around traffic patterns. "You'd have to be up for most of the night."

His brown eyes darkened. "I don't require a lot of sleep."

"You'll be exhausted."

"Where's that robot car when you need it," Jia quipped. "Seriously, though, I can come with, and we can switch off."

"That's unnecessary," Jas said quickly. So quickly, Katrina wondered if there was something she didn't know about Jia's driving.

Jas crossed his arms over his chest. "Katrina, I have stayed up much longer than a few hours and the longer we stand here arguing, the later it will get."

She inhaled the slightly smoky air. Someone on the hilltop must have their fireplace going. It felt odd to disagree with Jas like this. They were usually in agreement. "No."

They stared at each other silently for a long moment. Jas blinked first. "What if I promise to stop and rest if I get tired?"

Then they'd have to stay in a hotel, which would make her fret, but she'd figure something out, if it meant he could sleep. "Fine. You have to keep that promise." She gave him a hard look. "I mean it."

"Done. Pack a bag. I'll make the arrangements."

"I can help you pack," Jia volunteered. "And I'll watch Zeus. Give her oodles of cuddles."

Katrina would have liked to take Zeus with her, but it was better the cat stay with Jia. Zeus hadn't spent a lot of time in cars, except for the few vet visits Gerald had taken her to, and the report Katrina had gotten from her grim housekeeper was that the animal wasn't fond of her carrier. She assumed he'd been understating the situation, as was his British style. "Thank you." She came to her feet.

Jas caught her elbow, and this time she felt it. The zing. Still muffled, but clearer than before. "Everything will be fine," he said. His face was so familiar, his dark eyes steady. She clutched that steadiness to her, using it to ground her.

She nodded once and forced a smile. Yes. She would disregard the one-sided zing. She'd cling to that solid assurance. It was a surer bet. *Everything will be fine.*

Chapter Seven

THE SKY HAD turned light blue, the sun kissing the far-off horizon, by the time Jas finally turned down a dirt road so familiar he could have driven it blindfolded and backward.

This was the road where he'd learned to drive: first a tractor, then a car. This was also the first place he'd ever kissed a girl, Rani from Sacramento, in said first car.

He kept his gaze straight ahead, though it strayed now and then to the fruit trees that lined the path, his family's bread and butter. The bread and butter of so many of the families that lived in this town. In an hour or so, people would be out in the orchard. Harvest season was long over, and the trees were bare now, silently prepping for the next season, but there was still work to be done. The work was never finished on a farm, though it changed every month.

He blinked to wet his eyes, dried out from the air blowing from the vents. He'd only stopped once throughout the drive, and he was feeling it.

He came to a fork in the road, then turned right, then left, and there it was. The house was just as he remembered it from the last time he saw it, a two-story wooden structure. Big enough to raise a family and a couple of kids. Nikka ghar, they'd called it, growing up. The little house.

Jas turned off the engine and grabbed a bottle of water from the bag in the passenger seat. He glanced in the rear-view mirror.

Katrina had been silent for the first hour of the drive, the tension radiating off her in waves, but thankfully that frenzied anxiety that had gripped her in her kitchen had vanished. She'd either taken a pill or run herself down, because she'd fallen asleep the second hour in and hadn't stirred since.

He got out of the car and stretched, groaning. He placed his hands on his hips and glanced around. All was still and quiet.

And familiar. So familiar his back teeth ached.

Had it been just yesterday morning that he'd wished he could run away from worrying about McGuire and his own impending exposure? How ironic, to run away to the one place he'd once run *from*.

He gazed up at the no-frills house. It wasn't exactly small, as the name would suggest. His great-grandparents had envisioned multiple generations living here. Multiple generations had lived here. The farm hadn't truly taken off until he was ten or so. They'd lived here until the big house was built, his family of four, his grandparents, his mom, and him.

It had been comfortably full. Each of the three bedrooms had an attached bathroom, and the living room and kitchen were of a decent size, though nothing like what Katrina was used to. A wide porch wrapped around the front, with two rocking chairs his great-grandmother had bought still sitting right up front, the wood weathered by time.

He crouched and touched the soil. The dirt clung to his fingers.

Home. There was pain, yes, but also love.

The second Jas had had the idea to come here, his gut had told him it was the right move. As he'd driven through the night, he'd grown more sure. They could both run away. Two birds with one stone.

His grandpa wasn't in the country. He could stick close to the little house, and none of the employees would come this far west, to a nonworking part of the farm.

Jas dusted his hands off and rose. He'd get to help Katrina and satisfy that craving to see his home without actually having to deal with the biggest issues that came with it. A win for everyone.

He'd called his stepbrother to tell him they were coming and asked him to keep it under wraps. Bikram was the foreman, though he was only twenty-five. Unlike Jas, his little brother ate, slept, and breathed this farm and this little town. Ideally, Bikram wouldn't let his presence here slip to their parents. He didn't want his mom to get her hopes up.

Jas surveyed the heavy growth of trees that shielded the little house from view. He'd arranged for a 24/7 security detail. The first shift should be arriving soon, and the guards would stay out of sight. He'd told Katrina about the arrangement during their trip so she wouldn't be worried if she spied them.

He exhaled, his breath fogging in the cold early morning air. October was so much colder here than it was in Southern California. The cold wind blew through the valley, right through his thin cotton long-sleeved shirt. He'd packed warmer clothes, but he might have to borrow a heavier jacket from his brother as well.

He couldn't be grouchy about the weather. His knee might grow stiff soon, but the cold was his old friend, enveloping him in an icy hug, much kinder to him than the sun had ever been.

Jas opened the back door of the car and bent down. His hand hovered above Katrina's shoulder, unwilling to take even the slightest liberty when she was unconscious. "Katrina?"

Nothing.

He dared to use two fingers to poke her shoulder, grimacing as he did so. This was not smooth.

Or effective. Her breathing remained as deep as ever.

He finally shook her shoulder, then shook her again. "Katrina?"

Jas straightened, flummoxed. He glanced around, the cold air crystallizing his breath. He couldn't very well let her sleep in the car for the rest of the morning, and he was too exhausted to keep poking her until she woke up.

He scuffed his otherwise spotless shoe in the dirt. *You've carried her before.*

Only once, when she was having an attack and he'd moved her. Never from a car to a bed. He'd especially never carried her over a threshold.

He glanced at the structure. Over his ancestral family home's threshold.

He tried to shake her gently again, and thank God her lashes fluttered open. "Hmm?" she murmured, and the sleepy sound went to his gut.

"We're here," he said.

She gave a nod and stirred, though her seat belt stopped her from rising. He reached over her, careful not to touch any part of her, and unsnapped the buckle, then moved back.

He had to hold her arm when she got out of the car, but she found her balance quickly. "It's chilly," she muttered. She'd changed into a sweater and yoga pants for the drive.

"I know. Let's get inside." She looked so unsteady he hovered behind her as she walked up the two steps to the porch.

The door was unlocked, which was normal. Even if he hadn't told his brother he was coming here, the door would have been unlocked. Locking doors in this town was for tourists, not locals.

Consider him a tourist, so long as he was in charge of Katrina's safety. He glanced at the rusted dead bolt. Tomorrow he'd change the locks on it and the back door.

It was warm inside, which surprised him. At some point over the last however many years it had been since he'd visited, they must have installed central heat. He took in the large living room with a glance. The place was clean and furnished with an older, comfortable sectional and television, but that was updated from what he remembered too. His grandpa must have refurbished the big house and given this place the hand-me-downs.

Katrina slumped against the wooden post at the foot of the stairs and yawned. "Come on," he said. "Bedrooms are upstairs."

It wasn't until he led Katrina to a bedroom and turned the light on that he realized how tired he must be, because he'd accidentally led her to the room he'd used as a kid instead of the much larger master bedroom. *Noooo, you cannot put her in your childhood bedroom. That's so weird.*

Before he could stop her, she muttered, "Thank you," and collapsed on the mattress of the four-poster bed, not even bothering to get under his great-grandmother's quilt.

"Uh, Katrina," he tried, but all he got was a slight snore, her mouth parted.

He set his hands on his hips and glanced around. This wasn't really his room any longer. The walls were bare now, the magazine posters he'd taped on the wood paneling as a kid long gone. The door to the bathroom was wide open, and it was similarly empty but clean and dust-free. He was sure Katrina had brought her fancy toiletries with her, but he could see some small samples on the counter. His brother really had readied the place for him on short notice.

He closed the bathroom door, so the light from the window there wouldn't interrupt her sleep. He also closed the blinds. He was about to leave when he made the mistake of glancing at her.

She hadn't taken off her shoes.

So let her sleep in them.

But then she'd be uncomfortable and wake up. He wrestled with himself, but finally walked back to the bed.

It was impossible not to touch her while he removed her shoes, but he tried to remain as detached as possible, even when he had to briefly encircle her slim ankle with his hand.

Pretend it's a dowel, or a fishing rod, or a hanger. Not a perfect round little ankle.

He didn't dare take off her socks. If removing her shoes made him feel vaguely guilty, he didn't want to think how pervy he'd feel for stripping wool off her bare flesh.

He straightened and made for the door, but then did an about-face. Despite the warmth from the heater, it might get much colder up here than Katrina was used to. Jas stood above her and frowned. She was sleeping on top of the bedspread. How was he supposed to get her under it?

He envisioned multiple possibilities, but before he could act, her eyes opened and he froze.

"Jas," she murmured, and the sleepy, hoarse word made his stomach drop. His name on her lips was always torture, but that husky bedroom tone was too much, especially when deployed in *his* bedroom.

He clenched his hands tight together so he wouldn't be tempted to do something stupid, like stroke her hair and tell her everything was okay.

What is wrong with you?

He didn't know, except maybe the fear for her peace of

mind had discombobulated him so much he was no longer thinking clearly.

She closed her eyes again, which was good. He stumbled back to the door. His hand got to the doorknob before he mentally kicked himself.

The blanket.

He tiptoed back to the bed and grabbed the part of the cover she wasn't on and folded it over her body, turning her into the filling of the world's clumsiest taco.

Good enough.

He nearly ran out of the room when her lips parted. Maybe seeing a woman he had feelings for innocently sleeping in his old bed wouldn't affect another man at all, but it was clearly making his brain cells seep through his ears.

He closed the door behind him and sighed in relief to be out of there. *Don't think about it. Move on.* There was still work to be done.

First, Jas retrieved their bags from the car. They both had backpacks with their laptops and computer things. He had a small duffel and a bigger bag filled with security equipment. She'd packed a large roller suitcase, one he hadn't seen in a long time, which made sense, since she hadn't gone anywhere overnight in forever.

He grunted when he lifted her bag out of the trunk. He had no idea what was in it, but back when they'd traveled extensively with Hardeep, she always had carried a great deal of *stuff.* There had been bellhops then to handle the luggage.

He took their insulated bag of food into the kitchen and placed the few supplies they'd brought into the fridge, including a small jar that contained Katrina's precious sour-dough starter. That had been another thing that Katrina had always traveled with.

He carried the rest of the luggage upstairs and held his breath as he opened her bedroom door so it formed the smallest possible wedge. He shoved her suitcase inside like it was on fire, then closed the door quietly. He wasn't getting stuck in that trap again.

He walked across the hall and tossed his duffel on the bed there. The room was bigger, comfy and cozy with older furnishings, but also devoid of any sign anyone had actu-ally lived here. So, fine. He'd take the master and be okay with it. He supposed, technically, as the owner on the deed for this house, this was his room by right, even if it was weird to sleep in the room his grandparents had occupied.

He unzipped the second, larger bag. He took out the cam-eras and lined them up on the antique writing desk. His grandfather would grumble if he discovered Jas was drill-ing holes in the historic house, but again, it was Jas's house. And they needed cameras. He'd install them around the perimeter once there was more light.

He gathered up some basic gadgets and headed down-stairs. No alarm system, which he'd also have to figure out. For now he installed a simple doorstop at each door. The metal stick wedged under the doorknob wasn't the most so-phisticated way to keep intruders out, but it would be ef-fective enough for warning him if someone was entering the place. At each window he attached a high-decibel alarm sensor that would shriek if it was opened or the glass was broken.

Did he actually think someone would hurt Katrina? Not really. He genuinely believed it would be difficult for anyone to get through all the digital roadblocks he had in place to protect her home address.

At the same time, he also understood her reaction. The potential threat of doxxing was scary enough for people who hadn't been through what she had.

Jas shuddered, recalling the day of the incident. Her security had claimed they'd barely been a couple feet behind her. They'd heard a noise, glanced away for a second, maybe two, and she'd been gone. It had taken one whole harrowing day for the ransom call to come. Jas had been there a few days later for the handoff in the parking lot behind a deserted warehouse. Would he ever be able to forget the way Katrina had looked when she'd stumbled out of the van? Dirty, small, still in the now-torn clothes she'd been abducted in. Bleeding.

He shook his head. No, he'd been too far away to see the blood at first. It was only in his nightmares that he could see each drop of blood curving down her smooth cheek.

Hardeep had been told to stay away from the scene, lest he be targeted as well, so it had been Jas who had pulled her away while the cops swarmed, Jas who had held her hand in the ambulance, Jas who had stood by while a doctor stitched her cheek in the ER. It had taken her days to start speaking in anything but one-word sentences. Weeks for her to leave the house, and then only because Hardeep had gently browbeaten her into it, much to Jas's disapproval, though he'd only aired that with his boss in private. In Punjabi, because, though Katrina was quick, she hadn't picked up enough Punjabi to understand them when they spoke rapid-fire in their own language.

She doesn't want to go to a movie or dinner or anything, Hardeep.

If we let her hermit, she'll stay in here forever.

So?

Hardeep had sighed. *There's no use in coddling her.*

Jas's lip curled. *Coddling* was such an infantilizing word for respecting the wishes of an adult and encouraging them to take things at their own pace.

He scrubbed his hand over his face. Look at him, dwelling on the past. Must be the novelty of being in this house where so much had changed.

It was time to head to bed. He tested the front door one more time, ensuring that it was secure. Or as secure as it could be.

He wasn't sure what made him glance over into the living room as he headed to the stairs, but it was the mantel over the fireplace that made him stop.

So not everything had changed.

His steps were leaden as he made his way to the fireplace. When he'd been young, it would have been impossible to reach, but now he easily pulled down the shotgun hung up high in a place of honor.

It was old and worn, from his great-grandparents' time. Hung for décor, not function. It was unloaded, and there wouldn't be any ammunition left carelessly lying around the house.

He ran his hand over the old weapon, searching out the scratches and nicks. He'd grown up around guns, had known how to use them safely well before he'd headed to the armed forces.

He swiped his arm over his mouth. His upper lip had broken out in sweat. Jas hadn't touched a weapon more lethal than a Taser in years. That did make him an oddity in his field, but he'd learned to compensate for the lack of a gun.

He pivoted and made his way back to the front door, removed the security bar and jerked it open. He had the presence of mind to close it behind him, even though he wasn't going far, just to the SUV parked in the driveway.

He opened the trunk and dropped the shotgun inside, concealing it with a blanket and the luggage cover. Once it was enclosed in there, the tightness between his shoulder blades eased.

He was so exhausted he almost walked into the room he'd placed Katrina in, but turned away at the last second. That would be a true disaster.

Jas settled into his grandparents'—well, his now—bed. The bedding might have all stayed the same, but the mattress had been changed at some point. This one was memory foam, which he hated. Give him those old springs any day of the week.

He placed his phone next to his head, as was his habit, so he wouldn't miss any notifications. Or if Katrina needed him.

Really, it was the second thing he cared about most.

Chapter Eight

Katrina woke up in slow degrees from her sleepy cocoon. Without opening her eyes, she rolled over onto her stomach and buried her face in the pillow. She needed to get up soon. Read her paper, feed her sourdough starter, go make breakfast, get to work.

She groped next to her for her phone to check the time, but nothing met her hand. Katrina frowned.

The sheets didn't smell like her sheets. She'd used the same detergent and fabric softener combination for longer than she could remember. She ran her fingers up the cotton, which was rougher than her high-thread-count stuff. Wait. This wasn't her bed.

A surge of adrenaline coursed through her veins. Her eyes flew open and she rose up on her hands and clambered to her knees.

The place looked like it had been ripped from another time, with old wood-paneled walls and sturdy furniture hand-carved out of oak. The blue and white quilt she was tangled up in was clean, but deeply loved, the fabric worn.

Holy Laura Ingalls Wilder, where am I?

Not her room.

Because you're not at home, remember?

Jas's place. His family's farm. She breathed out through her nose, then did it again. That was right. She was safe.

"You're fine," she whispered to herself. "I know this is out of the ordinary for you, it's not what you're used to, but you're fine."

She wrapped her arms around herself to give herself a hug and took her time examining the room. It wasn't her bedroom, but now that the confusion had worn off, she could see that it was quite nice and tidy. There was an inviting, well-used fireplace in the corner and a stack of firewood next to it.

You'll like this place. You came here to feel better.

She inhaled and exhaled, letting the knee-jerk fear leave her completely. She reached into her jeans pocket, where her phone was uncomfortably wedged. She vaguely remembered staggering up here, but she must have only taken her shoes off before sleeping. This particular prescription always left her groggy.

Her thumb hovered over her Twitter app. She'd downloaded it yesterday, for this nightmare. She had little use for social media, and this hadn't made her want it. She got her news from print papers, connected with others who had similar panic issues on online forums. Social media was exposure.

She almost opened the app, but then backed off. She didn't

need to be in a fetal position immediately upon waking up, now, did she? Twitter and fetal positions could wait. For a shower, at least.

Her bag was next to the door, and she made her way to it and pulled out her toiletries and jeans and a long-sleeved shirt. She'd packed cool-weather clothes. A girl liked a nice blanket scarf and boots every now and then.

The hot shower revived her, as did her morning skin care routine. Each product she dabbed onto her face and neck felt like an extra protective layer, even if the essences and serums were watery and light.

She turned the lights off in the bathroom and went to her bag with determination. She would be here for a while, and she'd get used to it. Though she was in a new place, there was no reason she couldn't have a bit of order and discipline.

She unpacked her suitcase, hanging up her clothes in the closet and putting her undergarments away in the dresser drawers that smelled vaguely of lavender sachets. She frowned when she noticed a blue sweatshirt wedged into the corner of her bag. It was Rhiannon's favorite one. How had it gotten in her suitcase?

She pulled the hoodie out and shook it. A small scrap of paper fell to the floor. She picked it up and found Jia's handwriting.

> *Rhiannon told me to give this to you in case you need a hug. Does that make sense? I thought it was weird but figured I'd pack it for you.*

She clutched the cotton close to her. She was very lucky in her friendships.

She drew the hoodie on, even though it didn't go with her outfit. Rhiannon was taller than her and skinnier, and she couldn't close it over her chest without smashing her breasts down. That was okay, it fit fine. Sisterhood of the traveling hoodie.

Katrina grabbed her phone and took a selfie, sending it to Rhiannon and Jia in their group chat. She purposefully kept her tone light and cheerful.

> Everything's fine! Got here safely. Thanks for the present, Rhi.

Her phone rang immediately. She didn't know what time it was for Rhiannon, but she imagined her best friend must be dead-tired. She answered. "Hey. Are you at your hotel?"

"Just got here."

"How's India?"

"Hot and seen through jet-lagged eyes. I have been waiting for you to wake up. What the hell are you doing in Yuba City? Where is that, even?"

Katrina's smile was rueful. "Jia told you."

"No, I tracked you."

"Did you?" Katrina rubbed the skin under her ear. Funny, she didn't feel a chip there. "Ah. How'd you do that?"

"I have Find Friends set up on yours and Jia's phones."

"Oh right." When Jia had come to live with them, they'd

followed each other on the tracking app. Now that Katrina thought about it, she wondered if that made her phone less secure. She made a mental note to ask Jas.

"I'm glad to have it. I get worried. I listen to true crime podcasts."

"You know you're too paranoid to listen to those."

"Okay, fair. Now answer my questions."

"I'm north of Sacramento."

"I don't mean where literally, I mean, like . . . where in the grand scheme of things?"

"I actually don't know what you're asking."

"What the hell are you doing in the middle of nowhere, Katrina?" Worry dripped off her words.

"It's not the middle of nowhere." Katrina went to the window and squinted out at the landscape. All she could see were trees from here, and a little barn set off from the house, its red paint chipped and weathered. "I mean, it's rural and definitely small, but I skimmed the tourism page and there are many shops and restaurants. A Target."

"A Target is not a surefire sign of civilization. It's a sign that your wallet is empty because you walked in to buy milk and left two hundred dollars poorer. With no milk."

"Do you know the Target Effect is a real thing? Social scientists think it has something to do with the lighting—"

"Katrina. Stop trying to distract me. Why did you leave the house?"

Katrina traced a finger down the window, where her face was reflected in the glass. "I had to go."

"I've been monitoring since yesterday, even while I was

in the air. I'm certain this will blow over. If you let me tell Lakshmi, we can even make sure it does blow over."

Rhiannon's assistant was impressive, but Katrina didn't know how she'd make the internet bow to her. Katrina had already considered and dismissed flexing legal muscle yesterday. The tweets were, literally, everywhere. "You can tell Lakshmi, but I don't want her, like . . . hacking the CIA or whatever she might want to do."

"She has never hacked a government database."

Interesting, that left a lot of other databases for Lakshmi to hack.

"I know this sucks, but are you sure you shouldn't be home? I worry about you out there, in a place I don't even know, and me not in the country—"

"I told you I was kidnapped once," she blurted out. She'd given Rhiannon the barest of explanations back then, mostly to explain the scar on her cheek.

They'd met a few years prior, at a party, when Katrina was twenty-two. For once, Katrina hadn't needed to be prodded by her opportunistic dad to go speak to a wealthy person. Even in her twenties, Rhiannon had glowed with a confident, brilliant light. She seemed bigger than she was, her personality shining out of her.

Katrina had felt like the opposite at the time. Smaller than she looked. She'd craved what Rhiannon had. Her self-esteem had been so low, she'd been shocked when Rhiannon had seemed to return her desire for friendship.

Rhiannon sucked in a breath. "Is the kidnapper out? Because I'll kill him."

"Thank you for that offer of murder, but he's still in a British jail and will be for a while."

"Oh."

Katrina rested her forehead against the glass, the coolness grounding her. She didn't like to think too much about the small flat she'd been kept in for those few days or the fear Hardeep wouldn't be able to pay the ten million dollar ransom the kidnapper had demanded. Or that he wouldn't want to. Theirs had, after all, been an odd alliance—he got a pretty young escort and the satisfaction of saving her, and she got protection from her dad.

He'd paid it, though. On the day of the exchange, blindfolded and gagged, she'd struggled on the way to the van, certain the man was going to kill her. That was when he'd cut her cheek. Going by the way he'd cursed, she was pretty sure now it had been an accident, but she'd backed down, cowed.

She shook her head, lest the odor of that van invade her nostrils now.

Rhiannon cleared her throat. "You're scared someone might hurt you again like that?"

"Maybe."

"Or are you scared of your dad finagling his way back into your life?"

That scenario was more likely, but she'd drafted a plan to handle her father if he ever came back. It was her break-glass-in-case-of-emergency plan. She hoped she wouldn't have to use it, but it was there.

"Or is there something else?"

The breath she released was shaky. "I wanted to get away. That's all. I'm scared of people knowing who and where I am, of being exposed like that. It's not rational, not based on any one threat."

Katrina, sweetheart, you must come to the party.

Katrina, be rational. I can't not have my wife at this event.

Katrina, please get in the car. No one will hurt you. Face your fears.

Hardeep's well-meaning words rang in her ears. Being in public had been challenging before the kidnapping, never knowing where or when she might have a panic attack. After, it was like there were two threats always waiting for her. Inside her head, and around the corner.

She clenched her fists tight, part of her terrified Rhiannon would echo Hardeep's logical words and tell her to go back home.

Of course, this was Rhiannon, and there was a reason the woman was her best friend. "This place you're at, Target aside, you're safe?"

Outside the window, Jas came into view, striding to the car. If the glass hadn't been there, she would have fallen out, she pressed herself so tight against it. She couldn't see his face, but he wore a white long-sleeved shirt and jeans, and he held a ladder tucked under one arm, a black bag in his other hand.

He looked good.

"I'm safe. This is kind of an experiment, you know? Like how I expose myself to new establishments, but on a bigger scale. If I hate it, I can leave. Like any other typical person who goes on a vacation." Kind of. "I just woke up, but I'm already feeling better than I did staring at that Twitter thread all day yesterday."

"We all need to get away sometimes. I'm glad there's a place you could run to, however temporarily. Good for you, listening to yourself."

Her sinuses got a little clogged. "Thank you."

"Tell Jas to make sure no creepy clowns are lurking in the cornfields or anything," Rhiannon warned.

"There's no cornfields here." Katrina paused. "I mean, hopefully no clowns too."

"In my mind, corn and clowns and farms all go hand-in-hand. And bears. Are there bears?"

Rhiannon was being deliberately silly, and Katrina appreciated it. "That I'm not sure about."

"If you see a bear, run zigzag."

"That's a crocodile. Or an alligator?"

Rhiannon gave an exaggerated sigh. "Honestly, do *I* look like a farmer?"

Katrina was still chuckling when she hung up. She searched for Jas outside. At first she'd thought he'd disappeared, but then she caught sight of him at the top of the ladder next to a tree, a drill in his hands. Cameras, she guessed.

She tucked her phone in her sweatshirt pocket, adding her little gray fidget stone before she left the room. Though she couldn't zip up the hoodie, she did pull it tighter around her.

Katrina made her way slowly down the creaking stairs, clutching the wooden banister for balance. There were multiple framed photos on the staircase, like a small baby museum, full of chubby thighs and fat cheeks. The photos appeared to date back maybe fifty or sixty years—she assumed one of the more recent ones was Jas—ah, that one. For sure, this was him.

She paused at the last photo, smiling. Jas was maybe a couple years old, his eyebrows already beautiful at this young age, and he stared out at her with a militant glare.

She imagined he'd probably grunted at the camera as this was taken.

She ran her finger over the silver frame and looked up at the rest of the photos. There was history here, family history.

Katrina placed her hand over her heart. She'd stopped thinking of her maternal extended family long ago, but occasionally a memory or longing tapped on her consciousness. She tried to sit with that discomfort the way she did her fear, but it was a little too sharp today, exacerbated by the upheaval.

A schedule. She checked her watch. Too late for working on her latest project or the newspaper, not that she had one, but she could get to work on breakfast.

She walked through the house, taking stock. She'd lived in lavish houses for a long time, but this was about the size of her childhood home, and it was neither big nor small, but cozy, hugging her like Rhiannon's sweatshirt.

A sliver of excitement rose inside her. Some city folks paid big bucks to go stay in a well–kept up honest-to-God farmhouse like this.

She ran her hand along the chipped, gleaming Formica

counter in the kitchen and opened the fridge door. Completely empty, save for a box of baking soda and the small amount of food they'd brought with them. She pulled her starter out of the cold and placed it on the counter. "Been a while since we've traveled together, kiddo," she murmured. "I'll feed you shortly, once we get some good flour." Was talking to sourdough starter a step too far? Possibly.

She closed the fridge and walked a couple steps to the back door, where the glass window was covered by gingham curtains. She'd see if Jas could give her an update on what the grocery situation was here, if there was delivery.

Also, she'd see Jas. Possibly doing manly things with a drill. Nice.

Back to logistics. If the food was going to take a while, she'd have to rearrange her new farm schedule, move breakfast to after a check-in with her investment team.

She turned the door alarm sensor off—Jas had used these in hotel rooms when they traveled—and tugged open the door.

And promptly screamed and jumped back.

Chapter Nine

Her scream made the man outside also scream and dump the paper bag he held. It split open, food spilling everywhere. An apple rolled across the grass to stop at his feet.

"Oh my God," she wheezed, and pressed her hand over her chest. "I'm—I'm—"

The man mirrored her actions and straightened to his full height, big brown eyes wide. The handsome twenty-something guy was about as tall as her, solidly built, and dressed in worn, faded jeans with a big belt buckle, a plaid shirt, and a black turban. "What the hell? You scared me!" he yelped.

She braced against the doorjamb. Most serial killers crouching outside of people's doors probably didn't scream or lead with chastisement. "I'm sorry." She stretched her hand out to him. "I didn't mean to. I wasn't expecting anyone outside." He gave her a suspicious once-over and grunted, and it was with that grunt that Katrina realized who this must be. "You're Jas's brother, aren't you? Bikram?"

Before Bikram could answer, Jas came running into view, drill in his hand, fearsome scowl on his face. "What's wrong?

Why are you two screaming? Bikram, I told you to just put the bags outside the door."

"I did not scream," Bikram said with great dignity, and crouched to pick up the produce. "I yelped. I was startled by your . . . client."

"So was I. I'm sorry I startled you. Everything's fine, Jas." Katrina stepped outside and picked up an apple. An inappropriate urge to laugh came over her. Hadn't she thought yesterday that a solid meet-cute was someone dropping their fruit for pickup?

Well. She dusted off the dirt on the apple. That meet-cute didn't take into account the toll on the poor fruit.

Bikram only harrumphed. She helped the men with collecting the dropped items and took them inside. Bikram trooped in after her and unceremoniously placed the rest of the food on the counter, Jas following with the other two still-intact bags that had been sitting on the grass. He spoke to his brother over his shoulder. "I asked you to stock the kitchen last night."

"This isn't some Airbnb." Bikram placed his hands on his hips. With the three of them in here, the small kitchen was crowded.

She cleared her throat. "Jas, this is your brother, right?"

"Yeah. Bikram, meet Katrina King."

Bikram nodded at her, and she didn't think she imagined the frostiness in that one gesture. "Charmed."

She linked her hands in front of her. What a great first impression she'd made. "Thank you for your hospitality in letting me stay here. And the food. Again, I'm sorry I screamed."

"Yeah. Well. Jasvinder asked for a favor, and he doesn't do that often." He gave her another hard look she couldn't interpret, but spoke to Jas. "Gotta go work. I'll talk to you later."

"Wait." Katrina faltered when Jas's younger brother turned to her. "Would you . . . can I make you some breakfast?"

Bikram blinked at her, then shook his head. "No."

Jas grunted, a warning grunt, and Bikram straightened. "No, *thanks*. Bye." He walked out the door, tromping across the grass to get to the front of the house.

Katrina made a face at Jas. "Does your brother dislike me? For something more than startling him?"

Jas went to the sink to wash his hands. His shirt and jeans were pristine, even though he'd been up a tree. His brother looked like a rugged farmer. Jas looked like a model on a shoot where he was playing a farmer. Both men were making those looks work for them.

"How could he hate you?"

"Uh, well, I said dislike, not hate. You think he *hates* me?"

He turned off the faucet. "He neither hates you nor dislikes you. He literally met you five seconds ago."

That made sense, and she tried to shake off the vibe she'd gotten. A couple of times she'd asked Jas if his family would like to come for dinner, but he'd declined, so she hadn't pressed, unwilling to violate his boundaries.

Has he told them I'm a terrible boss? Or friend? Or human?

Nope. Jas would never do that, he was far too steadfast and loyal.

She had enough things on her plate. She'd shelve Bikram's

odd attitude for now. She started unpacking the bags. "I saw you outside setting up the cameras."

"Yes. Can you give me your phone? I'll add the surveillance app to it."

She handed him her phone and got to work putting the produce away, but not before admiring the lettuce. "So fresh."

"Almost everything is locally grown."

"When you told me all those years ago that you'd grown up on a farm, I pictured cows and horses, not peach orchards."

"Prunes, too. Or plums, I mean. I don't know why, we call them prunes whether they're dried or not."

She smacked her lips. "My favorites. I would have made you bring bushels back every summer."

"I thought mangoes were your favorite fruit."

"I have multiple faves. What's your favorite?" She asked the question casually.

He considered that with great gravity, like she'd asked him to pick a favorite parent instead of a favorite fruit. "I should say peaches out of loyalty, but I very much like strawberries."

She filed that tidbit away. Seriously, like a slow drip, getting stuff out of him. "Ooh, look." She waved a jar at him. "Canned peaches."

"We don't lack for preserved peaches, for sure." He held her phone out to her, his face expressionless. "I think you got a text."

She navigated to her messages, and nearly dropped her phone.

> Is it cold? Is the place nice? Is your hot bodyguard keeping your body warm?

Oh holy hell. Jia, to their group chat.

Her face flaming, she glanced up at Jas, but he'd turned away to put the rest of the groceries away. Normally she preferred doing that, but she was too mortified to say anything now.

Hot bodyguard. Oh, for crying out loud.

Her clumsy fingers managed to type one word, her cheeks aflame. Jia.

> What? See the man without a shirt on and then get back to me.

Katrina narrowed her eyes at the screen. Rhiannon beat her to a response. When did you see Jas without a shirt on??

> When I went to go get him last night. Answered the door shirtless. Hard not to whistle.

Katrina's arm jerked, and she knocked something off the counter behind her. "I got it," she said to Jas, breathless, but didn't get it.

Rhiannon responded with a 😊.

Katrina pursed her lips. She did not feel like rolling her eyes, she felt . . . jealous?

No, no way. Of Jia? No.

Jealous that Jia's eyeballs saw him shirtless.

The place is very nice. I'll call you after breakfast, Jia, for an update on #CafeBae. Hopefully that would keep her roommate from texting any more inappropriate things. She stuck the phone back in her pocket and faced Jas, who was putting the salt next to the sugar, even though everyone knew that the flour went next to the sugar.

She'd fix it later. The important thing right now was, had the text preview on her phone shown Jia's whole message? "Ah, that was just Jia. You know her." She did roll her eyes now. "Wild, silly Jia." She couldn't help it, her gaze darted to his wide chest. *See the man without a shirt on and then get back to me.*

"Are you okay?"

She shook her head. "Sorry. What?"

"You look flushed. Are you okay?"

She flushed harder. "Yes. I'm fine."

He walked toward her, and she pressed back against the counter. He was so big and tall and masculine, and he smelled so good, like a combination of the outdoors and that cologne he used that she liked so much.

He crouched in front of her and then rose to his feet. "Your baguette, madam."

She accepted the bread she'd knocked off the counter, her fingers digging into the soft dough. Maybe he hadn't seen

Jia's text, or only read the first few words when the preview popped up. He wasn't looking at her different or acting weird. She was the one acting weird.

She squeezed the bread harder. "What would you like for breakfast?"

"Whatever you'd like."

Standard response. She contemplated the ingredients Bikram had brought over and pulled out the flour and sugar Jas had put away and that would have to be rearranged anyway. There were strawberries and bananas and Nutella, as well as more savory fillings for Jas.

"I'll make crepes." That would eat up a lot of her time and delay her checking in on the internet. "It was kind of your brother to get us groceries."

"Hmm."

She suddenly hungered to fill the kitchen with words, like that might wipe out Jia's untimely text. "This is such a lovely home."

"I know it's not what you're used to."

"Actually, when I woke up, it reminded me of the house I grew up in." *And my mother.* Another pang. Now that she had flour, she'd feed the starter and think of the fond memories she held.

They lapsed into an easy silence as she made batter and cooked the crepes on the pan she found in the cupboard next to the stove. Behind her, she sensed movement and the sound of chopping. She almost told him to stop, that repetitive knife work was something she enjoyed because it calmed her, but it was possible he might need to work some energy off too. Besides, the two of them working together was also calming.

When the meal was ready, she placed a sprig of mint on her crepe and turned the plates around with a flourish. "Voilà, savory for you, sweet for me."

"Thank you." He accepted his plate and tipped his head to the round dining table, which he'd already set with silverware and coffee and orange juice. She followed him and sat in the chair he pulled out for her. They ate in silence for a moment.

"Good?" she asked, when he paused.

"Excellent." He dabbed the corners of his mouth with a napkin. "I was hungrier than I thought. Must be the fresh air."

She straightened up a little and smiled at him, warmth flowing through her at his enjoyment of the meal. "Good."

"You seem . . ." he eyed her. "Fine."

"I am, thanks." Her tone was light, but she understood what he meant. She was doing well, jumpiness over spotting a strange man right outside her door aside.

She traced her finger around the green ivy encircling the white plates. The plates and utensils were as old and worn as the countertops and equally sturdy. "So you own this house."

"Yes."

"Your grandfather doesn't live here, though?"

"No, my grandfather has a bigger house, on the other end of the farm."

"And the farm is . . ."

"Very large. Hundreds and hundreds of acres."

"I definitely feel . . . far away from everyone."

"In a bad way?"

"No. The internet, it has a way of making you feel like everyone in the world is in your living room. There's no one here. I like it." She smiled at him.

He polished off the last bite of his crepe. "Good. I'm glad you're getting what you want."

"Speaking of the internet though . . . Have you seen the hashtag yet? Are there any developments?"

He took a sip of his juice. "I checked. No one's found out who you are."

"And?"

"And what?"

"What else?"

"Isn't that all you care about?"

She made a face. "You know I need more details."

"Do you, though?"

If you look, then you can get on with the rest of your schedule. She pulled out her phone and opened the Twitter app. She clicked on the search button, but didn't have to type in the CafeBae tag. It was still trending.

Her stomach sank. So much for someone or something else absorbing the internet's attention.

She scrolled through, many of the tweets stuff she'd seen before. Becca the Witch's original post had grown exponentially in likes and retweets. It took her a few minutes to discover what was responsible for the unflagging interest.

Ross.

His smile beamed out from his avatar, and he was as handsome as ever. His handle was RossAlwaysWins and she was glad, on the basis of that alone, that she hadn't accepted his date invitation. The tweet after it cinched her certainty.

Haha, thought you were taking pictures. ☺ #CafeBae #itme

♡ 6k   ↻ 34k   ♡ 79k   ↑

A layer of cold settled over her. This. Dick. "Did you see this? Ross, the guy I sat with, he revealed himself." Her voice was dull. The sharp taste of fear came and went, but for the most part she was insulated by ice.

Jas's growl would have surprised her if she weren't so numb. It was so much louder and more ferocious than any grunt. "I did."

"What the fuck?" She stared at Ross's face, bewildered. "If he knew she was taking pictures, why didn't he stop her?"

"I don't know."

"Did he know this was going to happen?" Ross's tweet had been retweeted almost as many times as the original, and the numbers climbed as she watched.

"I don't think anyone can predict what catches the internet's attention."

Katrina clicked on Ross's profile and scrolled through his tweets, her ire growing as she read. His tweets were either retweets of other people virtually high-fiving him or more coy acknowledgments about him being the focus of the twittersphere. *I didn't realize I was internet famous til my mom told me, what a trip, haha,* she read from one tweet, then clicked to the next. *So #grateful for everyone who cares so much about our happiness.* She looked to Jas. "Our? Who the hell is our?" She shot to her feet. "Is he implying that we actually went out? Or that it was the love match this . . . this Peeping Tina spun it as?"

"Seems like it."

"This is bananas." She paced and scrolled, and scrolled and paced, growing ever more agitated as she read.

She stopped when she got to a quote tweet. *Did you really hook up with her?*

And Ross's gross, coy, winky acknowledgment. *I don't kiss and tell.*

Katrina swallowed her bile, feeling vaguely violated. No, not vaguely. Actually, genuinely violated. "I don't kiss and tell?" She shook her head. She'd been homeschooled for all of high school as she'd moved from modeling shoot to shoot, so she'd missed out on some experiences, but she imagined this was what it felt like to have the most popular guy in school tell everyone she'd gone all the way.

Only on a more massive, global scale. "Do you know what he's implying? That we . . ." She dropped her voice. "Had *sex*."

Jas's nostrils flared. "Yeah. I know."

"That's disgusting. What kind of man implies something like that to hundreds of thousands of people?"

It was amazing how much she could hate someone who had seemed so benign. *Your body knew not to zing. At least you didn't go out with him. That's something.*

Jas shifted. "No good man."

"We were only gone for a couple of minutes! Do these people know how sex even works? Have you ever *had* two-minute sex?" She bit her tongue as soon as she said the words. "Sorry."

"Don't be sorry."

She swiped the back of her hand over her mouth, trying to sidestep from that intrusive question that placed Jas in the same world as sex. "This could have disappeared if he hadn't revealed his identity. All these people will want to know who I am now, they're already asking. He fed the beast."

"You don't know that."

She didn't hear him. "I was having a normal, innocent chat with a stranger. And he and this woman seem fine—possibly even thrilled—about this attention. And they don't care that I feel . . ." *Terrified. Violated. Exposed.*

Furious.

She reached into her pocket, but the rock couldn't cool her anger now. "It's not fair."

Jas came slowly to his feet and braced his hands on the back of a chair. "It's not."

"Aren't you mad?"

"I am. I'm so mad for you."

But his voice was monotone. His growl told her he was upset about this, but she wanted him to *rage* along with her. "I want to throw something."

He picked up his mug, drained it, and then offered it to her.

She scowled. "I'm not breaking your mug."

"Okay." He shrugged. The loud crack as it smashed against the wall made her jump.

"The fuck, Jas?"

"It's not china. Pretty sure my mom got this stuff from a thrift store. In 1998." He offered her her empty plate. "Go on. Just one."

She eyed the plate. Before she could overthink it, she grabbed the ceramic plate and threw it on the floor. The crash was intensely satisfying. She looked up at him. "That felt so good. It was amazing."

"Better than two-minute sex, for sure."

She opened her mouth and then closed it again. Holy shit. Was that a . . . was that a slightly off-color joke Jas had just told? In her presence?

She and Rhiannon had cracked way more racy jokes to each other, but Jas . . . he was so proper!

Maybe he saw Jia's text, and this is his way of flirting with you?

No. Not a freaking chance.

She was processing for so long, she didn't move while he went to the pantry in the corner and returned with the broom and dustpan. "Oh, let me."

He waved her away. "Go work. Take advantage of how good you feel after some light destruction."

"Right. I'm sure I have spreadsheets or, um, something to look over."

"I'm sure you do." He swept up the mug shards.

She raked her fingers through her hair, his easy pragmatism grounding her. He always grounded her.

Driven by a foreign compulsion, she covered the distance between them and wrapped her arms around Jas.

It was a second, maybe two. Their chests pressed together, and she rested her cheek over his heart. He was stock still, his arms at his sides, the broom and dustpan still in his hands.

She didn't look at him as she released him and walked away. She'd never hugged him before, and, while new, it had felt . . . right. So right, she wanted to go back in for a second hug. Maybe a longer one.

Maybe a naked one.

Instead, she zipped her borrowed hoodie up, though it was too tight. It hugged her, too, and flattened her chest like his body had.

Whoa. Definitely don't think about that.

Yeah, that was . . . not where her brain needed to go, not at all. What had she been thinking? She'd managed to convince herself he hadn't seen Jia's text, and now she'd stress over this.

She was almost out of the room when he spoke. She flinched, but his words weren't about the hug.

"You should turn off your phone for a while. I'll monitor Twitter."

"I don't know . . ."

"How about this? You only look at the tag when you're around someone. Me, or on the phone with Jia or Rhiannon." His tone softened when she faced him. "I don't want you to be upset when you're alone. I don't think it's healthy to watch something develop in real time like that."

Yesterday's all-day computer binge *hadn't* been healthy. Plus, she had come here to get away from everyone. She capitulated, and if she did it a little quicker than she normally did because she wanted to get both of their minds off of that hug, that was between herself and God. "Okay. Deal."

She'd grab her computer and get to work, as he'd suggested, running on some semblance of her schedule. Real work, not monitoring the actions of strangers on the internet.

She pressed her hands over her warm cheeks as she walked up the stairs, trying to shake off the sensation of that hug.

Maybe he didn't say anything because he likes you, and doesn't mind your hugs or the prospect of you considering him hot.

She stopped, her pulse increasing, treacherous evil hope sprouting in her heart.

No, don't do this. How odd. Rarely did she have to counter positive thoughts.

Only this one was toxic positivity, bad for her in the long run. Hope this big and fresh would turn her inside out. Her romantic heart would take everything he did and said as a new spark of interest, and then when it came out that it was all nothing, where would she be?

Find something to kill it. Get rid of the hope.

She scrambled for her phone and hesitated on Rhiannon's name. Rhiannon was the most cynical person she knew, but telling her about this would result in so many questions. Plus, Rhiannon wouldn't truly crush her dreams.

She firmed her lips. She'd have to do it herself. Tell herself that it was nothing.

There. That sounded convincing.

It was nothing.

Chapter Ten

Jas squinted at the dying sun. The afternoon had turned out warmer than the morning, but it was now cooling in the early evening. The scent in the air, of grass and trees, was fresh and familiar.

It was good to get outside. He'd spent the day on his computer in the living room, while Katrina split her time between her bedroom and the kitchen, seemingly content.

> Is it cold? Is the place nice? Is your hot bodyguard
> keeping your body warm?

He closed his eyes, but Jia's text was emblazoned on the back of his eyelids too. His face flushed, the way it had wanted to when he'd read the thing.

He would have turned red from Jia calling him hot, but the rest of that sentence . . .

Jia being Jia.

Him keeping Katrina warm surely wasn't a common topic of conversation between the women. Surely she wasn't eager to have him . . . keeping her body warm?

She did hug you.

He placed his hand on his chest, where he could still feel the imprint of her body. It shouldn't have rocked him so much. His parents were huggers, his grandmother, his little brother too. He wasn't lacking for physical affection in his life.

Except for physical affection from Katrina. That had never really happened.

Nope, nope, nope. What he wasn't going to do was read interest into these small signs. That way lay disaster.

Jia's text had been a result of her usual outrageous sense of humor, and Katrina's hug had been nothing but a friend's display of gratitude.

That was the interpretation that had allowed him to spend the day buried in work, sorting out a tangled mess of a security system for a new start-up Katrina had invested in recently. It was a messaging app, and Jas had been disappointed but not surprised by its lax protocols. A Russian infant could have hacked it in about three minutes.

Consulting on these businesses was one of his least favorite parts of the job, second only to writing the reports recommending his fixes. He'd much rather get in there and build the systems than tell other people how to do it.

In between his work, and keeping an ear out for Katrina, he'd kept tabs on social media. He glanced at his phone, where Twitter lay wide open, exposing the bane of his existence. He didn't know how he was going to break this latest development to Katrina. She would freak out, and rightfully so.

He glared at RossAlwaysWins's tweet. *Can't wait to share this budding romance with the world tomorrow! Catch me on Good Morning Live at 8 a.m. with @BeccaTheNose.*

Wasn't the British royal family doing anything amazing this week that *GML* could cover instead? How had these two fools managed national TV coverage by making up lies about a woman who hadn't even come forward yet?

Budding romance, his ass.

His phone rang in his hand, signaling the call he'd come outside to take, lest Katrina hear. Lorne had texted him earlier, asking if he was free. Which he appreciated, though that 202 area code still made him anxious.

He swallowed and answered. "Jas."

"Hey, man." Lorne's voice was low and calm, as it had been years ago when they'd served together. "How's everything going?"

He glanced at the trees, where two of Lorne's guards sat in a well-concealed vehicle. "Not bad. Thanks for getting me the security on such short notice."

"Not a problem. Surveillance is a pretty plum assignment. I got two more headed your way, they'll stay in a nearby hotel when they're not on the property. Eight-hour shifts. You won't even know they're there unless you need them."

"Sounds perfect."

He could imagine Lorne in her cushy D.C. office, short red hair tousled, freckles standing out on her pale skin. "How are you doing?" she asked.

"Good." Jas paused. "Heard anything?"

Lorne didn't pretend to misunderstand. "Yeah. A reporter

contacted me. Said the pardon is basically a done deal. This week, most likely." Lorne made a disgusted noise. "What I want to know is, if it is so certain, why aren't the official sources contacting us?"

"I don't know," he said, trying to minimize the bitterness spilling over onto the words. *Because the official sources don't care about us. They used us until we were useless and then tossed us out, even while paying lip service to the ideals we we're told we served.* Jas had been prepared for some people to spurn him and Lorne when they'd accused McGuire. He hadn't expected McGuire to have way more supporters, powerful supporters, than they did. That the man had been convicted at all was a shocker.

"Well, I've put in some calls. You know, I was prepared when we had to testify for McGuire's parole hearing, for all the good that did. But a pardon?"

Lorne was right. A pardon was egregious, a mockery of the toll it had taken for a bunch of twentysomethings to hold one of their own accountable.

Jas hadn't expected medals. But when he'd testified in a courtroom, his injury still fresh, he hadn't expected to be brushed off either. "It was only a matter of time. You know how his parents have been spinning it all these years. Us against a poor soldier who was just trying to do his job." That had always been the defense. That McGuire had merely been exercising his best judgment and if the country punished soldiers for doing that, then where would it be?

Lorne sighed. "Yeah, I know. Sucks his parents are so well connected, huh?"

That's how life works. He clutched the phone tighter. "So the news is picking this up, huh?" He'd known that would happen. He shouldn't be so dismayed.

"For sure. His parents are so powerful. They'll want everyone to know their unfairly targeted son has been vindicated." Lorne made a rude noise, and he imagined she was giving her office the middle finger. It had always been her favorite gesture.

It was an apt one right now. He squeezed his phone harder. "Did you tell the reporter you would go on the record with a response?"

"I did. I think we have to get our side out there, too, right?" Lorne's tone was achingly gentle.

His stomach sank, though he'd been expecting the response. If Lorne voluntarily put her name in the news, he had to back her up. That had been his duty, and he didn't think he'd ever be able to shirk that sense of responsibility.

He thought of spilling his guts to a reporter, as he had in court, and at the parole hearing, only this time in front of a national audience.

He shouldn't be so worried about it. Sure, his name and picture would be in the paper. Jas wasn't as untraceable as Katrina, but it wasn't the kind of story that would inspire people to come looking for him. Lorne was right, for the sake of justice, they had to make a statement.

He'd have to open up that emotional wound, and do it while speaking calmly and concisely. Damn it. "I suppose that's the right thing to do."

"You don't have to do it, Jas."

"No. I want to," he lied.

The sound of hooves coming down the dirt road caught his attention. "I have to go. Can you call me when you hear anything more?"

"Absolutely. Hey, I'm going to be on your coast in a couple months. We should get together."

He thought of how fun it had been to go out with Samson and his friends. "That would be nice," he said, and he was surprised to find that he meant it.

Lorne sounded a little less grim. "Take care of yourself, Jas. Talk soon."

"You too." He hung up as Bikram came into view. Jas had already given Lorne's company the photos of everyone who might drop by, including his whole family.

He stuffed his thoughts and feelings about the pardon and McGuire and his service into a box, tied an anchor around that box, and shoved it into the deep dark hole of his soul. *As one does.*

Bikram stopped a few feet away and slid off his horse. In the nonharvesting months, the farm kept afloat with non-peach-related things, like boarding horses and stud fees. Their grandpa had always dreamed of having a stable.

Bikram's dappled horse was gorgeous. It had never met Jas, but that didn't matter. All horses reacted the same to him.

Jas looked at the creature, and the mare snorted at him.

Standard.

Bikram reached into his pocket and pulled out a white cord. Jas had only brought one phone charger, and he really preferred to keep two on him, in case one went kaput. He'd texted Bikram earlier with a request, since he knew his grandfather. The man had drawers full of cords and cables and chargers.

"Here's the charger you requested." Bikram stomped over and handed it to him. "Are the rest of your lodgings to your satisfaction?"

Jas raised an eyebrow at Bikram's testy tone. It was hard to look at this full-grown man and not see the toddler he'd been when Gurjit had married his mother. Especially when Bikram was pouting like he was now. "What is your problem?"

"What problem? I don't have a problem."

"You most definitely do have a problem." Jas crossed his arms over his chest and gave his brother his sternest look. If Bikram wanted to act like a child, he'd act like a parent. "Why are you mad? Is it Katrina?"

Bikram's chin jutted out. Ah yes. There was the stubborn kid he'd half raised. "I'm not mad at her."

"You were very short-tempered when you met her."

"She screamed at me."

"It wasn't at you. Anyway, you screamed, too." If he'd known Katrina was awake, he wouldn't have told Bikram to leave the bags around back.

"Hmph." Bikram rocked back on his heels. "Why did the princess leave her tower anyway?"

Jas automatically glanced in the direction of the house and tugged his brother away, until they were closer to the barn. He switched to Punjabi to be extra careful. "Don't call her that. Like I said, she needed to get away. Did you tell anyone she's here?"

Bikram didn't switch languages, since he wasn't as fluent. He could understand their parents and Jas in Punjabi, but tended to respond in English. "No. Only Mom."

Jas groaned. He should have been more specific. "That's *someone*, Bikram." A meddling someone. How had he not gotten ten calls from his mother during the day?

"Why did you need to get away?"

"It's a long story."

"It's October. No peaches to pick. I got time."

He debated how much to tell Bikram. His brother deserved to know some of what was going on on his farm. "She went viral, and we feared someone might figure out her identity."

"Viral? Like on the internet?"

"Yeah."

"For what? She doesn't seem like the type to, like, have a pet lobster that can play the piano or something."

"Not important."

Bikram shrugged. "I'm not really plugged in like that anyway. Does she have assassins after her? Did you bring a killer to our peach farm, Jas? Are we all gonna be on *Dateline*?"

No, this wasn't one of those suspense novels Katrina liked to read. "She's had some tough breaks. She wanted to go someplace where no one would know her, where she could feel safe. Think of it as a vacation." *Not to mention, I wanted to run away, too.* He leaned against the barn. The wood was rough, the paint peeling, and he'd leaned against this exact spot a million times growing up.

Home.

Twin bolts of pleasure and pain shot through him again at the thought. They'd been sparking all day, every time he came across something that he remembered or something that had changed—in effect, everything. He was kind of getting used to ignoring the pain, that happiness was so seductive.

Bikram studied his feet, then looked up at him. "Wouldn't think you consider this place safe."

"What's that supposed to mean?" Guilt coursed through him. He knew what it meant. It meant he'd stayed distant, had abandoned the property he loved and owned.

"Nothing. She must be pretty special, to bring you back here for an extended stay."

He reacted to the part of Bikram's sentence that ratcheted up Jas's defensiveness. "She's a client. This is my job."

Bikram snorted. "You sure are devoted to her, for being her hired help. Are you certain your feelings aren't all tangled up in Hardeep's widow?"

"It's a job," Jas repeated through gritted teeth. "I have no interest in Katrina beyond that."

"Sure." Bikram glared, which made his next question highly unwelcoming. "How long are you staying?"

"For as long as it takes for this to disappear, or until we decide to return." Or until his grandfather came back from Mexico, but he didn't say that. Hard enough to keep their presence secret from any employees on the farm, much harder to keep this secret from his eagle-eyed granddad.

"Until the parade?"

"No." Difficult to say that now, when he was standing in his hometown. He had so many fond memories of that parade. "Not that long."

"Hasan will be there."

He'd met his brother's fiancé many times over the years. Hasan was due to start med school next fall, at a university a couple hours away. Jas liked the cheerful young man.

Jas's parents considered them far too young to get married. Privately, Jas agreed. They were babies, the two of them.

Jas bit back his concern now. It wasn't his place to tell his brother what to do with his personal life. "I'll see him some other time."

Bikram pressed his lips tight together. "Fine. See ya."

"Hey. One more thing. Can you get me newspapers?"

"Newspapers?"

"Yes."

"Like . . ." Bikram mimed opening a paper. "Print newspapers?"

"Yes."

"Do you know what year it is? They're all online now, believe me."

"Can you get them or not?"

Bikram shrugged. "I'll see what I can do. I might have to time-travel."

Jas watched his brother ride off, his body strong and tall

in the saddle. He pulled his phone out with the intention of sending Samson an update about Lorne's phone call. That was when he heard it, the noise from inside the barn behind him. A half whimper, half whine.

What on earth?

He pulled the barn door open and peered into the dim interior. Light from the setting sun seeped in through cracks in the wood. As expected, it was empty, cleaned out long ago.

There it was again, the noise. An animal. A sick animal?

Dr. Dolittle he wasn't, but he couldn't ignore a sick creature. He flicked on the flashlight on his phone and shined it into the barn.

Chapter Eleven

Katrina stared at the cookbook open in front of her on the kitchen counter. She'd found the vintage book in the living room and had been pretty excited. She stroked the glossy sepia-tinted photo, though she wasn't really processing what she was looking at.

Katrina had had her first panic attack at seventeen during a photo shoot. She'd thought she was dying. They'd rushed her to the hospital, only for the doctors to throw their hands up after running a battery of tests and tell her nothing physical was wrong with her.

She'd had another one a few months later, with more tests and the same result, and then another one a few months after that. Instead of looking for a diagnosis, her dear old dad convinced her it was stress, exhaustion, she was simply too fragile, and only he could help her. Then he'd taken full control of her money, her career, and her time.

She'd had almost zero self-esteem by the time she was twenty-four, and her fear of having "a breakdown" at any given moment had made parties something to dread, even though she was naturally outgoing and social anxiety had never been an issue for her before.

Her father had carefully chosen her outings, all of them geared toward furthering her career, and an after-party at a popular photographer's house during Fashion Week in Paris had been one of them. She'd grown bored by the people in attendance and the increasing wildness as the night grew late. Since her dad had been too sick to come with her, she'd taken the opportunity to slip away into the empty library for a rare moment of peace.

Only it hadn't been empty. Hardeep had been sitting in a chair across from another man, also in his sixties, speaking rapid-fire in a language she didn't know. They'd both looked up when she'd entered, and the other man's face had hardened.

He looked a little forbidding, and she'd felt a moment of fear, but her future husband had spoken up. "She doesn't speak Punjabi, do you, love?"

She'd silently shaken her head, and the man had left. Hardeep had invited her to sit down in his place and quickly charmed her. Charmed her so much, they talked all night. She'd spilled her darkest secrets: her father/manager kept her almost under lock and key, she feared he was deliberately using her attacks as a way to maintain control, and she'd started to read stuff on the internet which suggested she could get help for her condition.

She'd forgotten about the meeting she'd interrupted, until she'd found out later that the guy had been a loan shark

Hardeep was encouraging to look the other way on a friend's debt. That was her late husband. Ride or die for his friends. Ride or die for her, the young woman he'd met and felt sorry for enough to save her from her abusive dad.

She hadn't lied back then. She hadn't spoken any Punjabi at twenty-four. But she'd always been quick, and she'd felt such a deep gratitude for Hardeep saving her, she'd spent the next three years learning his language. She'd downloaded apps, looked up a word here, a word there, and while she could only speak it at a very basic level now, she could understand enough of the gist of a sentence to figure out what was going on. It helped when the person spoke slow or sprinkled in some English words.

Words like *client*. Or her name, uttered in Jas's deep voice. *I have no interest in Katrina.*
She's a client.

Katrina braced her elbows on the kitchen counter and lowered her head into her hands. He'd been so far away, she shouldn't have been able to hear him. The wind must have timed itself just right, to carry those words to her ears. *You wanted something to kill your hope.*

Not so brutally, though, yikes. To go from giddily speculating Jas's tiny overtures meant something other than kindness to hearing from his own mouth that he didn't want her . . . oof.

She'd only gone looking for him because she'd wanted to check in on what the internet was saying about her. She'd come to a dead stop before she could turn the corner of the house when she heard what *Jas* was saying about her.

It had been such a good day, otherwise. Once upon a time, she had enjoyed traveling, and staying in a different place wasn't nearly as unsettling as she'd thought it would be. The silence here was beautiful, the only sounds those of nature. She'd slowly relaxed and tried to build an equally relaxed farm schedule.

She wasn't relaxed now. Her lower lip trembled, and she stilled it. She was self-aware enough to know rejection was not a good playmate for her. She needed to control her knee-jerk response to the revelation that Jas had zero romantic feelings for her.

She stuck her hand in her pocket and fondled the rock there. Doubtful that the rock would calm her right now, but it didn't hurt. Time would ease this painful discovery, surely.

Only she didn't get the time, because the front door opened and Jas called out her name.

She straightened and breathed deep, buttoning all those wayward feelings and hopes and dreams up inside her like she might zip up her sweatshirt. Those eyebrows were not meant to be smoothed by her fingers. So be it. This situation would be mortifying if Jas guessed that she'd come outside and overheard him and his brother. That would be even more mortifying than him witnessing Jia calling him hot. "In the kitchen," she replied.

He entered, and he was *smiling*, the jerk. Who gave him the right to look so cute and cuddly right now?

Be cool. "What's up, bruh?" *Not that cool.*

She'd so rarely seen such a wide smile on his face. "Come with me."

She slowly followed him from the kitchen to the front door. Was he taking her outside to shoot her poor soft heart and put it out of its misery?

Cool. "To where?"

"The barn. I found something that you may like."

Ugh, the last thing she wanted to do was go outside, where she'd eavesdropped on his convo. But since she couldn't tell him why she was sad—*I like you and you don't like me* was a really terrible color on anyone—she had no choice but to follow him.

The setting sun had turned the sky a pinkish-yellow, and she pulled her hoodie tighter as a ramshackle red structure came into view. She squinted at it, annoyed she had to return to the scene of Jas's disappointing conversation. "What are we doing here?"

He shrugged, but his smile remained. "You'll see."

She coughed when she entered the barn. "Is this place not used much?"

"No, not in a long time. I used to play in it when I was young."

His flashlight bounced over the punching bag in the corner of the barn, and Katrina wrinkled her nose. "Are you going to have me punch my frustration out?"

Jas frowned, but then followed her gaze. "Ah, no. Though I could teach you how to punch later, if you want. You asked me once, to teach you some self-defense. We never got around to it."

"I did ask you that." It had been after her kidnapping. Jas had seemed uninterested, so she hadn't pushed it.

He scooted around an old piece of machinery her city-girl eyes had no way to identify, and crouched down, shining the flashlight under it. "Don't get any closer. Look from here."

She stopped next to him and gasped at the sight. "Oh my gosh."

The black-and-brown dog blinked up at them from under the machine. She expected a growl, but instead it thumped its tail. "Where did this beauty come from?"

"No idea, or how it got inside."

"It's young." Katrina took a step forward. It was too dark to see very clearly, but the black-and-brown dog looked maybe a year old, and too skinny.

"I figured you'd kill me if you found out there was a dog on the property and I kept him from you."

"You know me so well." Oof. The wrong thing to remind herself of right now, how well he knew her. "How do you know it's a boy?"

"I don't." Jas held out his hand. "It won't come out. Here, boy. I mean, here, pup. Come here."

The dog cringed and whimpered. Katrina's heart melted and she got down on the ground, uncaring about the dirt on her clothes. "Hey, baby. Come here, doodlebug." She extended her hand and waited, making crooning noises. "Aren't you so beautiful? You're the most beautiful puppy I've ever seen."

"Now who's assuming it's a girl?"

"I didn't say she, I said beautiful. Every gender is beautiful," Katrina said firmly. "Come here, baby."

After a minute or two, the dog straightened, then inched out, one centimeter at a time, until its block-shaped head stuck out from the machine. "I was making a pie," she said to the pup. "Do you smell some peaches on me, Doodle? Do you like peaches?" She retreated and the dog followed her. Katrina's eyes widened as the dog seemed to elongate.

"Holy shit," Jas murmured. "Katrina, back up. It's way bigger than I thought it was."

She did not back up, but she did come to her feet when the dog was out from under the machine. The animal came almost to her waist. "Hello, beauty."

Jas ducked his head and then straightened. "It's a girl."

Katrina stroked the dog's head. Her eyes were big and sweet in the dim light. "No tags." She beamed at Jas, her upset fading with every pet.

He grimaced. "Sometimes out here in the country people don't tag their dogs. We'll have to ask around with the neighbors to see if anyone's missing one. Take her to the vet and see if she's chipped."

"Doodle must be a stray."

"Please don't name her yet."

"Fine." She snapped her fingers. "Come on, girl. Let's go outside, okay?" She continued to keep up running, soothing chatter until the dog was outside with her. There was barely enough light left to examine her properly, but Katrina ran her hands up and down her limbs and body. "She doesn't look injured. I'll give her a bath and a dinner. Even if she belongs to someone, they can't object to that, right?"

"I guess not," Jas said. "But don't go falling in love."

Impossible. She was falling deeper every second. Jas had declared himself out of her romantic reach, but she'd found another kind of love, almost immediately. Surely it was a sign, right? Life rarely made narrative sense, but sometimes it could take something away and give something else right back.

Doodle licked her fingers. Falling. In. Love.

"I'll call Bikram. He knows the neighbors better than I do at this point."

She cupped the dog's face in her hands. "I think she's definitely part rottweiler."

"The vet will know."

"Tomorrow," she said hastily, unable to look away from the puppy's soulful brown eyes. "Who knows, her owner may show up tonight to get her." Please, no. "It's too late now anyway, the vet'll be closed."

"This is farm country. There are after-hours urgent care centers."

"She's so hungry and tired. Let's give her a night of rest before we rush her off somewhere." Katrina was also hungry and tired and could use a night of rest with her new friend.

Jas moved closer and the dog side-eyed him and gave a warning bark. He stopped.

"Hey," she scolded the dog. "That's not nice. That's our friend." *And only our friend.*

"It's okay. Most animals don't like me."

"What? Zeus loves you."

"Zeus is a cat. How can you tell what's love and what's utter disdain?"

She scratched the rottie behind its short ears and spoke in a high-pitched voice. "We do not enforce terrible stereotypes about cats. Are we a cattist household? No, we are not."

Jas coughed, but it sounded more like a strangled laugh. "Fine. Zeus loves me."

She started walking, and Doodle—that was her name, damn it—followed right at her heels. "What a smart pupper you are. Let's get you some food and water, and then we'll give you a nice warm bath." She glanced at Jas in time to catch what looked like utter softness in his eyes.

But it must have been a trick of the light, because he blinked and it was gone. "Before you get preoccupied with the dog, there's something I need to tell you."

He'd known she was eavesdropping.

He'd seen Jia's text.

He knew she wanted to stroke his eyebrows.

He was going to tell her not to hug him anymore.

She stopped, braced for the worst. "Go on."

"It's about—" he hesitated.

The hug. My hotness. How little I like you like that.

"The CafeBae thing."

Oh right. The whole reason they were out here. "Oh."

He grimaced. "They're going to be on TV tomorrow."

"On TV?" Her voice rose on the second word.

"Yeah. *Good Morning Live.*"

"What the fuck?" Not the most elegant response, but he didn't seem to mind.

"That was my reaction."

"What is newsworthy about this? Is there nothing else going on in the news cycle? No one's won the Super Bowl? Or the National Spelling Bee?"

"The first one is in February and the second one's in June, so no." He shrugged when she squinted at him. "I follow football and the bee. They're both on ESPN, they're both sports."

She made a frustrated noise. "I guess we just watch tomorrow to see what happens," she said. As if sensing her worry, the dog leaned against her leg.

Unfortunately, the dog was big, and Katrina wasn't expecting the weight, so she almost toppled over.

"Whoa, there." Jas steadied Katrina by grabbing her arm. "Can you handle this dog?"

"Oh yes. She doesn't know her own strength, but she'll learn." Katrina petted her new companion. "Look, she loves me already."

"How could she not?"

The kind, too-personal words almost brought a tear to her eye, especially on the heels of learning what she had learned. *How could* you *not?*

"Do you need any help? She's going to be a handful to bathe."

"Oh no. We're fine." The last thing she wanted was Jas

being charming and sexy, especially near a bathtub. Let her be in love with one creature at a time. "Go on and finish doing whatever you're doing."

Jas looked away. "Oh yes. I'm very busy."

"Cool, cool. Me too." She forced a smile.

Handy trick her father had taught her, smiling even while she hurt, but it didn't fool her new dog. Doodle stuck close by her side all the way back to the house.

Chapter Twelve

IT WAS STILL dark when Katrina woke the next morning, which was quite normal. The heavy weight snoring next to her was not.

She was already smiling when she turned to greet the animal. Doodle was so *good* and well-mannered, from her potty-training skills to her stoic acceptance of her bath last night. But unlike most dogs, Doodle hadn't slept at her feet, but right next to her, giant block head on the pillow.

She wrinkled her nose at her dog's breath. "Where did you come from?" she whispered, and rested her hand on the dog's back. Doodle stretched, yawned, and continued lightly snoring. Doodle had been curled up in the kitchen next to the stove when Katrina had come upstairs to sleep. "Your sister doesn't like sleeping with me, so this'll be nice when we get home, though I do think you have to learn to sleep on the foot of the bed." It was probably premature to pair up Zeus and Doodle as cool crime-fighting animal siblings in her head, but she couldn't help it. They'd be such cute friends.

Her alarm beeped and she mentally groaned. She'd set it as a reminder about *Good Morning Live*, not that she needed one.

She shivered and burrowed deeper under the quilt. If she could stay here, bundled up forever, she'd do it. But that was impossible, and not only because the minute Rhiannon got back, she'd drive up here to check on her.

Without disturbing the dog, she slid out of bed. The weather had turned colder overnight, and her room was chilly.

She grabbed her phone from where it had been neatly plugged into the charger on the nightstand. She had multiple missed messages, and she clicked on Rhiannon's first.

I meeeeeeesssss you!

She smiled. She replied with a heart eyes emoji and moved to the rest of her texts.

There was a message from Andy, delivered a little over half an hour ago.

Hey Katrina. I know you get up early. Call me whenever you want, if you'd like.

She made a face. It was only a matter of time before Andy saw the CafeBae nonsense. Of course her therapist would recognize Katrina and the café and check in on her.

This was timely. And talking to Andy was good for her. So why was she so reluctant to talk to her therapist about all this?

She could wait, have some coffee, but if she did wait, she'd probably put it off longer. She'd learned a long time ago some things were easier to do at dawn, when no one else was awake.

She petted the puppy for moral support and dialed. Andy picked up on the second ring, her voice calm and alert. "Hi, Katrina."

"Hi." She scuffed her sock-clad foot along the floor. "You saw?"

Andy didn't pretend ignorance. "I did. Honestly, almost by accident, I ran across an article."

"Did you recognize me instantly?"

"Yes. But remember, I saw you a few hours before the photos were taken. I can't imagine anyone else would be able to figure out who you were."

Wow. Had it only been three days ago that she'd sat in that café with Andy? When everything was chaos, the days could feel like years, she supposed. "Right. That's what my roommates said, too. That chances are slim."

"I think so."

"I ran away."

Andy paused. "Did you now. Where are you?"

"At my bodyguard's family farm. NorCal." Katrina trusted Andy to tell her the exact location, but she probably wouldn't know the area.

There was a creak, and she imagined Andy sitting back in her leather chair. Katrina had never been to her office, but she imagined all therapists had leather chairs. "You went to stay somewhere else overnight. How are you doing?"

"Fine." She knew what the next question would be. *What did you learn from this exposure?* "I learned waking up in a different place isn't so terrible, especially if I try to keep some of my schedule the same. Actually, I'd forgotten how much I used to enjoy new experiences, and a farm is very new. There's a lot to like about being here, beyond the fact that it's not home."

"Yeah, it would be new for me too. And, yes. You can absolutely make the unfamiliar familiar in certain ways."

Katrina walked to the bureau to fiddle with her rock. "Those people—from the café—they're going on TV today in a few hours."

"I saw."

"It's going to bring more attention to me."

"Well, I'm sure you've already considered all the terrible things that could happen, right?"

"Yes."

"What are some alternative possibilities?"

Katrina made a face.

"Are you rolling your eyes?"

Was Andy psychic? "No. Um, I suppose . . . it could be possible people find out my name and nothing happens. Or it dies down on its own and I go back to my life."

"Those are definitely valid possibilities." Andy paused. "How's this for a suggestion? I know you work on this a lot, but be more vigilant to your thinking patterns in a time of stress like this. When you start to catastrophize, take a step back and acknowledge you may be overestimating the probability that the worst will happen."

That seemed like a reasonable enough suggestion. "Okay."

"It's not homework. It's a suggestion," Andy said, and there was a smile in her voice. "And remember to call me if you need me. Your support system is there to help you out when you need it."

"Understood. I'll try to focus on other things too." *Like how Jas will never love me.* No, maybe not that.

"Always good to stay busy. Remember sometimes social media is flat and overly simple. It's not the whole world, even if it seems like it sometimes. There's millions of people out there who have no idea who CafeBae is."

"Got it."

"I can't wait to hear all about farm life when you get back."

They said their goodbyes and Katrina placed her phone on the bed. She quickly showered and changed. No newspapers here, but she'd catch up on the world online. Then breakfast, then work.

She left Doodle sleeping and tiptoed into the hallway. She paused outside Jas's door. Was that a thud?

She stood in the dark hallway for a minute, and then heard it again. A thud, followed by a grunt. She knew his grunts. This was a pained grunt.

She knocked lightly. "Jas?" she whispered.

Nothing.

"Jas?" she said, louder.

She placed her hand on the doorknob and hesitated. Entering Jas's bedroom was fairly intimate, but if he was hurt, she didn't want to ignore him. She heard a low, tortured moan, and that made up her mind for her.

There was enough light coming in from the rapidly lightening sky to see Jas clearly. His head rocked back and forth on the pillow. He'd kicked the sheet off. He was naked except for a pair of shorts. Seeing that much skin might have normally sent her packing, but he was in so much distress, she couldn't leave.

His lips parted and he gasped. His brow was furrowed. She walked over to the side of the bed. "Jas," she whispered, but he was in deep REM sleep, his eyes moving rapidly under his eyelids. And what he saw wasn't making him happy.

"Shhh," she crooned, and placed her hand on his cheek. He immediately stilled. Jas shifted his legs and she glanced down. This was as much of his flesh as she'd ever seen, but she could barely register his lean stomach when the web of scars on his right thigh and knee existed.

She'd seen these scars before. The details were murky, but she knew he'd been injured in the course of duty, that he sometimes moved a little stiffly when it was cold out. Katrina wasn't a veteran, but she knew trauma. She knew scars, scars on the body and on the soul.

She studied the lines of exhaustion and pain etched into his face. Her heart melted. He was so focused on her, always. On her comfort and well-being.

Because you're his client.

Her lips twisted. Her silly romantic dreams were just that, dreams, and he couldn't help that he didn't feel the zings she did. Nothing else would come of this, but she considered him a friend. She'd be a better friend, his best friend. He had things going on in his life that had nothing to do with her, and she ought to be more sensitive to all the stuff he might be dealing with, the stuff he didn't show her or anyone else.

Katrina didn't want to wake him. On the contrary, she hoped he caught up on his sleep. Before leaving, she opened his window a crack so air could flow into the room. A poor substitute for her cool hand on his face, but probably a much safer option to mitigate his discomfort while he slumbered.

Chapter Thirteen

Jas had grown up with peach everything—peach cobbler, peach pie, peach jam, even peach sandwiches. He might not be a farmer but peaches ran in his blood, and occasionally his mouth watered when he remembered the taste of the first crop of the season, fresh from the trees.

So it was no surprise the delicious peachy scent of whatever was cooking lured him out of bed and downstairs in the morning.

He entered the kitchen and found Katrina at the stove, stirring something in an old cast-iron pan. She wore leggings and a soft cozy cream sweater that slipped off one shoulder, revealing a lacy bra strap and light brown skin. He kept his gaze above her neck. "Good morning."

Her beaming smile caught him off guard. "Good morning. How did you sleep?"

"Fine," he lied. His sleep had been fitful, as it occasionally was in times of stress. He didn't remember his nightmares perfectly, but the feelings always lingered in the morning.

For the most part, he could repress the memories of getting hurt, but sometimes . . . well, sometimes they popped to center stage. "You?"

The dog lifted her head from where she lay at Katrina's feet. He expected the animal to growl or huff at him, but instead she only put her giant head down and closed her eyes. Looking at Doodle's still big paws, he feared she wasn't quite done growing.

"Excellent. Doodle kept me nice and warm. Did Bikram get back to you about anyone missing her?"

Her words were casual, but he caught the hint of worry underlying them. Her attachment to the dog was very clear. "He hasn't responded yet. He seems to be a little annoyed with me, so he may be delaying." He hadn't meant to confide that last part. The nightmares must have loosened his tongue.

"Hmm. Maybe he's annoyed with you for the same reason he seems to dislike me."

"He doesn't dislike you," he said automatically.

She lifted a shoulder, and the sweater slipped farther. Not that he was looking.

"It might be he's resentful that you working for me has kept you away from your family for so long."

Jas shook his head. "That's ridiculous, I see them all the time," he said, even as he thought back to Bikram's visit yesterday.

She must be pretty special.

He frowned.

Katrina waved a spatula. "Something to think about before you see him next."

"If he doesn't respond in the next couple hours, I'll take the dog to the vet and see if she's chipped or if they know anything about a possible owner." Though that would entail leaving Katrina alone, and he wasn't sure if he wanted to do that.

"Well, if the vet doesn't know anything, you could get a temporary tag for her, just in case. It's Doodle with two o's, one l."

Jas didn't particularly want to do that, on the off chance Katrina couldn't keep Doodle, but he didn't want to crush her hopes either. "We'll see. What are you making?"

"Peach cobbler." She nodded at the windowsill. "I made a couple of pies earlier. There were so many peaches. You could perhaps take a pie over to your brother and any of the other workers?"

The men and women would be delighted. Everyone who worked on the farm carted home the non-sellable fruit, but an out of season pie was next level. "How long have you been up?"

"A while. You know I'm an early riser." She gave him a wry smile. "No newspaper here, so I did a bit of reading on this new start-up I found, and cooked."

That sounded more like her schedule, except . . . "You're not listening to any music here."

She swiped her hands on the towel tucked at her waist. "My headphones block out noise. I don't know this place well enough yet."

"Ah."

"How do you feel about a nice fruit salad for breakfast? Maybe a yogurt parfait. Something quick."

"Sounds good. Do you need help cutting anything?"

She waved him off. They were silent as she chopped fruit and assembled the parfait in little glasses she must have found in the cupboard, Doodle patiently sitting at her feet ready to gobble any fallen scraps. "Bikram did a great job stocking our fridge," she remarked.

Jas poured them both orange juice and coffee. "Let me know if anything's missing. I can place another grocery order."

"I'll do a proper inventory later." She placed the parfaits on a tray and cocked her head at the living room. "Shall we eat on the couch? The show's about to start."

He raised an eyebrow, and her gaze slid away from his face, though he didn't know why. "You want to watch the *Good Morning Live* segment?"

"Of course. Don't you?"

He'd planned on watching it, if only to keep up on what was happening. "Yes. Which is why you don't need to put yourself through that."

"Don't be silly." She sailed past him, and he had no choice but to follow.

"Katrina . . ."

"It's fine, Jas." She sat on the couch and switched on the TV. Katrina patted the place next to her. "Let's watch."

"AND NOW WE'RE going to turn to CafeBae and the viral romance that has captured the nation."

Katrina placed her spoon down. Next to her on the old floral couch, Jas rested his orange juice on his knee.

Now that this moment had come, she felt oddly disassociated, like she was standing outside her body, watching this show. "You know, I was on *Good Morning Live* once," she said casually. The camera panned over Ross in what she assumed was his house. The voice-over gave a summary of the nightmare, with the same rom-com spin, as Ross puttered around a kitchen shirtless and sat down with a staged plate of eggs and bacon. She knew it was staged, because only a masochist would cook bacon shirtless.

"When were you on *Good Morning Live*?" Jas asked.

"When I was maybe sixteen. It was a calendar that was being promoted, Teens against Tetanus." She shrugged at his puzzled expression. "Yeah, I don't know. I got groped by a correspondent during the segment. I told my agent, she told me to play nice, and I guess I wasn't nice enough, because they never asked me back." She'd also told her father, who had yelled at her to not make up stories. The joy of show business.

Jas placed his glass on the coffee table with a loud clink. "Where's the correspondent now?"

"Fired."

"Thank God."

On the television, Ross leaned against the railing of his balcony and laughed at something the interviewer said, and it cut in their audio. "Why do you think you went viral?" the reporter asked.

Good question.

Ross stroked his chin. His stubble had grown since she'd seen him in person, and he looked rugged and masculine, and conventionally attractive enough to fool the internet, she supposed. "It's a cynical world," the liar said. "I think people want love and romance and happy endings."

Katrina wanted those things, too, but she wanted them in reality. Not the fantasy these people were spinning.

"How do you feel about being the hero in this love story?"

Ross laughed. "You know, I think the real heroes are the ones who documented it for the world. Becca and her dear hubby."

Whaaaaat. The video cut to the studio and Becca and her *dear hubby*—gag—whose name turned out to be Alan, according to the chyron on the bottom of the screen.

Katrina squinted at the brown-haired man. Oh right. The entirely forgettable guy who had been with Becca at the café. Nice, she had another person to focus her ire on.

"We were so captivated by the thought that we were witnessing love in real time," Becca gushed. Alan nodded enthusiastically. "I suppose the rest of the world was too."

"There was no love," Katrina muttered. Jas took a measured sip of his juice, but was silent.

"I just want them to be happy, truly," Becca said, and tittered. "And maybe invite us to the wedding."

"They'll have to invite the whole internet to their wedding," Alan joked.

The video cut to Ross. "How did you feel when you first saw CuteCafeGirl, Ross?"

"Oh, I thought she was beautiful and stunning. Intelligent.

And we had so much in common, right off the bat." He pressed his hand to his hairless chest. Why was he still shirtless? Wasn't he cold? "We're both animal lovers, for one. And the more we talk, the more we find out about each other."

She jerked. Jas stilled next to her. What? Had he said *talk*? Not *talked*?

"So you two are still in contact with each other?"

"Yes." His dimples flashed. "Kat's a little shy, but she's as delighted as I am that our story has inspired so many people."

"Is there going to be a fairy-tale wedding?"

Ross winked. "Time will tell."

Katrina shut the TV off with a snap of the remote. "It's . . . he . . ."

"What a motherfucking asshole." Jas's calm pronouncement had her turning to face him. He met her gaze. "He's on TV saying you guys are still talking to each other. This is going beyond the lies he spun before. He's . . . he's enjoying this fame. So is the woman. And you had to leave your own damn home." He launched to his feet and ran his hands through his hair until it was spiked up. "This is so unfair."

She watched him, bemused. It was all stuff she'd said yesterday, when he'd sat so calmly and listened to her.

It was like a trade, she supposed. Now that he was upset, her own ire deflated. "It is unfair," she agreed. "But that's how it's going." Her smile was wobbly. "One superpower my brain gives me is that I'm always low-key prepped for the worst. This scenario wasn't one I considered, but it's not the absolute worst."

He growled.

"To be honest, I truly expected them to go on television and rattle off my name and Social Security number." Katrina winced. "He gave the internet my nickname, so, like, not great, but it really could have been worse." She rose and dared to place her hand on Jas's arm. "You know what? Next couple of days, let's try to focus on other things. Not stress too much until we have to. It's okay. We can handle this."

He looked down at her hand. "You're right. We can handle it."

She let her lashes conceal her eyes as she turned away and picked up their plates, Doodle coming to her feet, tongue sticking out in anticipation of returning to the kitchen.

It had sounded a little too much like a vow, those words coming from him. *We can handle it.*

She's a client.

She'd take her own advice and stay focused on other things, like enjoying this time, tucked away in this adorable little farmhouse, with her dear friend.

Chapter Fourteen

IF JAS DIDN'T leave the house soon, Katrina was going to kill him.

Okay, kill was, perhaps, too strong a word.

Tap, tap, tap.

Katrina's eye twitched. Or not strong enough.

Doubtful anyone else would be annoyed by Jas tapping a pen on the table while he worked on his laptop, but repetitive noises made her head ache. Especially since he'd been doing it for the last two whole hours.

"Katrina?"

She refocused on the computer, where her two employees were gathered around a conference table. Being an investor wasn't easy when one didn't leave one's home, but it was made simpler with a small staff of people she trusted implicitly to handle the face-to-face interactions and judgment calls that were necessary in this game. She leased a small, ridiculously expensive office in Silicon Valley for them.

So far, the system had worked. There was some speculation, but no one closely questioned who the wizard was behind the curtain of the KA Fund. Entrepreneurs were happy to get money, they rarely cared where it came from so long as they could keep building. "I'm sorry, Akash. Can you repeat that?"

Akash fiddled with the precise knot in his tie. He was her newest hire, and happened to be Rhiannon's assistant's cousin. Katrina trusted Lakshmi and Akash had struck her as clever and quick. He'd only worked for her for a year, but he'd done well in scouting out some good opportunities. They were working on his impulsiveness. "I was saying I think you ought to reconsider the handbag start-up."

Carol was already shaking her head before Katrina could respond. She was in her fifties, and had been Katrina's agent's assistant many years ago. She was solid and cautious, and possessed an uncanny ability to suss out diamonds in the rough. "There are a million sustainable purse companies out there now. There's nothing special about this one." She grimaced. "Their samples are hideous, too."

"It's not about the company, it's the people behind it," Akash argued. "Two Stanford Ph.D.s."

Tap. Tap. Tap.

Katrina glanced at Jas. He wasn't using the pen anymore, but he was typing. Loudly. Was it his keyboard that was loud or his fingers? "Carol?"

"Yes, ma'am."

"What do we say?"

"Just because Google was founded by two Stanford Ph.D.s doesn't mean we hand out money to every Stanford Ph. Dick, Tom, and Harry that walks in our door," Carol intoned.

Akash adjusted his glasses. "Of course, I wasn't suggesting that."

"I read an article that the 3-D printing company this start-up uses to make their purses shut down under some shady circumstances. They're having severe issues sourcing the product." Katrina read a lot of articles. Sometimes the information came in handy, and sometimes it was useless. She was happy this was a handy time. "It's not worth the risk as it stands right now."

"I missed that article." Akash nodded, once. "I won't bring it up again. I'm so sorry."

"Please don't be sorry. I'm fine with you arguing with me. Carol and I have had some epic arguments over the years, haven't we, Carol?"

The lines around Carol's light blue eyes crinkled. "Epic."

"Sometimes she's in the right, sometimes I am. I want you to feel free to air your opinions."

Akash perked up. "Yes, ma'am."

Click, click, click. That stupid pen again.

She gritted her teeth, then remembered her employees could see her. "Why don't we pick this up later?"

"Sure."

"No problem."

"Is there anything else urgent you wanted to talk to me about?" She held her breath. She'd been holding her breath for the past hour, waiting for one of them to bring up Cafe-Bae, but they hadn't and they didn't now.

She supposed there were still some people in the world

who didn't know she was trending. Or, they were too polite and kind and in love with their jobs.

She signed off, and turned to Jas with a determined smile. "Jas?" she asked sweetly.

He stopped mid-click on the pen. "Yes?"

"Do you have anything to do? Outside the house, perhaps?"

"Well I do have to take Doodle to the vet, but . . ."

Oh, wait, no. She didn't hate the clicking so much she would sacrifice her pup. What if the vet knew who Doodle belonged to?

However, Doodle needed to be looked over by the doc to make sure she was okay. Katrina wanted to be a responsible dog owner. "Okay. That's fine."

"Now?" Jas looked at the dog sitting at her feet, one big paw covering her foot.

Best to get this potentially hurtful thing over with. "No time like the present." She set her laptop aside and leaned forward. "Who wants to go for a car ride? Is it you, my sweet darling?" Doodle thumped her tail, but didn't rise. She'd really taken to being a spoiled pet.

"I'd have to leave you alone."

She stared at him, puzzled. "I'm home alone all the time back home."

"No. That's different. Gerald is around, and Jia and Rhiannon sometimes, plus the guards."

"Well, what do you call the people in the car parked behind those trees?" She cocked her head. "You're not my babysitter, Jas. I don't need a babysitter."

"I didn't say you needed a babysitter."

"There's cameras all around the place. Alarms. Guards. I'm fine."

"You could have a panic attack while you're here alone."

"So? I've had them before alone. I *prefer* to be alone, if I can't be with someone I trust." She raised a shoulder. "Take the dog to the vet. I will be absolutely fine." *And I will get all my work done, you beautiful distraction.*

She rose to her feet and made a kissy noise at the dog. "Come on, Doodle. Come on. Let's go to the car."

Jas rose to his feet at the same time Doodle did, and Katrina hid her smile. Her coaxing tone was pretty good, she supposed.

JAS LEFT THE vet and wrapped the newly bought leash around his fist. "You're not in the clear yet," he told the dog. "You may not be chipped, but you heard the vet. There could still be someone looking for you."

Doodle panted up at him. The black markings on her face made her look like a masked superhero.

He tugged on her leash, and she obediently followed. They'd settled into a grudging truce today. Doodle had easily gotten into the car. More important, she hadn't ripped his throat out while he drove.

He hadn't particularly wanted to bring her to the vet, and not only because it would leave Katrina alone, as he'd mentioned. He'd been tense, waiting for someone he'd grown up with to recognize him and stop him for an interminable amount of small talk. Small talk was the fifth horseman of the apocalypse.

He also hadn't wanted to leave because he'd enjoyed the rare glimpse he'd gotten of Katrina at work. She was so *smart*.

He was about to open the door to the SUV when he glanced across the street and paused. His brother had had the same truck for years, his license plate held in a commemorative frame from his alma mater.

Jas checked his watch. Noon, so it made sense his brother would be grabbing lunch at the restaurant in the little strip mall. It was a staple in the small community, so he'd undoubtedly run into someone he knew.

If Bikram was there, he could deflect that fifth horseman. Jas spoke to Doodle. "If the same couple still owns that place, they'll let you come in." He kept his distance from dogs, but he knew keeping them in a locked car wasn't a good idea.

The same couple did own it, the aunty at the register nodding and smiling at him when he walked in like he hadn't been gone for almost two decades. Sure enough, she didn't bat an eye at his dog. Jas inhaled deeply, the scent of curry and spices filling his nostrils. It took a second for his eyes to readjust to the darker indoor lighting, but then he caught sight of his brother sitting at a corner table in the not-so-crowded dining room.

Bikram *did* bat an eye at the dog that padded along at his side. "Holy shit, what is that, a hellhound?"

Jas looked down at Doodle, resisting the urge to cover her ears. The guys at the nearby tables gave the dog nervous looks. "She's the dog I asked you about." Jas sat in the chair across from his brother and brought Doodle in close to his leg. She barely fit under the table.

"She looked smaller in the pic. She likes you?"

Jas tried not to take offense at Bikram's incredulous tone. He was not an animal whisperer. The opposite, in fact, if that was a thing. "She seems to tolerate me."

"Weird." Bikram tore off a piece of naan and dipped it in the saag on his plate.

The owner appeared at Jas's elbow with a plate full of food. "Your hands looked full, so I got you a little of everything from the buffet," she said in her quiet voice.

"Thank you, aunty." He took the plate from her and placed it in front of him. He wasn't hungry, but he figured he'd make an effort to eat with his brother.

"How have you been?" she asked.

He braced himself. "Well."

"Good. Give my love to your mother."

Okay, that had been a lot less painful than he'd thought it would be. Jas turned back to his brother. "Have you heard anything about Doodle?"

"Doodle, huh?" Bikram shrugged. "I've asked around. So far, none of our closest neighbors are missing a dog."

Relief ran through him. It wasn't definitive, but he'd like for Katrina to be able to keep Doodle. "Good."

Bikram glanced under the table. "She looks pretty scrawny.

Couple of people haven't called me back yet, but she's most likely a stray."

"Probably." He accepted the basket of naan Bikram passed across the table. "What are you up to today?"

"It's slow. Figured I'd take advantage of that and run some errands I've been putting off since summer."

Jas nodded. He hadn't been here through a harvest season in a while, but he remembered how much work that was, how they'd all pitched in. Even his grandmother had been out in the orchard every year, grading the peaches to determine which ones were fit for selling. "Smart."

"How's everything going at the little house?" Bikram indicated the dog with a wave. "Animal surprises aside."

"Pretty good." He hesitated, the worry niggling at the back of his mind. Bikram didn't sound annoyed right this minute, but he knew his brother. If they didn't resolve whatever was bugging him, it would crop up again and again. "I have a question for you."

"Okay."

"Are you resentful of Katrina because you think she's the reason I don't spend much time here?"

Bikram chewed his bite of food and maintained eye contact with him. He swallowed and spoke. "Duh."

Jas squinted at him.

"I mean, I said as much, didn't I?"

"It's not Katrina's fault I live down south." He hesitated, unsure how to broach this particular uncomfortable subject. "If you're upset about the farm, Bikram . . ."

"It's not that." Bikram's nose flared. "You're the heir. I get it."

Jas leaned forward. "You know I don't want it."

Bikram's smile was sardonic. "Doesn't matter. You know Grandpa. Blood is thicker than water, blood above all." He took a sip of water. "I'm not blood."

"Bikram—"

"It's not about the farm, and this isn't about living a few hours away."

"Then what is it about?"

"It's about the fact that you barely know my fiancé. I'm marrying someone, Jas, and you haven't shown the slightest bit of interest!" Bikram sat back and glared at him. "Now, I get that you're busy with your job, but you didn't even stay overnight at our engagement party. You had to run back that night, you said, because Katrina needed you. This is the longest I've seen you in years, and we live in the same damn state."

Jas thought back to last month and the engagement party. No. That couldn't be right, right?

Only that was what had happened. He'd attended the party, toasted the couple, and left about ten minutes after the first person had gone home.

He may have used work as his excuse. He didn't remember now.

It was like Bikram had opened a spigot and couldn't stop. His brother thumped his fist on the table, making the plates rattle. "You've barely met Hasan. He could be a serial killer."

Jas drew back. "Is he a serial killer?"

"No! But you don't know that! You should be vetting my boyfriend. You should be telling us we're too young and haven't known each other long enough. That's what a big brother does."

Jas took a bite of food, if only to have a moment to think while he chewed. "Ask me something."

"What?"

"About Hasan."

"What are you talking about?"

"I mean, what do you want to know about him? Where he went to grade school? His MCAT score? His parents' favorite vacation spot?" Jas leaned forward. "This is my job. If you think I would *ever* let you marry someone without finding every crumb of information I could about them, you are mistaken."

Bikram slowly nodded, and there was a sheen of tears in his eyes. "Why don't you stick around when you visit? You always say it's work. If it's not, then why?"

Jas opened his mouth and then closed it again, his heart wrenching in his chest. He wasn't sure what to say to that.

He wished Katrina were here. She was empathetic and adept at soothing hurt feelings, counseling people through roadblocks, and he was not.

They ate in silence for a few minutes, and then Jas looked up. "Maybe . . ." he said, and cleared his throat, though the hoarseness remained. "Maybe you and Hasan can come down some weekend and I can get to know him better." He tried for a smile. "My search didn't turn up any serial killer tendencies, but it doesn't hurt to double-check."

Bikram eyed him suspiciously. "Yeah?"

"Yeah. That would be nice." And he meant that. "Also, actually, I do think you're too young to get married."

A smile spread across Bikram's face, and just like that, his brother was back to his usual sunny self. "We don't care what you think."

"Well, I'll—" Jas hesitated, trying to navigate this odd conversation. "I'll tell you what I think anyway. You're barely old enough to rent cars, the two of you—"

"Okay, that's enough opinion-sharing for now." But Bikram had a big grin on his face, and Jas returned it.

Bikram bumped his elbow. "This is the brother I know."

Jas's smile froze. No. He wasn't.

"Something wrong?" Bikram asked.

"No." He looked out the big tinted windows lining the front of the restaurant, toward the parking lot. "Can you do me a favor?"

Bikram looked wary. "What?"

Jas lowered his voice. "You remember that shotgun in the little house?"

"Above the mantel?"

He nodded. "I can't have it there."

"I doubt that firearm's still functional."

"It doesn't matter. I can't be around a gun."

Bikram stilled. "Jas," he said softly. "Are you okay?"

"Yes. I don't like the reminder. That's all." He could still hear McGuire's gun going off that night, the pain and the blood, but above all the *noise*. It had been so loud.

Bikram blew out a breath. "I'm sorry. I was only eleven

when the trial happened. Sometimes I forget, you know? What you must have gone through."

Jas shifted. He hated that sympathetic look Bikram was giving him. He was fine. Other men and women had it much worse than him. *Stuff those feelings back. Don't think about them.* "Actually, never mind."

"No." Bikram's tone was brisk now. "What can I do? Do you want me to pick it up?"

His desire to be rid of the thing won out. "I put it in the trunk of my car. It's wrapped in a blanket. Can you take it? It can go in Grandpa's collection in the big house." Their grandfather was obsessed with collecting pieces of family history.

Bikram reached across the table and grabbed Jas's arm. It was only then that Jas realized he was rubbing his ear. He stopped.

"Give me your car keys," Bikram said. "I'll take care of it now. You stay here with the dog."

He didn't argue with his brother, he was too grateful to be rid of the thing. He handed over his keys and stayed put. As if she sensed his discomfort, Doodle shifted so she could put her head on his thigh. He rubbed the spot between her eyes until they started to close.

Jas signaled the owner for the check, and pulled out two twenties when she came over with a pad in her hand. Her eyes widened at the cash. "It's fifteen ninety-eight."

Oh right. The year might change, but the $7.99 buffet was a constant. He handed her the cash anyway. "Can you pack up some food for me? A nonveg entrée, a samosa, and whatever sweet you have." Katrina was only cooking vegetarian food here because of him, and he didn't want her to not eat what she liked.

Bikram came back inside as the aunty brought Jas his go-bag. His brother handed him his car keys and nodded at the bag. "What's that? Bones for the hellhound?"

Doodle showed all her teeth, saliva dripping off them. The vet had given her a little much-needed teeth cleaning. Bikram took a step back.

"No. Food for Katrina." He stiffened when his brother smirked. "She has to eat too."

"Riiight." His brother tilted his head at the door and sat back down. "Your trunk is empty."

He swallowed. "Thank you."

Bikram shrugged. "I'll call you if I hear anything from the neighbors."

It was a dismissal, but Jas took heart in the fact that it wasn't a harsh one. Bikram and he might still have issues, but at least he'd aired his grievances.

When Jas got in the car, the vehicle felt lighter, like Bikram had removed a couple of tons of weight instead of one old shotgun. He was relieved now, that he'd asked for the favor.

Doodle poked her head out from the back seat and rested it on Jas's shoulder. The reflection in the rearview mirror made him smile, and he carefully maneuvered his phone out of his pocket and took a selfie.

He sent it to Samson. I think Katrina found a new best friend here.

The response was immediate. Is that a wolf?!

No, a rottweiler mix. She's very sweet.

Hang on, Dean and Harris will want to see her. Let me loop you into a group chat.

He thought about those words on the ride home, *group chat*, even while his phone lit up with message after message, from his new group chat.

The only group chat he was a member of was his immediate family's. He liked being in another one. Being a part of a *group*.

Doodle clambered out of the car when they got home and raced inside. Jas followed more slowly, coming to a stop when he peeked into the living room and found Katrina fast asleep on the couch, her open laptop precariously resting on her chest.

She never napped during the day, as far as he knew. But then again, she probably hadn't been sleeping much lately. She was going to be so annoyed when she woke up and discovered a nap had derailed whatever she'd planned for the afternoon.

He rescued the computer from toppling over with her next big breath and covered her with a blanket. Seemed like tucking her in was just his role in her life, and that was okay. Jas gestured to Doodle. "Stick close," he whispered, though the dog was already on it, climbing up on the big couch to rest next to her.

He turned his attention to his new group chat as he left the room, his thumbs already composing his replies.

Chapter Fifteen

Ugh, how could she have fallen asleep?

Katrina yawned and waited for Doodle to finish her business in the yard. She was so groggy, and if the dog hadn't woken her up to go outside, she would have easily slept for another hour. Watching the *Good Morning Live* segment this morning must have really sapped her of her energy.

She staggered back into the house once Doodle was done and nearly yelped when she saw her face in the mirror. She tried to make some order of her hair and rubbed her cheek in a vain attempt to get the sleep creases out. She checked her watch. Almost two o'clock. "Jas?" she called out. He must be back. Doodle was back, after all, and with a cute new red collar and pretty white teeth.

Doodle sniffed the floor and then paused in front of a door. "What's that, girl?" Katrina went to the door and opened it, startled to find stairs. She hadn't realized any houses in California had basements, but she supposed some of the ones built earlier in the century might.

The clang of metal on metal told her Jas was down there. She petted Doodle. "Good girl. You can go lie down." Doodle huffed as if she understood, and turned away, her tail thwacking Katrina hard on her thigh.

Katrina rubbed her leg and descended to the basement. This was no fancy place. The basement was one large cold concrete room, unfinished, so she caught sight of Jas immediately.

And promptly almost swallowed her tongue.

Welp.

He wore only gym shorts and reclined on the bench press, hefting the heavy weight above his head. His thighs were thick and muscular on either side of the bench, feet on the floor. His bare chest was sprinkled with dark hair, and it was wide and shiny with sweat. The muscles of his abs were clearly delineated, each one perfectly carved.

Save for his nightmare, when she'd been utterly distracted by his pain, she'd never seen him with so much skin exposed. So much . . . beautiful skin.

Katrina pressed a hand to her belly. Oh God, the zings. The *zings.*

She tried to mentally slap herself. This was Jas, not some piece of meat to ogle. He was like . . . well, she couldn't view him as some sexual fantasy come to life.

He placed the bar back into its holder thing and crunched to come to a seated position, which did all sorts of amazing things to those stomach muscles. He twisted to grab his water bottle from the floor and lifted it to his lips. It was inexplicably sexy when he tilted his head back and drank large gulps.

He lowered the bottle, and that was when he met her eyes.

He jerked back, like he was startled. Well, why wouldn't he be? She was hovering by the foot of the stairs like a polter-geist. "Katrina. Is anything wrong?"

She licked her dry lips. Yes. Things were wrong. She'd come here for a reason. A very specific reason. "Unf."

"What?" He swung his leg over the bench and rose to his feet. A trickle of sweat ran down his chest.

Remember that hug?

She'd carefully repressed that memory. But it came back to her in a rush now. His arms hadn't gone around her, but she'd felt the power in them. Had he hugged her, he could have squeezed her so tight.

Those biceps were gigantic. She was willing to bet he gave good hugs.

"Katrina?" He grabbed his T-shirt from where he'd slung it over another bench and pulled it on.

She snapped out of her hypnotized state. What had he been asking? Something about his pecs? Or the way the white T-shirt clung to his sweaty man chest? "Yes."

"Yes, what? Something's wrong?"

"Nothing's wrong."

"Then what do you need?"

"Yes."

"What?" He took a few steps toward her.

She shook her head. "I'm sorry. Did you say something?"

He spoke slowly. "Why are you here? Is something wrong?"

"Oh. No. Um. I woke up, and . . ." She hooked her thumb over her shoulder. "I was sleeping."

"I know. I saw you."

"Right. I fell asleep. I don't normally fall asleep, but here we are. I think I'm groggy. Yes, that is why talking is hard. Anyway, how was the vet visit?" *Yes, good brain. Go to a neutral non-muscle-related topic.*

"Good. Doodle is in great health. No chip, no one who's called looking for her. I ran into Bikram and he says he still has a few neighbors to hear back from, but no leads yet."

Yes, she would be happy about all of this when she could concentrate on what he was saying with his mouth and not what he was saying with his abs. "Cool."

"Are you sure you're okay?"

"Uh-huh."

"Okay, then. I'll go shower—"

No, he needed to stay looking like this. "Hey. Didn't you say you'd use this time to teach me self-defense?" she blurted out, and immediately nearly kicked herself. *Looking for ways to get closer to him? Control yourself.*

"Self-defense?" His beautiful thick brows drew together.

She tried to laugh. If she could play it off as a joke, maybe they could let this whole thing go. "A silly idea. Sorry. I was—" *Visualizing what it would feel like to have your hands touching me in any way possible.* "You know. It was a thought."

"It's a good thought. I did say I could show you some stuff," he said slowly, flustering her more.

She opened her mouth to protest, but then closed it again. Actually, though it had been born of sexual brain fog, it wasn't a bad idea. "Yes. Ahem."

"Do you want to do it right now?"

She stared at him. Why would he say that? Yes, she wanted to do it right now.

"Katrina?"

"Yes." She gave that yes a little too enthusiastically. "Sure." She glanced down at her clothes. "Are my leggings okay or do I need to change?"

He cleared his throat. "Leggings are good."

Chapter Sixteen

KATRINA TOOK A moment to compose herself while Jas chugged another bottle of water. *Be cool. Don't freak out if he brushes up against you or something. You're here to spar, that's all.*

Spar sounded sexual. How about *parry*? No. Never mind.

She bounced on her toes and made a right jab. "Okay, now I punch you, right?"

He cracked a smile that made her tummy flutter. "Not quite." He motioned for her to come closer. The basement was no state-of-the-art gym. The equipment in it was at least a decade old, maybe older. But there was a fairly thick mat on the floor. "Do you know martial arts or something?" she asked.

"No. I know surviving."

Ahh, that was a sexy answer. "Always good." She stood a foot away from him. "So where do I hit you?"

"You don't. First you breathe."

She raised a skeptical eyebrow. "What?"

"Close your eyes."

Confused, she followed his orders and shut her eyes. His footsteps were loud as he walked around her.

"This is stuff you're already aware of. When you're scared or get startled, it's instinctive to freeze up, hold your breath." His voice came from right behind her. Every single hair on her neck sat up and paid attention. "Totally normal human response. But you can't fight someone off if you can't get oxygen to your brain. I see you meditating, doing breathing exercises. You know how to deal with your panic when it's coming from inside you."

She did. Before she'd started going out to different places for exposure therapy, Andy had coached her on running up the stairs or turning in circles. Getting used to the physical sensations she felt during an attack in safe spaces, so she could start to associate them with safety.

"Apply what you already know to that. When someone startles you, you can get scared, but you have to breathe so you can think. If you can think, you can react." He released his breath in a big rush, and she echoed him.

"Good," he murmured, now from in front of her. He inhaled, then exhaled, loud, and she followed suit.

She matched his breathing, eyes still shut. She imagined curling up in his lap while they did exactly this.

Breathing exercises were her kink now? Okay.

She didn't know how long they stood there, but Jas was the one who finally spoke. "That's good."

She staggered back a step when she opened her eyes, the mild vertigo from keeping them closed hitting her. His hand hovered over her arm, but she caught her balance and he didn't touch her.

Touch me.

"So no hitting you?" she joked.

He shook his head. "Fighting basics: run before fighting, but if you have to fight, fighting and landing an injury, any injury, is better than no injury."

"Where'd you learn this? The Army?"

"Yeah, but before that, getting into fights as a kid."

She glanced upward. "You got into fights here?" Granted, she hadn't seen the rest of the town, but this little corner seemed so peaceful.

"My grandpa's fairly well-known in the community, my mom was an unmarried teen when she had me, my dad was some outsider, and it's a small town where all the locals know each other. Yeah, I got into some fights," he said dryly. She wanted to hear more about all that, but he changed the subject. "Let's talk about sensitive areas on a person."

"I've watched enough TV. I know the weak spots."

"Some of those weak spots are overrated. The groin kick? I've seen a man get up and still keep going after a hit like that."

She would not be titillated. He was talking dispassionately about groins, almost scientifically. Besides, *groin* wasn't even a sexy word.

Groin.

Groin.

Groin.

See?

"If you can hit the groin, of course go for it."

Okay, so maybe he was saying it differently than she was, it sounded sexy coming from him. Katrina shook her head. "Got it. Groin if possible."

"Show me how you make a fist."

She fisted her hand and he reached out and adjusted her thumb. "Like this. So you don't break a finger. Now hit me as hard as you can." He pointed to his stomach.

"Finally," she joked. Then she hesitated.

"What's wrong?"

"I don't actually want to hit you," she confessed.

Jas's lips twitched. "I promise, you won't hurt me."

"Ugh."

"Try it."

It was a halfhearted punch at best, like rapping her knuckles against a brick wall.

"Punching can hurt someone, but not if they're braced for it." He tapped her fist until she opened it, and arranged her fingers into a claw. "You know what really hurts? These puppies." He touched her nails. "Scratch, claw. Go for the eyes for maximum impact." He took a step closer. "Think of the other sharp parts of your body. You want to use them on the vulnerable parts of the attacker's body."

"Nothing on me is that sharp."

He took a second to reply. "Your knee. Your elbow." He placed his hand on her elbow.

Zings. Zings aplenty. Enough zings to power a nuclear plant.

Oh no, oh no, oh no.

It's your elbow. The unsexiest part of any body.

And yet.

His hand was warm and callused, the snags on his skin catching her softer flesh. She had a brief fantasy of those hands rubbing their way down the rest of her body. Her naked body.

"Katrina?"

His voice came from far away, like it was being filtered through Vaseline. "Got it. Eyes. Sharp parts of my body. Softer parts of theirs. Claws first."

"Or weapons. You have your pepper spray, right?"

After her kidnapping, when she'd been especially jumpy, Jas had given her a few pepper spray containers to keep around, and then refreshed them with new ones every couple of years.

The spray was the only kind of weapon she felt equipped to carry. Guns and knives scared her. When she'd asked Jas to move to California and be her main security, he'd quietly explained he wasn't capable of handling firearms, and only carried a Taser.

She hadn't needed him to elaborate. She wasn't naïve, and it didn't take a huge leap of imagination to understand why a wounded vet might shy away from guns. It hadn't been a deal breaker for her. She trusted him to protect her with every resource at his disposal. "The last ones you gave me just expired."

Jas frowned. "Why didn't you say something? I'll get you new ones."

She rubbed her nose, mildly embarrassed by imparting new evidence of her nerdiness. "I actually made a batch a couple weeks ago."

"You made it?"

"Yes. I read—"

"An article," he finished.

Katrina lifted a shoulder. "I was curious. I still planned on ordering new commercial ones, but it was a fun science experiment. I stuck one in my purse."

Jas narrowed his eyes. "Can you show me?"

"Um. Sure."

He followed her upstairs and into the kitchen. Doodle thumped her tail from her position in front of the front door.

Her large tote was on the kitchen counter. She pulled out a small unlabeled red bottle and handed it to him. "The biggest drawback is the pressurization, of course," she remarked. "The ones sold in stores are obviously more forceful."

"What's in it?" He opened the bottle and carefully sniffed it. His nose twitched.

"Peppers, cayenne, all stuff I had in my kitchen."

"Have you tested it?" He inhaled again. "I should be sneezing, at least." He shut the bottle.

"I definitely coughed when I took a whiff of it. To test it any more, I'd have to spray— Jesus Christ, what are you doing?"

Jas doubled over, choking and coughing, which made sense, because he'd just pumped a direct spray of the stuff right at his face.

"Oh my God!" Katrina grabbed him by the arm, helping him over to the kitchen table. "What do we do? We can't wash it, right? Why would you do that?"

"Bowl. Dish soap. Water." He choked the words out. They were punctuated with racking coughs.

She grabbed the items as quickly as possible, along with clean towels, then came back to the table. He was still gasping.

"I am so sorry, so, so sorry," she babbled, and dumped the dish soap into the bowl of water, until he indicated for her to stop. She watched, dismayed, as he dunked his whole face in the bowl for a few seconds, then came up and patted it with a towel, then dunked again. He kept repeating that while she stood around wringing her hands.

Unable to watch, she pulled out her phone and googled and found an article. "Take your shirt off, you may have gotten some spray on it," she instructed. Later, she'd think about what an absurd variation that command was on the good old *take your shirt off, it's all wet.*

While he stripped his shirt off, she went to the fridge and grabbed a gallon of milk. When she came back, he had stopped dunking his head, though he was still coughing slightly. He sat with his head tipped back, the towel over his face. "Here," she said softly, then pulled off the towel and re-placed it with the one she'd soaked in milk. "This may help."

He groaned in appreciation and touched the towel. "Yes," he said, his voice raspy.

Katrina didn't know what else to do, so she kept patting his shoulder as his coughing subsided. She didn't know how long she stood there. He finally pulled the towel off his face.

She flinched at his pink face, at his still-teared-up eyes. His chest was wet from the dish-soap antidote.

She couldn't stop patting his shoulder. But she had to know. "What." Pat, pat. "And I cannot stress this enough." Pat, pat. "The actual fuck?"

He blinked at her, and she couldn't tell if he was confused, or if he was still blinking out the pepper spray. "I wanted to see how effective it was."

Her mouth fell open, and her pats became harder. "Are you." Pat, pat. "Fucking." Swat, swat. "Kidding me right now?"

He grabbed her hand. "You don't swear often."

"Then you should understand how upset I am," she said, her voice hoarse. Hardeep had once noted that when she got angry, her voice got quiet. A function of her upbringing. She'd been perpetually angry at her dad, and she'd learned at a young age it was easier to push that anger down and deal with him quietly than to blow up.

She wasn't angry now, but incredulous. And okay, also angry. "You could have hurt yourself."

"Nah. I didn't spray it directly into my eyes. Now we know how someone will react to it. It's not as strong as the commercial ones for sure, by the way, it faded fast. It's not burning now."

"That was fast?"

"Relatively." He shrugged. "It was a good experiment."

"I beg to differ." So much for quiet. She'd shouted that sentence.

"Hey." He slid his hand up her arm. "I'm fine now."

And just like that, she was utterly distracted. His hand went down her forearm, then up again, against the grain of the hairs on her skin, lifting them up. And again.

She found herself matching his breathing again, without his prompting this time. She inched closer. His eyes were so watery she almost teared up herself. "I'm sorry," she whispered.

The corner of his mouth kicked up. "I did it to myself."

She bit her lip. "Actually, you know what? You're right. That was a ridiculous thing to do, and I am not sorry. You need to take better care of yourself."

He slid his hand down, until they were palm to palm. Their fingers didn't interlace or anything, but her thumb did curl over the side of his hand.

"I guess I do." His pinkie curled around the other side of her hand.

Oh no.

Now that the crisis was over, she could appreciate his bare chest once again. Truly, if only there were more less stressful situations where one could deploy the *your shirt is compromised, take it off* line.

She didn't know when she had moved closer, but suddenly she could count every hair in his beautiful eyebrows. With him sitting down, she had to look down slightly to make eye contact with him.

His eyes dropped to her lips and she held her breath. She swayed forward and waited.

His face came closer, and his hand tightened on hers, and her brain took a momentary break from functioning.

That was the only way she could explain why and how their lips met.

She'd been kissed before in her life, of course. Two men she'd managed to sneak away with while she lived under her father's thumb. A chaste kiss from Hardeep when they were wed.

This was like nothing else she'd ever felt. Like nothing else she'd ever feel. No tongue, nothing extravagant, nothing but the press of lips against hers for a minute, maybe more, and it was like a live current hit her body, restarting her heart. Like she'd been doused in the fiery hot spray, not him.

Actually, the fiery part may be contact with a trace amount of pepper remaining on his face.

Nope, it was him.

His lips moved against hers. They were dry and full, the scrape from the stubble on his face scratching her upper lip. She tilted her head and shyly opened her lips. Her hand came to rest on his shoulder. His naked, warm shoulder. She petted the skin, stroking now, grateful he'd removed his shirt.

His reaction was explosive. Her eyes flew open when he shoved away from her, nearly upending his chair as he came to his feet. "I'm going to go shower."

That was maybe the last thing she'd expected him to say. She blinked stupidly at him. "What?"

"I'm going to shower. Worked out. Sprayed. Need a shower." He nodded rapidly, and with every giant step he took as he moonwalked from her, her soul filled with dread. He bumped into the wall and pivoted, his feet moving only slightly too slow to be called a full-out sprint from the room.

Dear Lord. She may not have a great deal of experience, but a man running away after a kiss wasn't a great sign, was it?

Her heart sank and she thumped down into the seat he'd vacated, staring at the empty opening of the kitchen. "No, no, no," she whispered, horror filling the place that exultation had occupied.

What had she done?

Chapter Seventeen

WHAT DID YOU DO?

Jas glanced at the kitchen window out of the corner of his eye. His finally nonburning eye, thank God. He was only grateful that Katrina's concoction, while initially painful, had been relatively mild in aftereffects.

He and Katrina had avoided each other for the last couple hours. He'd come outside. She'd taken over the kitchen. He had no idea what she was cooking, except she was possibly using every ingredient in their pantry and kitchen, as well as every pot and pan in their house.

Jas stabbed his spade into the ground. He yanked out the dandelion and dumped it in the garbage bag. The garden around the house had been somewhat maintained. Not to his high standards, but not bad. He was mostly out here because he could keep an eye on Katrina through the kitchen window. All without actually talking to her.

He'd kissed her. How could he have done that? How had he allowed almost a decade of pent-up need and affection to escape? He prided himself on suppressing . . . well, everything.

He hacked at the root of a particularly stubborn weed. He'd slipped and let his feelings come out, done the worst possible thing he could do. He swallowed, the self-disgust nearly choking him.

He had to apologize. He rested his rusted spade on the ground and glanced up at the window. She came into view, tying her hair up on top of her head, her round face in profile. Her lips were bare of lip gloss, and they were perfect, the bottom full and pouty, the top a sweet bow. She'd showered and changed as well, and her loose green shirt was the same color as the emerald dress she'd worn when he'd first seen her.

He'd apologize, and explain that it had been a onetime thing, a mistake. He'd offer to leave if she'd like him to.

She wouldn't actually make him leave, right? She'd give him the benefit of the doubt.

He came to his feet, but stopped when he heard the sound of hooves from down the road. Why was Bikram here, when they'd only talked a few hours ago?

A flash of crimson came through the trees.

Oh no.

Another flash, and the shadow of a huge black stallion.

Oh *no*.

Had Bikram known? Surely he would have said something if he had.

The horse and rider emerged from the copse of trees. His grandpa came to a stop a few feet away, his devil horse's feet kicking up in the air a little. The old man had always been a showboat, and he wasn't becoming more discreet as he aged. His signature bright-red turban was the least dramatic thing about him.

Andrés Singh was locally and nationally known as the Peach Prince. Within the family, he was known as a tough son of a bitch. Jas had firsthand knowledge of how tough he could be.

The horse settled and Andrés lifted his chin at him, an action Jas immediately mirrored. They were similar in many ways: their thick eyebrows, their high cheekbones, their physique.

Their stubbornness.

Andrés slid off his horse and patted the animal on the neck before walking toward Jas. The man was as tall as Jas was, though age had stooped his shoulders. His denim shirt and worn jeans could be found on any other farmhand, but he'd always carried himself with an air of command. "Jasvinder," he said.

Jas took his gardening gloves off and slapped them against his palm. "Grandpa. You were supposed to be out of the country." And he'd be texting Bikram immediately to ask him what he thought Jas had meant by *don't tell anyone I'm here.* First his brother told their mom, now—

Ah. His mom. He should have known, since he hadn't gotten a single phone call from her in days. She'd surely blabbed.

His grandfather's dark gaze pinned Jas. When he was a kid, those eyes could have made him confess anything and everything that could be classified even moderately as mischief. "Plans change, boy. Sorry to disappoint you." His gaze slid over Jas's shoulder.

Jas's heart both sank and sped up. He glanced behind him. Katrina stood in the doorway leading to the kitchen, flour on her apron and face. With her rolled-up shirtsleeves and snug jeans, she looked like a farm woman with a penchant for baking, not a wealthy investor.

Katrina cocked her head and returned his grandfather's inspection. "Hello."

Andrés's mustache quivered. His beard hadn't grown any less thick and luxurious as he aged. "I presume you are Katrina. Hardeep's wife." It would be hard not to hear the disdain Andrés heaped on Hardeep's name.

This was a shit show.

"I am." Katrina came outside and extended her hand. "You're Jas's grandfather?"

"I am. Andrés Singh."

She shook his hand. "It's a pleasure to meet you." Her eyes met Jas's and skittered away.

He mentally kicked his own ass again. The stupid kiss.

"Thank you so much for your hospitality. Your farm, or what I've seen of it, is beautiful."

"No need to thank me. I didn't even know you were here."

Jas took a step forward. There was no need to make Katrina feel like she was imposing. "You didn't need to know. I told Bikram." *Who told Mom, who definitely told you.* "And this is my house."

Andrés gave him a tight-lipped smile. "Of course it is."

"Would you like some tea?" Katrina stepped aside. "I'm afraid I've been baking, so the kitchen is a mess, but if you don't mind that . . ."

His grandfather lifted his head and sniffed. "What's that I smell? Cookies, perhaps?"

"Mom said you're watching how many sweets you eat," Jas interjected, unable to help himself. Just because he was in a semi-feud with his grandpa didn't mean he wasn't concerned about his health.

"I don't need you to lecture me on my diet," his grandfather said coolly, and sailed into the house, past Katrina.

His grandfather was mad at him, too, but this went deeper than Bikram's annoyance with him for not staying longer at his engagement party. This went back almost two decades.

His grandfather froze when he entered the kitchen, and he turned in a slow circle.

Katrina wrung her hands. "I know, the place is a mess."

Andrés waved that away. "The kitchen hasn't been used like this since my wife passed twenty years ago. I don't come here much. Startling to see signs of life in it."

He hadn't known his grandpa had avoided the place. Jas softened.

Katrina visibly melted into a puddle of goo. She gestured to the table. "Please, have a seat."

Doodle padded into the kitchen and immediately made her way over to Andrés. "Who is this?" Andrés asked. The dog leaned into his petting.

"My new dog," Katrina said with pride. "Doodle."

"A stray we found," Jas said quietly. "Do you know of any neighbors who might be missing her?"

Andrés cupped the dog's face. "No. I've never seen a beauty like her. You know how it is. Lots of strays out here."

Doodle flopped down at Andrés's feet and Jas narrowed his eyes at the canine. It had taken Doodle a day to show him even a fraction of this adoration.

"Do you like tea?" Katrina asked.

"I like chai."

Katrina moved briskly to the cupboard. "I think I saw some masala in the supplies Bikram brought us. I can make that."

His grandfather's mustache quivered. "Can you make it well, though?"

Katrina gave him an amused look. "I can make everything well."

Andrés harrumphed. "We'll see. Not much cause for a fancy rich lady like you to be making her own tea."

Jas straightened, but Katrina only smiled. "If I don't make it, who will?"

"Hardeep would have never made his own tea."

She put a pot on the stove to boil, and pulled out milk. She picked up the takeout bag Jas had brought from the buffet and examined it.

"I brought you some lunch from the restaurant while I was out. Forgot to tell you," Jas explained, the tips of his ears going red as his grandfather's sharp gaze fell on him.

She glanced at him and nodded, replacing the food. "Thank you. Sit down, please."

Andrés settled into a seat at the kitchen table. Unsure of what to do with himself, Jas sat opposite the man. A tense silence settled over the kitchen, though Katrina hummed as she bustled around. When she was done making the tea and had arranged the freshly baked cookies on a plate, she finally came to sit down and gave Andrés a smile of challenge. "Let me know if it's to your satisfaction."

Jas's grandpa took a sip of the tea and a bite of the cookie, then nodded. "The tea could use more sugar. The cookie is perfect."

"Noted." She wrapped her hands around her own mug and leaned forward. "I thought Hardeep was a family friend, but it sounds like you didn't like him much." Her words were light, but her eyes were sharp.

Andrés sniffed. "His grandfather started this farm with my father. It didn't last long. The man was young and wasn't cut out for hard labor, he returned to India. The Aroras established their roots there in jewelry."

"I see. You kept in touch with the family."

"My dad was sentimental. He forgave his old partner quickly and they exchanged letters for years. Hardeep visited here with his grandfather from the time he was a child. He continued to drop in as an adult occasionally." Andrés's nostrils flared. "His flashy lifestyle might have been attractive to some people, I suppose, but I've never been impressed by money. We didn't have much for a long time."

Oh, come on. This revisionist history was ridiculous. "You live in a massive home and have for the last thirty years," Jas said bluntly.

"And before that, our family lived here, for almost seventy years. My parents built this house," Andrés explained to Katrina. "Nikka ghar, we call it now. Our little house."

"I noticed the photos on the stairs. What history."

His grandfather's eyes brightened. "You like history?"

"I love history." Katrina rose. "How about some peach cobbler? It's cool now. That's a fruit, so it's good for you."

Jas shook his head. "He's not supposed to be eating—"

Andrés growled. "I'm not a toddler, to have my food monitored."

"You're certainly not." Katrina moved to the windowsill and brought the cobbler to the table. She took a small amount and placed it on Andrés's plate. "Try that and tell me what you think."

His grandfather drained his tea first and then took a bite. He closed his eyes and sat in silence for a second, then opened them, eyes a little wet. "My wife used to make something like this. It's got a little spiciness to it."

Katrina indicated the living room. "I found an old cookbook on the bookshelf. Perhaps it's the same recipe she used."

Andrés sniffed and took another bite.

"It sounds like you objected to Hardeep's lifestyle more than to him," Katrina said softly. "He was a good man, and I loved him."

Jas shifted, impressed, though Katrina's diplomacy and brains had never been something he'd questioned. She'd disarmed his grandfather and sweetly and firmly stated her defense of her late husband, via a nice cobbler. "He was a good man," Jas agreed.

Andrés was silent while he finished the rest of his dessert in a few bites. "You will come to dinner at the big house. We will go over now," Andrés announced.

"That's not possible. Katrina needs to stay tucked away, for security reasons," Jas lied, giving her a complete and total out.

Not to mention giving himself an out. Dinner with his grandfather was only moderately bearable. His grandpa spent the entire night lobbing pointed remarks, and he responded in kind.

His grandfather shot him a frown. "Did I raise you to let a woman speak for herself or not? Besides, there will be no threat to her at our house."

"That's not the—"

"It's okay," Katrina interjected. "Jas hasn't told anyone much about me, I suppose. He's excellent at security. Very tight-lipped."

There was extra emphasis on his job title. He flinched. That kiss. She was putting him in his place, no doubt.

"It's difficult for me to go to new places. Sometimes I have panic attacks, and I get nervous about having them in unfamiliar locations," she continued.

Andrés scowled. "There is nothing bad at my house," he said gruffly.

"It doesn't have to be something frightening, to trigger it. I'm happy to try to come to your home for dinner, but it's possible I could have one. If I feel uncomfortable, I'll leave, and it may be abrupt."

Jas stared at Katrina. Never had he heard her summarize and speak so frankly about her panic disorder to someone new like this.

Whatever toughness Andrés had previously shown toward Katrina had been dissolved by the cookies and cobbler. He clumsily patted Katrina's shoulder with a big hand. "I understand. No big deal if you must leave. Please come."

"Very well." She shot Jas an unreadable look. "It would be nice to have the company."

He opened his mouth to disagree, but then thought about it. If they went to dinner . . . they wouldn't be alone for dinner. They could put off discussing the kiss. He was always in favor of shoving things down so he could avoid dealing with them. "We'll wash up and meet you at the house," Jas said.

"No need to dress too fancy, son."

Jas gave his grandpa a dour look, catching the dig at his city slicker closet. He didn't dress fancy, for most places, but he did appreciate quality clothes. "I've been gardening, Grandpa."

"I'm sure you're not used to dirt."

Son of a . . .

Andrés rose to his feet, gave Doodle a pet, and tipped his chin at Katrina. "Would you like to ride on my horse, over to my house?"

Katrina had completely won his grandpa over, clearly. No one got to ride that horse.

At her hesitation, Jas jumped in to give her another out.

He could not imagine her wanting the insecurity of being on top of a moving animal. "I'll drive her over."

"I'll bring the rest of the cobbler," Katrina offered.

"Do that." Andrés cleared his throat. "Bring the cookies too."

Chapter Eighteen

WHEN ANDRÉS HAD said he lived in the big house, Katrina should have been prepared. When the mansion that was about double the size of her own home came into view, she choked, breaking the awkward silence of the car ride. "*This* is the big house?"

The home was huge and white, with columns in front, like a mini–White House. Or maybe a White House to scale; she'd never been to the actual White House, and this looked presidential.

"Yup." Jas killed the engine and got out of the car. His answer was curt, which didn't surprise her. He'd been avoiding her since she'd made the god-awful decision—or non-decision, her brain hadn't been a part of that—to kiss him.

Which made sense. She'd barely been able to look at him, had welcomed the distraction of his grandfather's fascinating presence.

Jas came around the vehicle to open her door, and gave her his hand to step out. The first time he'd ever driven her anywhere, she'd tried to sit in the passenger seat, and he'd been mildly horrified. Hardeep had guided her to the back seat. It was a security concern, he'd told her, though she still didn't understand that rationale.

It hadn't seemed like a big deal, and she'd gotten into the habit of sitting in the back. Now, though, it seemed weird.

Because you kissed him!

Ugh, she needed to forget that kiss.

She craned her neck back to examine the home. "I don't think I understood the scale of your grandfather's operation."

"He has one of the biggest farms in the area. It's the largest producer of peaches in the state."

The pride he took in that was apparent. Katrina considered herself a fairly intuitive person when it came to most non-kissing-related things. She had easily picked up on the tension between Jas and his grandfather. It had been different from and more deep-seated than Bikram's coolness.

Andrés may have directed his invitation to her, but it was clear he had badly wanted Jas to come to his home, despite his gruffness whenever he'd spoken to his grandson. It was the frustrated affection in the older man's eyes that had prompted Katrina to impulsively agree to the meal. That, and she wanted to learn more about Jas and his family.

"Are you sure you want to do this?" he asked. "You feel okay?"

She checked in on herself. "Yes." She would treat this like she treated any exploratory foray to a new establishment. Actually, Katrina felt more confident coming to this home for dinner than she had walking into the pho place or the café for the first time. Part of that was the confidence she'd built from coming to this town at all. The rest was that it was a limited number of people, and one of those people was Jas. The familiar within the unfamiliar.

If he quits, what will you do?

She'd find someone else trustworthy to accompany her, that wasn't the issue. He was important to her for reasons unrelated to his job. If he were to quit over the kiss . . .

No, she wouldn't think about that right now. It would upset her too much, and she needed to focus on this new interesting experience.

Jas climbed the stairs. "Come on. Let's get this over with."

It didn't sound like Jas thought this would be interesting, but Katrina clung to her optimism. They walked inside and Katrina had to stifle another gasp. Hardeep had been wealthy, but not ostentatious, and he'd liked to frequent urban cities where homes were smaller.

This was wild. The floors were marble shot with gold, the walls were bedecked with gold-edged frames and fancy art, the chandelier was—no surprise—gold and dripping with crystals. Double staircases stretched to the second floor.

"You grew up here?" she asked Jas as they walked into the equally posh living room. What a puzzle he was. He dressed well, but not rich. He was subdued, not over the top. He'd grown up on a farm, but other than his penchant for gardening, he didn't seem to care much about agriculture or rural life. How had all this come together to produce him?

Jas surveyed the home with no expression. "Until my mom remarried, yes. It's—"

"My pride and joy," Andrés boomed, entering the living

room. "Jasvinder, Daisy's in the kitchen and wishes to speak with you."

"About what?"

"I'm not sure." Andrés scowled at Jas. "By the way, did you give Bikram the shotgun from the little house? That gun belongs there, not here."

"What shotgun?" Katrina asked.

"My father's gun. It was on the mantel," Andrés explained.

Katrina didn't recall seeing anything above the fireplace. She wasn't sure what this was about exactly, but given Jas's aversion to firearms, she could figure it out. When Jas didn't respond, she jumped in. "I don't like guns in the house." Not a total lie.

Andrés's face relaxed. "Ah, I understand. Jasvinder, Daisy is waiting."

Jas gave her a questioning look and she gave him a tiny shake of her head. It was such an automatic exchange it took her a second to realize that it was even done—his checking in on her, her subtly indicating whether she needed him or not.

How could she have potentially jeopardized this?

Later. You will apologize to him later for it. She stuck her hand in her pocket, settling her thumb into the groove of the rock. Yes. She would apologize. It would all work out. He cared about her, and he understood her, and he would understand that she had been overcome by emotion.

Which she had been. He never needed to know that that emotion had been overwhelming feels for him.

"Go on," Andrés said. "I won't eat her."

"Fine." Jas lifted the bag that contained the cobbler. "I'll put this in the kitchen too." He left after one more searching look.

Katrina turned to Andrés, determined. It wasn't imperative Jas's family liked her. It wasn't imperative anyone liked her.

She did like to be liked, though, and it was easy enough to surmise where Andrés's soft spot might lie. "This is a beautiful home."

Sure enough, Andrés beamed with pride. "Thank you. It was my father's dream to own such a place. I only wish he could have lived to see it." He gestured to a large frame over the ornate marble fireplace, containing a portrait of a young man dressed in silk, with a red turban and a thick beard.

There were hints of Jas in his powerful frame, his dark eyes, his stern visage. "He's very handsome. When was this painted?"

"I had it painted, from a photograph I have of him. From right before he came to America in 1910."

Katrina tried to bury the wisp of longing. Her mother had been born so much later, and yet Katrina had no photographs of her from her youth like this. "Wow."

"You like history, yes? Come here."

She followed him to a large display case running the length of the room. There were framed photos, clippings, household objects, and books under the glass, each painstakingly arranged and preserved. Andrés pulled out his phone and pressed something, and dim lighting filled the case.

She whistled, genuinely impressed. "I thought the family photos in the little house were cool, but this is like a museum."

"This is nothing. There's an actual museum dedicated to Punjabi-American history in town. I've donated many pieces for their exhibits there."

"It's wonderful you have this connection to the past that you can pass on to your community."

Andrés's chest puffed out with pride. "It's the least I can do. Our descendants should know about their forefathers, the part they played in this nation's history."

She drifted down the case, curiously absorbing the seemingly mundane articles that created a life. Bills of sale for livestock, correspondence for seed and supplies. "Did your father come to the States to farm?"

"He came here to survive. Farming was what he knew. He worked as a laborer when he first got here, earned pennies a day, until he found his own plot of land." He pointed to another faded photo. It was the same man from the photo above the fireplace, but this time Jas's great-grandfather was older, his face weathered. His turban and facial hair were gone, his hair cut short. The only tangible thing that remained from the large portrait above the fireplace was the iron bracelet around his wrist. "That was him in 1930. He had a couple acres by this time, worked them with his friend." Andrés rolled his eyes. "Your late husband's grandfather. He was younger and flightier and left, of course, after a couple years."

"Ah," she said, because she wasn't sure what to say. Hardeep had never spoken about Jas's family with anything but fondness, but now that she thought about it, he'd mostly talked about Jas's mother. He'd told Katrina he and Tara had been close friends in their youth, though they'd drifted apart as he made fewer visits to this part of the world, and he considered Jas one of his nephews.

It was a little weird when she thought of the fact she'd been married to someone who was of Jas's mother's generation, but her relationship with Hardeep had been a special case.

"That still upsets you, that he left? Enough that you resent his grandson?"

"That's not exactly why I don't like Hardeep."

"Oh?"

Much to her dismay, he didn't elaborate on Hardeep. "Yes, I do carry some bitterness over Arora leaving my father. Farming life can be lonely, and it was lonelier then. My father couldn't even own the land he farmed. Some of his friends put their land in the names of their citizen children, but my father felt the possibility of a family was out of reach for him."

"Why?"

Andrés gave her a measuring look. "Do you know about the Immigration Act of 1917? It was also called the Asiatic Barred Zone Act."

"I've heard of it."

"Not many have."

"My mother was Thai. She didn't care much for history, but I like to learn. It's my history."

Andrés rocked back on his heels, clearly at home in professor mode. "Well, then you know that the law barred immigration from most of Asia for decades. The majority of South Asians who came to America before that were men, and California's laws made marrying outside one's race difficult."

"He did have a family, though, eventually."

"Aha, yes. As I mentioned, theoretically California didn't permit mixing between the races. Theoretically." Andrés offered her his hand, and drew her along the case. "My father was older and resigned to being alone when he met my mother at a party. She always said it was love at first sight. She was Mexican, and they feared they wouldn't be able to marry. They took a risk, went to the courthouse, and to their great relief, all the clerk did was assess whether they were both brown." He pointed to an ornate frame in the case. "I have their wedding photo enlarged in the dining room as well."

A little ball of emotion caught in her throat. The stern-faced man from the previous photo was no more. He was looking down at the petite woman next to him with complete adoration. She was beautiful, in a simple white dress and lace veil, her heart-shaped face lit up with possibilities. "Your parents are beautiful."

"They were." His smile was tinged with sadness. "She passed away when I was young, in childbirth with my sister."

"I'm so sorry," Katrina murmured. "My mother also passed when I was young."

Andrés patted her hand in sympathy. "It's tragic. I was happy to have the time I did with her, and so was my father. They were an excellent example of compromise and love. My mama went to the Gurdwara. My dad went to church. Every Saturday we'd go to this restaurant in town owned by another Mexican-Punjabi family and have their signature dish, a roti quesadilla. After she died, my father took me to all those places on his own, tried to keep her spirit alive for me."

She smiled, wistfulness twining around her heart. Imagine, having a father like that. "Sounds like they built a good life."

"They did," he said simply, and jerked his chin at another wedding portrait on the other wall. This one was of a much younger Andrés and a beautiful Punjabi woman. She was dressed in bright red. Their brown skin glowed. "They were the example I followed when I married. That's my late Mata. We were childhood sweethearts."

Katrina didn't know how much more her tender, romantic heart could take. "She's lovely. Your family is lucky to have so many wonderful examples of love and marriages."

"You didn't have such examples?"

She tucked a strand of hair behind her ear. "No. My mother met my dad when she was in grad school, and they got married quick. It lasted about a year, didn't work out." Which was a massive understatement. Since her parents had split before she was born, she didn't know how bad it must have been, but knowing her dad . . . well. A nightmare, probably, for her mom.

Andrés gave her a sympathetic look. "I'm sorry to hear that."

"It was for the best." Thanks to that divorce, the first nine years of her life had been peaceful.

She rarely got so personal with someone she'd just met, but it was remarkably easy to talk to Jas's grandfather. He'd looked so forbidding when he'd thundered into the yard of the little house, but really he was a pussycat. Especially when it came to his family.

So why is he so mad at Jas?

Such a puzzle. "Thank you for giving me this history lesson."

"Perhaps at some point, I can take you to the museum. I know the curator well, we'll go after hours. My family, the other families around here, we've all contributed to it."

She softened at his thoughtfulness in subtly assuring her the place would be empty. "Sounds like you have a good community."

"The best. Our parents and grandparents started it, digging this soil with their bare hands. They took up space for themselves, carved out a whole new place for us. We have to nourish their legacy, or no one will." His fond smile vanished. "That's what I've tried to teach my grandsons."

She barely heard the last part. She froze, something in the words he'd said speaking to her soul. Realization crashed down on her.

She'd carved out a place for herself, too.

She could stand to take up some more space, though. No,

wait. Why not all the space? Yes, proactively take up space. Sit in the front seat, if she wanted to. Tap her resources to launch some sort of CafeBae counterattack instead of playing wait-and-see. Kiss Jas. Touch his eyebrows.

All you have to do is find out if he wants that too.

She could do that, right? The people in these photographs, they'd done way more, with way less. They'd built the nation. She could build her own life.

A chubby woman in soft black pants and a denim shirt hustled into the room. "There you are. Andrés, are you boring this poor young woman?" She was in her mid-sixties, and had a slight Indian accent and crinkles around her eyes when she smiled. Despite her casual farm wear, three gold bangles clanked on her wrist.

"She wanted to see the family history," Andrés said gruffly, but his eyes were kind as they rested on the woman. "This is my housekeeper, Daisy."

"Katrina, what a pleasure to finally meet you. Jasvinder speaks of you so highly." Daisy took Katrina's hands. "Would you like a hug?"

That the older woman would ask made Katrina want one more. "Oh yes." She stepped into the woman's arms. Something constricted in her chest as Daisy pulled her in tight.

It was so . . . grandmotherly.

She closed her eyes and breathed in deep, trying not to be a weirdo. Rhiannon's mom mothered her, or tried to, but she had no one in her life akin to grandparents. Not even her real grandparents.

Katrina stepped back, lest she linger in that comforting embrace too long. "I did want to see the family history," she confirmed.

"Well, Andrés can chatter at you about that later," Daisy said firmly. "Jas tells me you like to cook. Would you like to come help me in the kitchen?"

Ah. Jas had sent Daisy to rescue her, probably not realizing that she was enjoying this impromptu story time. "I would love to."

"Good. I sent Jas down to the chicken coop to get some eggs. I want to make a cake."

Andrés snorted as he followed them out. "The boy may cry if he gets his shoes dirty."

"Don't you make fun of Jasvinder, I see you polishing your shoes at night," Daisy said archly to her boss. "Jas grew up gathering eggs, it's a skill you never quite lose. Thank you for bringing that cobbler over, Katrina. It smells delicious. Jasvinder couldn't stop telling me about what an excellent chef you are." Her dark gaze was smiling but speculative, and Katrina wasn't entirely sure what she was speculating about.

"Oh no. I'm not a chef. I just like to cook for people."

"A chef is anyone who cooks," Daisy said. "We serve langar at the Gurdwara, a free meal for anyone who wishes it. That's what I tell all the sweet young people who volunteer to help cook, that they are all chefs."

Providing a meal to nourish anyone who needed it? Sounded like Katrina's dream. "That's fantastic. I like that."

"It is, isn't it? Come now. It's time for something other than these stuffy history lessons."

"Excuse me," Andrés huffed behind them. "I can hear you."

Daisy patted Katrina's hand but spoke to her employer. "I know."

JAS'S GAZE KEPT slipping to Katrina. She was too quiet, but her eyes were alert. He wished he'd been seated next to her, but Andrés had helped her to the chair closest to him.

"Pass me the salt?"

Jas handed his brother the saltshaker. Bikram had joined them for dinner, which Jas had learned was a nightly thing. His brother's skin glowed with health, and his body was relaxed. He and their grandfather had spent most of the meal so far chatting easily about the day's work. They were so alike in their pleasure in this place, so in sync, one would never realize that they weren't related by blood.

Andrés leaned back and gave Jas a narrow look. Jas braced himself. He didn't think Andrés would start anything with Katrina at the table, but he'd learned long ago never to count on his grandfather doing the expected. "I showed Katrina the family photos in the living room. She enjoyed seeing them all."

"She liked them, or you lectured her until she was bored into a stupor?" Bikram teased.

If Jas had teased his grandfather like that, he would have gotten a snarl, but Andrés only rolled his eyes at his step-grandson.

Katrina smiled. "I did enjoy it. I don't have anything like that documenting my family."

Daisy helped herself to more potatoes. She'd worked for the family for almost twenty years and had always eaten with them. "No photos, no records?"

Katrina shook her head. "No. I was an only child and my mom died when I was nine. I don't know my extended family on her side."

"And your father?"

Jas cleared his throat and tried to catch the housekeeper's eye. This was smacking of a gentle interrogation, a motherly prying, possibly since his own meddling mother wasn't in town and present at the table. Daisy purposefully ignored him.

Katrina lifted a shoulder. "No, we're not close."

"It happens that way sometimes," Daisy said comfortingly. "Do you want some more rotis?"

"No, thank you."

"Please, you barely ate."

"I'm truly stuffed."

"Welcome to my house," Jas couldn't help but say. "Daisy loves to make sure we eat until we burst."

Katrina shot him a small grin, and it distracted him so much he almost missed the clatter of Daisy dropping her spoon on her plate. "Excuse me," she said, and sniffed. Her eyes were bright. "I'm so glad you brought Katrina here, dear. To your house. Will you be bringing her to the parade as well?"

"No."

Daisy's face fell, and his grandpa scowled .

Great. It had been a peaceful dinner for as long as it lasted.

Katrina placed her napkin next to her plate. Daisy was right, she really hadn't eaten much, just pushed her food around her plate to make it seem like she had. If she wasn't careful, Daisy would grab her utensil and start making airplane noises. The woman was serious about making sure her charges were well-fed. "What parade?" Katrina asked.

Daisy leaned forward. "Every year we have a festival and parade here in town. It used to be a local event, but now tens of thousands of Sikhs come from all over the world. This year, Andrés is being honored for his charitable work and contributions to the community. It's in a couple weeks. We would love for you to come."

"Congratulations, Andrés. Unfortunately, I'll probably be back home by then."

"You are coming, at least," Andrés said to Jas.

"I have to work."

Bikram shot Katrina a speculative look, and Jas hastily corrected himself. Maybe he did use Katrina as an excuse far more than he realized. "I mean, I can't come."

Katrina's brow creased. "You don't need to work then. Go to the parade."

He couldn't. He simply *couldn't* go to the parade. He stabbed a piece of cauliflower and ate it, though it tasted like ashes. "No."

Andrés's face tightened. "The whole community will be there. How will it look if my own grandson doesn't attend?"

The knot in his stomach grew tighter. "Tell everyone I have to work."

"Your boss gave you the night off." Andrés pointed at Katrina. "You're coming."

Something in his brain always short-circuited when his grandfather used that tone. All he wanted was to do the opposite of what the man decreed. This time, though, he literally couldn't comply with his grandpa's orders. "I can't."

"You will."

"No."

Andrés slammed his fist on the table, rattling the dishes. "Damn it, Jasvinder, you will—"

"Okay," Bikram interjected. "Let's all calm down."

"I will not." Andrés threw his napkin on top of his plate. "I have given you everything you could have ever wanted. Every advantage. A company, land, business. And you have done nothing but throw it away, time and again."

"Andrés," Daisy implored. "Enough."

His grandfather shot to his feet. "Don't come to the parade. Embarrass me in front of everyone. But understand this: if you are not there, I will consider it a sign that you do not wish to be a part of this family."

Chapter Nineteen

AFTER ANDRÉS STORMED off, Daisy corralled Katrina into the kitchen with the excuse of showing her some cookware she'd just bought. Jas suspected it was a ruse so he and his brother could be alone.

So it was no surprise when Bikram came outside, to where he was leaning against the car. His brother had always come to console him after a fight and plead their grandfather's case.

Bikram's words were blunt when he sidled up next to Jas. "You have to come to this ceremony."

Jas rolled his lips in. "I can't."

"Listen, I know he's stubborn, and you two are like hissing cats the second you get in the same room together." Bikram leaned against the car as well. "Which I don't get at all. Grandpa's so easygoing with me and the staff and everyone else, and you keep your cool with everyone but him. Why can't you two chill with each other? This has been going on for as long as I've been alive."

Jas grunted. Their sniping had been going on for as long as *Jas* was alive. "You're more his grandson than I'll ever be."

"Ah, but that's not true, is it?" Bikram squinted at the trees that surrounded the paved driveway. "I'm not his grandson *by blood*. You are."

Jas's teeth almost cracked, he ground them so hard. There was no bitterness in Bikram's tone—he was merely stating a fact. Grandpa adored Bikram, he mentored him, loved that the younger man appreciated the land as much as he did.

But Jas was the one who was supposed to have been the heir apparent to the peach throne. He was the one who had chosen to enlist, and, in doing so, betrayed their great peach legacy.

"Hey, it's okay." Bikram knocked his shoulder against Jas's. "I'm fine with not being the heir. Relax."

"Easier said than done," he muttered.

Bikram sighed. "I'm scared he means what he says, Jas. That was harsh. Come to the parade."

He rubbed his hand over his chest. It ached at the thought of his grandfather considering them to no longer be family. "I can't come."

"I don't get this at all." Bikram's frustration was evident. "You were so willing to smooth things over with me when I was cranky with you. Why not him?"

Jas lowered his head. Because he didn't know how to tell his grandfather why he couldn't come to the big, noisy, crowded event. The words were there in his head, he simply didn't know how to force them past his lips.

Bikram pulled a pack of gum out of his pocket and offered it to Jas.

"Telling me my breath stinks?" Jas tried, a rough attempt at a joke.

"Nah, it's not too bad, but it could be better. Especially if you find yourself in close quarters with someone you want to kiss."

Jas froze.

That was his mistake.

Like a predator scenting prey, Bikram faced him. "Oh my God. You kissed someone."

"I did not."

"Who?"

"No one." Too quick, damn it. He had answered too quick!

His brother nearly bounced on his toes. "It was Katrina, right? I knew she wasn't just a client!"

Jas growled. "Shut up."

"I like her. This is great."

"You didn't like her this morning."

"I changed my mind. Have you eaten her cobbler? It's amazing." Bikram paused for a breath. "You kiiiiiiiissed her."

He resisted the immature urge to pull his brother into a headlock to get that smug look off his face. "Bikram."

"Admit it. Admit it, and I'll leave you alone."

He gritted his teeth. "I kissed her, okay?"

The words slammed between them and Jas closed his eyes. He hadn't meant to say that. He shouldn't have said that. Not to Bikram, not when he hadn't so much as apologized to Katrina.

Bikram whistled.

Jas scrubbed his hands over his face. "I didn't mean that."

"Uh-huh. When did it happen?"

"You said you'd leave me alone if I admitted it."

"I lied. You don't seem happy about this. Did she not like it? Are you a bad kisser?"

Jesus. How had they even gotten from talking about his grandfather potentially disowning him to this? "I don't think so."

Bikram's face turned grave. "You don't know if someone likes it when they're kissing you yet? Oh, Jas. That's so sad. How much did you come in? How much did she?"

"What?"

"There's a seventy percent test when you want to kiss someone." Bikram crossed his arms over his chest. "You lean in seventy percent. Then they lean in thirty percent. If they don't lean in, you lean back. How much did she lean?"

He replayed the kiss in his head, but trying to figure out the percentages of their *leans* baffled him. "I don't know."

"Hmm, yes, yes, I see." Bikram paced in front of him, stroking his beard. "What about eyes? Open or closed?"

"Mine or hers?"

"Both."

"I don't remember, Bikram."

"This is important stuff."

He threw up his hands. "I don't see why."

"Because I don't think you're upset about the kiss, you're upset because you don't know if she liked it. Like, if she had liked it, would you be okay?"

Yes. If she had liked it and wanted it, he'd be better than okay.

"Aha," Bikram said softly. "Knew it."

Jas tugged at his collar. It might be cool outside, but he was too warm. "Knew what?"

"One thing you learn when you spend a lot of time with crews is how to read people. Whenever you'd call, I would count how many times you said Katrina. Katrina said this, Katrina did that, Katrina's so smart, Katrina . . . after a while I had to stop counting. Especially after Hardeep died and you moved to Santa Barbara."

Probably because he'd no longer felt so guilty about coveting his boss's wife.

Bikram shook his head when Jas stiffened. "You were so gone on her, I think that's when I kinda started assuming she was keeping you wrapped around her finger." He pointed at the house. "But she's earnest and sweet, and she really loves that big dog, so if you are wrapped around her finger, I think that's okay."

Bikram was a sucker for animal lovers. "Where are you going with this?"

"I'm saying . . . I don't know if she likes you, or liked that kiss, but I know you like her and you liked that kiss. You could try telling her that and see what happens."

Like was too weak a word. He liked his mom's rotis and he liked the smell of rain.

He . . . well, he more than liked Katrina.

When he didn't reply to Bikram's suggestion, his brother

gave a half laugh. "Okay, fine. Bury down your feelings on this if you want, *or* you could have a conversation like damned adults. You might be surprised what comes of it."

"And if nothing comes of it?" Jas asked roughly. He would have disturbed their relationship more and could be left with nothing.

"And if something comes of it?" Bikram countered.

The words shut Jas up. Such a simple way to turn his own fear around. Both realities were possible. Right?

Bikram straightened away from the car as Katrina came out the front door of the big house. She held multiple foil packages in her hands, which told him Daisy had packed up the whole table for her to reheat later.

Bikram slapped him on the back. "Quit dancing around each other. It must be exhausting. Wouldn't it be so nice to stop fighting all this?"

Jas watched his brother walk away, the words hitting close to home. He was exhausted. Exhausted from shoving everything down. The other things he locked up tight in his soul, he did it because they made him feel bad.

His feelings for Katrina made him feel good.

Her hips swayed as she walked toward him, and the moonlight lit her hair a silvery brown. Jas opened the back door. She was so beautiful, and Bikram was right. He wasn't sorry he'd kissed her. He wanted to kiss her again.

He took the packages from her once she was close enough. She murmured her thanks and ignored the open back door to get into the front passenger seat.

"What are you doing?"

She buckled her seat belt. "I've always hated sitting back there. I'll sit here from now on."

Okay. What was that about?

She closed her door before he could ask. Jas put the food into the trunk and wiped his sweaty hands on his pants.

He felt like a teenager, or about as emotionally fluent as one. He started the car and searched for something to say, but she spoke first.

"You never talk about your grandpa."

There was no accusation in her voice, but his hands tightened on the steering wheel. "I don't." He coughed once. "You can see why. We have a complicated relationship."

"I can see that he loves you, but he's also deeply, terribly angry with you."

She deserved some kind of explanation for having to sit through that dinner. "My grandpa was mad when I joined the Army." That was an understatement. "When he was young, he protested wars, railed against the military complex. I think it's because his dad was in the British Army, and he saw what that short stint did to him. Grandpa didn't talk to me for a year after I was deployed. And then, after I was injured and discharged, I think he got madder that I didn't come home to the farm." Instead, Jas had gone to work for Hardeep. It had been a heaven-sent job, where he could contribute something and heal and learn new skills.

She angled her body toward him. "Did he want you to take over the farm?"

"Oh, without a doubt." Jas turned down the dirt road to the little house. "He puts a lot of stock in bloodline, as you see. I was supposed to be the heir. But I knew from the time I was . . . twelve, maybe, that it wasn't what I wanted. I like gardening, but not farming. I have no connection to the land, not the way he does. Definitely not the way Bikram does. But Bikram's not blood."

"Ah."

He parked in front of their house. Funny, how it was their house, when they'd only stayed here together for a few days. "I can take out Doodle," he said, when the dog came racing up to the front door.

She took the leftovers from him. "Thanks."

The dog quickly did her business, and they returned inside. Doodle went straight to her food bowl, which Katrina had freshened.

"Does it hurt Bikram? To not be in line to inherit the farm?" she asked, continuing their earlier conversation.

"I think so. I don't know. He refuses to talk to me about it. Always has."

She made a commiserating noise. "That puts you in a terrible position."

It was strange, to talk to someone about this. Someone on his side, who could see things more objectively than his family could.

It was nice, actually.

He busied himself with removing his shoes. "It does." It made him resent his grandfather even more.

"Do you think he'll actually disown you?"

Nausea churned. He nodded once, not eager to discuss that prospect.

She seemed to sense he was done talking. "Do you want wine?"

"I—yes." That was a good idea. They'd occasionally shared a glass of wine together. The wine would remind them of what good friends they were.

And then he'd . . . apologize.

Bikram's voice rang in his head. *Tell her.*

Either way, they could do with alcohol.

He accepted the glass of wine she handed him and followed her to the living room. She dropped down onto the couch. After a moment's hesitation, he sat down next to her.

He'd turned on the Tiffany lamp next to the couch, and she'd done the same with the overhead light. The dancing colors warred with the harsh light. Her sketch pad was spread out over the desk in the corner. She wasn't a good artist, even she admitted that, but she stuck at it.

She stuck at a lot of things. It was one of the bajillion things he admired about her.

She took a sip of her wine. Her face was so . . . peaceful, in a way he didn't usually see it at home when she was focused on a project or work. Except when she was cooking.

A sharp crack came from outside, and the peace was disturbed. She jumped. He jumped, too, but then relaxed. "It was a branch," he said.

Her shoulders slowly lowered from her ears. "Oh. Right. If it was a person, the guard outside would have notified you, right?"

"Yes." Lorne's people were discreet, but he trusted them to show up when need be.

They sat in silence for a while. There were a million things they could talk about or do. They could check up on the hashtag or he could contact Lorne, or they could talk about how his grandfather might really never speak to him again. But that would mean the real world intruding on their peace. And that was the last thing he wanted.

What do you want?

He moved his hand so it lay next to hers, his pinkie brushing her skin.

He was touching her. It was so small and almost something Katrina could explain away as an accidental brush.

Zing.

He moved his finger against hers.

Take up space.

He inhaled deeply. "Katrina—"

"I liked kissing you. I've been wanting to do it for a while."

He froze.

Though her heart sank in dread, she continued. Taking up space. "It seems that I have developed feelings for you at some point. I thought I could shove them away. Swipe them away with someone else. But I don't actually know if I can re-create what I feel for you with someone else. Anyway, um, I am sorry I didn't ask you first and sprang that kiss on you." She shut her mouth to stop the babble of words.

Jas set down his glass on the coffee table. "Katrina . . . I kissed you."

"No. I kissed you. Because I wanted to."

"No, I kissed you."

What was he talking about. "I'm pretty sure it was me who was the kisser, and you, who was the kiss-ee."

His brow furrowed. "Do you remember how much we both leaned in?"

"I'm sorry, what?"

He squeezed his eyes shut. "Nothing. Moral of the story, I wanted to kiss you, as well."

Her lips formed an *O*. "I see."

His eyes crinkled. "Do you?"

"No."

He looked like he wanted to say something more, but then he swayed forward, bridging the gap between them more than halfway. Then he waited.

It took her about half a second to close that gap.

The first brush of his lips against hers came as such a shock she jumped, though she'd wanted it.

His touch was soft and gentle, his lips exploring. He didn't suffocate her and for that she was grateful—this was too new to risk feeling like her air was being cut off.

Her head spun. Part of her brain tried to comprehend that this was *Jas* she was kissing. Jas, her longtime friend. One didn't kiss platonic friends, but here she was wrapping her arms around his neck and crawling closer.

Katrina had wanted sex, but in an abstract way. There was nothing abstract about this.

She wanted him. Not only for kisses, though this was nice. Oh no. She pressed closer to him, pushing him back against the couch so she could straddle him as they explored each other. His chest was hard against hers, his arms tight and steady. Because *he* was so steady. No wonder she felt safe and secure in his arms.

She pulled away and he blinked up at her, his eyes dazed. She imagined she looked just as confused. Her blood pumped fast in her veins, making it difficult to see or hear clearly. His fingers clenched on her hips and she nearly groaned when his erection rubbed against her.

He had an erection. For her.

To think she'd been so excited about hugs and kisses, and now she had his *erection* at her command.

She wanted it.

"Upstairs," she managed. "Bedroom."

He shook his head, and some of that dazed passion cleared from his expression. She braced herself for a denial, but instead he came to his feet in a rush, still holding her.

Any worry that she was too heavy for him disappeared when he easily took the stairs with her clutching him like a koala bear. He paused every few steps to kiss her, his hands roaming her back.

For a moment she wished they were at home, because she'd like to experience this in her own bed. That was okay, though. This was a different experience, not better or worse. She wanted every single experience.

He wasn't even winded when they got to the top of the stairs. He pressed his lips against hers, a hard, fast kiss. "Your room? Mine?"

"Doesn't matter."

He chose his. They entered and only got as far as a few steps in before he pressed her against the wall, his hands roving over her legs while they kissed again, deeply. They parted only for a second, so he could help her strip off his shirt, and then he was back. She didn't want to stop kissing him, because then they'd both start thinking. Maybe about all the reasons this wasn't a sound idea.

You're both adults, and you're both single. This is fine. Acceptable.

Wait.

Her lashes fluttered open, a fleeting worrisome thought worming into her brain as he kissed his way down her neck. Was there something else she didn't know about him? In all the time she'd known him, she'd never seen him with a date. What if he didn't bring them home? "Are you single?" she blurted out.

He paused and there was laughter in his voice when he answered, lips on the hollow of her throat. "Uh, yes."

"Okay, cool, just checking." She quickly mentally ran through any other anxieties she may have. In the moment, that is, because they didn't have time to run through all her anxieties. "I do pay you. Is the power differential coercing you into sleeping with me?"

Jas lifted his head. "No. Definitely not."

His words were so empathetic, she believed him. "That's good."

He studied her. "Anything else?"

Katrina's hands fluttered over his shoulders and she blurted out the words. "I'm not very experienced at this. I've only been with one guy, and that was over a dozen years ago." It had been out of curiosity and a silent rebellion when she was twenty, and it hadn't exactly inspired her to go looking for more conquests.

It was easy to do the math. A dozen years ago predated Hardeep. Jas didn't ask about her marriage, though, and she was grateful.

"I'm not that experienced either. I can't even tell you how long it's been for me," he admitted. "Years. I'm nervous too."

"Oh," she said soundlessly.

His finger coasted up her hip, pushing her sweater up a few inches. He squeezed the scoop of flesh that rose above her jeans' waistband, and her legs turned to jelly. "I think all you have to do is tell me what you want from me. We can fumble around and figure things out from there."

Her lips parted. What did she want from him? She didn't know. That was such a difficult question . . .

"Kisses?" he prompted her. Before she could reply, he pressed light, soft kisses along her neck. "Here?"

"Yes."

His mouth wandered down, to her cleavage, deep and plumped up by one of her best bras. He pressed his palms under the curves and pushed them up more. "More intimate kisses?"

"Yes."

He scraped his chin over the skin exposed by the deep vee of her sweater, his prickly beard making her gasp. "Here?"

"Yes."

She waited with bated breath for him to kiss her there, but instead he lifted his head. With great deliberation, he pressed his lower body tighter against her, so every inch of his erection was rubbing against her most sensitive, aching bits. "There?" he murmured.

She nodded like a bobblehead doll. "Yes, there," she whispered. "Kisses. And the other kisses. Everywhere." She wanted all of it. It all came with zings.

At her answer, his lips curved up. She'd never seen him smile like that, this seductive, warm smile.

Jas grabbed fistfuls of her sweater and pulled it over her head, neither of them tracking where it went when he tossed it aside. There was heat and fire in his gaze, and it flicked all her nerve endings awake. She reached behind her, and he visibly gulped when the cups of her bra loosened.

Were her breasts making him salivate? She liked her body quite a lot, but her confidence notched up a little more.

Katrina threw the bra aside to join her top. He pressed two reverent kisses on the top curves of her breasts, then slid to his knees. His fingers were quick and sure as they unbuttoned and unzipped her jeans. He pulled the material down over her hips, taking her panties with them.

She had to fight not to cover herself up when he looked up at her from the floor. She was naked while he was not and his mouth was right on level with . . . well, *there*.

Once upon a time, she'd always been camera-ready with a bikini wax in case she had to take most of her clothes off for a shoot, but that hadn't happened in a very long time. Whatever self-consciousness she felt flew out the window when he nuzzled the hair covering her intimate lips and pressed a kiss there. Then another. And another. His tongue found her, spreading her open, his fingers assisting.

She had never had this, someone's mouth on her in such a personal manner. She hadn't even been sure if she desired such a thing, but she was sure now, this was definitely something she would appreciate more of in her life. This was like . . . the pleasure one got from cotton candy and the beach and a book all rolled up into one perfect moment.

He drew her down to the floor. The rug was soft on her back. He pressed a hot, open-mouthed kiss on her clitoris, the burst of sensation startling her.

"You can put your hands on my head," he said.

She rested her fingertips lightly on his head, tentative. She'd never touched his hair in all the years she'd known him. That would have been too intimate a gesture.

His tongue is doing something way more intimate.

"You don't have to be gentle. Pull my hair. Show me what you like." His words were muffled against her body, the puffs of air from his breath hitting her in a spot that made her body shake.

"I don't want to hurt you."

His dark gaze met hers. He turned his head and nibbled at her inner thigh, making her stomach clench. "I don't mind that kind of hurt."

Her thighs clenched and she tunneled her fingers through his hair with more confidence, gripping the coarse strands, subtly urging his mouth back where she wanted it. She used her hands to direct his motions, but she was gentle, up until he pushed his fingers inside of her, so deep she arched up. She did pull then, and clutched him closer when he slipped his slick fingers in and out, moving together with his tongue.

She looked down her body, at his dark head between her legs, the moonlight gilding his hair silver. His eyes were closed, his brow creased, and the sight of all that concentration directed at her shoved her right over the edge. The spring of tension inside her snapped, and the pleasure washed over her. She bit her lip, savoring every sensation.

She let out a deep, breathy sigh and tugged at his hair. He nuzzled her one last time and lifted his head. "Did you come?"

Shy now, she nodded.

He smiled, and shifted so he could lie beside her. "You're quiet. I couldn't tell."

"I guess I am. Sorry."

"Don't be. Everyone's different."

She placed her hand on his chest, marveling anew that she was touching him like this. Touching him at all. "Your tongue should win an award."

He barked out a laugh. She slid her hand down, but he caught it before she could get to his jeans. "I, uh . . . I'm good."

"What?"

"I don't have any condoms. I'm guessing you don't either."

Condoms. Damn it. "No, I do not." She pulled her wrist out of his grip and unbuttoned his jeans. "We can do other things. As you've proven."

His breathing grew heavy, then heavier when she found his shaft. He helped her free him, raising his hips to kick his jeans and boxers off.

Katrina rested her forehead against his and played with

him. She wished there was more light, so she could see every detail of what she was doing, but she could follow the cues his sighs gave. She stroked him in long, slow pulls. Their breath mingled, and when his accelerated, she sped up her fist, too.

He was not quiet. He gave a deep moan as he came, and pressed his forehead tighter against hers.

"Good?" she asked.

"Amazing."

She'd thought so, but it was nice to have confirmation.

They lay there for a while, and then Jas stirred, helping her up. "Will you sleep in here?" he asked.

Her heart melted. "Yes."

They tidied up and then climbed into bed, both of them still naked. At some point, she'd want to examine his body in greater detail, but that could wait for now.

He pulled her close, so her head lay on his shoulder. Thoughts tried to nibble on the edges of her consciousness. The two of them needed to talk. It was very important they talk, actually. About what this meant.

If it means anything.

Katrina brushed that cynical voice away. It had to mean something. He said he wanted her.

He also told his brother you were just a client. Which one is true?

She calmed when his hand brushed over her butt and patted her there, like he knew she was fretting. "Go to sleep. We can deal with this in the morning."

Deal with this didn't sound romantic and lovely, now, did

it? But she was too exhausted to think about it and dissect it and take it personally. Sleep crashed over her, and she welcomed it.

WHEN KATRINA WOKE up from a dark dream in which she was running, running through an endless tunnel with no light at the end, struggling to breathe, she knew she wasn't going to be sleeping for the rest of the night.

Katrina was dimly aware Jas was lying next to her, but cuddling wouldn't help her right now. She slipped from the bed to sit on the floor, the rug and the plank floors underneath grounding her. She crawled away to brace herself against the wall. Her brain buzzed like a million bees had set up residence inside it. Her breathing grew short, sweat beaded on her forehead, her chest tightened with pain. The dark room spun around her.

Heart attack!

No. It wasn't a heart attack. She inhaled and exhaled, letting the panic wash over her. For her, anxiety was like a rip current. The harder she fought it, the more it dragged her out to sea.

In a real rip current, you got out of it by swimming perpendicular to the current. Here, she just had to tread water. Eventually it would pass.

It would pass.

It would pass.

Everything passed. Nothing felt the same forever.

More sweat, more tears. She doubled over, the pain in her chest becoming too intense. A light touch moved over her hair, but even a light touch felt too sharp. She shook her head, rejecting it, and it vanished.

Katrina let the storm thunder and rage, and slowly her heart rate began to slow, the pain growing less intense. She inhaled deep, dragging the oxygen into her lungs in greedy gulps.

When the attack had mostly passed, she tipped her head back against the wall and opened her eyes. Jas sat across from her on the floor, holding an orange prescription bottle. He lifted it up in question.

She shook her head. The anti-anxiety meds were on an as-needed basis, and other than her lingering nausea, she no longer needed them tonight.

Jas didn't ask her what had happened, for which she was grateful. She hated that question, because she rarely had a response. "You okay?" he asked quietly.

"Yes," she whispered.

He studied her, as if confirming that she was telling the truth. He placed the bottle between them. "Do you want a hug?"

Katrina wrapped her arms around herself. "I would very much like that, thank you."

He sat next to her and pulled her into his arms. She rested her head on his chest.

His naked chest.

Oh right, they were both naked.

She snuggled closer. That was fine with her. This was the stuff of dreams, naked-cuddling with Jas.

The zings were muted now, satisfied by physical exhaustion, but still there, comfortably hovering under the surface. These weren't the electric lustful zings from before, but cozy zings. The zings that invited cookies in front of a fire.

"Are you cold?" he asked.

"Yes, but I like the cold."

He shifted. "The winters here were my favorites. It can get over a hundred in the summer, but the winters make up for it."

"Yikes. Does it ever snow?"

"Once, when I was a kid. So not really."

"I miss the snow."

"Tahoe's not far from here. Do you want to go? The car's gassed."

She choked out a laugh, then looked up at him when she realized he wasn't laughing. "We can't get in the car and drive to Tahoe."

"Why not?"

She opened her mouth, but she had no explanation. "Because . . . well, that's wild."

"If you want the snow, we can go."

She ran an internal check of her body. They *could* go, if she wanted to. "What would we do there?"

"Have a snowball fight."

"I've never had a snowball fight. At least, not since I was a child." When her mother had been alive.

"I can fetch some mittens from Bikram."

Katrina smiled, charmed at the thought of tussling in the snow with Jas. "No. I'm too tired tonight, but maybe some other time."

He ran his fingers up and down her arm, soothing her. "Do you have bad dreams?" she whispered, though she knew the answer.

"Yes," Jas said, his admission coming faster than she'd expected. "I often have bad dreams."

"Do you want to tell me about them?"

He puffed up his cheeks. "Not now."

She wanted to touch his scarred knee, ask him to share, but didn't want to push him. "I had one."

"What was it about?"

"I don't remember. My dad, I think." All this talk about family and blood. She closed her hands into fists.

"Do you want to talk about it?"

She nodded, then shook her head.

She'd felt so strong and independent. Taking up space. She didn't want her dad's memory to taint that.

Then again, whenever she did think about her dad, it was like a boil welling up that needed to be lanced. Her therapist was usually who she went to for that. It wasn't even dawn yet, she couldn't call Andy.

It would make her happier to talk right now.

Happiness is a radical act.

"When my mom died in that car accident, they had to hunt down my father. I'd barely seen him when she was alive. That first day, when he picked me up from the social worker, he told me he would provide for me until I could get a job."

"You were nine."

She shrugged. "Yeah. I got scouted a few years later,

though. He was happy to stick around while I was making money and funding his lifestyle, so long as he could direct what I did and when I did it."

"What an asshole."

"He was an asshole. He controlled . . . everything. Where I ate, what I ate, what I drank, who I saw." He would have controlled who she married if she hadn't had a brief evening of rebellion the night she'd met Hardeep.

After they'd talked all night and she'd told Hardeep about her dad, the man had leaned forward. *Sounds like we could help each other. Marry me, and you'll get away from your father. You'll have money, comfort, a doting husband.*

She'd stared at him across the few feet that separated them in the library. *What will you get out of it? Sex?*

He'd snorted. *Oh God, no. I have no interest in sex. No offense, don't take it personally. No, I simply want some companionship, and you seem clever and kind. I don't plan on ever marrying someone else. I'd like the satisfaction of knowing I can help a young woman.*

She licked her lips. "Hardeep paid my dad off, with the demand that he not bother us. I don't know the exact amount, but I assume it was huge."

Jas squeezed her waist. "Yes. I knew about that. Hardeep put us on notice to make sure he didn't show up. I figured your dad must have been a terrible guy, but I didn't know the scope of the terribleness."

That had been another big attraction to marrying Hardeep. He'd had people in place to protect her.

A surge of love flowed through her at his memory. Her

husband had been so good and lovely and generous in so many ways. Hardeep had assured her the money was nothing to him, and it was a proper quid pro quo, but it was still hard to shake that feeling of being a bother. An expensive bother. "That bribe eats at me sometimes. Like Hardeep had to buy me."

"Whatever Hardeep did for you, I'm grateful."

"I only wish I could have done it on my own," she confessed. Her deepest shame, that familiar bitterness over the fact that she'd needed help. *A big strong man to save you.*

After the wedding, for a while, she'd tried to join Hardeep on his daily jogs before finally admitting she hated running. The only way she'd managed to get through those three-mile-long hilly jaunts was by concocting elaborate revenge scenarios against her father if he ever came crawling back.

They were dramatic and impressive scenarios where she placed her stiletto heel on his neck and laughed while he begged for money and mercy. She'd filed them away, and now she had a far more rational break-glass-in-case-of-emergency plan, a fund of money to ensure she could pay her dad off again if he ever tried to bother her. Keeping a well-stocked bribery account wasn't nearly as exciting as, say, forcing the man to eat a bug for every hundred dollars he wanted from her, but it was definitely more grown up.

"How would you have done it on your own? Sounds like you were barely able to breathe on your own, without him watching you. That you managed to find someone in a position to help you is a miracle. That you took that help is another one. I'm grateful," he repeated.

The words settled on her soul like a balm. It was the mushiest thing anyone had ever said to her, and her heart galloped. "Yes. I guess I am too."

He rubbed her back for a while in silence. "Katrina?"

"Yes?" She yawned.

"My knee is killing me and my butt is cold. Can we go back to bed?"

She gave a soggy laugh. So much for mushy romance. "Yes. Let's go back to bed."

Chapter Twenty

Katrina learned quickly over the course of the next morning and afternoon that reciprocated affection did not turn you into a princess with a perfect singing voice and talking woodland creatures.

It did, however, turn you into a space cadet.

She'd been delayed taking Doodle out for her potty break this morning and had to clean up the consequences, all because she had dawdled in the shower, soaping up her aching body and watching Jas brush his teeth through the steamed-up glass of her shower. She'd burned their quiche at breakfast because Jas had had the nerve to wear a pair of snug cotton joggers with a white T-shirt French-tucked into the front waistband. She'd almost knocked her cup of coffee over onto her laptop because Jas had had the further nerve to bend over in the aforementioned sweatpants.

He was so lean, but tightly put together. Like a very sleek sports car. A manual one.

Katrina rested her chin in her hand and stared out the window. Jas had left to go do something outside a few hours ago, and she'd been grateful. Out of sight, out of mind, and she could give her poor brain a reprieve from thinking about his butt and cotton and his butt in cotton, but alas, her focus seemed to be shot even when he wasn't sashaying in front of her.

"Katrina?"

Katrina's gaze cut guiltily away from the window and back to the open laptop on the breakfast table. "Yes?" she asked, and pushed her hair behind her ear. She pointedly shifted her chair so she wouldn't be able to see out the window.

Rhiannon peered at her. She and Lakshmi were sitting side by side on a couch, a tiny bit of their luxurious hotel room in India visible. On the split screen was Jia, who was, thankfully, painting her nails and hadn't seemed to notice Katrina's distraction. "I said, I'm glad you're ready to go on the offensive," Rhiannon repeated.

Katrina sobered. The single cloud hovering over her sex-induced happiness was the bane of her existence. Well, one of them.

Up until now, she'd avoided looking at Becca, Alan, or Ross's Instagram accounts, but Ross had done a live video for his "fans" last night. She and Jas had obviously been otherwise occupied, but once she'd come out of her haze enough to check her phone this morning, she'd found texts from Rhiannon and Jia.

Katrina had scrolled through Ross's Instagram before watching the video and had been disturbed by his recent posts with their vague as hell captions. A shirtless shot of him contemplating the ocean: *Sunsets are better with your sweetheart. #CafeBae #CuteCafeGirl #nofiltersrequired #theLordismyfilter.* A photo of him, again shirtless, holding his mom's dog: *Sandy's kisses can't compare to hers. #CafeBae #CuteCafeGirl #PuppyLove #CantWaitToSeeHer #weddingbells.*

Barf.

None of that had compared to the video, though. She'd watched it with Jas next to her, but even his presence hadn't prevented the cold ball forming in the pit of her stomach.

Over the course of twenty minutes, Ross fielded questions from people about his new nutrition company, his past as an athlete, and his exercise regimen. Then the questions about her had started. Where was she, why wasn't she coming forward, were they really seeing each other, what was her real name?

Ross had spouted some cutesy non-answers, but for the last one, the bastard had looked straight into her camera and winked. *I'm sure one of you super-sleuths can find out who CuteCafeGirl is. No one's truly impossible to find.*

A shiver ran down Katrina's back. The man had practically invited the internet to dox her.

Unacceptable. It was time to do what she'd decided on yesterday with such passionate fervor. Take up space. Use her resources, damn it.

She'd called her lawyer, who had been aghast and sympathetic. There were some legal options, but they'd have to be approached in a way that didn't end up calling more attention to the story and her. Her lawyer wanted to consult with some of her colleagues who had experience with cases like

Katrina's. In the meantime, they would compose takedown notices, though Katrina was aware that was kind of like trying to stuff a hundred thousand cats back into a sack.

After that conversation, she'd called this meeting of their brain trust.

Lakshmi rubbed her hands together. Rhiannon's assistant was stylish as usual, in a black-and-gold front-slit kurta, her hair slicked back, her blood-red lips a slash of crimson suited to her dramatic personality. "By the time I'm done with these people, they won't think it's so great to go viral."

That sounded vaguely ominous to Katrina. "You're not putting out a hit on them or anything, are you?"

"Of course not. I'm going to make them see the error of their ways."

That sounded even *more* like Lakshmi was going to put a hit on them. Katrina shifted. "Rhiannon."

Rhiannon placed her hand on Lakshmi's shoulder. "No one is going to hurt anyone. This will be a purely online information campaign."

"Purely online." Lakshmi's voice dropped. "Until it's not."

Katrina's eyes widened. "Rhiannon."

Jia looked up from her nails. The blue of her fingernails matched her hijab and the flowers on her embroidered shirt. "Guys. Wait." They all hushed.

Jia took a deep breath. "Do you like my eyebrows? I got them threaded at this new place."

Lakshmi turned to Rhiannon. "Is it necessary for her to be on the call?"

"Yes, *Lakshmi*, it is, and I can hear you." Jia's nostrils flared.

They'd only met a few months prior, but there wasn't much love lost between uber-efficient Lakshmi and dreamy Jia. "I was asking because I want to make sure my eyebrows are camera-ready when I go live shortly. BeccaTheNose *wishes* she had my following." Jia straightened, and her voice went up an octave. "You all can't for serious think this is an okay way to behave. Clearly CuteCafeGirl doesn't want to be found. Imagine if this was you, if you were, like, a busy professional and someone plastered your face all over the internet without your permission. This *is* a privacy issue, and it's also a feminist issue, a humanity issue." Jia subsided and gave the thumbs-up. "And so on for five minutes. I'll get my biggest influencer buds on board to spread that message."

Lakshmi sniffed, mollified. "It's not bad. I can help with the script, if you like."

"You'll make me sound old."

Lakshmi no longer looked mollified. "I am five years older than you, you little—"

"Jia, thanks," Katrina interrupted, eager to head off this fight.

"No thanks necessary. I mean every word I'll say. I'm terrified of going viral for all the wrong reasons."

"Are there right reasons to go viral?" Katrina murmured. If she could, she'd continue to avoid social media for the rest of her life on the off chance that this was ever repeated.

"Oh, you know, going viral for showing people how to eat a pineapple is a way different situation." Jia thought for a second. "Though I went viral for, like, an eyeliner hack once, and got death threats within two hours. So I guess, no. There's no right way to go viral on ye olde internet anymore. Not for some of us, at least."

Lakshmi produced a pad of paper, getting the meeting back on track. "We can start amplifying and flooding every possible Twitter thread with basically the same message Jia's going to spread. Use bots for good instead of evil. Turn the narrative so it's no longer about who you are, but how wrong this is."

"I don't want to sic a mob on these three, though." Ross might have the power to urge the world to dox her by virtue of the current spotlight on him, but she had her money, Jia's reach, Rhiannon's ruthlessness, and Lakshmi's . . .

Well. She had Lakshmi.

Becca, Ross, and Alan were outgunned, outmanned, outnumbered, and outplanned, but they'd never know it until it was too late.

"Define mob," Lakshmi said.

"I don't want them run off the internet or hurt." Katrina twisted her fingers together. "They're people, too."

Lakshmi turned her head, but her whisper to Rhiannon was picked up by the computer's excellent mic. "How is she so nice?"

"It's not about being nice. I've seen them in person, they aren't some nameless faceless usernames."

"Look," Rhiannon said, with her typical matter-of-factness. "Sometimes to disarm people and keep them from hurting you, to keep them from doing the wrong thing, you gotta put pressure on them."

Lakshmi perked up. "Physical pressure? 'Cause I know a guy—"

Even Jia looked alarmed at that offer. "No!" Katrina yelped.

"Okay." Lakshmi rolled her eyes. "Fine."

"Katrina?"

She glanced up at Jas's raised voice from outside, and Jia let out a singsong *Ooooh*. "How's things going with you and Captain Chesticles?"

Katrina stabbed at the volume button on her laptop, her cheeks on fire, though Jas wouldn't be able to hear the girl. She didn't want a repeat of the text about his hotness! "I have to go now, good talk, I'll call you later, bye-bye."

Jia howled, Rhiannon snorted, and Lakshmi cracked a grin before the screen went dark. Katrina pressed her palms over her cheeks, hoping she hadn't given herself away. She didn't want her friends to know about her and Jas yet. One, because it was too new, and two, because . . . well, she was a little worried it wasn't real. Like this was a simulation, an illusion that would vanish when they returned to Santa Barbara.

Jia and Rhiannon, and to a lesser extent Lakshmi, didn't need to get emotionally entangled with her and Jas being a thing if it wasn't going to happen.

"Katrina?" Jas yelled again.

She came to her feet in a rush. "Yes?" she called out, and made it to the door just as he bounded up the porch stairs.

His jeans had lost their city creases, and the sleeves of his flannel shirt were rolled up. His hair was disheveled, and he hadn't trimmed his beard. He wasn't her perfectly groomed bodyguard today. "What's up?" she asked, trying not to think of Jia's new nickname for him.

Her gaze flicked to his chest, then back up to his eyes.

Jas beamed at her, sensing nothing amiss. "Come with me."

She checked her watch. "It's almost three. I have to check in on the pizza dough if we want it ready in time for dinner."

"I'll help you with that later. There's something I want to show you. Grab your sweater."

"It's warm out today, though."

"Trust me, grab it."

She arched an eyebrow at him but complied, pulling her big comfy sweater from the hall closet before returning to the door.

He stopped before they rounded the house. "Close your eyes."

She gave him a quizzical look, but shut them. "This better not be a prank of some kind," she warned. "I don't want to stick my hand into something gross."

"No prank. Who would ever prank you like that?" He took hold of her arm and led her about a dozen steps. "Okay, look."

She opened her eyes. "Oh."

"Well?"

She walked forward a few feet and stopped. "It's, um . . . hay?" She ended it with a question, because she had honestly only ever seen hay in movies. But this looked like the movie hay, tightly bundled in small bales. Piles upon piles of hay.

"You said you wanted a snowball fight. Well, I tried to get a snow machine, but I guess it's not cold enough for fake snow and also we're not a ski resort."

"So you got . . . hay?"

"Yeah. I mean, I know it's not the same as snow, but I figured it was really the only thing you can bunch up and toss at someone. And not injure them. So . . ." He spread his arms wide. "I thought, why not a hay fight?"

Oh my. If she could see what her heart looked like right now, she imagined it would be aglow, throbbing in her chest. "You went through all this trouble because I said I wanted a snowball fight?" She gazed at the brown straw that was piled everywhere, overwhelmed.

Engineering a hay fight was one of the weirdest and nicest things anyone had ever done for her.

"It wasn't trouble. I had to call my brother to ask if he had a lot of hay."

A phone call wasn't too bad.

"He's running low. So I had to find out where to get the hay, go to the big house, get a truck, go pick up the hay, and then . . . do that like three more times to have enough hay. Not that big of a deal."

"Right, that sounds like not a big deal at all."

He didn't seem to pick up on her dry humor, because he shrugged. "Nope."

She leaned over and touched the hay in the bale closest to her. It was scratchy and dry, and would be hell on her delicate skin.

The idea of this was *so sweet* and also something she had

no interest in doing. "Um, Jas—" She yelped when something wet hit her shoulder and exploded. Outraged and confused, she whipped her head around to glare at him.

His delighted grin took her breath away. He tossed a bright red water balloon in his hand, and that was when she noticed the pail at his feet. The pail filled with more water balloons. "Unfortunately, after I paid for all that hay and got it all here, I realized no one actually wants hay thrown at them. And there's this thing called farmer's lung?"

She wrung out the chunk of her hair that had gotten wet. "Sounds like something we don't want to contract."

"Right. So I figured it would have to be a water fight. Water is closer to snow, anyway."

She crossed her arms over her chest, her outrage turning to amusement. "This isn't fair! I don't have any ammunition."

"I'd never water fight an unarmed woman." He nodded at a hay bale. "Right behind there."

She darted around the bale and crouched down, finding her full pail right where he'd indicated. She grabbed a balloon, poked her head over her hay barricade, then retreated when a water balloon sailed at her head. "What are you going to do with all this hay now that it's useless?" As quietly as possible, she lifted two water balloons, one in each hand, and waited for him to speak.

"Hay is never useless. My brother and grandpa will be confused and delighted by my gift to the farm."

Using his voice as her guide, she launched to her feet and fired two balloons rapid-fire. Her brain processed every action in slow motion—the windup, the release, the trajectory of the balloons as they launched through the air, landing and bursting against his face and chest.

A helpless giggle escaped her at his disgruntled expression. He wiped the water out of his eyes. "You'll pay for that."

"I'd like to see you try." She squealed and ducked when he tossed a balloon at her. They darted around and behind the hay and the air filled with their laughter and curses. Most of her shots missed. A good number of his landed. "Unfair, you're a trained soldier and guard. You have better hand-eye coordination," she puffed from behind cover.

"All's fair."

In love.

She reached into her pail and made a sound of dismay when she discovered she only had two balloons left.

She said a quick prayer and launched to her feet, hands full, and ran away from the makeshift obstacle course.

A balloon hit the back of her leg, and she sped up.

"Why are you zigzagging?" he called out as he chased her, and the asshole didn't sound out of breath at all.

"That's how you get away from bears." Another wet hit on her arm. How did he still have so many?

"I think that's a myth about alligators, and I'm neither of those things." The laughter in his voice was evident. Something smacked the ground at her feet, and she sped up. "Quit running. Stand your ground."

"Retreat is the better part of valor," she managed, though

she was huffing and puffing. It was warm today, and she was actually sweating a little despite her damp clothes.

She ran right into the copse of trees, darting around the big trunks. She finally stopped when she couldn't hear his footsteps behind her any longer. She tried to control her breathing, and then carefully peered around.

She narrowed her gaze at the undisturbed, silent clearing. No way would Jas lose her. "I know you're out there," she yelled.

Her phone vibrated in her pocket. She almost ignored it but she did hate to ignore phone calls when they could be for work or one of her friends.

It was one of her friends, but one who was pretty local.

I'm at 3 o'clock. Don't be startled.

There went her heart, all aglow.

She turned to face Jas. He leaned against a tree, his hair glossy from the remnants of one of her hits. He spread his empty hands in front of him. "You wouldn't hurt an unarmed man?"

She tossed a balloon in the air and caught it. "Nice try. Use camouflage balloons next time, I see the one you stuck in the branch above your head."

His lips formed a smile, and he reached up and grabbed the water balloon. "Good eye."

She threw one of her balloons to the ground and it burst. The water was harmless, but later, she'd come out and pick up all the balloon remnants. Though knowing Jas, he'd probably already considered the environmental impact of their little game here and had a cleanup plan in place. "Truce?"

He nodded solemnly and sacrificed his single balloon to the grass.

She lifted her other arm, considered him for a second, then let her second balloon fly, laughing when it smacked him in the stomach.

"We said truce!"

She laughed harder at his outraged expression. "You were the one who told me to use whatever tools I had at my disposal, remember?"

His eyes narrowed. "Oh right." He took deliberate steps toward her and she eyed him with suspicion. "What are you doing?"

He walked faster, bridging the short distance between them. "Using my tools."

She squeaked in amusement and feigned trepidation and tried to dart away, but he was so much faster than she was. He caught her by the waist and kissed her. She wrapped her arms around his neck and took a step back. In her mind, they would effortlessly make love against the tree, with her legs wrapped around his waist and absolutely no splinters in her bare ass.

In reality, she tripped on a root.

He tightened his grip on her when she stumbled, but that somehow threw his balance off-kilter, and the momentum toppled them both to the ground. He twisted at the last minute so he took the brunt of the fall. He grunted when she landed on top of him like a graceless sack of potatoes.

His shirt was damp and cold, and his hair was messier than before, with pieces of hay stuck in it. So bedraggled, so sexy. She scrambled up. "Are you okay? Your knee?"

"Yes." He stroked her back. "You?"

"I'm fine."

"Good." His fingers played over her sides rapidly.

She stacked her hands on top of his chest and rested her chin on them. "What are you doing?"

He frowned. "Using my tools."

"Your tools were your kiss."

"No, my tools are tickling you." His fingers moved with renewed vigor.

"Oh, I'm not ticklish."

His frown deepened. "I just need to find the right spot." His tickling attempt moved to her back.

She stared at him, then touched her fingers lightly to his side. He cringed and laughed immediately. "Stop!"

He was *ticklish*. Delight ran through her. The devil in her wanted to continue, but she'd give him a break. "This was very enlightening, thank you."

He grunted in acceptance. "I'll find your ticklish spot later."

She waggled her eyebrows. "Feel free to find all my spots."

His eyes widened, and she hoped she hadn't crossed some kind of line . . . double entendres with Jas would take some getting used to. But he chuckled. "Will do."

"My first snow slash hay slash water fight was quite fun."

His smile stretched ear to ear. "Agreed. A snowball fight might actually be boring after this."

"I'd like to try it. And snow cones. I've never had one of those."

His smile turned quizzical. "Never?"

She wrinkled her nose. "My childhood pretty much ended at nine, and I never went back after to try some of the smaller pleasures."

A muscle ticked in his jaw. "Someday, perhaps you could tell me more about your life with your father."

Her fingers curled into his chest. Her people-pleasing personality urged her to please him, but talking about her father *too* much made her want to throw up. It was a testament to how good her therapist was that she was able to listen to her body instead of her instant desire to make someone else happy. "I can try," was the best she could do.

"Whatever you feel comfortable with. In the meantime, next month, we could attempt a trip to Big Bear or Tahoe. Have some actual snow-related activities."

Her heart caught, then accelerated at the thought of a romantic couple's getaway. She didn't know where she'd be in a month mentally, but the thought of making even a small long-term plan with Jas was comforting. "I don't think I want to learn to ski." Strapping sticks on her feet and flinging herself down a hill held no appeal for her.

Jas's hand slid down her back, to her butt. He flexed his fingers. He wasn't demanding or coarse, just there, his touch light. "Skiing wouldn't be my priority."

Katrina was supremely conscious of his body under hers,

long and strong. "I'd like that," she said, and rubbed her nose over his chest. He smelled vaguely of musty hay. She'd never found the scent seductive before. She probably never would, on anyone else. "Or I'd like to try."

"If not, no big deal."

A surge of emotion rose inside her at his compassion, and it swamped her sense of self-preservation. She lifted her head to look him in the eyes. "I like you."

His lips curved up. "I like you too."

She inclined her head, and their lips met.

Oh the zings! The zings were different than they'd been the day before. Sweeter, familiar, more intense. What if the zings grew exponentially every day? Would she short-circuit at some point?

The kiss was closemouthed, but that didn't make it any less hot. Katrina didn't know how long it lasted, but when she lifted her head, they were both panting, and her heart was pumping in glorious time to his.

Her romantic little brain ran away with the implications of how dazed his gaze was. Even when he said, so romantically, "My entire back is wet and cold."

"I'm going to get a complex if you always complain about how uncomfortable you are when I'm on top of you," she teased, and shifted off of him to kneel on the ground.

His perfect eyebrows met as he rose to his feet. "It's not you."

"I'm teasing." She accepted his help to stand and dusted off her bottom. He recaptured her hand, holding it securely in his.

She'd never held hands with anyone. It was a singularly intimate experience. A different kind of intimacy from sex, the kind that came from showing off affection to the world.

Though there was no world here, only her and him.

"You'll probably want a hot shower," he said, and stroked his thumb over her palm.

Her stomach tightened. How was she not supposed to think of his long, hot body in the shower with her? Slick with soap, the steam rising off both of them.

"I'll want one too," he added. "But the water heater here isn't really big enough to withstand two people showering at the same time."

Oh. Katrina slid him a sideways glance, perfectly timed to catch *his* sideways glance. She cleared her throat. "Um. Well." She gestured as they walked closer to the house. "Why don't—what are you doing?"

He dragged her back, falling to his knees behind a hay bale and forcing her down as well. He checked his pockets and cursed. "I must have dropped my phone back in the trees. The cameras should have alerted me. Or the guards should have."

His face had gone hard and blank, like he'd flipped a switch. Her unease quadrupled. "Alerted you to what?" she asked, automatically matching his whisper, if not his flat affect.

"Someone's in the house."

Chapter Twenty-One

W_{HAT?}"

Jas ignored her incredulous question and held out his hand. This wasn't the man who had made love to her so sweetly or tussled with her amid the trees. This was a protector, a guard. If she wasn't scared at the thought of someone invading her home, she might find it sexy.

"Do you have your phone?" he asked.

She nodded.

"Give me. You have the camera app."

She handed it to him, and tucked a strand of damp hair behind her ear. "It could be your brother or grandfather, right?"

"The shadow I saw through the window was too small to be either of them." He pulled up the security video app and his lips went flat. He handed the phone back to her, and stood. "But not too small to be my mom. False alarm. No wonder the guards didn't contact me."

"Your *mom*?" She accepted his help to come to her feet, and took a deep breath to calm her racing heart. "Oh thank God."

"Yeah. Thank God," Jas said, with less relief.

Katrina trailed behind him to the little house, not sure if she should be a part of this reunion or not. Then again, she couldn't very well hide. Could she?

She smoothed her sweater, and then her hair, but without a mirror, it was a useless endeavor. "Should I wait in the barn?"

Jas opened the front door. "Absolutely not. Don't worry, this won't take long." He stopped, one foot over the threshold. "Unless . . . you'd rather not meet her?"

"No, no." She scraped her shoes on the old welcome mat in a vain attempt to get the mud off. "I would love nothing more." *Than to meet your mother when I look like a drowned rat that was rolling around on the ground.*

Katrina stifled the inappropriate urge to laugh.

This made perfect sense, didn't it? It made perfect sense, that the day right after she kinda slept with her bodyguard, his mom would crash the party.

FML.

"Mom," Jas called out as they went inside the house. "Where are you?"

A woman came bustling out of the kitchen, Doodle happily padding along at her side.

Jas's mother didn't look anything like Katrina had imagined. She'd had a vague picture of a woman as tall and imposing as her father and sons were.

Jas's mom was ethereal, petite and slender. Her henna-red hair was braided and hung over her shoulder. Her skin was a light, honey-kissed brown, her eyes big and lined with kohl in her smooth and youthful face. Despite the fall weather, she wore a long gauzy skirt and off-the-shoulder top, round blue designer sunglasses perched on top of her head. "Right here, my love," she said. Her voice was breathy.

Jas accepted her hug and looked down at Doodle. The big canine thumped her tail and gazed adoringly at Tara. "Some guard dog you are, Doodle."

Though Katrina would have given anything to hide shyly behind Jas and escape his mother's notice, she moved forward. "Doodle's not a guard dog. I don't want her to ever feel like she has to earn her keep." Katrina patted her thigh and Doodle obediently moved over to her side. "Hi, I'm Katrina. You've met my dog." She wiped her hand on her jeans and held it out. She hadn't been so nervous to meet Bikram and Andrés. They were far more imposing physically, and had been slow to warm up to her.

But this was Jas's mother. She'd never met the mother of the man she lov—was sleeping with, and she'd hoped to do it when she wasn't a mess.

"Doodle is a beauty, and greeted me so sweetly. Call me Tara." The woman beamed at her and spread her arms out. "I feel like I know you. I don't want to attack you with a hug, but would love to give you one."

Bemused, Katrina scratched her head. "Oh, well. I like hugs, but I'm afraid I'm a little messy right now. We were, um . . ."

"Working outside," Jas supplied.

"Yes, working."

"You put a guest to work on the farm, Jasvinder?"

"I love working," Katrina hurriedly said. Which wasn't a total lie. She did like to be industrious.

"Well, I'm a farm girl." Tara's sharp brown gaze tracked over her. "A little sweat never hurt me. Come on over here."

Tara's hug was lovely, and gave Katrina the same sense of homecoming Daisy's had given her. Katrina took a step back and smiled, her anxiety melting away. "It's lovely to finally meet you."

"And you. I always liked Hardeep. He was a good friend. I know he passed a while ago, but my condolences."

She relaxed. She'd tried not to take Andrés's annoyance with Hardeep to heart, but it was nice to have this, too. "Thank you. He was a great man."

"The nicest. So generous too. Whenever he visited, it was like Christmas in whatever month of the year it was."

Jas cleared his throat. "Mom, what are you doing here?"

"I came by to see if you were home. The door was open, and I wanted to ensure your kitchen and toiletries were stocked."

"I mean, what are you doing here, on the farm, in Yuba City?"

"Oh, I thought, my whole family's here, I should take a couple days off and stop in, too." Tara turned to Katrina. "I'm a teacher, so is Jas's stepfather. Unfortunately, he couldn't arrange the time off, or he'd be here to meet you as well."

Jas grunted. "What a coincidence that you decided to drive up after last night's—"

"What's all that hay doing outside?"

Jas rocked back on his heels. "It's . . . being stored here."

"That's weird." Tara moved closer to Jas and reached way up. They all stared at the tiny piece of hay she retrieved from behind his ear. "What kind of work were you doing out there?"

Katrina scratched her nose. *FML indeed.* "Jas, um, I mean, we had a mishap."

"Oh?"

"Yes. We were . . . making hay." Was that the right word? Or phrase? Damn it, why had she never read any articles about farming.

"Interesting."

"Katrina, why don't you go shower?"

She grasped on to Jas's suggestion like a lifeline. "Yes, let me do that. I'll be quick." She gave them both a wave and escaped, Doodle panting at her side as she accompanied her upstairs.

JAS WAITED UNTIL he heard Katrina close her bedroom door before he yanked the piece of hay out of his mother's fingers and tossed it aside. "Damn it, Mom."

Another woman might have scolded her son for cursing, but his free spirit mother had never been a conventional mom. Tara dimpled. "I'm sorry, I couldn't resist. You're so cute when you blush."

"You embarrassed her."

"By implying you two were rolling around in the hay together? I don't see why. Surely she knows I am aware my children might engage in sexual activity."

"Mom."

"Stop being so uptight, Jas, sex is a natural act."

He huffed out a breath. "Let's talk in the kitchen." He didn't particularly want to talk at all, but better to talk there than out here in the foyer, if his mom was going to go on and on about sex. Less of a chance of Katrina hearing them.

Tara rolled her eyes and spun around in a cloud of tiny bells on her anklets and a wave of her cotton skirt. His mother had always embraced the hippie aesthetic. When he was a child, he'd follow along behind her to bonfires and prayer circles, clutching her colorful loose clothes. She'd been so young when she'd had him, and until she'd met Gurjit, it had been her and him and his grandparents against the world. Sometimes Jas felt like they'd raised each other.

She was his number one weakness, but that didn't mean he couldn't get annoyed as hell with her. "You can't just barge in here. I thought you were an intruder," he said, when they were in the kitchen and out of earshot of Katrina. The pipes squealed as the water turned on upstairs, and he relaxed.

Tara leaned against the counter. "Don't be silly, who would break into the little house? It's safe."

Normally, that was true. Beyond the fact that it was a safe community, no one, not even a rebellious teen, would dare cross the Peach Prince of Yuba City. "I protect a rich woman, Mom. This is my job."

"Oh right." His mom shrugged, though, which told him she didn't quite get it. "I was surprised when Bikram told me you were here."

"He shouldn't have told you."

She ignored that. "Why are you here?"

His mom was paranoid and suspicious about the internet, convinced it was a tool used by capitalism to spy on her and sell her stuff she didn't need. Which, given the ads that were frequently served to Jas, he couldn't entirely defend against.

Tara grudgingly embraced only the parts of technology and the internet that could help her students. He didn't want to freak her out by explaining how Katrina had gone viral. "Katrina needed to get away. There were some problems for her at home."

"Oh no. Are they resolved now?"

Katrina had told him this morning that she and her roommates were plotting a counter campaign. He'd been too busy planning his hay/water/snowball fight to ask her how her talk with the other women had gone. "Soon, perhaps."

"Good! How are your friends in L.A.? Are you keeping in touch with them while you're here?"

"I've only been here for a couple of days, Mom."

"Yes, I know. But you do have a problem, I've noticed, staying in touch with people. You should text them, tell them what's going on with your life."

Jas was mildly offended. He knew how to keep in touch with his friends.

Do you? You mostly only kept in touch with Lorne because she provides you with a service.

He rolled his shoulders, disliking how he could kind of

see the truth in his mother's gentle criticism. "I'll text them more," he allowed.

"How are you enjoying being home?" Tara asked.

Like he was home. Pleasure. Hurt. The joy of being in his family's old home, his home. The pain of reopening old wounds with his grandfather.

She nodded when he was silent. "You don't have to answer. Katrina's dog seems to like you." She came closer and brushed a speck of dirt off his shoulder. "That's unusual for you."

That statement he didn't take offense to, because it was a fact. They hadn't been able to keep any indoor dogs when he was young because of how little they cared for Jas.

It had hurt his feelings when he was a child. Animals had a sixth sense about people, right? What did it mean when they decided you weren't worthy? "Doodle tolerates me." Which was the best he could expect from any four-legged creature.

"That's a sign."

"What's the sign with other creatures who don't tolerate me?" he asked dryly. He'd never been able to suspend skepticism for his mother's talk of signs and fate, not even when he was a child.

"That they weren't yours, of course."

What did that even mean? He changed the subject. "What are you really doing here?"

Her lower lip stuck out in a pretty pout. "I told you, everyone's here, and I felt left out."

"You told Grandpa that I was home, didn't you? That's

why he came back early? That's why you haven't called me since I got here, because you knew I'd know?"

She drew herself up, the picture of outraged sensibilities. "Of course not."

Jas studied her. Her lip twitched at the corner, which gave her away. His mom had a decent poker face, but she'd never been able to control that lip twitch when she was lying. "I don't believe you."

"Well, you can believe me or not."

He sighed. "Don't bullshit me, Mom."

Her lips firmed, and she turned away from him, taking a couple of steps away to the counter. "I spoke with Bikram yesterday night."

"Ah." His brother had snitched about the fight.

She examined an apple in the fruit bowl, then gave Jas a determined, toothy smile. "I am not going to let this foolish feud between you and your grandfather go on any longer."

Jas clenched his teeth together. "He's acting like a child."

"And so are you! Go to the damn ceremony, Jasvinder. It'll be in the high school auditorium, for crying out loud, in the midst of an event you know quite well. The only people there will be other people from this town, people you grew up with."

He didn't know any of those individuals anymore, but he couldn't tell her that when she'd just criticized him for not keeping in touch with friends.

Tell her why you can't go to the parade. "I can't," was all he said.

Tara collected herself and breathed deep. "You're killin'

me, Smalls. One of you has to bend, and I can tell you from experience it will not be my father. I refuse to see you disowned over this foolishness."

He folded his arms over his chest, in an effort to stifle the sharp pain that went through him at the thought of his grandfather cutting him out of the family. "I don't want to be disowned."

"Then do what he wants!"

"I can't!"

A throat cleared, and he and his mom both looked to the doorway. Katrina's hair was wet and slicked back from her freshly scrubbed face. She'd changed into a pair of leggings and an oversized sweatshirt, and she looked far younger than she was. "I'm so sorry to interrupt."

"It's okay." Tara gave Katrina a wry smile. "You must think we only yell in this family. I heard you were present for the blowup yesterday."

"I was." Katrina took a step into the kitchen. Doodle wasn't at her side, which meant her shadow had probably fallen asleep upstairs. The creature sure slept a lot. "I know it was hard on Jas."

He rubbed his jaw, ill at ease with both the sympathy in Katrina's eyes and this whole conversation. If they kept talking, he'd have to keep talking, and there were so many things he never wanted to talk about. "We don't need to have this conversation."

"Yes, we do," Tara said firmly. "And we'll have it tonight, at dinner, together."

Another family dinner? He groaned. "No. Mom . . ."

"For me, Jasvinder."

Damn it. He stared down at his feet. The thought of going back to the big house for another meal around that table. Ugh. "Fine."

"Let's do it here," Katrina interjected.

He lifted his head. "Here?"

"We can have everyone come here for dinner. I would be happy to cook."

Tara clicked her tongue. "Oh no. You're a guest here, Katrina."

"Right, and I would love to give you some small repayment for hosting me. Cooking is a pleasure for me, truly."

Tara's brow creased. "A pleasure? That I don't understand."

"If you'd rather not have it here because of my presence, I'm happy to give your family private time to talk."

"No," he said sharply. "Anything we say can be said in front of you."

Tara looked between them with barely suppressed delight, and he realized immediately he'd made a tactical error. He'd been acutely aware Daisy had been subtly grilling Katrina last night in his mother's absence. His mom was cool and relaxed and all, but she still wanted her eldest son married off with grandbabies on the horizon. "I mean . . ."

"We had dinner at the big house last night, is all," Katrina noted. "It might be best to try a reconciliation in a different setting."

Tara's eyes widened. "Oh, yes. Without the negative vibes clouding anyone's auras."

"Ah." Katrina cocked her head. "Sure."

Tara nodded. "Excellent idea. This is so exciting, it's been so long since we had a meal like this in the little house. I will help you cook, Katrina."

"You don't want my mom to help you cook," Jas muttered, and glared at his mother when she reached up and tugged on his ear. Hard.

"Don't be disrespectful," Tara ordered. "I was thinking more along the lines of running any errands, acting the sous-chef. My mean son is right, I'm not the best of cooks."

"Sure. I'd like that. Let me make you a list."

Tara smiled sweetly at him. "In the meantime, Jas, why don't you go get cleaned up? You have dirt all over your back. Those mishaps when you're making hay can leave you filthy."

Chapter Twenty-Two

I F JAS HAD been to a more awkward dinner, he couldn't recall it. Starting with the fact that Jas was almost positive his mom had tricked her father into coming here, because Andrés had shown up in overalls with a tool box, and had seemed pretty surprised to find a full meal laid out in the kitchen. Jas was pretty sure his grandpa would have stomped out if it hadn't been for Katrina's presence.

The little house didn't have a dedicated dining room, but Jas had added an extra leaf to the kitchen table so the five of them could sit there. He and his mom and his sullen, silent grandpa had instinctively taken the same seats they'd sat in when he was a kid. Bikram was on one side of Jas, Katrina on the other. Doodle sat at Jas's feet, head on his leg, mouth open.

He fed the dog a tiny piece of bread, and she gulped it down. Some might say he was bribing his way into her affections, but this was an insurance policy. He'd never cared if any animal liked him before, but they'd never been Katrina's before either.

Tara cleared her throat. "Katrina, this pizza is divine."

Katrina smiled. Her skin glowed. She looked the same whenever she cooked for anyone, like she was getting nourishment from nourishing others. "Thank you."

"What's the crust made of?" Bikram took a bite of his slice, the crunch loud and satisfying.

"It's sourdough."

"Katrina has a starter handed down from her mother," Tara enthused. "Isn't that lovely? She said it's traveled all around the world with her."

"I'm happy to give you some," Katrina offered.

"Daisy might like that." Tara wrinkled her nose. "You know now I'm no chef."

"You don't have to be a chef. Baking with sourdough requires some science and some patience, is all. It seems complicated, but using it is more heart and care than talent."

Tara took a sip of her wine. "Oh, there's definitely talent in this meal. Right, Dad?"

Jas's grandfather broke his silence with a grunt and helped himself to another slice of pizza. He'd devoured his salad and soup and his first helping, leaving only crumbs on his plate. He hadn't looked in Katrina's direction too much, which told Jas his grandfather might be embarrassed she had witnessed his outburst last night. "The food's not bad, Katrina."

Jas's repressed resentment toward his grandfather needed only a spark to ignite. "She cooked for hours. You can give her a better compliment than that."

Andrés plopped his slice onto his plate and pointed at his grandson. "Listen up, you little—"

"Nope, we are not doing this." Tara interrupted her father without raising her voice, and he immediately subsided. "If we cannot speak to each other in civil tones, we will not speak to each other at all."

Jas sniffed, and he busied himself with his food. His grandfather did the same. A tense silence consumed the room.

His mother finally sighed. "Oh shit. I should have known better than to give you lot the option of not talking at all."

Andrés finished off his second slice of pizza and reached for a third. Jas bit his tongue to keep from commenting on his grandpa bypassing all the other healthier sides on the table in favor of the pizza. "I don't have a problem with anyone talking. I do have a problem with us airing our dirty laundry in front of a guest who isn't family," his grandpa muttered.

"Katrina is my family," Jas snapped, and it was only as he said the words that he realized how true they were.

And, when Bikram choked and hid his laugh with a napkin, how telling.

Jas ducked his head and avoided looking at Katrina. They hadn't defined their relationship privately. It was beyond presumptuous to claim her as his family when—

"I've already seen your laundry." Katrina's tone was easy. "Last night, when you threatened to disown your grandson."

Andrés looked down at his plate, but didn't answer that pointed reminder.

"Would you like my completely unsolicited opinion?" Katrina asked.

"It's hardly unsolicited if you're family," Tara said to Katrina.

Katrina's cheeks turned red, but she continued. "You all love each other deeply. You have a family anyone would envy."

"Everything I have ever done in my life has been for my family."

Jas's throat closed up at his grandpa's fervent words. They were true. His grandpa had sacrificed so much for all of them.

Anger and resentment and guilt and love swirled together inside of him, creating the most annoying, overwhelming mix of emotions.

Katrina's tone was gentle. "You can't seem to talk to each other is all."

"That is an absolutely accurate assessment." His mother's eyes were wet with unshed tears. "You two are breaking my heart. I want you both to be happy."

Andrés surprised Jas by speaking. "Whenever I try to talk to him, he doesn't listen."

Jas took a sip of his water. "You don't listen either."

Bikram rested his arm on the back of their mother's seat. "The funny thing is, you two are each other's Kryptonite, and you can't even see it. You both interact like adults with other people. It's only when you're together that everything falls apart."

That wasn't entirely true. Jas wasn't exactly forthcoming with everyone else.

He slid a surreptitious glance at his grandfather's stubborn jaw. His immediate instinct was to stick his chin out, too.

Okay, there might be some truth to Bikram's observation.

"Dad, you cannot seriously consider never speaking to Jas again over something so foolish as him not attending the parade. You can't possibly be that angry."

Andrés's eyes glinted. "I'm not angry, I'm disappointed."

Tara scowled. "It's not only disappointment."

"So what? I'm allowed to be angry my flesh and blood turned their back on everything I worked for."

Bikram cleared his throat. "If I may, Grandpa: Mom didn't want the farm, either, but you're not mad at her for picking a different career path."

Tara sighed. "Because I'm a girl, my love."

"That's sexist." It was rare for Bikram to rebuke their grandfather.

"I'm not sexist. If she'd wanted the farm, I would have encouraged her," Andrés growled.

"You didn't expect it of her, though."

"Because daughters go off and start their own families. Sons stay with you. They build with you." His grandpa jabbed his thumb at Jas. "I built all this for my boy. And he threw it all away."

"Grandpa." Bikram shook his head. "He chose to enlist. You can't be mad at him forever for picking a different profession."

"I'm not talking about that. I'm talking about after he was done."

Jas stirred, weary of being discussed like he wasn't in the room. "What about after I was done with the military?"

"You were injured. You should have come home and let us take care of you, let this land take care of you. Instead, you chose to go live with a man who was of no relation to any of us. Blood is thicker than water, but you chose Hardeep Arora over me. The family of the man that abandoned my father? You abandoned me and this land to go live with *him*?"

The tense silence returned, but only for a moment. "You know, that saying is misused in modern times," Katrina said, her calm, reasonable voice a much-needed break.

Andrés shook his head. "What?"

"The whole phrase goes, the blood of the covenant is thicker than the water of the womb. People shorten it to mean that kin is stronger than all else, but the original meaning is that the bond between nonfamily members can actually be stronger than family."

"What on earth does that have to do with anything?"

Katrina grimaced. "Sorry. It seemed relevant."

Andres exhaled in a great rush. "I think it's time I go. This is useless." His shoulders drooped. "Jasvinder, you can do whatever you want. Of course, I'll never disown you. Come to the parade, don't come to the parade. I'll love you, even though you don't want me."

Jas clutched his glass. "I can't."

"Yeah, yeah. Like I said, if you don't want to, fine."

Jas couldn't take this anymore. "I didn't say I don't want to come. I said, I *can't*."

Everyone turned to him.

"What does that mean? Why can't you?" Andres asked.

"I can't . . ." The rest of the words stuck there, as they always did.

I can't because I am physically incapable of doing this thing you ask.

I can't because I'm not the man you used to know.

I can't because even though I look mostly the same, my brain is different now, and this thing you're asking of me, this simple, tiny thing that anyone else could do, will hurt me.

He swallowed, and tasted his self-disgust.

"Jas, it's okay," Katrina finally said, her voice soft.

It wasn't okay. Jas placed his napkin over his empty plate. He considered leaving, which was the safest option, but his mom, his brother, his grandfather. Katrina. All of them were looking at him with concern, even his grandpa. Jas touched the scarred wooden table. His great-grandfather had built it.

Jas had run away from this place, but deep down, he'd always been secure in the knowledge he could return someday. Except, if he didn't talk now, he might not get to come back, never feel this place that was heart-wrenchingly his. The place where his roots ran deep, even though he had no desire to farm.

Tell them. He forced the words out past the constriction in his throat. They came in a rush. "I can't come to the parade because big crowds and loud places are difficult for me since I was in Iraq. If there are fireworks or a car backfires, I think they're gunshots. If I get too hot, I feel like I'm in the desert. I . . . I *can't.*"

Tara inhaled, and Katrina shifted closer to him. She placed her hand over his.

His heart pounded, so loud it hurt his ears. "You have no idea—" His voice cracked. *Don't think about it. Put it back. Bury it deep.* Only it was out now, and he couldn't. "You only know what happened in the trial. You think that was the only terrible thing I saw there? You think I walked away fine?"

Andres dashed the back of his hand over his eyes. "You didn't tell us. How could we know what you don't tell us?"

Jas's inherent sense of fairness strangled his resentment back. He hadn't told his family anything. He hadn't wanted to tell anyone anything. No civilian could truly understand.

"You could have come back here, after. We would have taken care of you."

"I couldn't come back here, to this place that had stayed the same, when I wasn't the same person anymore. It hurts, to see all the stuff that was familiar. It hurts to see the things that have changed, the things I wasn't around for." The words were falling faster out of his mouth, like a wound had been lanced. This was a high, to have this drained out of him. He'd come down off this high later, but for now, he'd take this. The euphoria of unburdening himself numbed the pain of recalling it.

Jas raked his hand through his hair. "Hardeep heard what happened through the grapevine. He offered me a job out of pity, so I could escape. It's not that I hate this farm or what you built. I love it. It's just not for me to claim. It wasn't then, but it especially isn't now."

Tara didn't bother to hide her tears. "Hardeep was always very good at helping people in need," she said.

Katrina visibly swallowed. "Yes."

Andrés's shoulders drooped. "You rejected the business. It felt like you were rejecting me, like I had built all this for nothing."

Jas shot a glance at his silent stepbrother, who gave him a warning look, which he ignored. "You didn't build it for nothing, though. It's not like you don't have an heir who's eager and willing to take over the whole thing."

"Jas," Bikram hissed.

Andrés scowled and turned to his other grandson. "Well, of course I do. But what man doesn't want two heirs? Hell, it's only because I have Bikram that I'm still able to run this place. It's not a one-man job."

Wait, what?

"Two heirs?" Bikram sat back in his chair.

"Yes." Andrés's fearsome scowl grew. "You think Bikram won't inherit half this farm? What kind of a monster do you all think I am? Bikram is as much my grandson as Jas is. Tara adopted him, he was raised here, he works his ass off for this place. Of course my will is drawn up so you both get equal shares."

Bikram appeared dazed. "I had no idea. I thought . . . I thought I was just your employee."

"The hell you are. You should have asked me. You and Jas, together."

Jas shook his head. "I don't want any part of the operation.

I have this house, and it's enough. Give the entire farm to Bikram."

Andrés made a sound like a wounded bear.

"Why does that upset you so?" Katrina asked Andrés.

"I *am* the farm."

"No, you're not," Jas said, with some exasperation. "You're a person. The farm is a place. I know your whole identity is tied up in here, but my rejecting the farm is not a rejection of you. I don't want to be a farmer. I will always want to be your grandson."

Andrés huffed. "I can't help how I feel."

"You can if it means not seeing Jas again. Don't you think he'd come here more often, stay longer, if he wasn't terrified you hated him because of his life choices?" Tara snapped.

Andrés's shoulders lowered. "I . . . is that true, Jas? We'd see you more if I stopped pressuring you?"

The hope in his grandfather's eyes made Jas feel like a monster. "Yes." This trip had taught him that the familiarity and happiness of the little house had outweighed the pangs of hurt.

He brushed his leg against Katrina's under the table and let it rest there. He wouldn't have come if it hadn't been for her. This would never have happened without her.

"If I can make accommodations for you, will you consider coming to the ceremony?" his grandfather asked, more humble than Jas had ever seen him.

Jas blew out a breath. He wanted to decline immediately, but he hated to kill the hope on his grandfather's weathered face. "I'll think about it," he managed. It was the best he could do.

He could tell his grandfather wanted to insist, but Tara cut him off. "That's good enough for now. Grandpa is a reasonable man. Right, Dad?"

Andrés folded his arms over his big chest. "Of course I am."

Katrina's fingers stroked over his as she withdrew her hand. It ached, the loss of her touch, but he couldn't very well grab her hand. He'd already given away too much about their relationship to his too nosy family.

His family stayed later, all of them lingering over coffee. Katrina fit right in, chatting easily with Bikram and Tara now that the most serious topics had been exhausted. Andrés was quiet, but so was Jas.

The only cloud on the horizon came after dinner. Bikram pulled him aside. "Hey, uh . . . I have to talk to you about something."

"I do, too. I bought you a present. It's hay. I'll deliver it tomorrow."

Bikram squinted at him. "We need to work on your gift-giving. Anyway, two things. Um, I don't want to step on your toes, but Hasan's older brother is a therapist. Do you want his number?"

A muscle in Jas's cheek twitched. "I knew he was a therapist already. Maybe. I'll think about it."

Bikram beamed, then sobered. "Okay, second thing: I heard from the Smythes. About Doodle."

He stiffened. The Smythes were neighbors. "What did they say?"

"One of their dogs ran off a couple months ago. The description sounded like Doodle. They didn't sound too heartbroken, but they said they'll take her back if we'd found her."

Jas glanced at Katrina, who was chatting with his mother. Their heads were bent close together while Katrina carefully measured a portion of sourdough starter out of her jar and into another. Doodle lay on her back on the floor, tongue lolling out of her mouth, pink belly exposed.

If she went back to the Smythes, they'd treat her with benign neglect. For certain, she wouldn't have a quarter of the affection that Katrina showered upon her and received in return from the mutt.

"Jas?"

Jas pulled his attention away from the domestic scene. "Offer them five grand."

Bikram's eyes bulged. "Five thousand dollars?"

"Ten thousand. Whatever they want. I'll pay it." He had enough money. With no lodging expenses, a lot of his salary was banked.

"Yeah, it's clear you're not cut out to run any kind of business." Bikram patted Jas on the chest. "I'm going to offer them five hundred dollars on your behalf as a rehoming fee."

"What if they don't take it?" He'd be damned if he'd force Katrina to give her dog up.

"They'll be delighted to have it." Bikram rolled his eyes. "Love must have affected your eyesight, because that dog isn't exactly a purebred, brother."

Chapter Twenty-Three

Doodle, should we go into his room, or stay here?"

Doodle hopped on Katrina's bed and lay down, making it clear what her preference was. Between the excitement of having guests in the house and her full belly from all the food Jas had snuck her, the dog was visibly pooped.

Katrina should also be pooped, but she was way too wired to go to sleep. After removing her jewelry, she washed her face. Water dripped into her eyes and she groped for her washcloth. After drying, she braced her arms on the bathroom counter and stared at her reflection.

Coming to the farm had hurt Jas, and she hadn't known.

Katrina gripped the counter. That was only the tip of what she didn't know.

She hadn't known why Jas had taken the job with Hardeep. She had only a vague sense of what he'd gone through in Iraq. She didn't know the details around the testimony the Singhs had alluded to over dinner. She hadn't realized how deep his lack of communication with his grandfather ran.

Let's face it. You don't even know what his favorite breakfast food is.

Jas's reticence to talk about himself wasn't new. He had always been an enigmatic creature. She *knew* him. The important parts of him. His heart, his values.

Yet . . . phew. What a slap in the face this had been, to sit there at that dinner table, utterly clueless as to what was going on.

Katrina left the bathroom and picked up her phone from the bureau, then put it down again. She could talk to Andy or her friends, but she'd have to first navigate the fact that she had feelings for Jas, and she was too tired to explain everything right now.

There are things he doesn't know about you.

Yeah, that was true. He didn't know every little detail about her life, but he'd been around for so much of it. He'd seen her on the floor, stripped of all defenses. He'd protected her, knew about the threats she faced. It was literally his job to know stuff about her.

She took off her clothes and put on a camisole and yoga pants, despite the slight chill in the air. Guilt threatened to overwhelm her, but she tried to beat it back. *You can't control someone else's actions, you can only control yourself.*

She could be the best friend in the world to Jas, and she would make a more concerted effort to draw information out of him, but at the end of the day, she couldn't force him to talk to her or anyone.

What if he's never forthcoming? What if this is all you'll ever know of him?

She bit her lip.

Footsteps sounded on the stairs, and she went to the door. She hesitated for a beat, then opened it.

He stood with his fist poised to knock. "Hi."

"Hi."

"Everything's cleaned up downstairs."

"Thank you for that." She hadn't argued when he'd sent her away after their guests had left. Cleaning up was much less fun than cooking was.

"Thank you for cooking for us."

What a terribly formal conversation. She glanced over her shoulder at the bed. At home, her bed was big enough to accommodate them both and Doodle, but not here. "Do you . . . do you want to go to your room to talk?"

Jas's smile was faint. "Don't want to disturb Doodle?"

"Ha, yeah." She stepped outside the door and closed it behind her. She brushed up against him, and he looked her up and down. She shivered. He'd never really done that before. He'd always been so careful to keep his gaze above her neck. Sleeping together had changed some things.

"Have you told Rhiannon and Jia about Doodle yet?"

She fell into step next to him as they walked down the hall. "Not yet. I didn't want them to get attached if I had to give her up. I'll tell them next time we talk."

"You're already attached."

"Well, those are my feelings to deal with. No need to make someone else hurt if I can avoid it." *Can't control others.*

He motioned her into his room. She flushed at the sight of the bed where they'd slept last night.

She sat down on it gingerly and drew her knees up. He went into the bathroom and closed the door for a few minutes, then opened it again. He wore only a pair of those sweatpants she'd drooled over this morning.

Her misgivings and dismay flew out of her head. Had gray joggers always been the sexiest article of clothing a man could own, or had that happened recently?

He brushed his teeth and washed his face and she scooted back on the bed, fascinated. He had his own routine, only his was much more economical than her fifteen-step program. Such a mundane thing, to watch someone ready themselves for bed, yet so intimate. Especially when they were in those joggers. Those low-slung, drawstring-tied, easy to remove . . .

Katrina released the breath she was holding and fanned herself. She needed a distraction from those sweats. "What's your favorite food?"

"What?"

"Your favorite food. Like if you could have anything in the world for breakfast tomorrow, what would it be?"

He pulled out his floss. His biceps flexed when he lifted it to his mouth. Who knew good dental hygiene could be such a turn-on? "I like everything you make."

"But what's your favorite?" she insisted.

He finished flossing, and came out of the bathroom. "I don't have a favorite."

"Everybody has a favorite dish. What's the breakfast you used to eat the most as a kid, the one that makes you feel all warm and squishy inside when you think about it?"

"I was never actually much of a breakfast eater."

She stared at him. "You eat it every day when I make it for you."

"Because you make it for me."

Holy shit. "So let me get this straight: you don't even *like* breakfast, but for the last nine years, you've eaten whatever I make for you, every morning, instead of just *telling me* you don't care for the meal?"

Jas leaned against the armchair facing the bed. "I appreciate you cooking it, and it is an important meal. I'm happy to eat it."

She gave a half laugh. "Are you kidding me?"

"I don't see what the problem is."

"The problem—" she cut herself off when he rubbed the back of his neck. A rare show of exhaustion on his part.

Another shot of guilt. She should drop this. It wasn't that important, right?

Except as a symptom of a deeper problem. This should be an easy question, one she didn't have to badger him into answering. "Name one dish you actually like."

He was silent for a moment. "I like your waffles."

"The sourdough waffles?" She perked up. "Those are my favorites, too."

"I know. You're happiest when you can use that starter."

Her smile faded. He liked the waffles, at least partially, because she enjoyed making them. It was sweet and selfless, and still he was holding himself away from her.

"Is something wrong?" He rolled his shoulders, and she shook her head, burying her misgivings. It sounded so foolish to complain that he was too nice, yes?

"No." She scooted over on the bed. "Do you want to come sit here?"

His quickness in complying eased her worries a little.

They sat side by side for a couple moments. His hand slid over her thigh and squeezed, sending tingles of happiness through her body. "Thank you for being there tonight. I'm sorry you had to see this family drama."

"Oh no." Never let him think she didn't appreciate learning stuff about him. "I'm glad I could be there. It would have been a shame for you all to have an irreparable rift between you. Grandparents like that don't fall from trees."

He shot her a sideways glance. "Do you know your grandparents?"

"Not on my dad's side. My mom was born in America, but her parents returned to Thailand when she was in college. I met them twice, but I was too young to remember it. After she died, my dad blocked them from contacting me." Her smile was bittersweet, the same mix of anger and aching tenderness she'd felt when she'd found out what her dad had done. "I found letters my grandmother had sent me. Birthday cards with money still tucked in them. By the time I realized they had tried to see me, it was too late, they were already gone. If I'd had the courage to buck my dad a few years earlier . . ." She trailed off, her inner-therapist-trained counterthinking kicking in. "Well. What's done is done."

"I'm sorry."

"I considered seeing if I could track down any extended family members, but . . . I don't know."

"You should."

She lifted her shoulder. She'd been raised by a father who had seen her as his meal ticket, a pretty object to be photographed and used for financial gain and tossed when she was no longer useful. Her abandonment issues were severe. What were the guarantees that this family that didn't even know her would even like her?

She had made a family. Rhi, Jia. Everyone who worked for her. Jas.

She inhaled deeply, pulling air into her lungs to calm the prickle of tears at her eyes. She could always use more, though. "I'll think about it."

He nodded. "You do that."

How had they gotten back to her so easily? It was a habit, she supposed, him looking after her. "Can we talk about dinner? About . . ."

Your PTSD.

This testimony everyone was talking about.

Your relationship with your family members.

"I'm really exhausted. Can we not, tonight?"

Her nod was automatic. "Yes. Of course."

He leaned in close to press a kiss on her cheek. "Do you want to sleep together? I'm too tired to do more, but I'd like to sleep."

"Absolutely."

He turned the light off, plunging the room into darkness. They got under the covers, and she moved onto her side, in her usual sleeping position. He curved around her, spooning her.

She tried to shake the sense of something being wrong,

but her eyes popped open as a thought occurred to her. "Hey, is this your side of the bed?"

"I can sleep anywhere. I don't have a side."

That sounded like absurd talk to Katrina, but she supposed there were some humans in the world who didn't care what side of the bed they slept on. She craned her neck to look at him. "Are you okay with this position? Do you usually sleep on your side?"

"Are you okay with it?"

"Yes."

"Then I'm okay with it." He tugged her close. "I'm tired, Katrina."

The rebuke was as gentle as it could be, but she got the hint. "Okay, right. Good night."

"Night." In a matter of seconds, his breathing deepened and grew heavy.

She stared out into the darkness of the night, stroking her hand over his. In the history of the world, had any woman ever complained about having a partner who was *too* selfless?

Probably not. Despite that lingering sense of anxiety, she closed her eyes and did what she'd learned to do so well. She fell asleep with her breath matched to his, the heat of his body seeping into hers.

Chapter Twenty-Four

THERE WAS so much noise, and the sharp taste of sweat and metallic fear in his mouth. He wanted to leave, but he was pinned, cursed to witness the same horrific sequence of events again and again.

Hands on his chest held him down. He had to get away.

He lashed out, kicking and swatting, and it was only when he heard a grunt that his eyes flew open.

He expected to see McGuire's deceptively boyish round face over his, but that wasn't the case. Katrina was on her knees next to him, eyes wide.

The bed. The room. He was in the little house, and Katrina was with him.

"Oh God." Jas sat up and grasped her hands. They were cold in his, which didn't bode well. "I'm so sorry. Did I hurt you?"

"No, not at all. I shouldn't have tried to shake you awake. Are you okay?"

He looked around the room, his grandparents' old master bedroom. The climate was cool here, not hot or arid. Nothing smelled like blood. "Yes."

"Let me get you some water."

"That's okay."

But she was already clambering out of bed before he could finish speaking. He rubbed his knee through the blanket, but stopped when she came back from the bathroom.

She turned the light on the nightstand on, and sat on the bed next to him. "Does your leg hurt?"

Couldn't get much past her. "No. Thank you." He accepted the glass of tap water.

"You were rubbing it."

"Sometimes it aches when it's cold out." Or when he had this dream, where he was shoved back into that horrific night.

"Can I see?"

He didn't want to show her, but he couldn't deny her anything, so he shrugged. She flipped the quilt, shoved his sweatpants up, and examined his naked leg.

"It's ugly," he said gruffly.

She traced the scars with a feather-light touch. "No, it's just you."

He made a deep noise in his throat, and drained the rest of the water.

"Is that what you dream about? This injury?"

Jas shook his head. Then he nodded. Then shook his head again.

The door widened and Doodle came padding into the room. The animal put her paws on the bed and hopped up, shoving Katrina aside to plop on Jas's chest. Katrina chuckled. "She seems to really be warming up to you."

"I snuck her scraps at the table." Jas scratched the dog's head and let some of his fear and sadness seep into each stroke. "Most animals aren't so receptive."

"Why do you think they don't like you? Are you a werewolf?"

The unexpectedly silly question made him smile. "Do animals not like werewolves?"

"So I've heard. I also assume werewolves are taciturn and have perfect eyebrows."

He squinted at her. "Perfect eyebrows, eh?"

"Beyond perfect."

He shouldn't feel so happy over such an odd compliment, but it was still a compliment, so he'd take it. "I don't know why animals tend to be, at best, indifferent to me." He scratched Doodle's neck. "It used to make me feel bad, but I learned to get over it."

"Why did it make you feel bad?"

"Animals are excellent judges of character, aren't they?"

She side-eyed him. "Or they're animals, and somewhat fickle and unreasonable?"

His smile was faint. Doodle hummed and scooted closer to him. "I suppose that's possible."

"Can you tell me about your dream, Jas?"

He hesitated, that same warring urge rising inside of him. He wanted that euphoria of unburdening himself, but he also wanted to bury it deep. To compromise, he switched into as robotic a tone as he could manage, eager to get through this with as few emotions as possible. "I led my infantry platoon. There was a bomb, a roadside explosion that killed two of my men. We got a tip about this guy who they said was the weapons supplier for the cell that placed and detonated the IED. Our superiors questioned him for two weeks before letting him go. There was no proof he was connected at all." Jas had looked at the Draft Intelligence Information Report later. The suspect had been a civilian, by all accounts a quiet villager who lived with his mother and daughter. There had been nothing to tie him to the crime except a rumor.

She rubbed his knee, and he leaned back against the pillows. It was odd to have someone petting him like this, but the soothing massage calmed him.

"One guy, McGuire, he was best friends with one of the men who was killed. He and another soldier were supposed to take the suspect back to the village, but he stopped on the way."

"Oh no."

"Yeah." Jas squeezed his eyes shut, as tight as he could manage. He couldn't block out the memory, though. "I don't know if he planned the whole thing, or if it was a spur of the moment terrible idea. The sergeant with him, Lorne, she slipped away and came and got me. We raced back. We found the translator terrified and huddled away from the scene, the suspect naked and tied up, with McGuire screaming questions at him. The man had been hurt badly." It was getting harder to remain emotionless.

"Did he kill the suspect?"

"He tried to. The guy went to stand up, and McGuire shot

at him. Lorne and I rushed him, and he shot me twice in the struggle."

Katrina's touch on his knee turned soothing. "This is what you had to testify to at the trial?"

"Court martial. Yes. We all did." His eye twitched, recalling the angry glares of McGuire's parents and supporters. They'd called him and Lorne the traitors, held firm in their belief that their son had been doing his job the best he could.

Bullshit. Jas had seen the aggression and rage in McGuire's face, up close. All he'd cared about was exacting vengeance on anyone he could.

"Tell me he was convicted."

"Twenty-five years."

She sighed. "Good."

"He served five before he was paroled."

Her lips curved down. "Oh."

He ran his tongue over his teeth. "Looks like he's probably going to be pardoned."

She inhaled. "Oh dear."

"Yeah."

"What can you do?" She came to her knees.

"Nothing."

"But . . . but that's not fair."

It wasn't. He shrugged, her outrage making him feel a little better. "That's how it is."

"He tried to kill a defenseless, unarmed man. It's only because of your intervention that he didn't succeed. And he tried to kill you! And . . . nothing happens?"

"Right."

"Is your name going to be in the press or anything?"

"I'll make sure it doesn't lead back to you."

Katrina made an annoyed sound. "That's not why I'm asking. I'm asking for your sake."

"It's possible." Jas shrugged. "There's so much going on in the news now, that I imagine this will be a blip on most people's radars."

"How can you be so calm?" She clutched her hands to her chest. "Aren't you angry?"

"Of course." He hesitated, unsure of how to explain. "Anger can be a useful emotion, but if I'd stayed angry when I came back, I would never have been able to move forward. So I buried the anger down."

"Sounds like you buried everything down."

Jas thought of the love he had for Katrina. "It's not like I don't feel things."

"You just don't talk about most of those feelings," she noted.

"That's not—" He paused. "That may be true. I've never been forthcoming, but now I'm pretty far out of the habit of confiding in anyone."

"I'd like to know when things make you happy, or sad. I want to know when you're hurting, even if that means I can't get something I want. Like coming here? I had no idea it would hurt you. You should have told me."

He caught her fluttering hands and gave them a squeeze. "I came here because I wanted to, too. I missed this place, and since I'd gotten news of the pardon, all I'd wanted was to run away. I was glad to have an excuse to come here. Honestly." Every word he spoke came from his heart. He would never have thought to come stay here for days had it not been for Katrina. This trip had nourished him, like her food nourished his body, first thing when he woke up.

Her eyes were big and dark. The strap of her camisole had slipped down. He liked that little dip where her shoulder met her neck. It was such a tender, vulnerable spot.

"How do I know when you genuinely want something, though, if you don't talk to me?"

"I promise, I'll try to talk more," he said, as soothingly as possible. He'd say anything to get that worry off her face.

Her frown relaxed. She scooted closer to him. "Well, I'm glad you got something out of fleeing here with me."

"I got a lot out of it. All alone with a girl I . . . like." He'd almost slipped. Used the other *l*-word. *I love you*. But he couldn't say that. He opened his mouth, then closed it, tongue-tied and out of his depth, as he often was around her.

She nudged Doodle. "Puppy, can you leave us alone for a bit?"

The dog was brilliant, easily a ten-thousand-dollar dog. Doodle hopped right off the bed at Katrina's sweet command and padded to the door. If Doodle could have, Jas imagined she would have shut it behind her.

Katrina walked up the bed on her knees and straddled him, so they were face-to-face. "I like you too. I'm sorry all of these terrible things happened to you."

He automatically grasped her round hips. Her skin was warm and soft under the thin cotton of her pants. "I'm sorry terrible things happened to you."

The kiss was soft and sweet, and so was her embrace. "I should tell you," he whispered into her mouth. "I was so busy getting hay, I forgot to go to the pharmacy."

She closed her eyes and gave a helpless laugh. "Oh my God. Jas."

"I know."

Katrina grasped his face between her hands. "Are we ever going to get to penetration!"

"Probably not, if you call it penetration ever again. Least sexy word ever."

She collapsed against his chest, giggling. "Okay. You know what? This is kind of great. I never had that fumbling around period as a teen or young adult. I'll have it now. We'll thoroughly explore the bases."

That sounded fine to him, though he made about ten mental notes to pick up the damn condoms tomorrow. "Amazing."

"We'll make it amazing." A kiss fell on his forehead. "And hot." Another on his nose. "It'll be sexier than penetration."

He made a face at the word. She laughed. "I have an idea. Can we try something?"

Uh, yeah, he was game for anything. He was hard simply being this close to her. "Whatever you'd like. You can run the show, if you want."

Her hands fluttered over his shoulders, then rested there. "Good."

His toes curled when her lips settled on his, sipping away. The kiss was soft and tentative, and he leaned back until he rested against the headboard, to give her more room.

Out of politeness, Jas tried to keep his erection from pressing into her, but she sought it out, squirming against him. He captured her exhalation and gave it back to her. The kiss turned deeper, more intense, her tongue flirting against his lips. He returned the caress, and she sucked at his tongue.

She pulled away, and he flexed his fingers on her hips. "What do you want?" she whispered.

"Whatever you'd like," he repeated.

She sat back on her heels. "No. Tell me what you want."

"I want . . ." He didn't know what answer she was looking for. "I want to make you happy."

She huffed out a laugh that sounded vaguely exasperated. "Without turning it around to me, tell me what I could do that would bring you pleasure."

He almost said *anything*, but that would probably annoy her, even if it was true. "Can you take your top off?"

"Yes. Good start." She crossed her arms in front of her and grasped the hem of her tank top. The frothy, useless piece of cotton landed somewhere in the room, and he was faced with her breasts.

He couldn't help but stare. They were so lovely, the skin here a lighter golden brown than the rest of her body, her brown areolas large and puffy. He cupped the heavy fullness in his palms and traced a silver stretch mark. "Pretty," he managed.

"What do you want to do with them?"

He'd never heard that tone from her, that seductive purr. "Everything." Was he going to be reduced to cavemanlike one word sentences? He ran his thumbs over her nipples, cataloguing the way she shuddered. "I want to play with these. Lick them."

She slid her hands around his neck, and this time it was he who shuddered when she dug her fingers into the muscle there. "Do it, then."

He might have been embarrassed by how fast he snatched her closer and buried his face between her breasts, had her long moan not told him how much she liked it. He ran his tongue over one of her nipples while he played with the other.

She wiggled up until her bottom rested right on his crotch. Without his urging, her hips moved in a circle and he gasped and came up for air. "Don't . . . yes."

"Which is it?" Another circle, their hottest parts separated only by a few layers of cotton.

That *purr.* "Yes. Keep doing that." The tease was more exciting than he could have imagined.

She pressed hot, wet kisses against his neck, moving up to capture his ear lobe. "What else do you want?"

There was something so insistent and serious under that purr, it jolted him out of the seductive spell. "Is something wrong?"

"No." Her wet nipples brushed his chest when she lifted her head, and his mouth salivated. "I want you to tell me what you want. Not me. Focus on you. What do you need? What have you fantasized about doing to me?"

He opened his mouth, then closed it. What had he *fanta-sized* about doing to her? What hadn't he fantasized about doing to her?

She wrinkled her nose, misunderstanding his silence. "Nothing?"

"No. Everything. I can't narrow it down."

Katrina brightened. "Ah. Well, I can work with that. Better than the alternative." She traced her index finger over his collarbone and down his chest. "Can I tell you one of my fantasies?"

He nodded so quickly he got dizzy.

"You know the double doors on my bedroom balcony? Once I dreamt you came through them while I was sleeping and crawled into my bed. You woke me up with your mouth here." She brought his hands up to her breasts. "And here." She slid one of his palms down her soft belly and placed it between her legs. The cotton of her pants was damp, and grew wetter when he rubbed her through the material. "Do you want to do that someday?" she whispered. "Sneak in through my window, and lick me awake? I'd like that."

He nodded again, helpless.

"And what would you want me to do to you?"

His gaze dropped to her lips. "I'd want the same."

"Say it. Tell me what you need."

"I want you to . . . suck me."

"Suck you where?"

He slid his hand down his belly, under the elastic waistband of his joggers. He fisted his cock. "Right here."

A secret smile played over her lips, and she inched the

waistband down, until she had freed him. It had been too dark to see in detail last night, but the sight of her small hand around his erection was almost more than he could bear.

But wait, there was more.

She moved down his body, her ass high in the air. He gathered up handfuls of the sheets.

A dimple popped into her cheek. "Tell me if this is wrong. I've never really done it before."

"I've never really had it done to me," he confessed. It had always felt far too selfish and uncomfortable and awkward.

He felt none of those things right now.

She paused. "Really really?"

"Really really."

"Okay, then. That takes some of the pressure off."

He tipped his head back when her breath melted over the tip of his erection, but he didn't close his eyes. When her hand pulled a little too roughly at the head, he hissed, and she gentled immediately.

His gaze slit in pure pleasure when her lips fit over his penis. She was clumsy and a couple of times she tugged at his foreskin a little too hard, but none of that was important.

This was beyond anything he could have fantasized. She was hot and wet and perfect, and the fact she desired him enough to pleasure him like this . . . well, that was aphrodisiac enough, even without the visual of her lips wrapped tightly around his erection, her cheeks hollowing every time she sucked. Though that was nice too.

"Touch my hair," she murmured against the tip of his

cock, repeating the words he'd said to her last night. "Show me what you like."

His chest rose and fell and he tentatively let his fingers tangle up in her silky hair. He guided her gently, unsure of what would be too crass or forceful, but when she murmured in pleasure, he grew more confident. Her strokes sped up and the knot at the base of his spine drew tight. He tugged at her hair. "I'm . . . close."

Her fist slid up and down his shaft, spreading the wetness. "So come, then."

His thighs tensed and his breath came faster as she went back to torturing him. It was all too much, the feel of her mouth and hands and the sight of her. He grasped her shoulder and squeezed as his body clenched tight, the pleasure radiating up from the soles of his feet.

When the aftershocks of pleasure had faded, he stroked her hair, then urged her up. She gave him a startled look when he swiftly turned them so she was under him. "Wha—"

"My turn," he said. Or maybe he growled it. He wasn't sure.

"We did this yesterday, though."

"It's not a quota system, Katrina."

She gasped when he moved down her body, and moaned when he stripped her pants off in one smooth motion and pressed his lips to her pussy. He made a vee with his fingers to open her up, and feasted, the taste of her going straight to his head. This was *Katrina* he was tasting. He'd remember this for as long as he lived, even if this ended.

Don't think of the end right now.

He shook his head to dislodge the thought, and she whimpered, so he did it on purpose, moving his face, trying different positions, keeping up firm, slow strokes to her little clit. She wasn't shy now about grasping his hair, and he made a mental note every time she showed him what she loved.

She tasted like . . . he knew he was supposed to say sunshine and flowers, but that wasn't true, and frankly he'd be a little concerned if she did smell like roses down here. She tasted good, an indescribable flavor he doubted anybody could ever replicate.

He loved it. He loved her.

He wanted to tell her, but there had been far too many revelations tonight. No need to add another emotionally charged one to her basket.

Her muscles clenched up, and he gentled his touch. He didn't go far. He stayed there, resting against her thigh, giving her tiny, gentle licks, until she shifted beneath him. He wasn't ready to leave her yet, but he reluctantly gave her one last kiss before coming to his knees. He swiped the back of his hand over his mouth and looked down at her splayed, delicious body.

He met her brown eyes, and that vague sense of melancholy he always experienced after a particularly bad dream moved through him.

What if this ends when we get back to the real world? Cinderella at midnight, left with a pumpkin carriage.

"We never got our shower."

He blinked at the seeming non sequiter. "What?"

"Earlier, when your mom interrupted us. We were going to shower and didn't." She sat up and coasted her hand up his arm, then kissed his nipple. "I'm all sweaty now."

He looked down at her body, his mood lifting. He was willing to be charmed into forgetting all of the dark stuff for a night and let hope spark inside him. Hope that this was exactly and entirely where he belonged. "As am I."

"Shall we?"

"Absolutely. Can't wait to see what you want to try next."

Her laugh was low and throaty. This seductive, earthy side of Katrina was so new and exciting. All he wanted to do was wallow in that laugh and her touch.

She crooked her finger. "Follow me."

Easy. Truth be told, he'd follow her anywhere. A shower, a hot, wet, steamy place where they could get tangled up in each other? That was a no-brainer.

Chapter Twenty-Five

It's really too bad we're conflicted out of dating apps."
Akash sorted through the papers in front of him.

Katrina pulled her legal pad closer to her and smiled at
the computer screen. She was getting used to taking her
conference calls from the little house's living room. "Did
you come across something good?"

"Yeah, get this: it's called CatFishr. You can upload any
pics you want, so you never know what the person you're
talking to looks like until you meet. You have to go wholly
on the text conversation."

Katrina chuckled, then realized Akash was serious.
"You've got to be kidding me."

"Who the hell would want that?" Carol exclaimed.

"Oh, I don't know. I thought it was kind of revolution-
ary. You know, leaning into the fear people have with dating
apps. It's kind of like a surprise grab bag, and not knowing
what the person looks like is a way to focus on substance
over appearance."

Katrina rubbed her temples. Sometimes she felt very old.

What was the world teaching these youths? "Crush spends a great deal of money to combat bots and catfishing. The idea of a grab bag first date is ridiculous."

Carol popped her gum. She'd already gone through two pieces of nicotine gum during the call, which told Katrina her friend was deep in another quitting attempt. "Dangerous, too. Bet ya anything the creators are heterosexual men who are bitter about women not swiping right on them."

Akash gathered himself up. "Not all—"

"No."

"Nope." Katrina folded her arms on the table. "Think about what could happen if someone shows up for a date, and the person they've been talking to is their abusive ex."

"Or a stalker," Carol added.

"Or simply someone nefarious who doesn't want any trail of who they're talking to. I can think of ten other dangerous scenarios off the top of my head. Do you see why it may not be a great idea to have an app where people are encouraged to pretend to be someone else?"

Realization dawned in his dark eyes. "Oh. *Oh.*"

That was the nice thing about Akash. He was teachable. "Sometimes tech people get wrapped up in their own genius. You have to look ahead to the consequences. Conflict or not, I'd hard pass this one."

Akash made a note on his tablet, then moved on. "How about an AI system? It's so you can play with your pet when you're not home."

A loud crack came from the kitchen, and Katrina glanced

that way. Jas had been very quiet while she'd been on her call, thankfully. She smiled at this noise, though, the reminder that he was nearby.

They'd slept in this morning, and though she'd had grand plans to make waffles for breakfast, she'd been too tired to put together anything more complicated than oatmeal. She'd watched Jas carefully, and he'd eaten every bite with apparent enjoyment.

She still wasn't really sure of anything, except that they liked each other. That should have been enough. She should be satisfied with that, and the fact that he'd opened up as much as he had.

It *should* be enough.

"Katrina?"

"Yes." She cleared her throat. "Send me more details about the pet AI." It sounded absurd, but she was always willing to take a chance on the pet market.

"Will do." Akash closed his tablet cover with a satisfied smile.

"Is that all?" Katrina asked, her finger hovering over the end button.

"I actually have something I need to discuss with you. Akash, can you give us a minute?" Carol tugged on her bright blue blazer.

Katrina waited until the young man had left the office. "How's he working out?"

Carol's smile was faint. "He's smart and trainable. He's not Lakshmi yet, but I see some potential. They're definitely related."

"No one's Lakshmi."

"Truer words." Carol clasped her hands on the table. "How are you doing?"

The sympathy in Carol's eyes tipped her off. "You heard about the viral thing."

"Yeah. Don't worry. My lips are sealed." Carol twisted her wedding ring. "You have someone there with you? Rhiannon?"

Unease slithered through Katrina. "What's going on?"

"I have some bad news. Your dad somehow got my digits." Her lip curled. Carol had always seen right through her dad. Which was the main reason Katrina had hired her later. "He called me today and asked if I have a contact number for you."

Her mouth went dry. "That is bad news."

"I'm so sorry, Katrina. I stonewalled him, but I assume he's calling everyone you used to work with." Carol's gaze was worried. "If he digs and finds out I work here . . ."

"He'll probably rightly assume I'm behind the fund." Damn it.

You have a plan for this. You have multiple contingency plans in place for this. "Text me his number." She was proud of how well-modulated her voice was.

"Are you sure?"

"Yes." They said their goodbyes, Carol still looking worried. Katrina's phone buzzed almost immediately.

A number couldn't be evil. Could it?

Her finger hovered over the delete button, ready to exorcise it. There was no good reason to ever be back in touch with her dad, right? At the very least, she could have Jas or Rhiannon in the room with her when she did this. If she did this.

Actually.

Wait. Wait a damn minute.

Katrina straightened. This asshole had the nerve to come sniffing around, after everything he'd done to her? After Hardeep had given him bags of money to go away? Oh no.

She took a deep breath, and let the anger rise up. Anger was good, especially when it was this cold, fiery anger.

Katrina mentally flipped through those elaborate plans she'd crafted for just this possibility, until she found her favorite one. Yes, she was doing this. She *could* do this, and she could do it on her own. She wasn't the same scared child she'd been the last time she'd dealt with her father.

She rose and went upstairs quietly, to her bedroom, lest Jas hear. She masked her number first, so it wouldn't show. Even her number was too much information for her biological father to have.

The phone rang once, twice, and then a man's gruff voice came over the line. "Yeah?"

Sweat beaded on her upper lip, but her anger kept her cold.

"Hello?" he prompted.

Thomas King sounded different, and yet not. She hadn't spoken to him since the day after her wedding, when Hardeep had paid him a substantial amount of cash to go away. Actually, had she spoken? No, she'd stayed silent. She'd been too scared. Hardeep and her father had coldly worked out the financial arrangements.

That was okay, for who she'd been then. She was different now, even if he was not.

She took up space now. She was happy. Radically happy. "Hello," she said.

"Katrina." He sounded triumphant. He'd known she would call if he rattled some cages.

"Father. I hear you're trying to find me."

He paused, like he was surprised she'd confront him so bluntly, and maybe that was surprising to him. "The whole world's trying to find you."

She nodded, her suspicions confirmed. Blackmail.

She was numb now, the kind of icy control that came with pure rage. "So you recognized me in those photos."

"What man can't recognize his own daughter? Even if she doesn't look quite the same as she used to."

Her dad had always been freakishly obsessed with her face and body. They'd been, after all, tools to make him money.

Katrina wrapped her arms around her middle. She would not think one negative thing about her physical appearance. She loved it. She loved herself. He was a monster, and she was beautiful the way she was. "You have one minute to tell me what you want before I hang up. The clock is ticking."

He hesitated, but something must have convinced him she was being sincere, because he spoke in a rush. "The world wants to know who CuteCafeGirl is. I know you well, daughter, and understand how much you value your privacy, how fragile you are. So I wanted to assure you I wouldn't tell anyone who you are."

The ice thawed enough for her to shake. Fragile. That was the word he'd used to convince her that she needed him so much, that he was the only one who would be able to take care of her, that she was incapable of looking after herself.

Two panic attacks in public settings, two hospital visits. That was all it had taken for her father to get her fully under his control.

You're strong. You're not alone now.

Katrina wished Doodle were in the bedroom. "What do you want in exchange for your silence?"

"I would never demand anything." Her father clucked his tongue. "If you'd like to give me a gift, I'd consider accepting, but this isn't blackmail, love."

Bull. Shit. She swallowed. "Your minute is up."

"Why don't you think about how much your privacy is worth to you?" her dad said in a rush. "And call me back tomorrow for negotiations. I'm in driving distance to Santa Barbara right now. Perhaps we can meet in that charming café?"

The café that had once been her refuge, that she wouldn't be able to return to for a while, barring a better disguise than her baseball cap? This huge asshole.

"Don't wait too long, though. You know how quickly people dig up dirt on the internet."

She hung up without saying goodbye, his threat lingering in her ears.

She pinched the bridge of her nose. What would her friends do? Rhiannon would blow up his threat by exposing her face and name herself. Jia would do something similar, and leverage every contact she had in the influencer world for the biggest impact.

Katrina wasn't Jia or Rhiannon, so she couldn't handle it like they could. That was okay.

She inhaled and exhaled, until enough of her panic dissipated that she could think clearly.

She had to keep her privacy.

She had to neutralize the immediate threat of her father.

She had to try to address this media circus once and for all.

Okay. Katrina nodded. This was doable. Time to get to work.

She texted the group chat, blunt and to the point. My dad saw the story. He's blackmailing me. I'm coming back home. Will keep you posted on when.

Rhiannon's response came right away. I didn't listen to you, and I'm already on my way back. Be there by early am, pacific time. Lakshmi's staying behind.

Jia replied a second later. We'll think of something.

I'll call you later. I have some ideas. Katrina placed the phone carefully on the table and rose to her feet, grabbing the hoodie Rhiannon had sent with her.

She paused as she caught sight of herself in the mirror. She did look different from the sad-eyed woman her father had known, the one who had graced magazine covers and lounged on beaches. She ran her hands over her tummy. It was full now, protruding, the curve of it pronounced. Her thighs were dimpled. Her arms jiggled. She had changed, on the inside as well as the outside.

She'd never been fragile. She'd believed in someone who was supposed to protect her, and that belief had gone sideways. That wasn't her fault.

It's not your fault.

She repeated the words as she made her way downstairs, and found Jas in the kitchen. He looked up and smiled, his teeth white. "Hey, look at what Doodle can do. Doodle, sit."

The dog plunked her butt on the tile, her tail wiggling.

"Good girl," Jas crooned, and gave her a treat. She snapped it up and gobbled it down. "Isn't she brilliant?"

Her smile was forced. "Uh-huh." Even her fake smile faded as she caught sight of the food lined up on the counter.

He followed her gaze. "We have so many leftovers in the fridge, I figured we could clear them out. How do you feel about a smorgasbord— Katrina?"

The nausea caught her unexpectedly and she shook her head, darting from the room and out the front door. She clutched the railing and took in deep breaths.

A big hand came to rest on her lower back and Doodle pressed against her leg and whined, a high-pitched and plaintive sound for such a giant dog. "Are you sick?" Jas asked quietly. "What happened?"

The words spilled out of her, words she'd never confessed to anyone. "When I was young, my dad, he'd put a bunch of dishes on the counter for breakfast. If I completed everything I was supposed to—smiling, running, singing—I could choose one thing to eat. If I didn't perform well, he'd take away one plate as punishment for each infraction."

She expected him to be upset, but his "Holy *shit*" was violent, as was the embrace he pulled her into. "Katrina." His chest rumbled under her ear. "I'm so sorry. That's utterly abusive."

She breathed in through her nose, out through her mouth. His scent was better than any other kind of air. "It's okay."

"It's not. Let me go clean up the food. Or I'll make you something. You're always cooking, I wanted to give you a break—"

"I like cooking." She pulled away. "Rhiannon's on her way home."

He blinked at the seeming change of subject. "Oh. Good."

"I would like to go home, as well."

"Why?"

"Because my dad is blackmailing me, and I realized I'd like to be around all the people I care for more than I'd like to run away."

"Your dad is *what*?"

"It's okay." She patted his chest. The weak sunlight lit the porch, turning it into a golden cage. No, not a cage. She was here voluntarily, and she'd go home voluntarily.

She didn't have a sword, but she could at least have her rage. The rage, and her own intellect. She smiled through her anger. "I think I have an idea on how to head this off."

"What's the idea?"

"I'm going to write a statement."

He waited, then frowned. "That's it?"

"Yes. I'll beg for people to leave me alone. Appeal to everyone's sense of goodness."

Jas steepled his fingers under his nose and looked down at her from his greater height. "Your plan is to appeal to the goodness of . . . the internet."

She managed a wobbly smile. Cynics, she was surrounded by them. She wasn't a cynic, though. She couldn't afford to be. She had to believe there was good in the world, and so she'd appeal to that good first. "Yes. It's one thing for Jia to do a video telling the world that this isn't a fun love story, it's a damaging privacy infringement. It'll make more impact coming from CuteCafeGirl."

"Okay. Kind of see your reasoning. I don't think a statement could hurt you. How will this get your dad off your back though?"

"If people stop caring about who I am, there's no story. If there's no story, there's nothing for my dad to blackmail me with."

He did not look convinced. "I don't know. That sounds like a stretch."

I'll also crush him for good measure.

That part, she wouldn't share with Jas, not yet.

The rage flared again. The crushing? No white knight needed this time. That was going to be all her. "It'll work."

NOT FOR THE first time, Jas wondered if that woman with the camera had known, when she'd taken those photos and spun an elaborate story, that she'd be revealing Katrina's underbelly to the world. Had it even occurred to her that that would be a possibility? Or had she blithely only been concerned with entertaining her followers with a romance casting real people?

He puffed out his cheeks. "If you say so."

"I do." She moved closer to him. "I'm sorry."

"For what?"

Her grimace was deep. "For making everything about me again."

He snorted. "Last night, everything was about me."

"So we're trading?"

Trading sounded good. It sounded awfully close to sharing. He wrapped his arms around her.

She rested her head on his chest. Around the corner, the hay bales were still piled high. "I'll be sad to leave this place. Us being alone together."

"You hate me being around you when you're working."

"It's because you make *noises*." She pressed a kiss on his chin to soften the blow.

"How much time will you need to pack?"

"Not long, but I have to write my statement, talk to my lawyer, put some things into motion on the publicity side."

Another few hours with her, alone? Yes. "Right. Let's do it."

"Actually, never mind. You'd have to drive late into the night if we did that." She worried her fingers. "Times like this, I wish I felt confident enough to drive. But . . ."

But she didn't want to risk a panic attack at the wheel, and neither did he. "I'll drive you all night. Don't worry."

If anything, that brought more worry to her expression. "Are you only saying that—"

"Katrina." He shook his head, trying not to let his exasperation creep through. "I am a grown man. Trust that when I say I'm fine with something, I'm fine with it."

She nodded, and he bent down to kiss her nose. "Let's clean up and we can take the leftover food to the big house and say goodbye."

"Don't forget the hay."

"I could never."

Chapter Twenty-Six

GOD, I'M EXHAUSTED." Rhiannon lay on her back, her sweatpants and hoodie travel-worn and stained. She'd rolled off her international flight two hours prior. Gerald had picked her up.

"You and me both, sister." Jia slumped on the couch, her head resting in her hand. In deference to Jas's presence in the room, she wore a simple scarf over her hair.

Katrina shifted from her position on the other side of the couch and stroked Zeus, who was curled up into a tight ball in her lap. Doodle had easily gone off with Gerald to explore her new home, but Zeus had been clingy since they'd gotten home. Understandable. Anyone who said cats didn't feel affection for their owners had never had a sweet little cat like Zeus.

She glanced at Jas. He should have been the most tired, having stayed up late to drive them down, but no one would have known it after his quick shower and change of clothes. His shirt collar was crisp, his eyes alert but unreadable. He leaned against the wall next to the door, his sharp gaze on the television. The energy in the room was expectant and tense.

"Does anyone want any breakfast? Coffee?" Katrina asked. It was early still, barely eight.

Rhiannon yawned. "Nah. You said she'll be on soon, right?"

"Yes." This had been the only time slot *Good Morning Live* had been willing to give, but it was a good one. Late enough to catch the parents whose kids had headed off to school, early enough so people might see it before they left for work. Media spurred media, too, so she was sure clips of this would shortly be aired by other outlets and on social media.

She drummed her fingers on her knee until Zeus batted at them. She was nervous about this part of her plan, more so than the errand she had to run after this.

One thing at a time.

Jia stirred. "I think this was a smart move. I'm sure whatever statement you gave to Mona was wonderful and from the heart."

Jia's confidence soothed Katrina's doubts and second-guessing. "I hope so."

"Smart, picking Mona to read your statement," Rhiannon remarked. "She's far removed from you, and clearly trustworthy, or she would have given you up long ago."

Katrina nodded, feeling a rush of affection for the older café owner. It was true—Mona could have revealed a lot about Katrina, and she'd kept mum. So had the other owners of the mom-and-pops Katrina frequented in the area. She had multiple little teams in her corner.

Jia straightened. "Unmute. It's on."

Knots in her belly, Katrina hit the mute button and reached into her pocket to clutch her rock tightly. With her other hand, she continued smoothing Zeus's fur. Double the coping behaviors.

The perky newscaster, the same one who had interviewed Becca, came on the screen. "We have a new development in the CafeBae story we brought you earlier in the week. For those who don't know, this was the meet-cute heard around the world." He paused. "Or was it? A growing backlash has started on social media against the original poster of this possible rom-com in the making, with some saying that this was a gross invasion of privacy."

It was a bit rich for users on the same platforms that had helped invade her privacy to now wonder over whether that should be okay, but such was life.

"Please welcome Mona Rodriguez, the owner of French Coast, the café where CafeBae started."

The split screen showed Mona, standing behind her counter, beaming. Katrina had told her to make sure she wore branded gear. If nothing else, the woman should get free advertising out of this. Mona had informed her traffic had already gone up significantly in the last week. "Hello." Mona waved at the camera, and then cleared her throat. "I have a prepared statement from the young woman in this clusterf—ah, the woman who was unfairly targeted during this phenomenon."

"Please, go ahead." The host gestured to her, and the screen expanded so it was only Mona.

Mona squinted at the phone in front of her. Katrina had written the statement quickly, had thought it best to speak from the heart, but now her stomach churned. Had she said enough? Or too much?

"Last week, I went to a café. Because it was crowded, I agreed to share a table with a young man. I did not know him. I have not seen him since then.

"I had no idea that while I politely chatted with the man, someone was taking my picture, eavesdropping, and fictionalizing our entire interaction. I did not consent to any part of that.

"I believe real-life fairy tales exist, but this is not one of them. This was not a movie. This was not a meet-cute. These were lies, and a gross trampling of my privacy. Strangers have spent days speculating about who I am, so I'll tell you: I am you. A real, regular person trying to live their life. I do my best. I hope you do, too.

"Everyone's face and bodies ought to belong to themselves. I humbly beg you: please respect my privacy. Let this story end. Thank you."

Mona looked up and sniffed. "And this part isn't in here, but I'll add that I know this young woman, and she is one of the finest people I have ever met. If anyone out there continues to hound her after this, they can kiss my—" a bleep blocked out the rest of Mona's sentence, but she looked satisfied to have gotten her point across.

The screen cut to the show host, who appeared suitably concerned. "Thank you, Ms. Rodriguez." The camera zoomed out to include a panel of the other show hosts. "What do you all think of this? Is there a right to privacy in this world of cell phones and—"

Katrina muted the television. It was Jas who broke the silence. "Excellent."

Rhiannon rose up on her elbows. "Yes, concur. Couldn't have written a better statement myself."

Katrina released a breath she hadn't known she was holding. Her shoulders straightened, renewed confidence flowing through her. "Thank you so much."

"The fairy tale part was a little mushy for me, of course, Princess Katrina."

Her cheeks turned pink at Rhiannon's teasing words. She carefully avoided looking at Jas. "The fairy tale isn't just about the princess," she said. "There's also the fairy godmother." She inclined her head to Rhiannon. "The little mouse friend." She gestured to Jia.

Jia sat up. "Wait a minute, how come she gets to be the fairy godmother, and I'm the mouse? We all know I'm the one who would dress the princess for the ball! Rhiannon would have her out there in a sweatshirt and kicks."

"The mice sew the princess's dress, they are the fashion designers," Katrina argued.

Jia pursed her lips. "If I must be a cute creature, I want to be the dragon, at least."

Katrina smiled. "Fine. You're the dragon friend."

Rhiannon stood and stretched, her shirt lifting to reveal her flat belly. "I'm bushed. Gonna go to bed and get in a nap before Samson gets here." She winked at Katrina. "Proud of you, seeing how you handled this whole thing."

"It's not over," she fretted. Who knew if this would reduce interest in her.

No. She stuck her hand into her pocket, over her cell phone. The text she'd sent her dad earlier made it feel weighty. He hadn't responded, but she assumed he'd show.

"You took the teeth out of it. If someone does reveal your identity now, it won't be because they're trying to reunite two lovers, but because they're assholes, and they'll be treated as such. Trust me, people will be discussing a symptom of a larger issue, not you." Rhiannon yawned. "Good night. Morning? Whatever." She moved to the door, and paused next to motionless, silent Jas. The two of them didn't interact that much, but they had a cordial, polite relationship.

The hug Rhiannon gave Jas was personal, though. "Samson said he'd come by your cottage in the afternoon, once I'm done with him." Rhiannon clapped Jas on the arm. "Thanks for taking care of her, big guy."

Jas raised a perfect eyebrow at Rhiannon. "It's my job."

Katrina felt that sharp blow, and filed it away. He didn't mean it like he'd said it. She knew he had feelings for her.

Or it's his deep sense of responsibility rearing its head, and he doesn't really have any personal feelings wrapped up in this. You're his client.

Her fingers tightened on her phone.

Jia uncoiled herself from the couch and bounced to her

feet. "I'm going to get to my Insta and break this down for my followers."

The door closed behind the two women, and some of Katrina's anxiety disappeared when Jas crossed the distance between them in a few steps. His hug felt so good and necessary and right.

She drew away and rubbed her nose against his. "Sometimes there's a prince in the fairy tale too."

Oh, there it was. Officially the mushiest thing she'd ever said in her whole damn life.

He didn't seem to mind, though, if his smile was any indication. Or the kiss he gave her.

The sound of the door opening had them both breaking apart and glancing guiltily in that direction. They found two pairs of big brown eyes on them, one almost black, one almost hazel.

"*Damn* it," Rhiannon said.

Jia's expression was smug. "I will take my hundred dollars in tens and fives, thank you." She waggled her fingers at them. "Go back to whatever you were doing, kids, Mama needed to earn some Vegas money."

Katrina pressed her forehead against Jas's chest and huffed out a laugh. After a second, he joined her. "We would have had to tell them sooner or later," Jas murmured.

They would? Because this was going somewhere? Her heart soared, but it was brought back to the present with the beep of the alarm on her phone. She pulled away from Jas. "I . . . can you drive me to the café?"

He cocked his head. "What? Why? So soon after the broadcast?"

She swallowed. She couldn't keep this a secret indefinitely, but she knew Jas wouldn't like her answer, or who she was planning to meet. "I'll tell you when we get there."

Chapter Twenty-Seven

Jas glanced at Katrina in the passenger seat of the car as he pulled into the alley behind the café. Her shoulders were straight, a frown creasing her brow as she looked pensively out the window. She'd changed into a pair of jeans and a sweatshirt when they'd arrived this morning. Her hair was pulled back from her face in a ponytail. A couple of light brown strands had fallen out to caress her cheeks.

He parked the car. She'd been silent for the entirety of the short drive, and that had only deepened the vague sense of unease in his gut. "You're not here to see Mona or Andy, are you." It was a statement, not a question.

She licked her lips. "No."

"Then who?"

He didn't miss that she opened the door and had one foot on the ground before she answered him. "My dad."

It took him a second to overcome the shock of that statement. By the time he'd closed his mouth and wrestled himself out of his belt, she was already out of the car and opening the back door for Doodle. The dog sauntered next to her mistress, their long legs eating the ground.

"Your father?"

"Yes."

Thomas King. He'd kept his dossier on the man updated, but that didn't mean much. "Why are you doing that?"

"It's something I have to do."

"I do not think that's a good idea." That was an understatement.

"I know. I need to talk to him." Katrina adjusted the bag on her shoulder.

"You should have told me." He went silent when Mona bustled into view. The woman beamed at both of them, but Jas nearly cursed. He couldn't argue with Katrina in front of other people.

"Whoa, who's this girl?" Mona held her hand out for Doodle to sniff, which the dog did daintily.

"This is Doodle."

"She's gorgeous." Mona straightened. "Did you watch? How did I do?"

"You were magnificent," Katrina said, and hugged her.

Mona graced Jas with a smile, and then turned back to Katrina. "I know you may not feel comfortable coming back here during business hours."

Katrina's smile froze, and his heart clenched.

"Please know my place is open to you whenever you wish." Mona dropped a key into Katrina's palm and closed her fingers over it.

Katrina swallowed. "Thank you. I appreciate it very much."

"Not a problem. You asked for my office." Mona briskly shepherded them to the small room. "I'll bring your guest here when he arrives."

"Thank you." Katrina moved behind the desk and pulled a stack of checks out of her bag. She proceeded to lay them out neatly on the table.

Jas took two steps to the desk. "Katrina. This is unwise. That man shouldn't be near you."

"He already knows about this place, and that I come here. Came here." She straightened, and her gaze flicked to him. There were ten of the checks lined up on the otherwise bare surface, facedown, little soldiers.

His confusion grew, but so did his concern. "This is a security issue," he tried again, desperate to change her mind. Doodle sauntered over and sat next to him. At least the dog was on his side. "You kept me in the dark until the last minute. I haven't investigated him. There's no extra security in place."

That stopped her. "I'm sorry, I know. I thought you and Rhiannon and Jia might try to change my mind, and I didn't want to be swayed." Loud footsteps came from the hallway and they both looked in that direction. "Please. Trust me." She placed her phone on the surface of the desk and sat behind it.

He looked at Doodle, who gazed back at him with a weary expression on her face, as if in commiseration.

He marshaled his face into expressionless disinterest when the door opened. Back to being a shadow, unnoticeable.

"Katrina!" The older man swept past Mona and came barreling into the room.

It was hard for Jas not to sneer. Thomas was still handsome, his blond hair now a pure silver. He'd given his daughter a solid bone structure and frame, as well as his sharp cheekbones, but his piercing blue eyes held a cynical coldness Katrina's brown gaze lacked. His delight to see her felt like a thinly applied mask.

Jas emerged out of the shadows. Thomas faltered at spotting Jas and the dog, but his face grew annoyed when Jas approached him and gestured for him to spread his arms. "Is this really necessary?" Thomas barked.

"It is if you want to see her," Jas replied, before Katrina could speak. He didn't really expect the guy to be packing a weapon, but this was his job, even if Katrina had tried to hamstring him.

Plus, he bet it would be galling for Thomas to be searched by the help.

Thomas grumbled, but he let the pat-down commence. Jas pulled a pen knife out of Thomas's pocket. It was a harmless small blade that wouldn't do much damage, but Jas kept it out of sheer pettiness. He stepped away.

Thomas opened his mouth, but something in Jas's expression must have been forbidding enough to shut him up.

Katrina gestured at the seat across from her at Mona's desk. "Sit, please."

Thomas shot Jas another wary look.

Now that the man was seated, Jas felt free to melt back into the shadows. All he wanted to do was run Thomas out of the room and take Katrina home, where she could be safe. He clenched his fists. How could she not tell him about this?

"It was so good to hear from you," Thomas gushed. He glanced around the office and Jas had to fight not to tackle the man over the avariciousness in his gaze. "What a lovely city. And an expensive one. Did your husband leave you a home here?"

"No." Katrina didn't elaborate.

Thomas rallied. "Well, good for you, buying a place for yourself. Seems like the little nest egg I put together from your career really paid off."

Her smile was thin. "The nest egg wasn't that great once you'd skimmed your take off the top."

He gave a wounded pout. "I only took my fair share as your manager, Katrina."

Katrina ran her tongue over her teeth. "Look, why don't we get this over with? No need to waste time on pleasantries neither of us means."

The mask slipped. "You summoned me here."

Katrina crossed her arms over the table. "Because you tried to blackmail me. I simply wanted to make sure you got your money."

THERE WERE FEW things Katrina had ever found more satisfying than catching her father off guard, she decided. Blunt truth was the best weapon she could possibly ever use against this lying snake of a man.

A quickly cut-off growl caught her attention, and she spared a look at Doodle, but maybe Jas had made that noise?

His fists were clenched, his eyes glittering as they regarded Thomas. Those were the only signs of his disquiet. Otherwise, he was still and emotionless.

"Blackmail's an ugly word."

"It's an accurate one." She paused. She'd spent years rehearsing how this meeting would go, but now the path seemed clear, she knew exactly what she wanted to say.

She tapped her pen on the desk. Her father's gaze went straight to it, and she didn't stop the rhythmic noise. She hated sounds like this when she was working, but she was well aware he hated them all the time. "Congratulations. You've made a nice little life for yourself in Vancouver. A house, a community, friends you go to the track with. You even have a girlfriend, Lord help her."

"Are you spying on me?"

"I've kept tabs all these years. In case you decided to come crawling back, hunting for more money. That's why you're here now, right?"

"I—"

Katrina gestured at the checks spread in front of her. Like Jas, she'd shoved a great deal of her rage and bitterness down over the years, but she welcomed it now. "Do you remember this game? You used to play it with me, only it was food back then. You'd take a plate away if I refused to do whatever you wanted. Auditions, voice lessons, piano, photo shoots. If I behaved, then I got rewarded with the basic fucking thing you were legally obligated to give me."

If I can go to ten places, then I can date someone.

She blinked. Whoa, now was not the time to have a

therapeutic breakthrough, but Jesus. She was still motivating herself in that absurd, if-I-do-x, then-I-get-y mind-set, wasn't she?

She made a mental note to talk the implications of all that through with Andy later. For now . . .

She touched the check on the far left. "Ten million dollars. That's what that ransom was for, right?" She touched the paper on the far right. "Over here, one million dollars." She sat back. "I will pay you if you admit you tried to blackmail me yesterday." She tapped her phone, and the recording icon lit up. She made sure he could see it.

Sweat had broken out on Thomas's brow. "There's nothing to admit!"

Doodle's deep bark caught everyone's attention. The pup came to her feet and took a menacing step, teeth bared, a growl rumbling in her throat. For the first time, Katrina could see why some people may be startled by her dog's size. "D—"

"Death, heel." Jas's sharp command cut through the dog's growl.

Death. Katrina hid her smile, but Doodle did heel despite the strange name. She supposed *Doodle* wasn't very intimidating.

"Don't raise your voice to Katrina again," Jas said coolly. "Death doesn't like it, and neither do I."

Katrina cleared her throat, delighted despite the tense atmosphere. "Where were we? Ah yes. Confess to the blackmail, and you can take the money and go. You never contact me again. You don't tell anyone anything about me. My name never so much as passes your lips. If it does . . . well, I make sure that everyone in the world knows what a piece of shit you are." Katrina's eyes widened. "Imagine that. People discovering that CuteCafeGirl is a former cover model who disappeared would be titillating, but finding out her sordid history, how awful her father was? How he manipulated and controlled her for years? How he blackmailed her?" She tsked. "Have you ever gone viral? It's not everything it's cracked up to be. You can avoid that, though. Admit that you're blackmailing me."

"I will not."

"Cool. I take a million away for every second you waste my time."

"This is preposterous," Thomas spluttered.

She picked up the ten-million-dollar check and ripped it in half. "Nine million left. Don't worry, the millions you lose will be donated to charity," she added, almost as an after-thought. "I'm not a monster."

"I'm not incriminating myself on tape."

Another check ripped. "Eight million."

Thomas scrubbed his face. "How can I trust you won't go to the police with that recording?"

"You can't." Another rip. "Seven million."

Another check bit the dust. "Six million." This was so sat-isfying. "Five million."

"Okay, stop. Wait. Let me think."

"No." Rip. "Four million."

"Fine! Fine, I'll take it."

Katrina paused with her hand on the four-million-dollar check. "Say it."

His face contorted, like he was swallowing something bitter. She hoped it did taste like that, like the grossest medicine a person could imbibe. "I tried to blackmail you."

"Say you were a shitty father." She paused. "And a worse manager."

He repeated the words through gritted teeth.

"Thanks. That was lovely." She slid a paper across the table. "Sign this."

"What is it?"

"Basically everything you just said, in writing. I like to cover my bases."

He scowled, but signed it.

She waved the check in front of him. "You are officially gagged. Are we clear?"

"Yes. Fine." Thomas grabbed the check and tucked it into his suit pocket. He rose to his feet and sneered. "Goodbye, you crazy bitch."

Chapter Twenty-Eight

I THINK WE'RE DONE." If nothing else, Jas was done. Katrina's cheeks were flushed, her eyes sparkling, her back straight. She looked magnificent, not cowed, but he'd be damned if he'd let Thomas insult her, especially after she'd given him millions.

Jas grabbed the older man's arm harder than he needed to, and marched him to the door. "Don't say another word," he breathed as the man opened his mouth, no doubt ready to launch another insult at his daughter. Doodle—or Death, he'd had to think quick—obediently followed behind them.

Mona had left the back door open. "Oops," Jas murmured, as he knocked Thomas into the frame of the door.

"Oh, so sorry," he added, when he stuck his foot out as they descended the back steps. After he fell, Thomas scrambled to his feet and glared at him. His cheek was scraped, blood welling.

Jas had a flashback to Katrina all those years ago, injured and bleeding, and he felt a sudden, violent urge to destroy Thomas, even though the man hadn't been responsible for that particular wound. Something in his eyes must have telegraphed his rage, because Thomas stumbled backward, tripping on his own feet and landing on his ass in the alley.

Jas didn't believe in violence as a rule, but if anyone deserved to get knocked around a little, it was *this* guy.

"Let me help you up." Jas bent down and grabbed the older man by his shirtfront and turned and slammed him against his own car, a bright red brand-new Ferrari. Jas brought his lips close to the man's ear. "If you don't leave Katrina alone for the rest of your life, being smeared isn't the only thing you'll have to fear. I will kill you. But first I'll make it so you beg to die. Are we clear?"

Doodle barked and growled behind Jas, as if to add her own contribution to the threat.

He didn't release Thomas until the man gave a short nod. "Apologies," Jas added, when he opened the car door into Thomas's midsection. "Have a nice drive home." He shoved the still-doubled-over man into the vehicle and shut the door, only narrowly missing Thomas's foot.

Jas waited until the guy left. Life had been so much easier when he'd stomped all his feelings down. This swirling mess of worry and concern and anger was rough.

He'd deal with the concern first. Then the rest.

KATRINA WAS BENT over, head between her legs, when she heard the office door open. Jas. She could tell by his footsteps.

His shiny black loafers came into view, along with Doodle's four brown paws, and then he was crouching down in front of her, lifting her chin to inspect her face. Doodle licked her cheeks. Jas pulled out his handkerchief, and did a better job of drying her tears. "Are you okay?" he asked.

"Yes," she sobbed.

"I don't believe you."

She took a deep, shaky breath. "I hate the thought that that man is my family."

He stroked her hair back from her face. "What's that saying again? The blood of the covenant is thicker than the water of the womb? You chose your family, and it's not him."

She took the handkerchief and blew her nose. He held out a gold watch. She stared at the Rolex. "What . . . ?"

"It'll take him a while to realize he doesn't have it."

Her mouth dropped open. "You took my dad's *watch*?"

"I was going to take back the check, but figured that may cause some problems down the line."

Dumbly, she accepted the watch. It was a Submariner. Pricey. "What on earth do I do with this?"

"I don't know." He bared his teeth. "I couldn't let him leave feeling like he'd gotten away with everything. It's not a four-million-dollar watch, but it's an expensive one. Pawn it."

An odd urge to laugh came over her. "I'll give it to Mona. A thank you gift." Her smile came from deep within her soul. Yes, it had cost her millions of dollars, but now it was done. Her dad wouldn't come back. And if he did, she had leverage. He liked his reputation. He wouldn't want it smeared.

She inhaled. Most important, she'd done this herself.

The shame that she'd harbored over Hardeep saving her

slipped away. It had taken her years to get to this point. She would never have been able to do it in her twenties. It was truly okay for her to have gotten help when she hadn't had these financial or emotional resources.

She smiled through her tears. "I did it, Jas."

"You sure did it."

The unusual inflection in his tone had her glancing up. "Is something wrong?"

"Is something wrong?" He laughed, and it was a hard laugh she'd never really heard from him. "To quote you, what, and I cannot stress this enough, the fuck were you thinking?"

She squinted up at him. "I don't want to live my life waiting for the other shoe to drop any longer. I wanted him gone."

Jas took a step back and placed his hands on his hips. "What if I hadn't been here?" he asked, his voice raspy.

"You were here," she said simply.

"What if he'd attacked you, and I couldn't stop him?"

"Physical violence isn't his style." No, it had always been psychological and emotional abuse her dad had gone with. "In any case, you and Doodle could have handled anything."

He raked his hands through his hair. "You should have *told* me. I'm your security."

Oh dear. He was really upset. "Okay." She held out her hand, which Doodle licked, then nuzzled. "You know what? You're right. I should have told you."

"Don't patronize me."

"I'm not." She wasn't only trying to placate him. Her common sense had been mildly blinded by her emotions and anticipation of this showdown.

She may have also been thinking of Jas more like her boyfriend and less like her security. Which wasn't an excuse she particularly wanted to share with him. "I see your point. You're my bodyguard, it's your job to know about this stuff. Had it been anyone else, I would have given you a heads-up. I didn't think that through, and I'm sorry." She licked her lips. "I needed to do this, very badly, for myself, and I think my anger blinded me to the practical logistics of this meeting."

Deep lines bracketed his mouth. "You can't keep things from me."

She paused. Something about that command scraped. A year ago or even a month ago, she might have stuffed her annoyance down, but she didn't now. "I agree I should have shared this with you," she said. "But you can't tell me I can't keep things from you when you regularly keep things from me."

"Don't turn this around on me."

"Don't . . . I'm not turning this around on you. I'm bringing up a legit issue. You know everything about me. Getting you to talk about yourself is like pulling teeth." It wasn't until she uttered the words and felt a boulder fall off her shoulders that she realized how much this had upset her. "I don't even know what you like to eat for breakfast, damn it."

"Breakfast again?" He shook his head. "I told you—"

"You told me you like waffles because I like making them, that doesn't mean you like them for the sake of liking them!" She tried to control her rising voice. This wasn't about breakfast, or rather, not just about breakfast.

"I don't understand this. It is my job to know you."

A client. "Am I a job or am I something else?"

That stymied him. "What?"

"I heard you telling your brother that I was your client. Is that all I am? Or have things changed?"

"When did I . . ." His mouth fell open. "Hold up. Hold up. You speak Punjabi?"

She waved that away. "Enough of it."

"Wait—"

"What am I?"

Jas raked his hands through his hair. "You're not only my job."

"Then you gotta talk. You can't shove everything down. I'm so worried you're so focused on meeting my needs you'll never tell me your own." Her knuckles had turned white, her fists were clenched so tight. "It's a pattern. It's so hard for you to tell anyone what you need. Your family, your friends. That's important, to have that support system. It's important, for you to have that support."

"Katrina—" His phone rang, and he cursed and yanked it out. His face grew pale as he read the text.

Katrina sat forward. "What is it?"

"My grandfather's sick."

Her hand fluttered to her throat. That robust, energetic man? "Oh no. What's wrong?"

"I don't know. He says it's not an emergency." He typed out a reply, then looked up. "I should go."

"Of course." Katrina grabbed her phone. "But you can't drive, you haven't slept. Take the car to the airport."

"No. I'll take you home first."

She bit her tongue. Now wasn't the time to get into how he was doing the exact thing she'd just told him she was concerned about, seeing to her needs instead of his. It would be quicker to humor him. "Fine." She came to her feet and opened an app on her phone. "I'll get you a flight."

She waited for him to argue, but he was silent. "I hope Andrés is okay," she said.

He held the door open for her. "Me too."

Chapter Twenty-Nine

You're faking being sick now? Grandpa, come on."

His grandfather's lashes fluttered open at Jas's flat pronouncement. Andrés should have looked weak and small in the hospital bed, but it was hard to dull the ruddy flush in the man's face or his big size.

Still, Jas supposed Andrés could appear fine and still be sick. Unfortunately for his grandpa, Jas had run into his mother downstairs in the hospital. Undoubtedly the man had dragged his daughter in as coconspirator, because his mother's lips had been twitching up a storm as she'd covered up for her dad.

Andrés coughed. "What's that?" he said hoarsely. "I can't hear you."

"I thought you had the flu." Jas dropped down into the chair next to the bed. "The flu affects your hearing?"

"It does when you have the flu and an, um, sinus infection." Andrés coughed again.

Jas placed his palm on his grandfather's forehead. "You're cold as ice."

"The fever comes and goes."

"What the hell, Grandpa? This is extreme and ridiculous, even for you. I haven't slept all night. I don't have any extra clothes with me."

"I can loan you some clothes for as long as you're here," Andrés croaked.

Jas opened his mouth to answer, but a nurse came in. She smiled brightly at Jas. "Sir, can you wait outside for a few minutes?"

He gave his grandpa a suspicious look, but he couldn't call the older man a liar in front of witnesses. He slipped out of the room and pulled his phone out. He wanted to text Katrina, but they'd left things far too unfinished. They needed to talk in person.

He groaned when he saw Lorne's text. They'll announce the pardon tomorrow. I'm sorry, Jas.

He hit reply. That's okay, he typed. Except it wasn't okay. *It's so hard for you to tell anyone what you need.*

He looked up and down the deserted hallway, then hit Lorne's name. She picked up on the second ring. "Hey. Sorry to deliver the bad news via text. I tried to call, but it went straight to voicemail."

"I'm visiting my family, the reception's spotty here." He paused. "It's certain?"

"Yes. I don't know if you've seen the news at all but the press is already spinning it as the vindication of an American patriot."

Jas stared blindly at the blank off-white wall. "What

about us?" If McGuire was the patriot, what were they, the ones who had stopped him from murdering an innocent? The ones who carried the scars of that night?

"We're forgotten. Unless we make it so we're not."

"You want to go to the press."

"Yes. There shouldn't be only one narrative out there. I have two reporters chomping to get the story."

He closed his eyes, stomach churning. He had to back Lorne up. That was what was right.

What do you need?

"I don't want to talk to anyone," he said, enunciating every word carefully. "I can't go through this again. I can't bring those memories up. The nightmares. They're so bad, Lorne." His voice cracked on her name.

"I absolutely understand. I have to do this, but I get that you can't." Her tone was extremely gentle. "You had my back that night. I'll have yours now. I'll do my best to run interference so no one comes looking for you."

He released a careful, shaky breath, the anxiety and fear leaving him. A dogged reporter might run him down, but he'd deal with that if and when it happened. "Thank you."

"No worries." She hesitated. "Listen, you can tell me it's none of my business. Are the nightmares a regular thing?"

"Sometimes."

Lorne made a sympathetic noise. "For me too."

He scuffed his shoe on the linoleum. "Yeah?"

"Absolutely. You're not alone."

Jas swiveled away as a man bustled past him. He waited

until the hallway was clear before he spoke, his voice low. "I feel alone sometimes."

"Have you ever tried therapy?"

"Briefly." Right after he'd come back home, before he'd gone to work for Hardeep. After that, his therapy had simply been to run away and forget.

"It helped me. Especially with the nightmares. I still go in for a tune-up." She cleared her throat. "I can ask around, send you some names of good ones near you."

He shifted. Bikram had offered the same. If multiple people were going to bombard him with referrals, he had to call someone. "Might not be such a bad idea."

"Roger that. Hey, I'll text you the dates I'll be in California, too. We'll get that drink."

"Sounds good. Thank you for handling everything."

"Not a problem. We all deal with things in the ways best for us. Take care."

He hung up. He didn't know how long he stood there, slumped against the wall, the relief like a drug in his veins.

"Son. How are you?"

Jas straightened. "Fine, Dad. Good to see you." He hugged Gurjit, squeezing him extra-tight. His stepfather looked like an older version of Bikram, with the same stocky build. Jas inhaled, the familiar scent of Old Spice calming him.

"Whoa there. You okay?" His father's big hand patted him on the back.

Jas hugged him tighter. "Yes. Everything is great."

Gurjit paused, then whispered in his ear. "Your mother

filled me in regarding dinner the other night. I'm proud of you, son."

Jas coughed to clear the frog in his throat, then stepped back. "Thanks." Gurjit was dressed in khakis and a black button-down shirt, which told Jas that his father must have driven here straight from work. The man didn't wear anything but jeans when he was off.

Gurjit examined him closely. "You look tired."

"Haven't slept much. I drove home, then had to turn right around." He gestured to the door. "Give it to me straight. He's faking, right? This is some elaborate ruse? That nurse is in there chatting with him, not taking his vitals?"

His stepfather's face went blank, but his gaze darted around the hallway, which was a dead giveaway that he was looking for his wife. He scratched his head. "Uh . . ."

"This is completely ridiculous. I expect this sort of thing from Mom and Grandpa, but you? You drove all this way from the city for these shenanigans?"

Gurjit winced, but didn't confirm or deny anything. At some other time, Jas might admire the man's loyalty to his wife, but not today.

The nurse opened Andrés's door and smiled at them. "You can go in."

"How much is he paying you for this farce?" Jas demanded of the nurse, and her eyes widened.

Gurjit's laugh was strangled. "Sorry, ma'am." He herded Jas inside the room and shut the door behind them.

Andrés smirked at them from his bed, clearly having heard Jas. "Done embarrassing yourself, boy?" He coughed.

It was the fakest cough Jas had ever heard. "You are not sick, and I want to know what's going on."

"I *am* sick, and you can ask my doctor, if you want. The nurse said he should be by shortly."

"You know what?" Jas rocked back on his heels. "We don't have to wait for him. I'll go ask one of the other doctors. Or at the nurses' station. Surely they can tell me all about my dear grandfather's flu."

Andrés glared at Jas, and Jas glared right back, both of them silent.

Gurjit's exhale broke the standoff. "Andrés. I think the jig is up."

"I don't know what you're talking about," Andrés tried.

"He's going to go out there and find a doctor who isn't your old housekeeper's son, Andrés. Or a nurse who wasn't in the delivery room when Tara was born. Tell Jasvinder the truth now." This was probably the same tone Gurjit used on his most mischievous students.

Jas strode to his grandfather's bedside. "You better have a damn good reason for—"

"I was scared you wouldn't come back!"

Jas's mouth gaped open at that admission. "What?"

His grandfather folded his arms over his chest. He looked decidedly not sick now. "I said, I didn't know if you'd come back. For the awards ceremony." His voice dropped. "Or ever."

Jas sat down in the chair with a thunk. "So you were going to pretend to be bedridden until the awards ceremony?"

His grandfather nodded.

"This is the most outrageous thing you've done in a long time. I hope you know that. I am so angry with you."

"I told them it was a bad idea," Gurjit interjected. "So did Bikram."

"Damn it, Grandpa. I said I would try. How could you—" He closed his eyes, hearing Katrina's voice in his head.

He hadn't told anyone in his family what was really going on in his head for over a dozen years. He had deliberately avoided spending extended time with them, even when it was a huge occasion, like Bikram's engagement. How could Jas think one dinner would make his grandpa trust he would actually try to come for this thing that was so important to him?

He clasped his hands between his knees. "I'm sorry I've disappointed you so much over the years—"

"No." Andrés cleared his throat and shot a glance at Gurjit, who nodded his encouragement. "I was disappointed you weren't a carbon copy of me, it's true." His smile was the gentlest Jas had ever seen it. "You know, the first generation that comes here, the immigrants, they keep their head down. They do their best to fit in. And then the first generation who are born here, I think we feel like we have so much to prove, we have to make all of our parents' sacrifices worth it." He sniffed. "I got so caught up in proving my family's worth, I lost sight of what we want for the ones who come after us. The American Dream, eh? Pursuing whatever they want. Even if that means it's not what I want."

Jas cleared his throat. Now he was the one who sounded hoarse. "You didn't let me finish. I know I've disappointed you by not communicating with you as well as I could have. I'm going to be better, more honest. I want to be in your lives more."

Gurjit coughed. His eyes were suspiciously misty. He squeezed Jas's shoulder.

"If you do come to the parade, I got you some really good noise-canceling headphones," Andrés said gruffly. "So it won't be too loud. And I already cleared it with the committee to keep the backstage area clear so you can watch from the wings. You won't have to be in the crowd. We'll have a car waiting by the back door so you can leave if you need to. Any other accommodations you want, I'll do. If I can't do them, I'll find someone who will."

If his grandfather could get multiple people to help him pull off a ruse like this, Jas didn't doubt he'd move heaven and earth in this community to get Jas every accommodation possible. "That sounds great," he managed.

"If that's still not enough for you, I would love it if you would come home anyway then. We can have a small party after. Family only."

The pressure lifted off his shoulders with those words was immense. "In that case, I'll come. I promise."

"I love you, you know. I don't say it enough, because I assumed you knew I love you. But that's the problem. Sometimes we think a person doesn't need to hear something because it's obvious, because they know what's in our hearts. But that's not how the world works. We have to say the things." He cleared his throat. "So, I love you. I want you to be happy."

Jas swallowed the lump in his throat. "I love you, too. I am still extremely mad at you about this ruse."

"Fair."

"I don't quite understand how you pulled this off. Is this legal?"

"Pshaw." His grandfather puffed out his chest. "I am the Peach Prince. Favors have been called in for this."

Jas glanced around. "Do we need to leave?"

His grandfather grinned. "It was lots of favors. We can stay here for a minute. Open that drawer, son."

Jas opened the nightstand drawer and couldn't help but chuckle at the bottle of scotch inside. "Grandpa, honestly." He glanced up when there was no response, to find Gurjit and Andrés exchanging a look.

"Haven't heard you laugh in a while," his dad explained.

Aw, jeez. Jas had something in his eye. "You'll hear it more, I think." He pulled out the bottle. "Who wants a drink?"

Chapter Thirty

I LOVE YOU."

"No, I love you."

"I love you more."

"Ugh." Jia dropped her phone on her stomach and glared at Katrina and Rhiannon. "Being sober around drunk people is so annoying. Is this how Lakshmi feels when she's around me?"

Katrina laughed and rested her head on Rhiannon's shoulder. They sat on their patio, enjoying the cool evening air and relaxing after dinner. Katrina had grilled burgers for them. Then they'd opened the wine. Then they'd drunk the wine.

And now she and Rhiannon were ensconced side by side in a chaise lounge, the chair too small to really hold both of them, but that was okay. Katrina did love cuddling.

"How is the internet doing, Jia?" Rhiannon's words weren't slurred yet, so Katrina figured they hadn't drunk enough wine.

"Pretty good, actually. The internet is amazing." Jia twirled a thread on the hem of her dress between her fingers. She wore a flowy embroidered caftan this evening. She looked like a garden princess.

"Amazing," Katrina echoed sardonically, but she was amazed at how quickly her statement had been embraced. Think pieces upon think pieces had been furiously written all day.

She was sure there was an ugly section of the internet that had sneered at her earnest plea for privacy, but she wasn't living for them. She had a web of people who had protected her, even if some people hadn't. Her family. People who, even if she was exposed, would shelter her.

"It helps that those Japanese zoo escape drills went viral." Rhiannon tucked Zeus under her chin and scratched the kitten. Doodle was happily snoozing in the garden. "You couldn't hold anyone's interest, really, when up against a man in a panda suit running away from tranq guns."

"So glad I'm less attractive than a six-foot-tall man-panda." Katrina stretched her legs out. "I hope the couple and Ross don't get too much hate, though."

"Ugh, Lakshmi's right, you're so nice," Rhiannon said.

"I'm not nice. There's nothing wrong with giving people the benefit of the doubt. Perhaps they'll learn from this and grow."

"Too. Nice."

"For what it's worth, I'm on Rhiannon's side. You are too nice." Jia came to her feet. "I'll get you guys some water."

Rhiannon set the cat on the ground. "I don't mean anything bad when I say you're nice, by the way. I think it takes a certain kind of strength, when the world is hateful or mean, to come out on the other side with your heart and your kindness and your humanity intact. I honestly don't know how you can be so optimistic after everything you've been through."

Katrina gazed at the sprawling city in front of them, the sun setting over the ocean in the distance. She'd bought this house partially for the privacy, but mostly for the view. "I think I have to be hopeful *because* of everything I've been through. That doesn't mean I'm not angry. But if I didn't have hope or believe in others, what's the point?" She shook her head. "Humans aren't meant to be indefinitely bent into pretzels. We bend until we snap, and then we put ourselves back together and hold steady until someone or something bends us again. Every part of that process requires strength, and hope, I think." *Even the breaking. Even if you need help putting yourself back together.*

Rhiannon nodded. "I get it. Everything may not be perfect all the time, but that doesn't mean you shouldn't hope for more."

"Happiness is a radical act."

"What?"

Katrina's smile was self-conscious. "I saw it on this sign in French Coast and it kinda spoke to me. I was raised to make sure everyone else was happy. So now, when I'm truly happy, it feels . . . radical. To be happy, or even to have the possibility of happiness, when the world tells you you shouldn't, it's downright subversive."

Rhi's eyes shone. "Like you're *showing* everyone who made you unhappy."

Katrina nodded.

"I used to tell myself success was the best revenge. But I like your saying better."

"Whatever works."

Rhiannon took her wineglass, set it on the table, and then hugged Katrina tight. "Cinnamon roll. Too good, too pure for this world," she whispered against Katrina's hair. "I'll protect you with my life."

Katrina laughed. "Hopefully it'll never come to that."

Jia came back out to the patio and handed them each a water bottle. "Drink this, or you'll be miserable tomorrow. Now, who did we drunk-text while I was gone?"

"No one. Samson had to go to bed early." Rhiannon gave Katrina a questioning look.

She rolled her eyes. "Jas is with his sick grandpa, guys!"

"Have you heard from him at all?" Rhiannon asked.

"He texted me when he got to Yuba City."

Jia wrinkled her nose. "That's it?"

"Yes." Katrina took a sip of her water. "What more do you want?"

"I dunno, your smooching this morning looked way more fiery than *hey plane landed* texts."

"Like I said, his grandfather's sick."

"He's not dead, right?"

"Jia," Rhiannon snapped.

"Sorry, sorry. What I mean is, you could still text him a supportive emoji. A kissy face or a hug."

Rhiannon stuck her tongue in her cheek. "Or the eggplant."

"I'm definitely not doing that last one."

"What's up with you guys? You haven't figured stuff out yet?" Rhiannon asked.

"No." Katrina made a frustrated noise. "He doesn't say anything. That's the problem. I know him and love him, but I can't read his mind."

Rhiannon's lips pursed in a soundless whistle. "Play back what you just said."

Katrina pressed her fingers to her temple. She'd said what she said, and she meant it. "I know. I do love him. I think I have for a long time."

"Omg. You should ask him how he feels," Jia whispered, clutching her hands to her chest.

Rhiannon shook her head. "No, she shouldn't have to badger him about how he feels. He should be able to talk about his feelings."

"Even if he does, I'm worried he won't be telling me the truth. What if he says he loves me because it's what I want to hear?" She shook her head. "You guys, he is so damn devoted. It all feels so one-sided, like he's seeing to my every need, and I can't do the same for him."

There was silence for a minute. Rhiannon put her water bottle down. "So let me get this straight: you, a heterosexual woman, in our current modern dating hellscape, are complaining that the man you are seeing is . . . *too* selfless."

"I love you very much, Katrina," Jia remarked. "But please don't be offended if I kind of hate you right now."

"Samson is almost a saint, but I'm with you, Jia." Rhiannon made a disgusted noise.

Katrina choked out a laugh. "Okay, well. It sounds silly when you say it like that."

"Boy, does it." Rhiannon squinted at her. "Look, I'm still not entirely sure that Samson's as good as he seems. Like, I'm finally pretty sure he's not being nice to me so he can kill me, but who can tell? That's the whole leap-of-faith you kept pushing me to take."

Katrina's smile was faint. "I have new respect for the leap I was telling you to make."

"You have no idea how terrifying it is." Rhiannon paused. "Isn't it entirely possible that Jas is so devoted to you because he loves you too?"

She made a face. "I don't know."

Rhiannon gestured between them. "I mean, we love you, and we are very cool people. He would be in excellent company."

"Ha. Right."

The chair they sat on rocked a little as Jia perched on the arm. Her slender hand came to rest on Katrina's shoulder. "How long has Jas been with you?"

"Years." It was hard to remember a time when Jas hadn't been with her. Or rather, she didn't want to remember the time before Jas was with her.

"You've cooked him breakfast every morning for every one of those years, right?" Jia asked.

"Yeah, that's not—"

"What I'm saying is, yes, he should tell you more about his needs, especially if you feel like things are getting one-sided, but pretty sure if he does, you'll trip over yourself to make it equal, and then he'll trip over himself to do the same." Jia's smile was fond. "I've never seen two people more suited to each other, to be honest. You're equally considerate and kind. In fact, you might have a spiral death match to out-kind each other. I only have one reservation."

"What's that?"

"If you get married, you cannot hyphenate your last name." Jia wrinkled her nose. "God, Katrina King-Singh? You'll sound like a Dr. Seuss character."

Katrina and Rhiannon both chuckled.

"It's not funny, names are so important." Jia pursed her lips. "Anyway, send a text, open the door. See if he'll walk through it and be emotionally vulnerable."

Rhiannon toasted the younger woman. "Good advice, Jia."

Katrina gave a decisive nod, and pulled out her phone. "What if I say *How's the*, and . . ." She squinted at the tiny emoji keyboard. Phew, she must have drunk more than she'd thought. "Peach. For peach farm! His grandpa."

"Wait, no!" Jia grasped her arm. "Think what a peach means, Katrina."

She gasped. What had she been thinking? "I sent it."

Jas's phone dinged. He picked it up from where he'd dropped it on the hospital bed and peered at the display. He was on his third scotch, and he felt great.

He read Katrina's text once, then again, trying to puzzle it out.

His grandfather broke off from telling a story to a laughing Gurjit. "Ooooh. Is that Katrina?"

The alcohol had lowered Jas's inhibitions. "It is, but I don't understand this text."

"What does it say?"

"It says, *How's your peach?*" He glanced up.

"Oh, son," his grandfather said with pity. "Even I know what the peach emoji stands for."

Jas's eyes widened as realization dawned. "Oh, uh." His phone dinged again and he snorted. "Okay, this makes more sense. *I meant, how's your grandpa?*"

"She's asking about *my* peach?"

"Ew." Jas made a face. "No."

Andrés sniffed. "You don't have to say *no* like that."

He kept reading. "*Sorry, peach for peach farm.* There, that's cleared up."

He typed out his reply. My grandpa faked the whole thing to get me to come home because he was scared I wouldn't come to his ceremony. I'll be back tomorrow.

RHIANNON READ JAS's reply out loud. "Well, his grandfather sounds like he's a few peaches short of a—"

"He's very sweet," Katrina said repressively.

"Okay, so respond." Jia nudged her.

"What should I say back?"

"Whatever you want."

Katrina thought about it for a minute. "*I miss you.*"

"Wait, that's way too vulnerable," Rhiannon yelped.

Katrina cringed. "I hit send again."

"Katrina!" Rhiannon swiped the phone out of her hand. "We gotta work on this. You have a real problem with premature transmissions."

I miss you.

Jas sucked in a deep breath.

"What did she send now? More butts?" his grandfather demanded.

Gurjit leaned over and looked at his phone before Jas could hide it. "Aw. She says she misses him." His mustache jumped in delight. "Jas! This is so sweet. When do I get to meet her?"

"She is very sweet. Think carefully about what to say in reply, son. You have to woo her," his grandpa warned.

Gurjit scoffed at Andrés. "Let the boy write whatever's in his heart."

Jas tapped the phone against his leg. "I can't tell her what's in my heart."

"Why not?"

"Because . . . we kissed for the first time like a minute ago. It's too soon."

"So you have strong feelings for her! Listen, when you know, you know," Gurjit said dreamily.

"I changed my mind," Andrés counseled. "Tell her how you feel. If you don't you'll regret it. There's lots of things I regret not saying to your grandma."

"Are there things you regret saying?"

"Yes. But less of those."

Jas looked down at his phone and typed all the words in his soul. I love you.

Delete.

He hesitated, then typed again. I love you.

Delete. No. That was something to be said in person, not over text.

He typed, a third time.

He only started panicking after he hit send.

Chapter Thirty-One

"WHAT DOES IT say?" Rhiannon shoved Jia aside, but Katrina held the phone against her chest protectively.

"It's private."

"You don't want help answering?" Jia bounced. "This is so exciting."

"What did it say?" Rhiannon repeated, this time asking Jia.

"I don't know, she was too fast."

"Katrina, we are *invested*."

Katrina came to her feet and walked away from her friends, and then reread the message.

I love you. I always have.

Holy motherfucking shit balls.

She couldn't stop the leap in her chest, every romantic part of her bursting into action. She placed the cursor in the reply box, then paused. She did need help. "He told me he loves me."

"Oh my God." Jia clutched her face. "Say you love him too!"

Katrina started typing, then deleted. "I don't know."

"Okay, now that he's made himself vulnerable, you are free to make yourself vulnerable," Rhiannon lectured. "But not in excess of his vulnerability. That's the rule."

Katrina waved the phone. "Tell me what to say."

"Okay, right." Rhiannon leapt to her feet. "*Thank you very much. I return your affections.*"

Katrina tried that, and immediately erased it. "Never mind. I'll do this on my own."

"WHAT DID SHE say now?" Andrés demanded.

Jas dropped his head in his hands and stared at the phone in his lap. The scotch had made his head fuzzy, but not fuzzy enough to dull the pain of this torture. "Dots. Three little dots." *Evil dots.*

"What does that mean?"

Gurjit hushed Andrés. "She's typing."

Typing, typing, typing. Forever.

When the text did come, Jas almost passed out releasing the breath he was holding. "Well?" Gurjit clutched Andrés's hand. "What's the verdict?"

His smile could probably light up the hospital.

I love you, too. Hurry up and come home.

"Grandpa?"

"Yes?"

"Got any pilots who owe you a favor?"

Chapter Thirty-Two

Sleep came slowly to Katrina, but the alcohol helped. She would have slept straight through to morning but a noise woke her up.

Her eyes popped open. It was still dark in her bedroom, but someone was knocking on her door.

She breathed deep. *Don't freeze.* Katrina reached under her pillow and groped for the little spray bottle she kept there, because she was paranoid as hell. She crept to the door. "Who is it?"

"Jas."

What! Delight shot through her. She flung the door open.

The reciprocal excitement on his face flipped to alarm. "Don't shoot. Not again."

Katrina followed his gaze to the pepper spray in her hand. "Never again. I didn't know who was at the door." She backtracked and placed the bottle on her bureau.

Jas entered the room and shut the door behind him. "It's a good thing I didn't go with my first idea and sneak in through your window to try that fantasy of yours."

His smile made her hot, and his gaze tracking over her body made her hotter. He made a startled sound when she launched herself at him, but he caught her close. "Hi."

She looked up at him. There were shadows under his eyes and his shirt collar was no longer crisp. Jas looked about as close to bedraggled as he could ever get. He was so beautiful. "Hi. How's your family?"

He pulled her tighter to him. "Good. My grandpa's ridiculous, and I chewed him out. I also gave a firmer commitment to try to go to the parade, and he's going to move heaven and earth to make it accessible for me."

Now that Jas was here, she felt nervous, more nervous than she'd been when sending those texts. "That's so nice."

"How's the internet treating you?"

"Jury's still out, but there was this video with a man dressed like a panda—actually, it's not important. Everything's fine, so far. Can you hug me hard?"

He did, and they embraced for a long time in the middle of her bedroom. He finally brushed his lips over her hair. "I try to remember when I fell in love with you. But I can't. It feels like it's always been there."

She swallowed, joy filling her from top to bottom. "I love you too. I don't know when it started either. All I know is, I woke up one day, and it was like I'd been looking for you my whole life. And there you were."

He shook his head, chagrined. "We could have had this conversation years ago."

"Or we were meant to wait for right now. Like everything led to this, you know?"

"Always the optimist." He pulled away and gazed down at her, lingering on her braless breasts under her shirt.

The zings. From his eyes alone.

"Tell me you stopped at the pharmacy."

Jas's grin could rival the sun for brilliance. "I got some goodies in my pocket."

"Can we try it then?" she breathed. "The fantasy?"

He started to unbutton his shirt, and indicated the bed. "Get in and close your eyes."

It was hard to keep a straight face as she waited for Jas under the duvet. The bed depressed next to her, and then his naked legs were tangled up in hers, the crinkly hair scraping her skin. She kept her eyes shut as his hand moved down her stomach, until he got to her sex. His fingers slid under her panties and combed through the hair there, and then he pushed them inside, moving slowly. "So wet," he murmured.

She let out a sigh when his thumb found her clit and he rubbed it in tight circles. He kissed his way down her neck, and over the curve of her breast through her nightshirt. Her breath came faster, though his strokes remained steady and controlled.

He left her for a second, but only to tug off her nightshirt and panties. He lifted her breasts and licked each nipple, holding her steady for his mouth. He alternated licks and sucks, each caress tightening the knot in her belly, until she only wanted to *do* something.

So tell him. "Fuck me," she whispered, and he stiffened.

For a second, she thought he might be scandalized by the words coming out of her mouth, but then he rose up on his knees, and the dark need in his gaze told her he was into it. He grabbed a foil square from where he must have stashed the supplies on the nightstand.

Putting the condom on took a second, and she wished there was more light in the room so she could see, but then he was back over her. The head of his erection pressed against her thigh. She only had a fleeting moment to worry he was too large, and then a tight, burning sensation came as he entered. He stopped immediately when she winced.

"It's okay," she said, and pressed her palms on his shoulders. "It's been so long."

He gave her an incredulous look. "It absolutely is not okay. Hang on." He pulled away and reached over to the nightstand again, this time retrieving a small bottle.

Katrina gave a helpless laugh. "Wow, you really came prepared, huh?"

"I wasn't taking any chances." He poured the clear liquid on his hand, then stroked it over his cock. He drizzled more on his fingers and pressed them inside her, chuckling when she jumped. "Like that," he murmured. "Let me make you nice and slick for me."

She softened and grew more wet. Yes, she was slick. For *him*.

This was right.

She lifted her arms and he slipped into her embrace and her. This time when he thrust inside her, it was easy, natural.

Their bodies moved together, her legs and arms wrapping around him. There was a spot deep inside he kept rubbing against . . . right *there*. Her eyes rolled back as he tapped it again and again, taking cues from her body.

It was perfection. It was glorious. It was everything she could have dreamed of.

She cupped his face above her. His eyes were hard and focused, brow furrowed. When she clenched down on him in a shivering climax he let himself go, fucking her in short rapid strokes. His groan echoed hers through the silent room.

He straightened up on his arms to take his weight off her, his big chest rising and falling. "Sorry that was so quick."

That was quick? "I enjoyed it," she said. What an understatement.

Jas kissed her deeply, then got up. "Be right back." He went into the bathroom. She lay there and thought about how her body felt. Different, yet the same. Satisfied. For now.

Katrina made a happy noise when he got into bed and lay down next to her.

He kissed her nose. "It's toast, by the way."

"What?"

"I love toast. It's my favorite breakfast food."

She laughed, surprised. "That's . . . such a simple thing. I wasn't expecting that."

"When I was young, my grandma used to bake bread, and she'd let me have the first slice in the morning, slathered with hot butter." His smile was fond. "I love toast."

"I will make sure you get toast. You do have to eat breakfast in the kitchen from now on. With me. That's the difference between a boyfriend and an employee."

His smile took her by surprise. "This is probably a good time to tell you I'm quitting."

"Please, let me fire you. You could collect unemployment," she teased.

He sobered and played with her fingers. "Samson's friend, he said I should consult for their organization that they're a part of. The CTE one? They want to expand to vets."

"When did this happen?"

"Before we left. I went out with them. But I think instead of consulting . . . I'll ask him for some resources." He grimaced. "McGuire is getting pardoned tomorrow, and Lorne said she would handle the media by herself, but I know it'll stir things up. I think I'll take some time to decide what I want to do with myself. I'll probably stay in cybersecurity but I need a minute to get some help and sort stuff out."

"Oh." There went her heart, soaring. "I think that's smart."

He pulled her close. "You were right. I do need to ask for what I want more. I've been thinking about it since I left you, and every time I've done it lately, asked for what I needed, I've been happy after."

He sounded so mystified by the concept of feeling good because someone saw to his needs. She cuddled closer to him and slung her arm over his chest. His delicious, beautiful chest. *Focus.* "Yes. Makes sense."

"I'll keep building my support network while we build something together."

"I like that." She rose up on her elbow. "There's something I've been dying to do to you," she said, with great bashfulness.

"Oh yeah? Go for it."

She stretched up, and placed a delicate kiss on each of his perfect eyebrows. Then she smoothed them with her fingers.

With a satisfied sigh, she rested her head on his chest. "Thank you."

"That was a very weird thing to do, but you're welcome."

Could she time her pulse to his? "I'd also like to big-spoon you eventually."

Jas's chest rumbled under her ear. "You'd be more like a backpack, wouldn't you?"

"It would suffice." She interlaced her fingers with his. "You feel that? Those zings?"

"Zings, huh?" He kissed her fingers. "Okay. Let's call them that."

"Yes." She pressed a kiss on his pec. They were silent for a long time, their breathing in sync.

Katrina tried to close her eyes, but she was so happy and excited and hopeful, they kept popping open. She readjusted herself and gazed at the dark ceiling. "Jas?"

His voice was sleepy, but he answered. She knew he'd answer. "Yes?"

Her heart was aglow, and she needed to share it. *Radically happy.* "I've always thought it would be romantic to have a meet-cute with someone, but I think actually we're in a perpetual meet-cute, you know? Like it's never-ending, us finding each other."

His response to her mushiness was as perfect as his eyebrows. "Works for me." He rolled over, pulling her under him. He captured her mouth, then whispered into it, "It's always a pleasure to meet you."

About the author

About the book

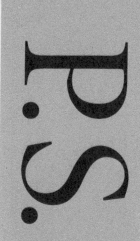

Insights,
Interviews
& More . . .

Meet Alisha Rai

M. Ladrigan

ALISHA RAI pens award-winning contemporary romances. Her novels have been named Best Books of the Year by the *Washington Post*, NPR, Amazon, *Entertainment Weekly*, *Kirkus*, and *Cosmopolitan* magazine. When she's not writing, Alisha is traveling or tweeting. To find out more about her books or to sign up for her newsletter, visit alisharai.com.

A Letter from the Author

Dear Reader,

I'm often asked where the inspiration for my books comes from, and I'm never quite sure what to say. It's basically a mishmash of things I've seen and heard and learned, combined with pen ink and a pinch of pepper. *Girl Gone Viral* is unique, though, because I can trace the inspiration for its setting to a single source, one you may have caught in the text.

The roti quesadilla.

(Did a heavenly light just fall upon this text? Normal.)

This delight was described in the Eater feature I found during a late-night hungry internet binge as "melted cheese, onions, and shredded beef sandwiched inside a paratha . . . served with a curry chicken dipping sauce." I feverishly searched for where to find the goods, only to discover that Rasul's El Ranchero, the small family-owned restaurant that had created it, had closed in 1993 after a run that spanned almost forty years, beginning in 1954.

After I grieved that I would never taste this delicacy for myself, I went back to the article. It was the dates that caught my attention, as well as the location, a small city in Northern California. Mexican/Indian fusion fits right into our trendy global foodie scene today, but it must have surely ▶

3

been unusual a half century ago, yes? Especially in relatively small agricultural Yuba City, the seat of Sutter County.

Except this dish wasn't a trend. It was representative of a whole community.

As Jas's grandfather noted, thanks to a rising tide of anti-Asian sentiment, South Asian immigration was effectively halted in 1917. The borders weren't fully open again until 1965. I know about the immigrants who came after: my parents, my grandparents, my aunts and uncles and cousins. I knew much less about the ones who came before and paved the way for the millions who came after. Like most early immigrants, they struggled against the odds to carve out a home for themselves and their families. Like most immigrants, they are a vital part of American history.

In the early 1900s, thousands of South Asians, mostly men, predominantly Sikhs, from the Punjab province in India came to America to work on the railroads and in agriculture. Places like Yuba City, with its rich farmland, became home to Punjabi settlements. Many pressing problems faced the farmers, not the least of which was a dangerous level of racism and hostility, but two major legal stumbling blocks directly challenged their dreams of becoming Americans.

First, a Supreme Court case, United States v. Bhagat Singh Thind, held that South Asians were ineligible for citizenship. (For context, Thind worked his way through Berkeley and served as a sergeant in the U.S. Army during World War I. He was granted citizenship after the war, but the Bureau of Naturalization appealed it.) Under California's Alien Land Law, only citizens could own property. South Asian immigrants, some of whom had been naturalized and then retroactively stripped of their citizenship following the case, could not legally own the land they were pouring their sweat and blood into.

Second, the combination of a scarcity of South Asian women, the closed borders, and California's anti-miscegenation laws, which prohibited people from marrying outside their race, made growing a community seem almost impossible.

In theory. In reality, the court clerk signing marriage licenses often didn't look very far past skin color. One source estimates that around four hundred marriages between Punjabi men and Mexican women took place between 1910 and 1940. These unions resulted in children who were automatically American citizens by birth and could hold title to their parents' property. A hybrid Punjabi-Mexican community emerged—and with it, establishments like Rasul's El Ranchero.

The culture thrived for at least a generation, but as laws around immigration and citizenship changed, and the children of these unions grew ▸

up and moved and had families, so did the makeup of the community. Once the borders opened, South Asians naturally gravitated to places like Sutter County, where they had friends and family. Today, Yuba City is reportedly home to one of the largest populations of Punjabis outside of Punjab. The Yuba City Annual Sikh Parade and Festival draws over a hundred thousand visitors from all over the world every November.

I visited Yuba City on a summer day when the temperatures soared so high my car overheated. I parked it in the shadiest spot I could find and explored. I walked through peach orchards where farmers picked fruit; was warmly welcomed at the three local Gurdwaras; toured the Becoming American Museum, dedicated to Punjabi American history; gorged myself on a $7.99 buffet I would easily make an eight-hour drive for again (shout-out to Star of India, the saag was truly divine); and sampled tacos and snacks at roadside stands. This is the American heartland, I thought. A rich and beautiful tapestry of faces and languages and food.

If you'd like to learn more about this volume of American history, I'd recommend starting with the Becoming American Museum's digital exhibits and archives, W. Kamau Bell's Emmy Award–winning *United Shades of America* episode "Sikhs in America," and *Making Ethnic Choices: California's Punjabi Mexican Americans* by Karen

Leonard. Please excuse any liberties
I may have taken with the city in this
book. All errors are entirely my own.
    Psst. If anyone can recreate that
legendary roti quesadilla? I'm still
hungry.

Best,
Alisha

Reading Group Guide

1. Katrina goes viral because of a voyeur eavesdropping and embellishing her conversation. In a society where anyone and everyone has a camera or recording device in their pocket, do we have any expectation of a right to privacy outside of our own home?

2. Ross really ran with his fifteen minutes of #CafeBae fame—making the talk-show rounds and creating a false social media impression detailing his "relationship" with #CuteCafeGirl. What do you imagine the fallout in his own life might be when the truth of the situation finally comes to light? How will he be affected—if at all—on social platforms and in his daily life?

3. Do you understand why Katrina wanted to get away from her home following the viral explosion of #CafeBae?

4. Jas was a witness to war and his testimony helped put McGuire away. Yet this criminal's family is quite well-connected and a pardon is certain. What is the emotional impact on Jas, and

all the other soldiers who testified, when the offender walks free?

5. Do you agree with Jas's decision to not make a statement to the media because it would be too painful for him?

6. Are you annoyed that Katrina didn't tell Jas she was meeting with her father because she felt driven to do it on her own? Would you be as annoyed if it had been Jas withholding similar information from her?

7. Do you think Katrina was too lenient or too harsh with her father?

8. In the end, Katrina feels some empathy for Becca, despite the position the other woman put her in. Do you empathize with Becca? Would you feel differently if Becca hadn't embellished the original story? If she hadn't taken photos but had simply tweeted Katrina and Ross's conversation?

9. Should Becca and Ross feel guilty? Would you feel guilty if something you tweeted about someone else (without their knowledge) went viral? ▶

10. Jas and Katrina have just scratched
    the surface of their new relationship.
    Do you think Jas quitting is the right
    move? What do you think the future
    holds for how this relationship will
    evolve? ∽